OCEANS ON FIRE

OCEANS ON FIRE

MARTIN GRANGER

RedDoor

Published by RedDoor
www.reddoorpublishing.com

This is a work of fiction. Names, characters, places and incidents either are products of the author's imagination or are used fictitiously. Any resemblance to actual events or persons, living or dead, is entirely coincidental

Hardback ISBN 978-1-910453-02-5
Paperback ISBN 978-1-910453-03-2

A CIP catalogue record for this book is available from the British Library

Cover design: Sheer Design and Typesetting

Typesetting: www.typesetter.org.uk

Printed in the UK by TJ International, Padstow, Cornwall

One

The ice-biting wind hurled itself into the ship's anemometer. The needle on the bridge flickered, forty-two knots and rising. A man in glistening yellow oilskins leant over the rail and stared at the black waters heaving towards the horizon. The waves must be reaching nearly eight metres. It was a strange sensation, here he was somewhere in the Southern Ocean in a maelstrom and yet he could balance a coffee cup in the palm of his hand without spilling a drop. He stretched out an arm to prove the point. The deck he was standing on was as sound as rock. It was a scene that he must have described a hundred times to the various dignitaries or students who had visited the vessel. What was the line he opened with? *'Even in the roughest seas this ship can drill through six miles of water and three miles of rock.'*

It was a great line but, unless he had seen it with his own eyes, he doubted whether he would have believed it. The *IOD Revolution* was held steady by means of a computer-controlled positioning system. Sam Armstrong's speciality was ocean floor sediment and the Earth's climate; and he just had to know how this thing worked. The ship's engineer was only too pleased to have the opportunity to tell him.

'We put a beacon on the sea floor right next to the drilling point. There are a number of hydrophones attached to the ship's hull that pick up the signals. Our computers work out the arrival times and send messages to the ship's twelve bow thrusters to keep us in position.'

Sounded simple, yet, when you were standing stock still on what you knew was a ship floating on thrashing Antarctic waters, it still felt crazy. He drank the last of his coffee and was tempted to throw the plastic cup into the waves. It was one of those 'standing on the top of a cliff' moments – an imperative for him to jump off. Sam was a dyed-in-the-wool environmentalist, a geologist dedicated to removing the threat of climate change. He opened the flap of his oilskin's pocket and dropped the cup into it.

A shout came from the deck above him. He looked up and tried to lip-read the words over the noise of the wind. The first officer was waving at him like a traffic cop on speed.

'Trouble?' he shouted back. It was useless; his question was just wrapped into the air and taken away with the spray. He pointed to his ear and shook his head violently. Then he pointed upwards and mouthed the word 'up'. Why he mouthed it and didn't shout it he couldn't work out. It was just one of those things you did. Maybe if someone couldn't hear, it was done to bring some sort of equality into the conversation. He made his way gingerly across the drenched deck to the nearest stairway. The ribs on the iron steps had been painted so many times they were almost smooth and he had to hang onto the handrail to stop himself from slipping.

The first officer grabbed his hand to help him up the final rung.

'You're needed on the bridge. The chief engineer wants to start drilling and the captain needs your advice.'

This wasn't the first time Sam had been called in to act as a referee. The 'International Ocean Drilling Project' was over time and over budget. They had set out six weeks ago to drill ten kilometres of core samples from the southern ocean floor. This would tell them about the state of the Earth's climate in the Antarctic region over the last ten million years. Their various government sponsors were impatient for the results but the seas had been high and, even with computerised positioning, it had been difficult to drill. To date, they had only brought up half of the target cores. This had led to tension on the bridge. The captain and the chief engineer were standing like chess players on either side of the chart table.

'Come in, Sam,' invited the captain without taking his eyes off the chief engineer. 'Otto here thinks we're in an ideal position to drill.'

Otto began to protest. 'I didn't say ideal, I said …'

The captain raised his hand. 'Otto has informed me that the sea conditions are well within the tolerance of the drilling rig, and that we should start drilling the next core. I've pointed out to Otto that I'm responsible for the safety of the crew on this ship and, no matter what the international committee says, I'm not going to risk the lives of these men for a few feet of clay.' The captain arrested Otto's next interruption with a military stare. Otto closed his mouth without saying a word.

'Even …,' The captain turned to face Sam, '… even if that clay gives them an argument to keep their jobs at the next election.'

Sam was aware of the undertones of this statement. For days now, discussions around the captain's table had centred on the ethics of their task. Some governments were leaning heavily on the scientists to come up with data to show that their economic policy of burning fossil fuels would have little effect on the climate; others wanted figures to prove a case of impending doom.

'Captain, I'm a scientist and, as a scientist, I want to know the truth. Otto, on the other hand, is an engineer and if he says that it's safe to drill, I believe him.'

Otto looked at the captain and shrugged as if to say 'I told you so'.

The captain turned to the bridge's instrument panel and studied the mass of flickering needles and blinking lights. Cold hard rain started to hammer against the windscreen. The pause was just becoming uncomfortable when the captain turned to speak.

'Okay, you two, let's get this straight. I will position the ship for drilling and your team will play it by the book. All procedures to be followed with no shortcuts. I want to be informed about any sign of trouble immediately. Then the decision will be down to me. If I say abandon the bore and cut the drill string, you cut it. Is that understood?'

Otto was about to say that there wasn't going to be any trouble when Sam took him by the arm and started to guide him out of the bridge.

'Absolutely, Captain,' he said. 'We will give you the drilling co-ordinates and procedures in writing within the hour.'

Sam half ushered, half pushed Otto down the stairs to B-deck. From the colour of Otto's neck he could see that he was fuming. This was confirmed when they reached the operation's cabin.

'What the fuck do you mean?' exploded Otto. 'Give you the procedures in writing. He knows what the bloody procedures are, and if he doesn't, he should do by now. What a waste of fucking time. As if we haven't got enough to do in this bloody storm.'

'Calm down, Otto, we've got our way. He says you can drill, just get on with it. I'll ask one of the university trainees to fill in the forms. I'm supposed to be teaching them something, anyway.'

'I hope they learn fast because I'm not waiting any longer. This sea's getting rougher by the minute. We've already dropped the guide cone onto the sea floor. If we don't get that drill string in soon we really will be in the shit.'

The pieces of drill were made up of rigid steel pipes nearly half a metre in diameter. When they were all screwed together to make a six-mile-long drill string, it behaved just like that, a piece of string. It wasn't easy to get such a long drill to bite into hard rock so Otto and his team had come up with a way of making it stick. Ten minutes later Sam was explaining this to his university trainee in his cabin.

'Okay, so they've lowered this huge aluminium cone onto the seabed. Technically, we should have logged this operation into the project book, so you can do that now and make up some sort of figure in the time column. Now the next thing we do is to use sonar to find its exact position and keep adding on bits of pipe until the drill bit wobbles around in the inside of the cone.'

The trainee seemed genuinely interested. 'How do we know when it gets there?'

'We can see it; there's a camera on the end of the drill. We can even take a photo to show the captain it's there.' Sam's right eyelid flickered. 'Keep him in the loop, if you know what I mean.'

'And then?'

'And then we fill the cone up with concrete so the drill tip stops wobbling and bites when we switch it on.'

'Amazing! How far down will we drill this time?'

'Three miles; enough core sediment to show the changes in climate over the last ten to twenty million years. But before we go too deep we have to bring up a sample from a few hundred metres. It's a pain but it's procedure. And with the mood the captain's in right now we can't afford to skip it, however stupid it seems.'

'What do you mean "stupid", Sir?'

'Well, it's never happened; a gas bubble, that is.'

Sam could see that he was losing his trainee. The poor boy had been thrown in at the deep end. Three years at university studying oceanography and then, as some sort of government PR exercise, a two-month postgraduate jaunt on the *IOD Revolution*, the most sophisticated deep-sea laboratory drilling ship in the world. No-one had really thought through what to do with these students. Once on board, there was no way they could get off before the end of the trip. Two of the three had spent the last few days throwing up below decks. The survivor was an enthusiastic lad, although not the sort of experienced assistant Sam would have chosen.

'You've seen some of the clay cores that we've brought up in the lab, haven't you …' Sam said this rather as a statement than a question. 'They are soft cylinders of striped sediment encased in plastic tubes, yes? Well, when the first core hits the deck someone rushes up with a syringe and sticks it into the clay. They pull the plunger out and literally run back to the lab to see if it contains any gas. If it does, we get the hell out of there as fast as we can.' Sam folded his arms and waited for the inevitable question. It didn't come so he asked it himself.

'Why? The theory is that if there is gas in a core, there could be a gas chamber in the sediment under the ocean. And if our drill punctures that chamber it could release the gas into the ocean as a massive bubble. A bubble you don't want to be sitting on top of.'

The student sat there trying to think of something to say. Sam made an upward waving motion with his fingers. When his hands had reached eye level he clapped them together.

'Bloop,' he said and then laughed at the look of surprise on his trainee's face.

'You needn't worry, I've checked the surveys; we are nowhere near any gas fields. Tonight, you're going to do the syringe sample and take the negative results to the captain because …?'

'Because it's procedure, Sir.'

Sam handed over the paperwork to his student and began to struggle back into his wet oilskins. 'Absolutely, young man; you should go far.'

On deck Sam could hear the familiar rumble of metal pipes as an underscore to the high-pitched, gusting winds. Otto had given the order to prepare the drill. It was an odd system, partially automated but with the final joints being made manually by two riggers on either side of the drilling rig. The fifty metre-long drill pipes had to be brought up horizontally from the hold and then turned through ninety degrees to hang in the cage-like derrick. Two 'fucking idiots', as Otto liked to call them, then positioned one pipe on top of another so that they could be screwed together. Drilling on a stable oil platform is dangerous; drilling on a ship in high seas borders on the insane. Sam found Otto on the viewing platform.

'Jumping the gun a bit, aren't you? I said I'd give the captain the co-ordinates in writing.'

'Well, give them to him then. By the time he reads them the bit should be near the seabed; that is if the bloody sea hasn't snapped it off by then.'

The noise from the drill rig and wind was now so loud that Sam had to cup his hands like a megaphone and scream out his words. 'I thought you said the conditions were okay for drilling.'

He couldn't hear Otto's reply and it was obvious that Otto wasn't going to make the effort to repeat it, so he pulled his oilskin hood over his hard hat and headed for the instrument room.

The front of the ship was a haven compared to the metal mayhem of the drilling quarters. Three floors of pristine laboratories packed with screens, computers and scanners. Bespectacled, white-coated technicians shuffled between rock samples and the space-age technology. Normally, Sam would have stopped to ask for some of the latest paleoclimate results but this evening he headed straight for the positioning computer terminal.

'I need a printout of the entry cone location for the captain.'

The technician turned to look at him. 'I could just phone it up to the bridge, if you want.'

'Not today. We have to do it by the book. I'll send one of the students down to collect it. Oh, and while you're at it, could you show him how to analyse the test core gas sample; I expect the captain will want that in writing too.'

The technician gave him a knowing look. 'Sure thing, Sam. You look whacked, why don't you take a rest? It will be a while before we cut the first core. Promise I'll wake you when it comes up.'

The hammering on the cabin door was getting louder. Surely the drilling hadn't started yet; he had only just closed his eyes. Sam turned over in the bunk and pulled his arm from the blanket so that he could look at his wristwatch. The muffled noises outside had now reached fever pitch.

'Dr Armstrong, open the door, open the door!'

Sam leapt from the bunk and threw the catch. His trainee was standing there, his face as white as the paper he was clutching. Sam, still drowsy with sleep, tried to take in the scene.

'What the hell do you think you're doing?'

'It's the sample core; it's got gas in it.' The piece of paper was thrust into Sam's hands. 'Sixty per cent hydrocarbons; it could be a gas field.' Sam looked down at the paper.

'Calm down, Jeremy, there are no gas fields around here.' He nodded to the charts on the table. 'The surveys are pretty clear about that. Who took the measurements?'

'I did, Sir. The "chem ops" person showed me how to do it.'

Sam reached for his shoes and belt and began to put them on. 'Has he checked these results?'

'No, Sir, I came down here as soon as I saw the figures. You said it could be dangerous and that we would have to get out quickly.'

Sam smiled. 'I said we would have to get the hell out of here. I also said no-one's ever heard of a ship being sunk by a gas bubble. Look, it's the first time you've done this test and ... well, never mind that. Let's go up to the lab and we'll stick another syringe into that clay.'

Sam was still smiling as he led the trainee across a wave-swept A-deck when it happened. The ship bucked like a rodeo bull. Sam was thrown into the air like an athlete off a trampoline. The breath was crushed out of him as his body smashed back onto the metal surface. The skin on his face started to rip as he slid down the seawater-soaked incline. His arms and legs flailed to take a grip but the deck was now nearly vertical. The guard rail hurtled towards him – the only thing between him and the ocean – when he was pulled up sharply with a jolt and a sharp pain stabbing through his thigh socket. A thick coil of metal chain had wrapped around his ankle. For a moment his body dangled in the air, crashing from side to side into the air vents. A screaming, howling noise and then icy darkness. The foam and black freezing water entered his lungs. Sam tried to kick free but the huge iron links of the chain around his leg were pulling him down. He tugged frantically at them but it was pointless; they were impossibly tangled. Below him was six miles of water. He would either die of cold or the pressure would crush him like an imploding drink's can. He thought about inhaling a deep draft of seawater when his bruised hand caught on something. In his belt was a large serrated work knife. He pulled it from its sheath, screwed his eyes shut and placed the blade just below his knee bone. To his surprise he didn't feel a thing as it made the first deep cut into his flesh.

Two

The lobby at the Marriott in Boston was unusually quiet. The receptionist, who had caused so much trouble earlier, was now haranguing a young man about his minibar bill. Apart from two smart suited women drinking coffee in the corner, it was empty. It should be easy to recognise him, even if he didn't look much like his photo.

'Over there.' Joel saw a grey-haired man passing through the glass rotating doors. Nathalie dropped her magazine and got up to look.

'Nothing like him.'

A television screen flickered high up in one corner. She could never fathom out why, in an age of stereophonic sound, hotels displayed these silent images in public spaces. An immaculately turned-out news presenter was mouthing something at her. Cross at herself for being distracted by the mesmeric screen, Nathalie was about to look away when she was held by a superimposed caption *ANTARCTIC OCEAN ON FIRE.* The pictures turned to an aerial shot of an ocean landscape scattered with burning wreckage.

'Great shots,' said Joel. 'That's what we should be taking, not these crummy interviews.'

Nathalie looked around. Privately she agreed with Joel but when she was offered this job she had grabbed it with both hands. A trip to Boston filming a real-life senator sounded good at the time. The guy was hours late but if he did turn up suddenly she didn't want him hearing that he was just a 'crummy interview'; she had had a bad enough day already. The production company in London had hired the vice presidential suite for the interview but had failed to tell the hotel that they were going to use it for filming. As soon as the reception had seen the camera equipment coming in they were stopped and interrogated – the hotel did not allow photography on its premises. They had been caught out before; pornographers had hired the rooms and the hotel logo had been recognised by some trouble-making journalist. The bad publicity had lost them business and the police department were still making noises about a prosecution under the indecency laws. Nathalie thought it ironic that she had had to use all her feminine charm with the hotel manager to get him to understand that they were not about to record anal sex, only an interview about the Law of the Sea Convention with a member of the US Senate.

'We think it important to show that the United States has an interest in fairness towards developing countries and climate change,' she had said, exaggerating her English accent. 'And I'm sure the senator will be most grateful for your co-operation,' she had added, waving the official letterhead in front of him.

The manager had succumbed but all that now seemed pointless. Where was the bloody man?

'Miss Nathalie Thompson?' She had been so wrapped up in the television footage and her own thoughts that she hadn't noticed the guy in the grey flannel suit enter the lobby.

She began to turn around. 'Yes. Senator Cronkar?'

'No, I'm afraid not. I am a representative from the US Environmental Protection Agency. Due to personal circumstances I regret that the senator will not be able to give you an interview. I'm so sorry about this; I do hope this doesn't inconvenience you too much.'

Nathalie had become used to the unpredictability and frustrations of film production and had learned to keep a cool exterior. But on this occasion she was tired; a seven-hour flight from London, a night without sleep and the cancellation of the key interview for her only job this year made her lose it.

'*Inconvenience*!' she screamed. '*Inconvenience*! You have no idea how much time and how much money we have spent in setting up this shoot. Senator Cronkar personally promised to give us his views on the Law of the Sea Convention and no-one else that you offer us will do because he is the man who is going to sign the treaty.'

Nathalie's face was red with rage, her small frame stood there defiantly breathing heavily, waiting for a response.

The official was taken aback. He wasn't expecting such an outburst from this skinny girl and it was obvious from his delivery that he was blurting out more than his pay-grade allowed.

'I'm really sorry, Miss Thompson, I'm afraid the department won't be offering you anyone else; and I'm sorry to say that the senator doesn't have any permission to speak on the matter as he no longer has the authority to sign the treaty.'

Nathalie inhaled deeply, closed her eyes, paused and exhaled again. For a moment, everything in the lobby seemed frozen in time. Joel, the cameraman, looked first at Nathalie and then at the messenger of bad tidings who was bracing himself for another onslaught. But Nathalie had composed herself. When she at last opened her large brown eyes they were dilated and impassive.

'Well, Mr Representative, are you at least offering an explanation as to why the senator no longer has any authority?'

The man from the department was inexplicably unnerved by the presence of this young woman. He reasoned that he was an official in his own country and she was a mere visitor but his words didn't seem to come out with the authority that he intended.

'The department ... My authority from the department is to explain that the senator will not be making a statement today. We apologise for this, but in the circumstances ... I'm afraid I can't at present ... I'm sorry,' and with that he turned to make for the revolving door. At the same time a large-framed customer was entering the lobby, making him wait at the entrance.

'You'll read in the papers tomorrow, anyway,' he said guiltily, as he propelled himself through the rotating gap.

'Well, isn't that just great?' said Nathalie to no-one in particular. 'A six thousand mile round trip, film crew hire and the vice presidential suite, all for bugger all. The production company will be pleased.'

'Well, you've paid for the suite so why not make use of it?' said Joel. 'Buy me a beer and I'll fix it with the facility company that you only get charged half a day for me and the camera gear.'

'You're on,' said Nathalie, slinging her laptop over her shoulder and heading for the elevator.

The vice presidential suite contained a couple of easy chairs, a glass coffee table and a large flat-screen television, as well as the standard king-size bed and bedroom furniture. Joel threw the camera kit onto the bed and made for the minibar.

'Heineken or Coors?' he asked.

'Hardly a choice,' replied Nathalie. 'Anything that's cold.'

'So does this no-show mess up your movie?'

Nathalie put the neck of the bottle to her lips. She paused to take in the pleasure of the first cold mouthful.

'Mess up is an understatement. Without it there is no film. It's a training film for the IMO; three interviews and a few archive seascape shots with an amateur voice-over. Most of the budget has been used up in getting me here. My own fault; I said an interview with this guy was essential.'

'IMO?'

'International Maritime Organization. They want to teach their staff about the latest developments on the Law of the Sea. Sounds boring, is boring. Apparently the rest of the world has spent the last fifty years writing a charter to see who owns the oceans. The United States are the last to sign up. Our senator friend was going to agree the treaty tomorrow. It would have been a coup to get an interview.'

'We Yanks always seem to be the last ones to sign things. Remember that Kyoto thing? Bad news for the car companies. Could be worth chasing up why he's off the case.'

'Beyond my remit. And shit, shit, shit, I haven't even completed this one! You know what these bloody production companies are like. Doesn't matter what the excuse, it's the director's fault if you don't get the shots.'

Joel looked at his watch. 'Well, you can't do anything about it now;

it will be late in the day there. Set your alarm and ring them first thing their time, after they've had a good night's sleep.'

Nathalie knew he was right, cameramen were always right. They could afford to be; they didn't have to carry the can.

She accepted a second beer and flicked on the television remote. The screen displayed the same Barbie face as the one in the lobby. CNN's rolling news programme.

The elaborate graphics showed the daily fluctuations in the Dow Jones Index. Local weather would be next, followed by the world news' headlines. Nathalie relaxed into the armchair and watched the screen with only half an interest. Joel was muttering something about his next shoot in downtown Boston when the pictures of the burning ocean appeared.

'How do we turn this sound up?' she asked, wrestling with the remote.

Joel reached over and hit the volume key.

'Fucking amazing,' he said. 'How in the hell did they get those shots?'

The newsreader was describing the scene. The world's largest drilling ship had disappeared somewhere in the Antarctic Ocean. No Mayday call had been given. The coast guard had been alerted by concerned scientists who had stopped receiving their regular bulletins. A fly-past of the area where the vessel had last been sighted had revealed debris and a sheet of fire. Ships in the vicinity were now being directed to the location to see if there were any survivors.

'Can't see any chance of that,' said Joel. 'If the poor bastards didn't burn to death they'd soon be ice in that water. Wonder what happened?'

Nathalie looked at him in an 'if you shut up, we might hear' sort of way.

The newsreaders were as mystified as Joel. The usual experts were rolled out to speculate on terrorism, engine explosion and freak weather. It soon became obvious that no-one knew the answer and nor would they for months.

The guy who said it was too early to speculate, having just speculated on the disaster, was unceremoniously cut off by the Barbie doll.

'*Breaking news this hour. Reports are coming in of a scandal in the Whitehouse. Aide Senator Cronkar has been caught on film allegedly taking part in a sadomasochistic romp with a known call girl circle.*'

A clip of blurred footage appeared on the screen. Nathalie stood up to take a closer look at the face of the naked middle-aged man who was being strapped to a black wooden cross.

'Shit, it looks like him. No wonder he didn't turn up.'

Joel's eyes were glued to the television. 'You mean he preferred to do that than talk to us?'

'No, you idiot, he's been exposed. The next thing we'll hear is that he's resigned, another way of saying "been sacked."'

But CNN obviously hadn't got the sources for that yet. The rest of the reel consisted of shots of the exterior of Cronkar's empty home and a number of government officials who were saying nothing.

'They must be pretty sure to show footage like that,' offered Joel. 'Guess this makes a big hole in your "Law of the Sea Treaty" thing.'

Nathalie wasn't listening. The television was now showing the weather and she had unzipped the case of her laptop and was entering the hotel's WiFi code.

'YouTube,' she said before Joel could ask.

They watched the whole of the ten-minute video. It was pretty explicit – rubber aprons, riding crops and a group of energetic silicone-breasted women. Despite the extravagant action Nathalie noticed that much of the footage was spent on the pained face of her aborted interviewee.

'Pretty hard-core, but I've seen better,' said Joel, who was about to press the replay button. Nathalie took the laptop from him.

'Looks authentic. The footage doesn't look tampered with or, if it was, the editor's bloody good.'

Her fingers flashed across the keyboard, chasing the source. Minutes later she had read most of the internet chatter. There were the usual crazy conspiracy theories, though one article had some well-informed background. It cited the coincidence of the exposure of a senator at a vital stage of the ratification of a treaty that had been fifty years in the making. This treaty was highly controversial in that it called for the sharing of the resources of the sea by all countries, including those that were underdeveloped or landlocked. America, with its vast coastline and advanced technology, had most to lose with these egalitarian principles. The blogger ended by suggesting that many people in the United States had a lot to gain from Senator Cronkar's embarrassment.

Joel sat there watching the flickering reflection of the screen against Nathalie's face.

'Anything more on the dirty old bastard?'

His attitude made her cross. 'I don't give a damn what he does in his private life, Joel, but it looks like someone else does and just on the day before he's about to sign a treaty.'

She found the original posted clip bearing the strapline *Wacky Senator turns Red*, and there the trail ended. Joel made to get up and go.

'I'd best check this kit back in,' he said, grabbing the camera case. He laughed. 'A pity the old sod didn't turn up. We could have shot a porno movie in the vice presidential suite and given the manager a coronary!'

Nathalie was too deep in thought to see the funny side. 'Thanks for your help, Joel. If you can get the facilities house to reduce the fee I'd be grateful.'

Joel gave her an American Navy salute and said he would do his best. An hour later, exhausted by jet lag and television channel hopping, Nathalie had fallen asleep, fully clothed, on the Marriott's king-size bed.

It took a few minutes to realise where she was. Somewhere her mobile phone was ringing persistently. She struggled off the bed and reached into her bag. Although it was dark she could read the caller in the blue flashing light.

'Nathalie Thompson,' she said gruffly, and then had to repeat it as she realised she hadn't pressed the answer key.

'Nathalie, sorry to ring you at this time, I know it must be early there,' said the voice down the phone. 'We just had to get you before things got out.'

The numbers on her phone showed 3.20 am east coast time. Nathalie tried to drag her head out of the fog it was in.

'Is this Sheila?' she asked, trying to buy herself a little bit of time.

'I'll get to the point,' said Sheila's distinctive voice. 'We just want you to sit on the tapes. Then get back here on the first flight. Don't talk to anyone about it in America.' Nathalie tried to get her head around this.

'Nathalie, are you there? Do you understand? Don't talk to anybody.'

'About what?'

'The interview. It didn't happen. On reflection, don't sit on the tapes, wipe them. They might be checked at customs.'

'Sheila, what on earth are you talking about?'

'What do you think I'm talking about? The Cronkar interview. We've just been rung by our clients, who have pulled the plug on the project. They want all signs of it scrubbed – script, recordings, the lot. Apparently they want to distance themselves from this guy. They're paying the full whack and we signed confidentiality so that's fine by us.'

It was starting to dawn on Nathalie that the working day in London was just beginning and the production company didn't know that she really hadn't done the interview.

'Don't worry, you'll get your fee,' rasped Sheila as an afterthought.

'Okay, wipe the tapes, take the first flight back to London and forget the rest of the job.' She said it slowly but her mind was racing. How much did London know about the Cronkar sado video? Were they interested in the media mileage in this sort of story? Of course they weren't. Sheila ran a hard-nosed corporate video company. She kept clear of investigative television because most of those she would find herself investigating would be her well-paying clients.

'That's about it, Nathalie. Bring your paperwork and the empty tapes back to the office and I'll give you your cheque. Pity more jobs can't end up like this, eh?'

The blue light of the mobile phone flashed in the darkness, giving the hotel room an eerie glow. Another incoming call at three-thirty in the morning. She was becoming popular.

'Okay, Sheila, I'll keep my mouth shut and give you a call when I land. Goodnight or morning, whatever it is.' She pressed the keys to flip to the other call.

'Geoff, long time no speak, what on earth are you doing, calling me at this time in the morning?'

'Sorry, I forgot you start late,' said Geoff. 'I just thought you'd like first-refusal on a new film we're making.'

Nathalie was now awake enough to rationalise the situation. Geoff Sykes ran Bagatelle Films. Unlike Sheila's outfit, it was an edgy London production company that made investigative documentaries. Geoff was an early riser but, of course, he wouldn't have a clue that Nathalie was in Boston.

'No problem, Geoff, it's just that I'm in the States and it's half-past three in the morning here. As it happens, I'm awake anyway, so what's this job?'

'I'm so sorry, Nathalie, I'd call you back later but I need a response now. Although it seems like you're already tied up.' That's an irony, thought Nathalie, thinking of the last film she'd done for Bagatelle when she had got herself kidnapped.

'As it happens, I've just finished a job, Geoff. Fire away.'

'Well, I need a director who has some knowledge of ships and I thought of you.'

Like hell, thought Nathalie, you've rung all the directors you know and they're all working. 'Go on.'

'It's a documentary about using the oceans to solve the climate change problem. The broadcasters have just moved the transmission slot forward and we need to get a move on and start shooting. We've got some of the locations set up already. You'll like the first one. It's in the Antarctic, on the biggest drilling ship in the world …'

Nathalie interrupted him in full flow. 'Geoff, I don't suppose you've had the time to look at the news this morning …'

Three

From her window seat Nathalie could see the stunted neon lights trying to illuminate the fogbound peripheral road around Heathrow. Apparently, the lamp posts were shortened to protect low-flying aircraft. One could only guess at the mayhem that would be caused by any jumbo jet coming in that low. The flight was overdue and the darkness and glistening tarmac made their final approach uninviting.

She had whiled away her time over the Atlantic by going through her papers and filling out an expenses form. No matter how many times she had recalculated she was always out of pocket by tens of dollars. She thought of entering them as receiptless coffees and tips but, knowing Sheila, she thought it better to just write it off. Things could have been worse; at least now she didn't have to explain the empty videotapes. They had been left with Joel, and he could verify that they were now blank. She had rehearsed tomorrow morning's meeting a number of times. The less she said the better. She would stick to handing in the script and research papers, and calmly ask for her fee and expenses and to be considered for the next job.

The touchdown was smooth and she spent her time removing her papers from the basket in front of her and neatly stacking them into her bag as the plane taxied in. As usual most of the passengers, heads awkwardly bent, were trying to stand up in the aisle, waiting to exit. Nathalie had no idea why they did this, it wasn't as if they would get out of the plane faster or be awarded priority at the baggage carousels. She sat comfortably back in her seat, waiting for the doors to open and for the jostling queue to make its way through the cramped fuselage.

The bored taxi drivers stood behind the aluminium rail, holding up their cards like ice-rink judges; Kowlofski, Hedges, Turner – no

Thompson. She was told that there would be a cab for her. As the plane was over an hour late they'd probably moved on to their next job. Still, they had her number and they could have easily left a text. Nathalie was too tired to harangue the cab company so she wheeled her trolley-bag to the black cab rank, grabbing a copy of the *Evening Standard* on the way. She needn't have bothered; the cab driver was full of it.

'Dirty bastard, in charge of the country and plays around with whores. Gets his kicks by being spanked on the arse. Must be a nutter. Wouldn't let him in charge of my cab, let alone the United States of America.'

In the gloom of the cab Nathalie tried to read the small print under the headlines and lurid photographs. Nothing about the Law of the Sea Convention. Someone in their press office must be good. She let the cab driver rant on. For a man who was repulsed by this perversion he seemed to take more than a salacious interest in it.

'Have you seen the pictures on page four? Bloody contortionist, if you ask me.' Nathalie wasn't asking him, she was rifling through the paper to the middle pages of world news. The senator's story was taking up most of the opening pages. At last she found it as a small column under the science section – *Climate change ship goes missing in Antarctic.*

Drilling ships were obviously not the editor's strong point as there was little other than what she had heard on CNN. In fact, some of the copy looked like it had been lifted straight from their newsreel.

It was nearly ten o'clock in the evening when the taxi entered the familiar streets of Fulham. She asked for a receipt and told the driver to add ten per cent to the fare. He took the money without comment, then started complaining about his back problem as Nathalie heaved her bag out of the taxi. She was tempted to ask him what sexual exploits he'd been up to and thought better of it. People like that were prejudiced enough; she would only make things worse.

Her flat was cold and damp. The fridge had been left on but there was no milk in it. She hated black instant coffee yet that's what it would have to be. It was five o'clock in the afternoon in Boston and, from past experience, she knew that there was no way she would get to sleep. She couldn't face unpacking so she powered up her laptop and flicked through her e-mails. One from Geoff had invited her to afternoon tea at The Ivy Club, wherever that was. Despite the disappearance of his first filming location he still seemed keen to go ahead with this project. He had attached a number of documents on low carbon emission energy schemes. Nathalie had always been a bit sceptical about corporate exploitation of green issues. Even the phrase 'green issues' got up her nose. It seemed to her that large corporations thought they could make more money just by adding the phrases 'climate change' and 'carbon footprint' to their advertising. Still, knowing Geoff, there would be some sort of exposé of the facts if he found any foul play. She opened up a couple of the papers. They seemed a bit technical – articles on ocean thermal energy, kinetic wave machines and tidal power stations. All a bit too heavy after a long-haul flight. She would glance at some of them in the morning. The thought reminded her that she would have to take all her stuff back to Sheila. A lot of the papers were in an old box file wedged between the Yellow Pages and her back editions of *Broadcast* magazine.

She pulled it out, cursing at the magazines that now, unsupported, spilled all over the floor. She knelt on the carpet, pushed the magazines to one side and opened the file. Most of the stuff in there was rubbish. Sheila was welcome to it, but some of the letters and papers had taken a lot of effort. Nathalie made two piles either side of the box file. Sheila would want all of it, although Nathalie didn't see why she shouldn't keep copies of some of the more interesting stuff. You never knew when it might come in useful. She didn't have a photocopier but she knew of a Parsi all-night corner shop that did. It was five pence a copy. Nathalie handed him the twenty sheets and asked for a discount. She was the only customer and the shop felt like a warm Aladdin's cave in contrast to the dark, wet London streets. The shop owner recognised her and took part in some playful bargaining. Fifteen minutes later she emerged with her photocopies, a disgusting carton of UHT milk and Abrasham's full family history.

It had started to rain again so she pushed the sheaf of papers under her coat and hurried back to her flat. She put the milk carton in the kitchenette and took the photocopies into her bedroom.

'One for you, one for me,' she said, separating the sheets of paper onto the bed. She put the top copies into a bag with her shooting notes and call-sheet. In the distance the church clock on the towpath chimed twelve. The room was warming up and the immersion heater beckoned a hot bath. Nathalie grabbed a clean towel from the airing cupboard and turned on the hot tap. The mirror clouded over as the steam began to rise.

Sheila opened the door herself.

'Good morning, Sheila, no receptionist today?' asked Nathalie.

'Little bitch says she's got 'flu,' said Sheila, making her way up the narrow staircase. 'More like a head cold, if I know her. Did you wipe the tapes?'

No client ever saw the inside of Sheila's production offices. They were two white emulsioned, anaglypta-lined rooms above a minicab shop in Chiswick. When she held meetings they were either scheduled at the client's offices or in some fancy restaurant in Soho. Staff, on the other hand, were different. They were either given one of the stalls – a four-foot space on a Formica table separated by plywood dividers – or a chair around the large table in the so-called boardroom which doubled up as Sheila's office. Today it was the boardroom. Sheila sat down and nodded for Nathalie to do the same.

'The tapes?' Nathalie neatly side-stepped the question by handing Sheila her research documents and the various drafts of the script.

'All clean and with Joel in Boston. He said if he kept them, he wouldn't charge for them.' Nathalie offered an envelope across the table. 'I put my expenses form in with my invoice, if that's okay.'

'Of course, we'll send you a cheque as soon as we get paid. You're sure that all the tapes have been wiped clean?'

'I'm absolutely sure that they're completely blank, you can check with Joel, if you like. I thought you said that you would give me my cheque if I came in today?'

'It's no problem, should be with you in a few days. Cash flow, you know?'

Certainly Nathalie knew. Sheila's company was one of those that didn't pay up until they had got the money out of the client. Sometimes this could be six months. Nathalie thought the whole point of production companies making a profit was to take the risk. Freelancers like her, on the other hand, were paid by the day. By rights, they should get paid as soon as the work was done. In this case though, the work hadn't been done so Nathalie thought it best not to argue.

'Okay, Sheila, as soon as you can, please, okay? Anything else on the horizon?'

Sheila got up to indicate that the meeting was over. 'A few irons in the fire, I'll let you know. And remember, you've signed confidentiality on this last one, not a word to anyone about the project, okay?'

'Of course, Sheila, not a word,' said Nathalie, making her way to the narrow staircase and the pokey empty receptionist's desk at the bottom.

It was too early to meet with Geoff and too late to go back to her flat so Nathalie decided to make her way into the centre of town to find a friendly coffee shop. There she would mug up on the stuff that Geoff had sent her. She took the District Line to Earls Court and changed to the Piccadilly. The underground was unusually quiet and Nathalie had plenty of space to sit back and read the free newspaper that she found on the empty seat beside her. It was full of pictures of her senator. If he liked pain, he was certainly getting it now. His private world of pleasure was now a global event. *Resigned to a Beating*, read one of the headlines.

Poor guy, thought Nathalie. Just about to do the world a favour and he's forced to quit his job. Nathalie didn't believe in political coincidences. Perhaps she should mention it to Geoff, although perhaps not yet. No point in muddying the waters when she was about to be offered a new job. Also, she didn't have much to go on. Geoff was a stickler for sources and facts. He hated people who told him they had a great idea for an investigative documentary.

'I've got thousands of ideas for investigative documentaries,' he would say. 'What I haven't got is the money to make them or the facts and sources that will keep me out of court.'

From her Google search she had discovered that The Ivy Club was somewhere near Leicester Square tube station. Their web entry was intriguing. It was a private members' club and you couldn't even access the website without a password. She strolled down Shaftesbury Avenue looking for a coffee shop with comfy chairs and free WiFi. It didn't take long to find one and she grabbed a cappuccino and a window seat for her makeshift office. She opened the PDF files. Most were from respected scientific journals, others just selected articles from broadsheet newspapers. Nathalie skimmed the abstracts. The facts about carbon emissions and climate change were hardly controversial; the more carbon dioxide in the atmosphere, the hotter the Earth would get. What scientists were arguing over was by how much, in what time. Geoff's film proposal concentrated on the oceans. Huge energy projects were being set up around the globe to produce carbon emission-free energy from the seas. Did these projects work and were they worth it? Three coffees and a tuna wrap later Nathalie's head was buzzing. Some of these things were amazing. Machines that made energy from the waves, mile-long pipes that took heat from the sea and, the one she liked best, tidal power stations that made electricity from the moon. She definitely wanted to make this movie.

Theatreland in the gloom of a wet October afternoon didn't seem as exciting without its evening crowds and inviting lights. There was still another half an hour before Nathalie's four o'clock appointment so she took her time walking slowly towards West Street. She had heard of The Ivy Restaurant, a place where you had to book six months in advance unless you were a celebrity, but The Ivy Club was new to her. She walked the length of West Street without finding the place. She checked in her Filofax, where she had scribbled the address. Number 9. Retracing her steps she noticed a green-coated doorman standing just inside a small, exotic flower shop. She peered into the interior. A lobby decked with orchids and lilies surrounded a chrome and glass elevator. The man in the green coat had noticed her interest. The door opened and she was invited inside.

'Can I help you?'

It dawned on Nathalie that this was no ordinary flower shop. It was obviously a front to deter nosey passers-by.

'I'm here to see Geoff Sykes.'

'Certainly, Madam, please take the elevator.' The doorman gestured to the glass cage. The door slid silently open as she walked towards it. She entered and looked for the buttons. There were none. The door closed as silently as it had opened and a huge chrome piston pushed the glass floor upwards. Very impressive, Geoff, thought Nathalie. Even more exclusive than the Groucho.

A young woman greeted her as the glass compartment came to a smooth halt. She took her coat and guided her into a large bar area. Nathalie looked at her surroundings, wishing that she had dressed more suitably for the occasion. She needn't have worried; Geoff bounded towards her wearing an old pair of ripped jeans and a Ralph Lauren sweatshirt.

'Great to see you, grab a seat. Tea or coffee?' She hesitated, not knowing whether to shake his hand or kiss him on both cheeks. The moment passed so she just sat down. From nowhere a waitress appeared beside them. Nathalie noticed that Geoff had a steaming coffee in front of him so she ordered the same.

'Like it?'

'Cool. How long have you been a member?'

'Not long. Costs a fortune but it certainly helps pull a few strings.'

Nathalie laughed. 'Is that what you're trying to do with me?'

'I just had a meeting with Channel 4's Head of Docs. I thought you might be amused by the place.'

Nathalie tried to look hurt. 'Oh, I thought this was all laid on for me. No, really, it's fun, especially the flower shop thing; very James Bond.'

Geoff nodded towards her laptop, 'What do you think of the stuff I sent you? Interested?'

Nathalie had known Geoff long enough now not to bluff. He was old enough to be her father, and on the last occasion had even acted as one. There was no point in playing hard-to-get.

'Of course I am, especially if you'll let me direct it.'

'I think you're ready. I hear you've been doing a few corporate jobs. This will be tough but I think you're up to it, if you can commit the time.'

It was usual to flick through the diary at this stage to see if you could fit someone in. In this case Nathalie didn't see the point. 'I'm completely free from today. You name the schedule and I'll do it.'

'Good, because I'd like you to fly out tomorrow. All travel and crew are set up. Around the world in fourteen days, shooting in five locations. How does that sound?'

Nathalie sat back in the leather buttoned couch. She knew that this wouldn't be bullshit. Geoff didn't do bullshit. She took a deep breath, stared at the wall above his head and after a five-second pause gave him the answer.

'Sounds good. Also sounds like I've got some catching up to do.'

Bagatelle Films' offices were in Soho Square. It took Nathalie about twenty minutes. Geoff, having achieved his objective of recruiting a director, had stayed on at his club for another meeting. Nathalie would get all the information she needed from his PA. Any problems and he was always on the end of a phone. She had a thousand questions she'd have liked to have asked him. What happened to the drilling rig location? Why such short notice? How come he trusted her on such a difficult shoot? She could guess some of the answers.

Someone had opted out at the last moment. The arrangements had been made and cancellation would be expensive. She was inexperienced as a director but she had worked for him before and 'the devil you know'. Still, it was nice that he thought he could trust her, even if she was the last resort.

'You look drenched,' said the receptionist. 'Let me take your coat. I'll tell Stefanie you're here. Take the lift, second floor.'

Nathalie always got a buzz out of Bagatelle's offices, they had a creative excitement about them. Dramatic pictures flickered on multiple screens, freelancers mingled with in-house production people, and camera crews with their dimpled aluminium boxes wandered in from exotic locations. The lift door opened and she was met by Stefanie with a hot mug of coffee in her hand.

'You're going to need this; we've got a lot to get through.'

Nathalie followed Stefanie through a series of glass-panelled rooms to a neat videotape-lined production office. A far cry from Sheila's Chiswick outfit.

'Draft script, call-sheet, carnet, airline tickets, and float. I hear you've got a US Visa. The cameraman is John McCord, I think you've worked with him before. He'll meet you at Heathrow with his kit. You'll pick up sound and lights on the trip. I'll give you some time to look this over and then you can come and ask me any questions.'

Even at six o'clock in the morning Heathrow was heaving. Nathalie had only had a few hours' sleep and was beginning to wonder why on earth she had been hustled into this job. It seemed only a minute ago she was collecting her baggage from the arrivals hall; now she was checking it back in again. She looked at her watch. It was almost unheard of for cameramen to be late. They hid in some coffee shop an hour early and then casually strolled around the corner right on cue. Stefanie was right, Nathalie had worked with John McCord before. He was one of the best, and one of the reasons she hadn't felt too scared about taking the work. He had been everywhere and shot everything, from jungle swamps to war zones. If you got into trouble it might as well be with John. So, half an hour late made her feel uneasy.

'Nathalie Thompson?' The voice had a strange lilt to it, a mixture of Scandinavian and Antipodean. Nathalie turned around.

'Charlie Linde,' the fair-haired man offered his hand.

'Excuse me?'

'A bit of a shock, I'm afraid. John has been involved in a car crash; a couple of broken ribs and a fractured leg. I'm his replacement.'

Four

The seatbelt light went out with a reassuring ding. Nathalie opened her eyes and looked around the cabin. Charlie was already unclipping his seatbelt and making to move into the corridor.

'Sorry, I must go to the loo, didn't have time with all the rush.'

Nathalie nodded in acknowledgement. She was still trying to get her head around what had happened in the last frantic hour: the scramble to get eight metal boxes full of camera gear through customs and into the plane's hold; the last-minute panic to rush into their seats watched by rows of delayed passengers; and the mixture of relief and anxiety as the aircraft lifted into the air. She hadn't had time to ask Charlie any questions and she had a thousand of them. At least his toilet break would give her time to compose herself. She was meant to be the director and she didn't want to be seen as 'uncool'.

Charlie slipped back into his seat. 'Okay, fire away.'

'What do you mean?'

'You must have a lot of questions. I'm not sure that I can answer all of them but I'll have a go. We've got plenty of time, there's ten hours before we touch down in Los Angeles.'

Nathalie felt herself relax a little; this Charlie was obviously a pro. Like all top cameramen, just the way he spoke gave the impression that he'd been there and done that. She tried to adopt the same style.

'Okay, perhaps we could start with John McCord. How is he and who told you about his accident?'

'Your producer, Geoff Sykes, telephoned me early this morning. He said that you would be concerned about John. Apparently he was on his way to the airport at around four this morning when a car jumped the lights. It was a nasty one but he got away quite lightly. He should be back at work in a few months.'

Nathalie forgot that she was trying to play the experienced film director and her next questions came out in a rush.

'How do you know Geoff and how on earth did you get to the airport with all your gear within a couple of hours of the accident, and what about the paperwork?'

Charlie smiled, 'Well, to take those one at a time: I don't; I was at the airport already; and I had the paperwork on me.' He took in Nathalie's puzzled look. 'No, that's not fair. I'll tell you the whole story. I'd just finished a job in Sweden and had checked my gear out of Heathrow. I was queuing up at the taxi rank with all my stuff on the trolley when I got a call from your producer. He'd been given my details by a company that I've done a number of corporates for in the past. He sounded desperate; cool but desperate. His cameraman had met with an accident, would I turn around and take a plane to Los Angeles? Two weeks' work, double pay. I was tired. I also happened to be free so I asked him if he would give me five minutes to think about it. I called my contacts at Ocean Tech, who had recommended me, and they told me that they were part sponsoring the programme and that the deal was kosher. I rang Geoff back and here I am. He told me that he would e-mail you confirmation and that you would fill me in with the details.'

Typical Geoff, thought Nathalie, get a problem, sort the problem, and leave the details to others. A phone call to her at the airport would have been nice. Of course, he wouldn't have done that because she might have tried to back out of the project. As it was, she was so taken along by events that she didn't have time to think about it. And here she was, sitting on a Boeing 707, about to start a two-week trip around the world with a cameraman she didn't know. Well, she had always wanted to be a fully paid-up documentary film director. She wouldn't get a better chance than this.

Los Angeles Airport was a nightmare. Travel agents who don't travel with eight metal boxes that have to be imported and exported through international borders don't understand the time it takes to change planes. There was only an hour and a half before their internal flight to Hawaii and, although the queue looked short, it was an illusion contrived by the airport authority as on closer inspection it snaked for hundreds of yards through a system of zigzagging barriers. Travel agents and airport authorities also don't understand the difficulty of two people moving along these barriers with eight valuable heavy metal boxes without any trolleys. Nathalie and Charlie moved the boxes along in a series of relays. Every time a gap appeared Charlie would move a couple of boxes a few yards while Nathalie stayed with the others. This was beginning to irritate the other passengers in the queue. It was also becoming evident that they were going to miss their inter-connecting flight. Great, Nathalie thought, we've overcome the miracle of an injured cameraman to be thwarted by a stupid travel agent because, if we miss this flight, we will miss all the other flights in the two-week schedule.

'Where are you going?' asked Charlie.

'To see if I can get some sense out of this stupid system,' replied Nathalie, walking towards a solitary official at a desk on the other side of the hall.

'Excuse me,' she said to the uniformed woman, who refused to look up at her. 'Excuse me, but we're making a film for the British Government about the environmental concerns of the United States. We have an important appointment with the Governor of Hawaii. I'm afraid that without the stamp on our immigration papers we will miss our flight.' The woman continued to look down at her desk as if she didn't hear her.

Nathalie persevered calmly, 'If you could kindly stamp our papers, we, and I'm sure the British Government, would be eternally grateful.'

Without moving an inch of her head, the official slowly put out her open palm. Nathalie placed the papers into it and watched in amazement as they were rubber-stamped.

'Shit, how on earth did you do that?' asked Charlie as Nathalie wheeled up a trolley and told him to get the gear onto it and follow her.

'No idea, but if we don't hurry, they might change their minds. The departure lounge is this way.'

'Shouldn't we cancel the thing?' asked Stefanie, throwing the *Evening Standard* onto Geoff's desk. 'First this, and then John. We've no idea what this Charlie is like and the poor girl has never worked with him before.'

'If I cancelled every film that had a few problems we'd be down in that street handing out these newspapers, not reading them; and she's not a girl, she'll handle it.'

The editor of the *Standard* had at last grasped the importance of the sunken drilling ship for there it was, or the flotsam and jetsam that were left of it, plastered all across the front page of the late edition. An aircraft carrier on exercises had diverted to the location for search and rescue. Despite all the speculation they were still no further with the causes of the disaster.

'Think of it this way,' said Geoff. 'It's a good job we didn't get the money earlier; John could have been on that ship filming it. Instead, he's just laid up in hospital for a few weeks with bruises and a few broken bones. As for his stand-in, it couldn't have worked out better. If the guys who are putting up most of the money for this job think he's good, he probably is. If he's crap, it's their fault and they'll just have to put up more money for a reshoot.'

'That's a bit cynical, not worthy of you, Geoff. I'm only thinking of Nathalie, it's her first real big job.'

'Yeah, and I think she's ready for it. If I pull it on her now it'll only undermine her. If she gets through this one with five stars she really will have made it.'

'Okay, if you say so,' said Stefanie doubtfully, looking at the row of international clocks on the office wall. 'She should have landed in Honolulu by now. Don't you think you should give her a ring?'

'The last thing she'll want is a producer on her back every few minutes. She'll be knackered, anyway – I've done it, dragging all those boxes through customs, seventeen hours in the air. She'll just want to get her head down, let her be. And you should get off home too; being woken up at four o'clock in the morning to sort out crewing problems is above the call of duty.'

'What about Ocean Tech, shall I update them with the situation?'

'No way. Now we've got the co-sponsorship money the less we communicate with Ocean Tech, the better. They are a bit too keen for my liking; I've never had a company so interested in putting money into a project. That's great when you're looking for a commission from a broadcaster, although not so good when you're making the film. They think just because they've put up some cash they have a right to script it, film it and edit it. They've recommended a cameraman, and that's where it stops; from now on the creative input is all ours. We'll have to put up with a bit of politicking, of course. From past experience we should keep them well away from the cutting room otherwise it'll end up like that drilling ship, a bloody disaster. Goodnight, Stefanie. Get your coat before you can think of anything else you can do. Reception has gone already so I'll lock up.'

Five minutes later he was to regret persuading Stefanie to go. The phone rang and it was Nathalie.

'Glad to catch you, Geoff, we have a small problem …' Nathalie was surprisingly calm and succinct, Geoff thought, as she told him about her arrival in the Hawaiian hotel and her various phone calls with the rest of the crew she was supposed to pick up.

'No insurance set up, apparently. I've persuaded them to come along with the lights but the sound guy says without documentation he can't bring along his digital recording gear. Can you get Stefanie to fax some paperwork to him otherwise it looks like we're going to have to shoot the whole thing mute. I'm sure we can dub some sound in for the ocean shots but the interviews are going to look a bit weird.'

'Well, I'm glad to see you've kept your sense of humour,' said Geoff, already dialling his mobile with his other hand. 'Stefanie's gone home. I'll see if I can catch her and ask her to sort things out. Give me the guy's fax number.'

Nathalie read out the number and was on the verge of asking Geoff about Charlie and Ocean Tech. The continuous tone told her that he'd already put down the phone. It was nine o'clock in the morning Honolulu time. She had left London nearly twenty-four hours ago and had only cat-napped on the planes. Hawaii was apparently an exotic location. All she had seen so far was the inside of a windowless hotel room. Charlie had crashed out in the room next door. She was exhausted yet couldn't sleep. According to the schedule she was to meet with the rest of the crew after lunch and set off for the docks to board the vessel that was meant to be their first filming location. If Dan, the soundman, didn't get that fax it was going to be pretty pointless. She had done all she could on that front so to make use of the time she lay face down on the bed and opened her laptop.

Ocean Tech's website was pretty primitive – a few shots of oil rigs and some standard blurb on offshore drilling with the usual palliations about green issues. A recent posting claimed that they were a small independent offshore oil company thinking of diversifying into alternative energy. That was it. No mention of a board of directors, what their actual plans were, or about the fact that they were sponsoring a film on ocean energy. Perhaps this project was a way of them checking out the situation, or maybe just a way of publicising their name. Geoff hadn't been very forthcoming on the situation; to him they meant cash that enabled the series to get off the ground. The broadcasters liked the idea but there was no way in the current climate that they were going to put up all of the money. Still, it was strange that there was so little information available on them. Nathalie was good at internet research. There was usually a way of digging up material somehow although, this time, no matter how many avenues she tried, all she could establish was that they were a small rundown sort of outfit that had recently updated their website. For Geoff's sake she just hoped that they had enough cash to finish the project.

A ringing from the bedside telephone entered her head. Nathalie peeled her face off her laptop keyboard. She must have nodded off. It was Charlie on an internal call.

'Nathalie, we are meant to be meeting the others in fifteen minutes. Shall I meet you in the lobby?'

'Sure,' said Nathalie, trying to stretch out the blotchy indentations on her cheek. 'See you down there.'

The argument could be heard from the elevator. As she turned the corner into the lobby Nathalie could see three men shouting at each other. Jeans, white trainers, with mobile phone in hand, they were obviously her film crew. The tall one with the shaven head was protesting to Charlie.

'It's not your gear, we are on a bloody ship! If it gets damaged I'll be the one who'll have to pay.'

No fax then, thought Nathalie. 'Hi guys, good to see you.' She offered her hand. 'Dan, the soundman, I presume,' and then turning to the short one, 'and you must be Luke, the sparks.'

The three men stopped in their tracks. She could feel Dan's and Luke's eyes wander over her body. They hesitated, and then in turn shook her hand. Dan looked embarrassed.

'I was trying to explain to Charlie that your outfit hasn't come up with the insurance for our gear.' The abrasiveness had gone out of his voice and this was spoken in a soft Californian drawl. Nathalie quickly weighed up the situation.

'Well, Dan, as you can appreciate, Charlie and I have just spent the last twenty-four hours travelling halfway round the world to make what we think should be a great film. I hear you two guys were recommended to Bagatelle Productions as the best on Hawaii. It would be a great shame if we couldn't do this thing together just because of some stupid paperwork. Tell you what, I'm prepared to give you my personal bank details to guarantee your sound gear. If there's a problem I'll pay you out of my own pocket and it will be my responsibility to get the money back from Bagatelle. What do you say?'

Dan was still trying to work out this impish-looking female with the confident British accent. She sounded experienced and as if she knew what she was doing.

'We're not trying to be difficult, it's just that we've been stitched up so many times in the past. Foreign film companies come here and use local crews because they can't afford the travel. Sometimes they can't afford us and our gear either. I can risk my daily rate but the sound kit is my life.'

Nathalie just stood there and put her head to one side.

A smile broke out across Dan's face. 'Okay, you're right, we are the best and it would be a great shame if you ended up with crappy sound and lighting. We'll bring along the kit. Forget your bank details, I'll trust you to get your producer to pay if anything goes wrong. That's right, isn't it, Luke?'

Luke sat on his lighting box and grinned. 'What could go wrong, Dan? You're so anal with that stuff, anyway.' He turned to Nathalie. 'Treats his digital audio like a bloody baby, doesn't let it out of his sight.'

Charlie interrupted before Dan could reply. 'Okay, if that's settled, we'd better get all this gear into your truck. Dan, I'll be shooting 24 FPS, so perhaps you could synch to that. Luke, I don't know what sort of voltage they have on the ship but I expect you've done this sort of stuff before. I'll only be using a few "redheads" and "mizars" for low-key stuff.'

Nathalie hoped the guys didn't see her shoulders relax with relief. This was better, the safer common ground of film talk, and the prospect of getting something in the can. She had established her authority with the crew and that would make directing a lot easier. Game on.

Five

The first filming location was a bit of a let-down. Instead of the anticipated high-tech scientific survey vessel, they found a rundown trawler taking up the berth.

'Are you sure this is it?' asked Charlie. 'Looks more like a fishing boat to me.'

Nathalie looked at her call-sheet. 'It says here we are to meet at Berth 4B. The contact's name is Pearce. Stay here with the gear, I'll check it out.'

She made her way across the makeshift wooden gangplank. The trawler stank of oil and seaweed. Above her head was a large mounted crane. To the aft, a yellow torpedo-shaped object set in a white metal cage and, towards the front, a superstructure which she assumed was the wheelhouse. Somewhere a metal door began to open. She was turning to see who it was when she slipped on a thick coil of tarred rope.

'Careful there, we don't want you breaking a leg before we've started.' A weather-beaten man in oilskins lifted her to her feet. 'Nathalie Thompson, I assume.' Nathalie was more embarrassed than shaken.

'Yes, sorry about that, not a good first impression, I'm afraid.' Then, gesturing to the deck of the ship. 'So this is The Lone Ranger, and you must be Captain Pearce.'

'You're right on the last front but the vessel's called the *Cambrian Explorer*. It's the sonar that's called The Lone Ranger; gimmicky name for Long Range Inclined ASDIC Device. If that's your crew on the quayside, tell them I'll get someone to help them aboard.'

Their cabins were cramped and hot. Dan and Luke were squeezed into one, and Nathalie and Charlie into another, further down the narrow corridor next to the ship's galley. No room here for the prudish. Against the wall were two high-sided wooden bunks.

‘I’ll take the top one if you want,’ said Charlie, throwing his bag onto the bed.

‘That’s chivalrous of you,’ said Nathalie, sarcastically.

‘Not really. I prefer the top bunk, used to have one as a kid. I’d feel a bit strange in the bottom one.’ So, for the first time a chink in the armour, thought Nathalie, a cameraman with a background; interesting.

She left Charlie and the crew to store away their equipment and climbed the metal stairway to meet with Captain Pearce and the scientific director. She had been on the island of Oahu for twelve hours. So much for the glamorous location of Hawaii. All she had seen so far was the inside of a hotel room, a few palm trees on the way to the docks, and the inside of a smelly, confined trawler.

The chart room was also claustrophobic. A pale-looking man with small dull eyes and a pointed nose pompously introduced himself as Dr Phelps, Director of Scientific Ops.

‘Sorry about the accommodation. What with the ship’s crew and the sonar operators and interpreters, I’m afraid this is a tight ship. We’ll be underway in half an hour so I’ll brief you quickly on the project and lay out some simple rules for the film crew – health and safety, and so on, When we are at sea I’ll introduce you to one of our riggers, who will tell you where you can set up your camera.’

The brief was just that, brief. The scientific director obviously didn’t have much interest in the making of their film. He’d probably been coerced into having them on board by his clients, who were after the publicity. The trawler just happened to be the cheapest and most practical vessel they could hire from which to launch their precious Lone Ranger system. That was the yellow torpedo thing that Nathalie had seen earlier. Apparently, they simply dragged this object behind them in the deep ocean and it sent out pulses of sound in a thin, fan-shaped beam on either side of the ship’s track.

‘What’s the difference between this and the sonar that they use for detecting submarines during the war?’ asked Nathalie.

Phelps was outraged. ‘This isn’t any old sonar; it’s the fastest, most accurate deep mapping device in the world. It’s unique. It can survey vast areas very quickly, and the data can be printed out in real time.' He held up some strips of paper. 'See these, we stick them together to make a detailed 3-D picture of the seabed. In fact, our next job is to update the maps of the sea floor around the whole of the United States' coastline.'

'Is that anything to do with the Exclusive Economic Zones and the ratification of the Law of the Sea Treaty?' interrupted Nathalie.

She could see from Phelps' face that she had dropped a bombshell. The casual off-hand arrogance disappeared; instead he reddened and began to stutter.

'Well, I'm afraid that's client confidential. I understand your purpose here is to film the work we're doing on energy from the ocean.' He scrabbled for a chart and hastily circled an area with his finger. 'You see, our current project is to determine if there are possible areas of deep-sea volcanic fissures near the coast of Malachi, for our present client to exploit geothermal energy.'

He rolled up the chart and made his way towards the wheelhouse, muttering something about having to prepare for casting off and checking the deployment systems. She had obviously shaken him with her knowledge of the Economic Zones and she wondered whether his future clients had anything to do with her well-spanked senator. Small world!

Nathalie didn't believe in coincidences so she hurried to her cabin to unzip her laptop. The trawler's engines had begun to rumble and she could hear movements on the deck above her. No internet signal. She was surprised because the ship, although looking like an old clapped-out trawler, was stuffed full of technology. She thought it unwise to ask if they had satellite reception. They would only be at sea for two days; she would do some digging when she got back. Until then she would have to concentrate on the job in hand, getting good footage of the Lone Ranger at sea and, if what she had been told was no exaggeration, the instant 3D printout of the deep sea floor.

Suppertime on board was at the strange hour of five o'clock in the afternoon. Sailors ate early, went to bed early and got up early.

Nathalie realised that she hadn't slept properly in two days so she joined the boys in the galley. The floor of the ship had begun to heave. Dan and Luke took one look at the half-cooked greasy bacon and left the room without a word. Nathalie grabbed some tongs, pushed a few scraps of meat into two bread rolls, and handed one to Charlie.

'Filmed at sea before?'

He nodded, munching into the bacon sandwich. 'You?'

'A few times. I felt like Dan and Luke at first but you get used to it.'

'Any luck with the boffin? He didn't look too enthralled to meet us.'

'Something not quite right there. You'd think he would be really keen to talk about his stuff on camera. Instead, he's asked one of the subcontractors to look after us. You know, the guys who stick that sonar torpedo into the water, or "marine deployment" I think they prefer to call it. They're from an outfit called Marine Corps. I've already talked to one of them. They sound cool, a lot cooler than our boffin. I don't think we'll have any problem with them helping us get the shots we want. I've warned our minder that we have to do things again and again from different angles and he seemed to understand.'

'Not like most people then. They think we can make a half-hour film in half an hour; not three minutes of usable footage in a ten-hour day.'

'Well, I'm aiming at five so you better up your game,' said Nathalie, making for the door. 'Take your time with your sandwich, though. I'm going for a wash and to put my head down, and I promise I won't steal your precious top bunk.'

It was dark, the whole world seemed to be moving and she was being shaken violently. Charlie's voice came from somewhere above her.

'Wake up. It's five-thirty and they're about to launch the sonar.'

Nathalie couldn't make out why someone would wake her up the minute she had dozed off. 'I've only just fallen asleep; they told me they weren't going to do it until tomorrow morning.'

'It is tomorrow morning; I've had to put up with your snoring all night. You better hurry up, I don't think they're going to wait for us. Dan and Luke are already on deck. I've asked Luke to set up the tripod, all we need now is a director.'

She struggled into her jeans and sweatshirt and followed Charlie onto the swaying deck. She was completely disorientated but the early morning fresh air and the ocean spray soon made her come to her senses. Looking to the aft of the ship, it became obvious why the scientist had chosen the trawler. The stern had opened up with two metal doors revealing a gap where the nets would have been cast out. Now, instead of the nets, there was a swivelling crane between two gantries hanging over the ocean. Two men were already moving into the gantry cages and clipping themselves on with ropes and harnesses. It looked bloody dangerous. Nathalie swung into action.

'Charlie, grab a static wide-shot from where you are, and then pick up close-ups on those two guys. Dan, get as much dialogue as you can, we can get rough sea atmos any time later. I understand it's difficult in these conditions, just do your best. Luke, I know it's not your job; as lighting is impossible on this deck would you act as Charlie's camera assistant.'

'Good idea,' shouted Charlie. 'Luke, can you stand on this tripod spreader; I'm finding it difficult to keep it on the deck. Dan, I'll give you a signal when we're on the tight-shots so you can get your boom in closer. I'll let you know if you get into shot by shouting "Get your fucking boom out of shot." Slate ready? Mark it.'

The four of them swung into action. To an outsider it would have looked as if this film crew had worked together for a lifetime, yet they had only met twenty-four hours ago. It was a strange occupation; wherever you went in the world to pick up crew, they always turned up on time, slipped into events like a well-oiled machine, and got paid at the end of the shoot. No contract, no fuss. This was the part of her job that Nathalie really enjoyed. It was like conducting an orchestra; they all knew their role and could probably do most of it without her but she had to put all the pieces together and if anything went wrong, it was she who would carry the can. The yellow torpedo in its white cage was now being inched from the horizontal to an alarming angle into the ocean. The two guys on either side were shouting instructions to the winch house. The end of the sonar was now immersed in the sea and the buffeting was making the operation even more difficult. Nathalie tried to imagine the story she would be assembling in the cutting room.

'Take a close-up of the end going into the water,' she shouted to Charlie. 'Then a mid-shot of the winch house.'

Charlie moved closer to the ship's guard rail and raised up the tripod to get the angle he needed.

'Careful there,' the rigger behind him pointed to a snake-like metal rope on the deck. 'When she goes in that will uncoil like a whip; it could take your leg off.'

Charlie nodded and moved his position. Although the rope was only about five centimetres across it was made of twisted steel and attached to the front end of the yellow torpedo. He could see the rigger's point. As soon as the sonar was fully in the water this rope would be played out to drag it behind the ship. Once it had started to uncoil there would be no way to stop it.

'Good shot here, Nathalie,' he mouthed to her across the deck. 'Just like a silver serpent.'

'Go for it. Just don't miss the final launch in the ocean because of the arty stuff. I'm thinking of mixing into graphics to show how it works at that point.'

The sea conditions were making things difficult. Finally they got the thing into the ocean. Just as the rigger predicted, the narrow metal rope shot across the deck and suddenly became taut as it took up the strain. It was surprisingly strong for such a narrow gauge. The winch man played it out until the Lone Ranger slowly disappeared under the water, some eighty or ninety metres behind them.

'What happens now?' asked Nathalie.

The rigger beside her gestured towards the wheelhouse. 'That's all you are going to see out here. What we do now is to tow her at a constant eight knots; that way, she stays fifty metres below the surface.

Any slower and she'll sink. You had best set up in the printer room. We should be getting some readings soon.'

Nathalie knew it would take Luke at least an hour to set up his lights. She followed the rigger down into the bowels of the ship to check out the room. It was even smaller than she had imagined. Crammed with oscilloscopes and electrical metres it reminded her of her old physics lab at school, the difference being the print table in the middle. A wide strip of paper was horizontally stretched across a flat bed with a needle poised on its surface, like a seismic recorder. The needle wasn't moving, but something was. Crammed into the corner of the room was a small table containing a computer-like object bucking like a rodeo bull.

'That's pretty weird, what's it doing that for?' she asked.

One of the scientists, a girl wearing a T-shirt with the caption 'Time is God's way of stopping everything happening at once' on it, walked over to the machine and placed a pencil vertically on its surface. The pencil rock 'n' rolled with the table and amazingly, didn't fall over.

'It's not the table that's moving, it's on a gimbal. It's you.' Nathalie suddenly felt queasy. Evidently, the table and the pencil were absolutely still. It was the ship that was heaving around. She tried not to think about it and to concentrate on her job.

'There's not much room in here. We will need to light it; do you know which electrical sockets we can use?'

'The ones on that wall are fine. You'll have to strap your lights down; could be dangerous if they go crashing into our equipment.'

'I'm sure Luke will be careful. I'll just tell Charlie what shots I'd like to take and then leave them to it, if that's okay with you?'

'Fine, go ahead. When the printer gets going we'll have our work cut out, okay?'

The printer had been rattling away for at least half an hour when Charlie came to tell her that they were ready to shoot. The paper printout was better than Nathalie had hoped for. It really looked like a monochrome map of the deep sea contours. She could pick out each canyon and ridge.

'Bloody amazing,' she exclaimed. 'What detail.'

The 'Time is God's way' girl pointed to a place on the chart.

'More amazing than you think. See this shape here?' Her finger outlined a cone-like structure. 'It's half of a volcano four miles under the ocean's surface. If you go on deck you'll see the other half. It's the island of Malachi. Millions of years ago the volcano sheared into two and part of it slumped onto the seabed. Geologists were pretty sure of this because the scars of the resulting tsunami can still be seen on the neighbouring island of Oahu. Now we are the first people to actually show them that it's true. Worth going to sea for, eh?'

From the excitement on her face, Nathalie could tell that this is what these boffins lived for.

'Will this help your client with their ocean energy study?'

The girl shrugged. 'Don't know, we just publish the charts. It's up to them to do the interpretation.'

'Will the States be able to use this stuff for their Exclusive Economic Zone mapping project? I think the treaty lets them exploit the ocean floor two hundred miles from their coast line, doesn't it? And Hawaii is theirs.'

The girl looked uncomfortable. Not the first time that the mention of the EEZ had caused a squirm, thought Nathalie.

'No idea. As I said, it's our job to make maps. What the boss does with them is up to him. Don't mean to be rude; if you've got enough stuff down here, why don't you go back on deck? We could do with the space.'

'Okay,' said Nathalie. 'Guys, it's a wrap here. Let's get the gear out and go for a cup of coffee.'

Charlie unlocked his camera from the tripod. 'You go on ahead, I've got to get a new magazine from the cabin. Mine's black with two sugars.'

The galley was always laid out with bits of food and pastries for snacking sailors. Nathalie took a couple of mugs from the shelf and filled them from the coffee urn. She munched on a charred piece of shortbread. Some minutes later Sam and Luke joined her.

'Charlie not with you? His coffee's getting cold.'

'No. You want us to fetch him? He might want some help with loading the magazine.'

'Let him be, most cameramen I know don't like …'

But Dan and Luke would never find out what most cameramen didn't like because their conversation was interrupted by a scream in the wind from the deck above them.

Six

It had started to rain; hard, hot rain mixing with the salt spray on the deck, making visibility very difficult.

A sailor in an orange lifejacket was shouting 'Man overboard!' repeatedly but not in panic. Nathalie's heart was in her mouth. Had Charlie become a little bit too adventurous? She ran up to the guard rail and was told to get back. Two more men in lifejackets swept past her. One rushed to the winch and started the motor to haul in the sonar. The other went to help the sailor at the rail. Through the spray she could see they were grappling with a wire which was hitched onto one of the gantries. Now she understood what was happening; someone had fallen overboard. Fortunately they were still attached to the ship by a lifeline. An orange shape was thrashing around in the water behind them. One minute it was there, the next it wasn't.

Someone grabbed her shoulders from behind.

'What's happening?'

Nathalie felt a flood of relief flow through her body. Charlie's voice. Without turning, she shouted back at him.

'One of the riggers has fallen in the water; he's still on a wire and they are trying to haul …' She was stopped by a searing noise of metal and motor. The winch had begun to slip and the silver metal rope holding the sonar was beginning to lash backwards and forwards on the pulleys.

'Shut it off,' screamed a sailor at the rail. 'You'll kill him!'

'Keep it going,' another voice had joined the mêlée. 'That's millions of dollars worth of sonar; if the rope breaks she'll go to the bottom.'

The scientific director was running towards the winch house. The winch man slammed the door on him. The winch motor stopped but the metal rope continued bucking. Phelps had reached the winch house and was hammering on the door, only Nathalie had seen something else. High above them on the crane the metal rope had slipped its pulley. Half of the rope appeared to be cleanly cut in two. The other half, strand by strand, was beginning to unsplice. The sailors on the rail were right; if the rope broke it could whiplash into the sea and sever the lifeline or, even worse, the man on the end of it.

The sea conditions seemed to be getting worse. Wave after wave of water smashed onto the deck. It was like watching a scene in a strobing nightclub; the action broken up into jerky, slow-motion frames. Phelps had realised that, now the rope was off the pulley, even the winch motor was rendered useless. He started to remonstrate with a rigger about climbing the crane to weld the rope, an almost impossible job on land, let alone in a violent sea. The two men at the rail were having more success; metre by metre they were pulling in the lifeline. The victim was nearly at the ship's hull. Their next problem was to stop him being smashed against the side. Someone had grabbed a mattress from one of the bunks, tied ropes to it, and was attempting to use it as a fender. The body was limp and it was obvious that the man couldn't help himself, so the rescuers used all their strength to pull at the line. The harness was halfway up the hull when it happened. With a whistle like a firework the sonar winch rope broke. It flew like a fighting kite through the air and threatened to cut the rescuers in two. At the last moment it struck backwards and plunged into the trawler's wake. At the same moment a final heave brought the body onto the deck. Years of training snapped into action. If anyone could revive him it was these men.

'We've lost the fucking sonar!' screamed Phelps. He was ignored, by every one of them.

The Soho offices of Bagatelle were in their usual state of creative chaos when Nathalie's phone call came through. A film crew, returning from a story with the London Fire Brigade, were stacking their aluminium boxes in reception; a production assistant, waiting for an interview, was asking how long it would be; and the switchboard was alight with outside calls. Despite this, the receptionist kept her cool.

'Mr Sykes is in a meeting right now but as your call is urgent I'll see if he can be interrupted. Do you want to give me your number in case we get cut off?'

'He's got my number and tell him he will want to be interrupted.'

Geoff Sykes was used to urgent interruptions. Fortunately, so were his clients so it was agreed that they would all take a coffee break and resume the meeting in fifteen minutes. Geoff found a quiet room and picked up the receiver.

'Fire away, I'm all ears.'

Nathalie calmly told him about the disaster at sea; the lost sonar and the man overboard. The rigger had nearly drowned, though they thought he would pull through. In the aftermath there had been an emergency meeting to investigate the causes. A row had broken out between the scientific director and the riggers from Marine Corps.

'Say that again,' said Geoff.

Nathalie repeated that there had been a row.

'No, about the riggers, where did you say they came from?'

'Marine Corps. They've been subcontracted to the sonar project. Why? Is it important?'

'Just checking, carry on. What was the outcome of the row?'

During the voyage Nathalie had been taking notes and so she could unemotionally report the sequence of events. She carefully related the facts, her personal observations of the actual incident, and other people's ideas. The casualty was thought to have been trying to repair the half-severed metal towing rope when he had been thrown into the sea. Luckily he had attached himself to the ship by a safety line. They hadn't got the full story yet because he was still in a bad state. There were a number of theories about why the towing rope had broken. The riggers had said it could be something to do with it being caught in the ship's rear doors but Phelps, the project's director, was claiming that it was sabotage. That was the beginning of the row.

People wanted to know who on earth would want to sabotage the survey. Phelps had his own ideas yet wouldn't tell anyone. The meeting had ended in acrimony and the captain had set sail for Honolulu. The moment she had picked up reception for her mobile Nathalie had phoned Geoff to ask what she should do next. They were due in within the hour.

'And how are you and the rest of the crew?' Geoff probed.

'Physically fine, a bit shaken up seeing the state of that guy, and a bit upset about losing our storyline on ocean energy. We got stuff in the "can" though, so I expect we can do something with it.'

'So what's your theory? You sound a bit, how do I say, cautious on that front.'

'It's only a feeling, I can't put it more than that. Ever since I stepped on board I felt something wasn't quite right about this lot.'

'Okay, speculate. What do you think's going on?'

'Not really sure but there is one thing. I've mentioned a couple of times about something called Exclusive Economic Zones. I know about them from my last project. Phelps dropped that he was about to be commissioned by the States to do a marine survey. I asked him if it was to do with exploitation of their EEZs. He went scarlet and shut up like a clam. Later, I said something similar to one of his assistants. By her reaction, you would have thought I'd asked her about her private sex life. And on that point, did you read about that senator who was fired?'

'The guy who was going to ratify the Law of the Sea Treaty?'

'The very one. Makes you think, doesn't it?'

Geoff was already reaching for the internal phone and keying in his PA's number. He put the external line temporarily on mute and asked Stefanie to get hold of Nick Coburn. He flicked back the switch.

'Okay, Nathalie, this is what I want you to do. Keep the crew on, and plan for your next location on the call-sheet. Don't tell them anything at the moment. I think we've got a potential investigative documentary here. We'll have to shoot it in parallel with our Ocean Tech sponsored stuff but if we plan it carefully, they won't even know about it. It's a risk and may not turn out to be anything at all. Bagatelle will put up the extra funds. Are you game?'

Nathalie wasn't sure what she was about to be game for but Geoff sounded as if he knew what he was talking about so she simply said 'Yes.'

A few hours later Nick Coburn knocked on Geoff Sykes' office door and poked his head around. The two men had met on a past production and had since become great friends.

'This had better be bloody important,' said Nick, throwing himself into a comfy chair and putting his feet on Geoff's desk. 'I'm missing a Harlequins match because of you.'

Geoff had heard that Harlequins was a rugby team and he couldn't fathom why watching a bunch of grown men groping each other in swathes of mud would interest anybody.

'I'm sure they'll win without your support, might do better in fact without your tuneless "Swing Low" rendition. Also, I've got better things for you to do.'

'Such as?'

'Such as fly to New York and check out a senator who has been a naughty boy.' Geoff threw a pile of papers into Nick's lap. 'And while you're about it, you could see what this lot are up to.'

Nick looked at the pamphlets advertising the services of Marine Corps. He liked this type of job. Ever since he had left the army he had been a self-employed itinerant; no job too big or too small, too crazy or too dangerous, that was his motto. People knew this and because of it he ended up with the big, dangerous jobs. Geoff knew nothing of his other work and had the sense not to ask. All he was interested in was that, if he had a risky research job for a film, Nick was his man.

'Something's not right in the state of ocean research,' mused Geoff. 'A couple of so-called accidents involving a drilling ship and a survey vessel. Both touched with the fingerprints of a company called Marine Corps. And here,' he handed Nick another file, 'someone in America isn't very keen on sharing their coastal resources with the rest of the world. I'm not sure if they are connected. That's what I'm paying you to find out.'

Nick flicked through the papers. 'What's this climate change stuff about?'

'Oh yes, that's my theory for what it's worth. The petroleum-backed anti-climate change lobby has got a lot to gain from the failure of these projects. If it's too dangerous to get climate data or carbon-free energy from the sea it could be another weapon for them against the alternative energy lobby.'

'And?' Nick began to read from the file in front of him. 'These EEZs, what's that got to do with signing treaties and climate change?'

'Not sure, haven't thought that one through yet. Think we need more pieces of the jigsaw before we start putting a programme exposé together. Nathalie Thompson is in the Pacific at the moment; I've asked her to get any material on ocean stuff that she can. As and when a story develops, I'll be able to give her more of a pointer.'

At that moment Nathalie Thompson was lying on her hotel bed, wondering what on earth she had got herself into. Shooting one film was hard enough. Shooting two, one that had to be kept secret from the other and without a storyline to boot, was going to be dammed difficult. She studied the call-sheet, the only crutch she had – a step-by-step itinerary of the proposed locations and contacts for the shoot.

Most foreign tourists tend to call the island of Oahu 'Hawaii'. In fact, Hawaii is a chain of islands. The eight larger islands include Maui, Molokai, Oahu and the largest island, Hawaii. To avoid confusion this largest island is known as 'the Big Island'. This was scheduled as their next port of call. The accompanying paperwork was very technical and Nathalie had delayed studying it until the last possible moment. She picked out the most user-friendly looking document, *OTEC is a reality in Hawaii…Now* read the title. After studying it for an hour she had come to the conclusion that the title was misleading. OTEC stood for Ocean Thermal Energy Conversion. It was a way of extracting energy from the temperature differences between warm surface water and deep cold water. Apparently, Hawaii was the perfect place for this; a subtropical island surrounded by deep ocean, filled with a cold Antarctic current. The problem wasn't in the word OTEC. The paper clearly explained how heat exchangers made the pollution-free electricity. What was misleading was the word 'Now'. A research programme had been operating on the Big Island for tens of years. To date, no practical facility was producing electricity on a large scale. She checked the briefing notes that Geoff's researcher had given her. They looked hurriedly put together and she deduced that the United States had decided to make a huge effort to get something up and running. Climate change propaganda was plastered all over it. A handwritten note was scribbled alongside the contact name, *Be careful of this guy, he was very touchy on the telephone, very green and all that*. Nathalie was used to filming with difficult customers but she was glad of the note; Professor Bernard Lake would be treated with kid gloves.

'Anybody there?' Charlie was knocking on the door.

'Come in, door's open.'

'Just wanted to know what the plan is.'

'The plan says we should still be at sea filming deep-sea floor mapping. But, as their device is at the bottom of the sea and they haven't got another one, we've got a day to spare.'

'Yeah, shame. I was changing the magazine. Would have been great to have got all the action; looked spectacular.'

Nathalie looked at their windowless, uninspiring surroundings. 'I've got an idea. If you like the spectacular and you're up for it, why don't we drive to the north coast and film some surf? It's not scheduled but we will see some of the island and I could use some GVs for a title sequence.'

'Sounds good to me, I'll go and tell the others to load up the truck.'

They took the downtown freeway out of Honolulu. An enormous plaster pineapple loomed up on one side of the road. As they drove on Route 99 through the centre of the island they realised its significance; the pungency of sweet pineapple was everywhere.

'If you want, you can take one back to the mainland; it's the only fresh fruit that the airlines will allow,' said Luke, slowing the pickup down. 'I'll dig one out, if you like.'

'Luke's a mine of local information,' laughed Dan. 'If you don't want to get locked up for being an accessory to pineapple theft I suggest you ignore him.'

'Our onward ticket takes us west,' said Charlie from the back seat. 'So we won't be going back to your so-called mainland anyway.'

Nathalie joined in. 'I hear Charlie's going to get a grass skirt as his souvenir. If you see a store selling those, you can pull over, Luke.'

The pickup shot forwards as Luke put his foot on the pedal.

'He'll be able to get plenty of those at Sunset Beach; coconut bra too, I expect.'

'I'll wear it if you do, Luke,' laughed Charlie. 'I could get a great shot of you on a surfboard.'

Nathalie grinned. 'This isn't meant to be a holiday. I hear that Sunset Beach has some of the best waves in the world and I want some really good pictures of Hawaiian surf. Natural power and beauty sort of thing, not Luke on a surfboard, wearing a pair of coconuts.'

They all laughed at the image. Although it wasn't meant to be a holiday, it did feel like one; an open pickup and tropical sunshine. Luke turned up the radio. The four of them looked ridiculous as they began to head-bang and sing at the tops of their voices.

Nathalie's source was right. Sunset Beach does have some of the best waves in the world. The wind drives the water over thousands of miles before it hits the north coast of the island of Oahu. As the truck pulled up on a grassy ridge above the dunes they could see the massive turquoise rollers tipped with white boiling spray. A small bleached beach hut sported violently coloured surfboards stuck in the sand. Brightly logoed T-shirts hung on a rail and a rusty Coca-Cola sign swayed in the wind. All the signs of beach-bum life.

Charlie was the first out of the truck. 'We can do all this mute. I'll use a long lens and just pick off some shots. Can't go wrong in this light with a location like this.'

Nathalie grabbed the tripod and stood beside him. 'I'll give you a hand. Dan and Luke, why don't you take it easy? Stroll down the beach with the audio and grab a few FX.' She pointed to a parasol-shaped thatched hut. 'We'll meet you at that beach bar when the light goes.'

It was late afternoon and the light was getting lower, picking out the rocks and surf in 3D. Charlie slapped a UV filter on his lens and got to work. They manoeuvred their way to the edge of the bay, stopping now and then to put the camera on the tripod. In the distance, Nathalie could see the real pro-surfers just lying on their boards, waiting for the big one. A roller started to come in and she could sense by their movement that this might be it. She rammed the tripod into the sand and cupped her hands around her eyes to make what she thought was the best view.

Shit, those tourists on the beach are slap-bang in the way. She shouted at them. 'Hey, you there, can you move?'

The small group of tourists looked up in puzzlement. Nathalie repeated her shout, this time adding a very loud and elongated 'Please'.

Not a sign of movement.

'They can't understand you, they're Japanese. The island is full of them, it's their top resort.' Charlie waved at the group, '*Jama ni naranai yō ni idō shite kudasai.*'

Whatever he said, it seemed to work. They smiled, bowed and shuffled out of the way.

'*Arigatō*,' he added, putting the camera onto the tripod and pointing to it. They waved and nodded vigorously. Charlie put his eye to the soft chamois eyepiece.

'You're going to like this one,' he said, turning the camera over.

The ocean roll began to swell and break. The small group of surfers paddled furiously to keep up. One by one, they stood on their boards. They were taken up on the crest and zigzagged their way through the iridescent tube. The sun had begun to set and its last rays splintered into thousands of pieces as it hit the flecks of surf. Nathalie was breathless.

Charlie flicked the switch off, stood back and shook his head. 'Awesome.'

The two of them stood there on the sand, watching the sun sink below the black rocks. Nathalie felt Charlie's arm resting on her shoulder.

'Where on earth did you learn to speak Japanese?' she asked.

Seven

The Alex wouldn't have been his first choice of hotel. He hated midtown Manhattan but it was clean, modern and a six-minute walk from the United Nations. Nick Coburn was a downtown sort of man, more at home in the multi-ethnic streets of SoHo and the East Village, yet work was work and he wouldn't have much time for walking the streets and eating out. He had taken a cab from JFK and the hotel had held his small holdall in the lobby while he checked out another room; the one they had given him was no use as a temporary office. The suite on the thirteenth floor suited him best; a bloody nuisance about the elevator ride, although the separate room and the desk with an internet point would make up for that. He haggled on the price, claiming that having to wait for the lift to the extra floors wiped out the extra space. The argument was lost on them as they didn't understand the word 'lift', but this large-framed man with the ice-cold demeanour was not to be argued with, so he got his way.

'Computer World' was teeming as usual. He purchased the cheapest laptop they had and asked them to throw in a few memory sticks. He never owned or travelled with a computer, you never knew who would look inside it. In a side street nearby he found a two-bit phone store; a few dollars bought him a basic handset and a pay-as-you-go card. He texted his new number to Bagatelle. A couple of hardback files for the paperwork Geoff had given him and he would be set up. He found some in a discount place next to a liquor store. Some cold beers wouldn't go amiss, and he wasn't going to pay minibar prices so he grabbed a few six-packs and took his stash back to the Alex. He had just settled down to watch the evening news when his new mobile phone rang.

'Geoff?'

'Good trip?'

'Had better. Bloody security's ridiculous, all show. Hours queuing with my shoes off, when I could have waved a gun in their face and they wouldn't have seen it.'

'Are you online yet?'

'Nearly, just have to load some software and set up an address. Why? You're not going to send me any more stuff, are you? I haven't finished reading the lot you gave me for the plane journey. Lot of shit that was too.'

'Afraid so. Nathalie has sent me an e-mail saying she's got some research on the Law of the Sea Treaty. Good stuff apparently, personal contacts and so on. It's in her flat. She says her mother has a spare key. As soon as I get it, I'll scan in anything that looks useful and mail it to you.'

'Wonderful,' Nick said, as if it was anything but.

'Don't worry, I'll weed it. She was doing some corporate for the IMO. Knowing Nathalie, she'll have some good leads with numbers and addresses. Could save you time in the long run.'

'Okay, I'll e-mail you my address as soon as. I'll look at it in the morning. Only, no more, yeah? I'm not going to get anywhere by reading all day, I need to talk to people.'

'Sure, Nick. Keep it to talking, okay.'

Nick flicked the red button on his phone and switched the TV sound on again.

The newly appointed governor from the US Environmental Protection Agency was fielding questions on climate change and US energy policy. Nick tried to analyse his speech. Like those of most politicians, although it sounded impressive when you boiled it down the content contained absolutely nothing.

The morning was bright and crisp. Long shadows fell across East 45th Street. It was only a two-block walk to the UN building and Nick had plenty of time. Geoff was right about Nathalie's contacts. A guy called Philippe Charday, from the media department, had agreed to meet him for mid-morning coffee. He hadn't actually met Nathalie in the flesh although they had had many chats by Skype and e-mail. He said that they had got on professionally, both being in the media. Nick could tell that he really fancied her. A good place to start, better than Geoff's ticket to the lecture on climate change. Philippe sounded like he would do anything for Nathalie.

He walked past the iconic row of international flags and showed his lecture ticket to the guy at the turnstiles. The vaulted visitors' lobby was full of tourists milling around the exhibition stands. He looked around for Philippe. In front of him were a number of white-walled, open-planned floors reaching to the ceiling. To one side a webbed barrier guiding visitors to the exhibition and, on the other, the coffee shop. A reflective young man with a goatee beard was sitting at one of the tables. Nick held out his hand.

'Philippe, by the description. Nick Coburn. Thanks for seeing me at such short notice.'

'No problem, glad to help. I feel a bit bad about letting Nathalie down with her interview.'

'Letting her down?'

'She was really keen to promote the UNEP so I'd set her up with this meeting with Cronkar.'

'UNEP?'

'United Nations Environmental Program. We need all the good publicity we can get so, when Nathalie explained she was doing an educational film for the IMO, I agreed to help and told her the best guy to talk to would be Cronkar. Didn't turn out that way, though, the perverted bastard.'

'You knew him?'

'Thought so, but apparently not.'

'Who's taken his place?'

'A guy called Governor Cain. I wouldn't recommend getting him to talk about the Law of the Sea stuff, though.'

'This for me?' asked Nick, nodding towards the Styrofoam cup of cooling coffee.

'Sorry, yes. Do you want me to get you a fresh one?'

'No, this will be fine, thanks. Go on, you were saying you wouldn't recommend this Governor Cain.'

'Completely different, how do you say, "pot of fish"?'

'Kettle,' supplied Nick. 'Kettle of fish.'

'Yes, kettle of fish. Ambiguous on climate change, has stalled the ratification of the treaty, and is keen to promote the United States EEZs. Sorry, that's Exclusive …'

'Economic Zones,' completed Nick. 'Yes, I've heard of them.' He held up his ticket. 'So why is this guy giving a lecture on climate change?'

'That's it, he's not. The lecture topic changed this morning. "Environmental Protection and the Economic Zones." I had to prepare the slide presentation for him. He's making out that if the States are given full control of the ocean floor they will be able to protect the environment as well. Doesn't add up to me. A lot of this stuff is oil company backed; they just put a green flag on their logo and pretend they're environmentally friendly.'

Philippe was certainly an intense young man but he had a point. Fitted Geoff's theory about oil companies too.

'Is this stuff about double-blind exploration sites true?' Nick pushed an old copy of *The New Yorker* onto the coffee table.

Philippe glanced at the title of the article. He almost knew it off by heart.

'That's the proposition. One of the biggest sticking points on the Law of the Sea Treaty. Think about it, ninety per cent of wars are about territory. Two-thirds of the planet are underwater and aren't owned by anybody. Up to now it hasn't mattered. There's nothing there that anybody wants and, if there is, it's almost impossible to get at.' He drained the last of his coffee and held it upside down for Nick to see.

'Now, let's suppose someone has the technology to get to the deep-sea floor, exploit it for energy, oil or gas. Whose is it?' He drew a question mark on the bottom of his Styrofoam cup with a Biro and pushed the cup into the middle of the table.

'Let's say it's five hundred miles from the nearest coastline. Do you measure who is closest, or,' Philippe smiled, accentuating his accent, 'how do you say it, finders keepers?'

'So they want companies to operate two sites if they find anything?'

'Naturally. If you can exploit the seabed, which you don't own, it's only fair. You make two sites – you keep the profits of one and you share the other with the international community.' Philippe picked up the two empty coffee cups on the table and put them behind his back.

'So you can't cheat, you give the international community a blind choice of the sites.'

'I can see why a governor of a high-tech state wouldn't think that a good idea,' said Nick, tapping Philippe on both shoulders and putting out his hands for the cups. Philippe handed them to him and pointed up to the gallery.

'That's him now. He'll be heading for the lecture hall. We should go.'

A stocky, silver-haired man accompanied by a leggy blonde started to descend the staircase.

'Who's the diva?' asked Nick.

'I wouldn't let her hear you call her that. It's Viveca Olsson, she's senior operations manager for the Environmental Protection Agency. Used to work with Cronkar, now been assigned to Cain. Tough cookie.' Philippe's accent became stronger again, as it did whenever he fell into colloquialisms.

'Can you get me to meet her?'

'I could try; we used to bump into each other quite frequently when Cronkar was around, but nowadays, her diary seems quite full.'

'Are you unhappy that Cronkar resigned?'

'Of course. He would have signed the treaty, only he didn't because he got caught up in that scandal.'

'Perhaps he got caught up in that "scandal", as you call it, because he was going to sign the treaty?' Nick proffered, crushing the Styrofoam cups and throwing them into the bin. 'If you don't mind, I'll give the lecture a miss. There's someone else I must talk to.'

Pumas Gentlemen's Club and Restaurant was in a nice part of town. It was a nice sort of club. 'Gorgeous topless dancers, happy hour drinks and delicious food' went the blurb on the website. The word 'Gentlemen's' was a bit of a misnomer because they also advertised bachelorette parties. Nick had known the manager for years. What Victor didn't know about New York club life, you could write on a girl's G-string.

'Can I get you coffee?' asked Victor, pulling up a gold-backed red velour chair to the spangled table. Nick sat down beside him and looked around at the empty stage.

'Only if you make two and I get to choose,' he replied enigmatically.

'You want two?'

'No, sorry, an in-joke. I just had one. A beer would go down fine, if it's not too early for you.'

'It's never too early for me,' said Victor, clicking his fingers at the young man vacuuming the stage. 'Billy, two beers, and cut that machine, we're trying to have a quiet conversation over here.'

Nick laid out a newspaper and a few blown-up photographs onto the table.

'You seen this guy?'

Victor didn't even lean over to look at the pictures.

'Of course, hasn't everyone in Manhattan? His face and arse have been plastered over every rag and television screen in the States. Weird, I thought he was a soft porn sort of guy.'

'What makes you say that?'

'Well, he wasn't regular but he's been here a few times – corporate do's, entertaining celebs, you know. Never asked for anything stronger.'

'Stronger?'

'The stuff we do here is pretty Disney – topless, lingerie, bikini.' He waved at the photographs. 'Anything like this is usually at private clubs; we get clients asking for the addresses.'

'Do you pass them on?'

'Sometimes, though less and less now. You can get most of this stuff on the internet.'

The beers arrived. The young man was moving the photographs to set them on the table when Nick noticed he did a double-take.

'Thanks. Naughty boy, wasn't he?'

'Yeah, it's just that I haven't seen these pictures so blown-up before.'

'Meaning?' said Nick, passing him one to look at more closely.

'I wondered where they went; looks like she took him to Spankers.'

'Pull up a chair,' said Nick.

Billy filled in the gaps. Cronkar had arrived at Pumas with a B-rated celebrity and two young women. One of them fitted the description of Viveca Olsson. They had ordered sushi and champagne before taking their coffee in the lingerie room. All very elegant and above board; girls in exotic underwear serving top-priced brandies. By the end of the evening Cronkar had almost certainly had one too many and the Olsson woman had asked for a couple of cabs. Billy had hailed two for them and noticed that Olsson had shepherded the senator into one with the other woman. She had given the cab driver instructions before getting into the other with the celebrity. He now knew where they had gone.

'See this ratchet thing on the side of that sort of mediaeval black rack? I've only seen one like that at Spankers. And if you look carefully in the background, there's the edge of some red neon lettering. It's cropped a bit but looks like it's the first letter of their logo that's above their dungeon bar.'

Nick thought that Billy knew rather a lot about the interior of this S&M club. He didn't bother asking why.

'So what's the address of this place and how do you become a member?' he asked.

It promised to be a long night so Nick strolled back to the Alex to put his feet up. He lay on the king-size bed, ordered a pastrami sandwich from room service and looked at the other stuff that Geoff had e-mailed him. Marine Corps seemed to be a name that cropped up more than once. They described themselves as ocean engineers. Their CV claimed that they worked on anything from oil rigs to submersibles. Geoff, or rather one of Geoff's researchers, had discovered that they had provided a support role to the International Ocean Drilling Project, as well as supplying engineers to the Lone Ranger survey. Worryingly they also had a team on Nathalie's next filming location, the Hawaiian OTEC Project. He looked at his watch; Hawaii was five hours behind, she was probably there right now. From the literature, these Marine Corps people were all over the place so it would be surprising if they weren't on big-time ocean projects. Just because there had been two incidents didn't mean ... Well, there wasn't much he could do about it from a New York hotel room. Internet research was more Nathalie's thing. He was better at getting information from people on the ground. Marine Corps didn't seem to have any offices in New York so he would bat that one back to Geoff. He turned over the card that Billy had given him – Spankers VIP Membership. Now underground nightlife was more up his street. The address was in the East Village, only a block from McSorley's Old Ale House. It was an area he knew well. The club didn't open until one in the morning, the very time that McSorley's closed. Would fit in nicely. He would sleep the afternoon off, take in some beers and a cheese plate at the Ale House, and turn up at the club just after one. He kicked his shoes off and put his head down.

McSorley's was a legend in New York. It claimed to be the city's oldest ale house. Irish origins, after the potato blight. A public house set up by one John McSorley, a mid-19th century immigrant. To Nick it seemed to want to keep it that way – sawdust on the floor, no cash registers and layers of dust on the bar.

It was quarter to midnight when he entered from the street and was hit by a wave of sound. It was three deep in the front bar, so he made his way into the back room. The beers came in twos here, one light and one dark for each order. Only half the glasses were full, the rest made up with froth. Nick knew from past experience that pouring one into the other made a good 'half and half'. He called for three pairs and some food, knowing that it would take some time before he could put in another order. Seeing the size of him a group squeezed up to let him have space at a table. The beers came at once, the food took a little longer. Nick had downed two 'half and halves' before the cheese plate was put in front of him. He wondered whether raw onion breath was part of the sadomasochism scene.

At exactly 1.00 am they were all politely but firmly asked to leave.

'Please respect our neighbours,' shouted the barman, 'they've had to put up with us for the last hundred and sixty years.'

The regulars must have heard this joke many times. They laughed anyway. Nick's VIP card insalubriously informed him that the entrance to Spankers could be found at 'the side door next to the parking lot'. He walked south towards 6th Street and ironically past a building with a plaque bearing the title of *The Women's Prison Association*. Founder members of Spankers' dungeon, Nick mused. He turned the corner to see an orderly queue of people in the dimly lit parking lot. They were a mixed bunch – young, highly made-up women in buttoned-up raincoats alongside what he could only describe as grey-haired lawyer types. He filed in behind them and pulled out the membership card from his wallet. The girl in front of him was given a leather paddle by the doorman.

'Welcome to Spankers,' he intoned without enthusiasm. 'Every tenth female guest receives a free paddle.'

She took it from him with a giggle and slipped through the small, scratched, iron door. Nick showed his card and was nodded through. The lobby was a bare brick, painted corridor lit by one small, naked red light-bulb. An iron stairway led to the basement. Although he had done many strange things in his life, he wasn't sure that he was ready for this one.

Eight

At the bottom of the staircase Nick was greeted by a very large bouncer with a gold ring through his right nostril. He scrutinised Nick's VIP card, sized him up, and gave him a locker key.

'Sadie will meet you in the bar after you've changed; she will be your hostess for the night,' he grunted, nodding towards the male cloakroom.

Billy had told him that this would be the form. The VIP card would give him access to one of the girls he knew in the club. He was only to talk to her and play along with the S&M scene. If he broke the rules, or tried getting information from anybody else, things could turn nasty.

'Just act as if you're enjoying yourself and you'll be fine,' Billy had said in parting.

The girls coming out of the ladies' cloakroom were doing just that. He now understood the buttoned-up Mackintosh uniform in the queue. Most of them were either wearing thin leather harnesses or schoolgirl kilts and tight little white shirts underneath. He felt distinctly overdressed.

The men's locker room looked very much like the one in his local squash club; steam, sweaty socks and some not-so-fit flesh. The difference was in the kit they were changing into. City types were buckling on impossible leather costumes, and elderly men were sporting shorts, ties and old-fashioned school caps. Nick looked at his key and found a locker with his number on it. The things he had to do for Geoff Sykes. The locker contained a pair of leather jeans, a small leather waistcoat and some cowboy boots.

Nick was just thinking that this was not too bad when he discovered that the jeans had no seat to them. A card on the inside of the locker spelt out the club rules.

No penetration.

No spanking of non-consenting participants.

No drugs.

It also revealed tonight's safe word: *'RED!'* This was the word that, when uttered, would stop whatever game was being played. One to remember, thought Nick.

He felt a complete idiot as he shuffled to the bar. Sadie was waiting for him, perched on an aluminium barstool. She was dressed from head to toe in a tightly laced rubber cat-suit. On any other evening Nick would have appreciated the outfit. Tonight, all he was conscious of was his bare backside. The club was getting into full swing. People were pairing up and settling onto the different types of equipment throughout the room. It was set up as some sort of mediaeval dungeon; the walls were painted black, the floor tiled with cold stone. In one corner a black iron cage hung from the ceiling; in another, a red wooden chair was festooned with manacles; in the middle was a strange, unpainted, rough wooden structure. This was made of two wide planks that slid between the side struts, just like a pair of stocks but with only one very small hole in the middle. Nick suddenly twigged what this was for.

'Bourbon?' Sadie slid him a drink across the bar.

'How did you guess?' Nick asked, downing it in one.

'You look like you need it. Your first time?'

'How did you guess?' repeated Nick.

'Is that all you can say? Billy said you had some questions.'

'Yeah, it's about that senator guy, the one all over the papers.'

Sadie looked around, and watched the woman in the plaid gymslip being spanked with a ruler.

'Don't look yet. See the dominatrix behind us? That's Geena, she runs the club. If she catches me talking to you, the game that these people are playing will look like tiddlywinks.'

'Can we go somewhere private?'

'This is as private as it gets. I'm meant to be hostessing you as a VIP. If Geena sees that we're just talking, we're both in trouble.'

'What do you suggest?' As the words were coming out of his mouth Nick started to regret saying them.

Sadie led him over to a strange-looking, worn red leather dentist's chair; it had a double seat. She sat Nick in one and sat astride the other, facing him.

'Just do as you're told and you can ask me questions between the pain,' she said, smiling and buckling the arm straps around his wrists.

'I'm not sure this is a good idea,' said Nick as she began to open his waistcoat.

'You were asking about the senator.'

He tried to concentrate.

'Billy thinks that he came here. Did you see him?'

'Of course. He stood out like a sore thumb.' She dangled a pair of small, shiny crocodile clips in front of him. 'Just like you.'

'Was he with anyone?'

'Yes, he arrived with a glamorous model type. Didn't seem sure where he was. Kept saying he was waiting for someone called Veronica or something.'

'Not Viveca?'

'Yes, that's right, odd name. The girl told him that she was delayed and Geena kept plying him with spiked champagne.'

'Did Viveca turn up? Ouch, what are you doing with those?'

'Just playing, keep still and they won't pull. No, she didn't. He kept protesting that he had been taken to the wrong place. After a few drinks and the attention of a few of the girls, he seemed to forget about it.'

'The video showed him getting involved in some pretty hard stuff; I can't see that torture rack thing in here.'

Sadie deliberately reached out for a candle next to the chair and began to trickle the hot wax over his chest.

'It looked like Geena had prearranged a "Special". There is a separate, intimate dungeon for the really hard-core stuff. Most members don't know about it, and probably would report it to the authorities if they did. They're usually respectable sorts of people who just like playing games.'

'Funny sort of games. You said "prearranged"; you think it had all been set up beforehand?'

'Yeah, sure of it. The rest of the girls were warned off; keep to our own clients and not to talk to him. You know something? When he was led away I couldn't help thinking he thought he was going to be the audience and not the show.'

To Nick's relief she started to undo his wrist straps.

'Now, if you're warmed up, I think we should go for the stocks,' she said, curling a little rubber cat o' nine tails around her fingers.

'Can't believe we're getting paid for this,' said Charlie, poking an ice-cube around his coconut shell with the small paper umbrella. 'Piña Colada cocktails, lobster dressed with pineapple, and an ocean view out of a holiday brochure.'

Nathalie nodded, the evening was surreal. They had landed at Kona Airport and been taken to their hotel by a courtesy minibus. Not the normal film crew economy accommodation. A marble staircase curled around a central lobby fountain leading towards their luxury bedrooms with balcony view. She had spent most of the day e-mailing the office between long pauses of catlike slumber, eyes closed, taking in the waves of pleasure through the sun on her face. The concierge had recommended a trip to Kailua Village, an historic seaside resort a few miles along the coast. Dan and Luke had been there before and preferred to chill out by the pool with, what they claimed would be, a 'few' beers. Nathalie and Charlie decided to take the rare opportunity to be tourists and hired a taxi to the Oceanside Restaurant. Charlie even bought an Aloha shirt to get into the spirit. The tables were wedged between slanting palm trees hung with webs of coloured lights. The shoreline could be heard through the twang of live music, and the aroma of suckling pig wafted from the barbecue. It was either corny or romantic, depending on your point of view.

'So, what's in that Chicken Lu'au?' asked Charlie between mouthfuls.

'Chicken,' laughed Nathalie. 'No, it's with spinach, onions, long rice and sweet potato. Want some?'

Charlie shook his head. 'Sounds too healthy for me. I'll stick with the surf-and-turf with fries.'

'Chips with everything,' said Nathalie, remembering an old television programme her father used to talk about.

Noticing the moisture in her eyes, Charlie placed a hand on hers. 'Everything all right?'

She sniffed and nodded her head. 'What could be better than this? Just thinking of my dad, he would have loved it here.'

'Would have?'

'He died five years ago. A bit of an adventurer; crashed a light aircraft into the sea. '

'Sorry, I didn't mean to …'

'No, don't be. It's good to remember him, especially in a place like this.'

Charlie had kept his hand on hers. She didn't remove it. This was getting difficult. Charlie was being paid to shoot a movie on Ocean Alternative Energy. She had been told by Bagatelle to get additional footage for a possible conspiracy documentary. She had asked how much she should tell the crew and Geoff had told her to play it by ear. Charlie had been recommended by Ocean Tech, and Ocean Tech was sponsoring their film. How much loyalty he had to them Geoff didn't know.

Most cameramen are independent hired guns. Pay them well and they'll work hard, he'd e-mailed. *Suss him out about Ocean Tech. I'm sure he won't mind shooting back on back if we pay him a bit more.*

Trust Geoff to give her the dirty work. Should she come clean and involve Charlie in the documentary, or should she just tell him to take certain shots and pretend they were for the Ocean Tech script? Geoff treated cameramen as mercenaries. Who knew how close Charlie's relationship with Ocean Tech was. If she was honest there was the danger that he wouldn't play ball. He seemed a really nice guy, though; how could she lie to him?

'Do you get a lot of shoots in exotic locations?' she asked, after a long pause.

'Had my fill. That's why I shoot with an Arri. Most people have given up on sixteen-mil. When you travel to hot damp places in the middle of nowhere, she goes on and on; long after a video camera would have packed up. Deserts and jungles seem to be my speciality. I've had my share of cardboard box-making factories but, in the main people choose me because of my experience on foreign location stuff. It's a different game to domestic shooting. Getting back in one piece with the film cans intact is as important as being able to frame a good shot.'

The moment had passed and he removed his hand.

'But obviously you know that. You must have had a lot of fun with carnets and X-ray machines.'

'Yes. Good job that you already had the carnet details for your equipment when I met you at the airport. Ocean Tech job, wasn't it? Do you work for them often?'

'Now and then. They're quite a reliable client. Do a lot of movies about oil rigs. Once you've shot one it's easy. The set-ups are pretty much the same.'

'You have a good relationship with them then?'

'So so. Their daily rate isn't great. They usually call me when they have a job. Internal DVDs for their staff mostly. Not too complicated so he gets me to direct it as well.'

'He?' Nathalie thought Charlie looked a bit fazed; perhaps it was the drink.

'A guy called Oyama. He's head of their corporate communications in Tokyo.'

'Ah, so that explains the Japanese.'

Charlie laughed and downed another Piña Colada. 'Good joke. Yes, I lived there for a year. Bit rusty now, though.'

'Good joke?'

'Ah so. Or "*ah so desa ka*", "so that's how it is".'

Nathalie suddenly twigged. 'Stupid me. Unintentional, I assure you. Look, it's a full moon. That's your fourth cocktail, and I need a sober cameraman tomorrow. Why don't we pay up and go for a walk on the beach?'

The air was balmy. They took off their shoes and dragged their feet through the gentle foam on the shoreline. A silver rope of light held the sea to the horizon. She slipped her hand into Charlie's.

'I think it's only fair to ask you something.'

He took her hand naturally, like two kids at school. 'Go on.'

She told him about Geoff's idea of a second film; the idea that Senator Cronkar had been compromised, the fact that Marine Corps were associated with two marine disasters, and the possible involvement of the anti-climate change lobby.

'Sounds great, what does he want us to film?'

'You don't have a problem with doing it alongside the Ocean Tech stuff?'

'Why should I? I told you, I work for myself. They just hire me on the occasional job. As long as we get the shots that they're paying me for, it's up to me what else I do. You did say Geoff would pay a bonus for the extra work?'

'Yes, by the hour at your top rate,' said Nathalie, making up a figure.

'Well, that's fine then. What are you looking so worried about?'

'I wasn't sure you'd play ball.'

'Shooting a conspiratorial documentary, with a beautiful woman, in paradise. Not go along with the idea? You must think I'm crazy.'

Nathalie stopped, put her hands together and bowed. '*Ah so desa ka*,' she said seriously, before breaking into a grin. She ran down the beach. The spray soaked his new shirt as he chased after her. He caught up, spun her around and they kissed.

Dan and Luke were waiting for them on their balcony as the cab pulled up outside the hotel at midnight.

'Thought you two were going to brief us on tomorrow,' slurred Dan.

'We are,' shouted back Nathalie. 'See you in the bar in ten minutes.'

'Shit,' muttered Dan. 'I was only joking.'

'Keep the jokes to yourself next time,' said Luke. 'I've got a feeling that we're going to get the whole bit; who's who, target audience, scientific background. All I need to know is where to put the fucking cables.'

But Luke was wrong. Although Nathalie did look a little flushed with excitement as she re-entered the room she began her briefing succinctly and professionally.

'First thing in the morning we'll recce the OTEC plant and ask the director where the best interiors are. Dan and Luke, you'll set up for the interview while Charlie and I take some GV's. Luke, are you getting this?'

Luke looked up from manicuring his fingernails. 'Yes, you'll take some general views in the sunshine while we cable up the hot, sweaty room.'

'Exactly; so you'll be all set by mid-morning when we'll shoot the interview. Overhead Sennheiser mic, no lapel-clip in vision. I'll take the interview off-camera so won't need my questions full quality. We'll then break for lunch before deciding the schedule for the afternoon. I'll need some cutaways so these shots will depend on the sort of stuff we get from the interview. Any questions?'

Dan had sobered up a bit. 'Sounds good to me. I'll bring along some stands for the interview and a muffler in case you want to do vox pops outside in the afternoon. Luke?'

'As long as we can get power I'll be fine. I've got a hand basher if you need it for shady exteriors. Otherwise, if you want to go natural, I can always help Charlie out as a camera assistant. Seemed to work well on that boat.'

'Ship,' corrected Dan. 'That ship.'

'Ship, boat, what's the difference?' argued Luke.

'A boat's a small thing. We were on a bloody big ship.'

'Well, we are not on a boat or a ship tomorrow,' intervened Nathalie, aware that the effects of alcohol had not worn off completely. 'We are working at the Hawaiian onshore OTEC laboratory.' She nodded knowingly at Charlie. 'Which reminds me, so are some engineers from a company called Marine Corps. They're a bit shy about their work and I haven't got permission from their company so I want you to be discreet when we're filming them.'

Luke looked puzzled. 'Discreet?'

'Yeah, you know. If Charlie points a camera at them don't stick a light in their face or a microphone up their nose.'

'You don't want them to know we are filming them?'

'Yes and no. Yes, as part of the scenery; no, not specifically at them in detail. We are meant to have permission forms for all close-up participants and I don't think I'm going to get that, so I just want to be careful.'

'No problem,' said Dan. 'We are the souls of discretion, aren't we, Luke?'

'Absolutely,' said Luke, not having a clue what a 'soul of discretion' was. 'When it comes to discretion we are it.'

Dan noticed that Nathalie was looking anxious. 'No Nathalie, seriously we get it. Film these guys and get what sound we can without being obvious. Not a problem, we've done it a thousand times.'

The call time was for eight in the morning, and Nathalie was emotionally exhausted. She was relieved that she had cleared the air with Charlie about the second film but the kiss, what was that all about? Had he kissed her or had she kissed him? They hadn't spoken about it since, although it was obvious that things had changed between them. She wasn't sure how she felt. It wasn't the thing to do to have an affair with your cameraman. It was supposed to be a professional relationship. And she realised she didn't even know if he was married or not. Perhaps she should ask him. Or perhaps she shouldn't. It may have been a one-off on a moonlit beach. People had done worse.

'One for a nightcap?' suggested Charlie.

Nathalie looked around at the empty bar. They were the last ones. Four bodies slung together to make a film. This is what it was about, camaraderie and teamwork. As their leader it was her job to keep them together.

'Why not,' she said. 'Mine's a Piña Colada.'

Nine

It was blisteringly hot. The Jeep's tyres ripped at the tarmac. The aircon wasn't working properly so they kept the windows open; hot moving air was better than no air at all. They had hired the vehicle at the airport for its roof rack, which was now laden with the aluminium dimpled boxes containing their film gear. Charlie sat in the passenger seat trying to keep the film cans cool under a black changing bag. Nathalie, who was driving, swerved to miss a pothole in the road. The last thing she wanted was to pitch the camera, lenses and lights off the roof. Dan and Luke were in the back, playing with their smartphones, they had seen all this before. The north-western coastline was barren, yet spectacular. Rough, jet-black blocks of lava stretched into the cobalt-blue sea. A moonscape with a water's edge. The surrounding terrain was treeless scrub and so they could see the sign to Keahole Point long before the dusty turnoff. Luke jumped out to lift the barrier, a rather crude, rusty red-and-white painted poll stretched across the rutted track. There was no guard, no lock, only a sign. '*Hawaiian Department of Alternative Energy. Authorised Personnel Only*'.

Nathalie drove through and stopped the Jeep to let Luke back on board.

'Great security,' said Luke, wiping his hands on his jeans.

Nathalie put her foot gently down on the pedal and with that pleasing crunching gravel sound the Jeep crept its way to the coast.

The plant looked like a low-rise oil refinery; pipes and aluminium cylinders everywhere. Nathalie had done her homework. This set-up had been one of the first experimental OTEC plants in the mid-1970s. Since then it had had its ups and downs with sponsorship and wrangles over whether it was all worth it. More recently, the surge of the climate change lobby had renewed interest and money had been pouring in again. The Research Director, the infamous Professor Bernard Lake, was a leading light in this revival; constantly on the news banging the drum for renewable energy. She had watched him on YouTube. Bagatelle's researcher was right, only he seemed a tetchy, neurotic sort of character. He was also a pro UNCLOS person. Nathalie had already picked up the jargon for the United Nations Convention on the Law of the Sea. This treaty considered offshore OTEC plants as artificial islands. A minefield when it came to territorial rights of the sea and its bed within two hundred miles. His adversaries had claimed that if you wanted to exploit a fishing ground, all you had to do was set up an OTEC plant nearby and you could own it. His response was vitriolic. Good TV. She had to be careful, although with delicate questioning, she might be able to get material for both of her films. She and Charlie had worked out a system. He had taped a spare magazine with the letter B on it. Whenever Nathalie wanted a sequence for her investigative documentary she would ask him to shoot on the B-roll. B-roll was a common term in the film industry with a number of obscure meanings and so Luke and Dan wouldn't have a problem with it. They had decided that this was the best way of separating the projects and being able to cost it out at the end of the shoot. In that way, they were being fair to both Ocean Tech and Bagatelle.

Bernard Lake met them at the entrance. A thin, bronzed, jumpy-looking man wearing a strange pair of faded yellow dungarees, he introduced himself curtly.

'Professor Lake. Welcome to our OTEC centre. Come into my office and I'll tell you what we have arranged for you.'

No handshake, just an imperative command and a turnaround on his heels, followed by a quick march to a nearby Portakabin. Nathalie didn't like the sound of 'what we have arranged for you' but she decided to bide her time and fall in with Professor Lake's ideas for the time being. The cabin was ice-cool compared to the stifling heat of the air outside.

'Air-conditioned by deep sea water,' proclaimed Lake proudly. 'After years of research we have produced a prototype of the most sophisticated natural energy system on Earth.'

He reached into a map drawer and pulled out a piece of A3 paper. Nathalie had been through all this sort of stuff before. An eager boffin wanting publicity for funding, with his own ideas of how to make a film. This usually consisted of an incomprehensible interview lasting an hour, accompanied by a hand-drawn diagram containing small type to give the film 'colourful graphics and excitement'. The fact that the graphic was neither legible nor exciting on a television screen failed to dawn on them.

'This chart shows the working of a closed cycle system,' he began.

Nathalie glared daggers at Charlie, who was about to intervene. 'Let them burn themselves out and grab what you can' was her motto. She would fix the pictures later.

'Closed?'

'As opposed to open or hybrid,' he raced. 'You see, a closed system uses fluids with low boiling points, such as ammonia, to power a turbine to generate electricity. We pump warm surface seawater ...'

Nathalie was aware of Charlie, Dan and Luke hanging back by the doorway. She was also conscious of the time slipping away.

'Professor, I'm sorry to interrupt you but would it be possible for the film crew here to set up your office for an interview while you show me around the plant to explain how it works?'

'But this diagram ...'

'Yes, it's brilliant,' Nathalie lied. 'We would love to film it if we have your permission but we would need to light it and the boys could do that while you show me the real thing, if that's okay?'

She said it in a way that was difficult to refuse, even by someone as insensitive as Lake. He conceded ground and led her with route march pace towards the heat exchanger units.

'Two chairs, key light and fill, and the Sennheiser stand,' she shouted over her shoulder. 'Charlie, come with me. I'd like you to suggest the order you'd like to shoot the sequences.'

Lake rattled off his presentation as if it were to a potential sponsor. Nathalie tried to visualise the story as pictures in her head – shot of the deep seabed, probably from archive, followed by the warm, shallow surface water; a few palm trees to show they were in the tropics. Hawaii was a perfect place for OTEC – a volcano growing almost vertically out of the deep ocean. The temperature difference between the seafloor and the surface here was around twenty-five degrees. By pushing the hot surface water through a heat exchanger to vaporise ammonia you could turn a generator. Pumping the cold water through a second heat exchanger condensed vapour, which could be recycled through the system. All you had to do was get the cold water to the surface. Then you had a perpetual eco-friendly energy machine. Sounded perfect.

'How do you get the cold water up in the first place?' asked Nathalie, nodding to Charlie to take a closer look at the heat exchangers.

Lake was in his element. He ignored Charlie's inspection and strode towards the desalination plant.

'We have two ways of retrieving the cold water.' Lake gestured towards the ocean. 'You see that large yellow pipe? It goes straight down the side of the volcano into the deep ocean. We can pump cold nutrient-rich water from a depth of one thousand metres at the rate of twelve thousand gallons a minute.'

Nathalie wasn't very keen on statistics; all she needed was a simple story to share with her viewers.

'Yeah, but how do you get it to the surface?'

Lake gave her an irritated stare. 'I was saying there are two ways. One, we can pump it up with kerosene generators or, two, a more bio-friendly method where we can desalinate the water, which makes it lighter and float to the surface. This also gives us a great product for high nutrient, fresh water aquaculture. That's what we do here. The profits are offset against the cost of the plant.'

'You breed fish?'

'All sorts of things. Freshwater lobster, oysters and mussels, you name it. I'm sure if you ask the aquaculture guys they would be only too pleased to let you take some shots.'

That's better, thought Nathalie, relax. A few more conversations like that and she would have him eating out of her hand. But the whole atmosphere changed with her next question.

'I understand that you have some Marine Corps engineers working on the desalination plant.'

'Not of my choosing,' he said abruptly. 'Sometimes the sponsors bring in their own teams. I can't say I always agree with them. Now, if you'd like to follow me, I'll show you our latest project on offshore bio-fouling and corrosion research. It's quite revolutionary.'

They came to a halt by the quayside. An enormous crane loomed like a giant spider over its prey on the projecting pier. A red and yellow painted construction of metal tubes and canisters was being attended by a number of hard-hatted operators. One of them was pouring a liquid onto the concrete and scrubbing at it with a large brush. Lake left Nathalie's side and ran at him, screaming. He kicked over a container, spilling the liquid on his overalls, and hurled abuse at the man. Nathalie couldn't hear the exact words over the noise of the crane but it was obvious that the guy had done something inexcusable for he bowed his head, shrugged his shoulders and sloped off.

She caught up with the professor, not knowing what to say or do.

'Stupid idiot. I told you, that's Marine Corps for you.'

'Are you okay? What did he do?'

'What did he *do*? He's just tried to scrub rust stains off the concrete with bleach. That's what he's done.' He pointed at the contraption beside them. 'Believe it or not, this underwater buoy is used for our offshore bio-fouling and corrosion research. Call themselves engineers. We didn't used to have this sort of thing before … it's outrageous!'

Before what? thought Nathalie, but she kept her powder dry and tried to calm him.

'It must be difficult for you.'

'*Difficult*! Difficult, being given engineers who don't know basic chemistry. Even first-grade kids know about low standard reduction potential.'

Nathalie doubted that but she decided to keep quiet and wait for the rant to subside.

'Easier to oxidise, doesn't remove the rust, makes it set harder. And now it's all over my fucking overalls.' This was the first time that Nathalie had heard him swear. Human, after all.

'Would you like to get changed? We could interview you in jacket and tie, if you like.'

'No, I would *not* like to get changed. This is how I work, and this is how people will see me.' His eyes seemed to perk up with the next thought. 'Besides, I want to show you my coup de grâce. Your cameraman must get a shot of this.'

He seemed to forget all about the incident and charged towards the end of the pier. Nathalie discreetly took a quick picture with her phone of one of the Marine Corps engineers working on the underwater buoy before jogging after Lake. He proudly pointed at his new toy; a bright yellow, Perspex-domed submersible. Looking at Lake in his yellow dungarees beside it brought The Beatles' song to mind. He lifted up the transparent cover and showed her the controls.

'The engineering of the OTEC system is quite straightforward,' he explained. 'The problem lies in underwater maintenance. With this beauty I can observe at first hand the rate of bio-fouling and corrosion and how to remove it.' Lake was in his element, his excitement palpable. 'Tomorrow morning we are going to lower the buoy into the ocean, and then I'll use the submersible to make observations.'

'Will we be able to film that?'

'The buoy being lowered into the sea, yes, but not from the submersible, I'm afraid. It only takes one.'

'But we can get you entering it and submerging from the side of the pier?'

'For sure. I'm going to have a dry or, should I say, wet run this evening.' He smiled at his own joke. 'Just to get it right, you know, no cameras then.'

'Understood. Pity we can't get any underwater shots, though. Perhaps you could take some with your mobile phone through the cockpit window.'

She could see that Lake was warming to her filming ideas. The interview was going to be a lot easier now. Nathalie knew that the best material came when you knew a little about what they were going to talk about and they trusted you. She sensed that Lake had begun to trust her. Time to press a little harder. They started to make their way back to the office.

'These Marine Corps guys, you said you didn't pick them.'

'No, there's been a bit of a regime change. The staffing used to be down to me but budgets have suddenly become tighter.'

'The economic downturn?'

'Partially, but we used to have a champion for the cause in high places. Now he's gone, so has a lot of the money.'

They reached the heat exchangers where they found Charlie squatting on the ground, scribbling in his notebook.

'We can get some good shots of this,' he said, getting to his feet. 'Better in the early morning, though – low light at the right angle.'

'You're coming back for the launching of the buoy late tomorrow morning. Why don't you film it just before that?' asked Lake.

'Well, I had scheduled it for this afternoon,' broke in Nathalie, 'but we could always swap things around. Professor, do you know where we could hire a chopper after lunch? I'd love to get a shot of Kilauea from the air. Set the scene sort of thing, show that the island is just one big volcano.'

'Sure, Big Island Helios do tours all the time. You can ring them from my office.'

On a scale of one to ten, the interview turned out to be a six. He had difficulty in not overlapping her questions and couldn't quite get the idea of trying to wrap the question up with an answer. Nathalie kept trying to explain that her questions wouldn't be used and that his sentences would be stand-alone, so purely saying 'yes' or 'I agree with that' would be pretty useless to the audience. He was also a little stiff and kept glancing at the camera lens for approval. When she tried a different tack and told him to just talk to her in general terms about why he thought OTEC was a good thing, he did better. After about an hour and several rolls of film, she had got the facts that we were threatening the planet by burning fossil fuels, and that OTEC was one hundred times more efficient than other ocean energy alternatives such as wave power. The descriptions of the technology and equipment were so long-winded that she guessed she would have to use a narrator over pictures of the plant. Perhaps no bad thing. Nathalie clapped her hands.

'Absolutely fantastic, you're a real natural.' She turned to her crew. 'That's a wrap for this morning, let's break for lunch.'

Dan and Luke began de-rigging the equipment and stripping the windows that had been taped with neutral density gel to balance the light. This was going to take some time so Nathalie used the opportunity to ask Professor Lake if he could spare her a few minutes.

'Sure, I hope you've got all you need,' he said, showing her into the back office. He offered her a Coke from the fridge and pulled out a small stool from under the desk. Lake was a boffin and, although wrapped up in his own world, he was no fool. 'I sense that you are a bit unsure. Aren't you happy with what you got?' he asked, a little anxiously.

'Yes, absolutely. The interview was great for the science programme we're making. Really explains how large-scale OTEC could solve a lot of environmental problems.'

'But?'

'Not so much a "but", more of an "and".'

'Okay, "and"?'

Nathalie decided to come clean.

'And, I'd like to explore some of the more political aspects of your job. The difficulties you face in getting funding and persuading people that you are doing the right thing. You mentioned there was a change of regime.'

'That's no secret. Our torch bearer was a guy called Cronkar. Campaigned for legislation on climate change and rustled around for natural energy funding. He was here a few weeks ago. Got us sponsorship for the submersible. Then there was that sex thing. I don't know what his private life had to do with anything but that's politicians for you. It happened almost overnight – funds were pulled, cheaper engineering companies put in. I've done all I can to stop the whole thing closing down.' He paused to peel the ring-pull from his can. He took a long, cold draft before continuing. 'Then there's this UNCLOS issue. Our new government representative won't even ratify the thing. Even tries to claim that offshore OTEC plants will affect private enterprise property rights. But who's going to listen to me when he controls the whole government publicity machine?'

Nathalie noticed Charlie at the door. She beckoned him in.

'That's exactly where Charlie and I can help,' she said quietly. 'If you're prepared to say what you just have on camera we could get it out there. There's something not quite right with this Law of the Sea Treaty and its effects on ocean energy and we would like to expose it. We could do the recording when we come back tomorrow morning.'

'I would have to think about it, might make things worse.' Lake paused and slowly put his hand up to his chin. He looked thoughtfully into the distance before resuming, slowly but deliberately. 'Mind you, there is one thing that I could …'

He was interrupted by a knock at the door. The Marine Corps engineer whom Nathalie had clocked earlier was silhouetted in the frame. Lake hurriedly rose to his feet.

'What is it now, Webster?'

'It's the underwater buoy, Sir; we'd like you to give it one last check over before we lock it up for tomorrow's launch.'

Lake raised his eyes in exasperation. 'I thought I told you …, but never mind, I'll come along.' He turned to Nathalie as if he had finally made a resolution. 'Miss Thompson, I'm sorry to be rude but I must leave you now. I'll consider your proposal and see you first thing tomorrow morning. I do hope you enjoy your helicopter trip, it's quite spectacular.'

Ten

They had nearly reached the barrier by the junction when Luke remembered his sound sheets. Nathalie patiently turned the Jeep around and drove back to the plant. They waited at the entrance while he ran off to retrieve them. The early afternoon had become even hotter and the seatbelt buckles were almost too scalding to touch. The vehicle's fan had started to make a complaining noise so Charlie jumped out and opened the hood to see what was going on. He was still tinkering ten minutes later when Luke appeared around the main gate, waving his sound sheets aloft. He climbed back into the cab.

'Sorry, I've got everything in here: levels, retakes, atmos. Editor would have gone spare; can't do without them.'

'That's okay,' drawled Dan with sarcasm. 'Can't do without my arse either. Suppose I have to, now it's welded to this plastic seat.'

Charlie slammed down the hood of the Jeep, shaking his head. 'The fan on this thing is fucked so no relief there, Dan.'

Nathalie looked at her watch, put the Jeep into gear and drove off. 'If you gentlemen are now settled we'd better get a move on or we're going to be late for that helicopter.'

They headed inland. The penetrating blue sky gave way to a mist and then a bank of cloud. As the altitude increased the temperature dropped. Despite the open windows, the atmosphere in the Jeep was still uncomfortable. Luke explained that the blanket of grey swirling air around them was something that the Hawaiians called 'vog'; volcanic fog produced by a combination of hot ash and condensing humid air. Charlie asked if the chopper would be able to climb above it to view the volcanic crater. Dan expressed the view that speculative filming of volcanoes was a waste of time, especially in the daytime, as the lava always looked better at night. He couldn't understand why every film crew that ever came there wanted to reinvent the wheel. It was best left to the local experts who were willing to sell their archive by the minute. Nathalie chipped in that archive came with conditions. You had to state your context and were restricted to a number of broadcasts. She wanted use of the footage, where she wanted it, when she wanted it. For her, it was the last resort.

'Less fun too,' insisted Charlie.

'Not fun, bloody dangerous,' said Dan from the back. 'Especially when you guys take the doors off and hang over the edge. All held up by a rotor blade and a few ball bearings. No thank you.'

'Lucky there's not much sound to be got from a helicopter then, isn't it?' spat back Charlie.

Nathalie joined in. 'Now then, children, there's only going to be room for the two of us anyway, so let's not fall out over it.'

'Yeah, the last thing we want you to do is fall out, Charlie,' smirked Dan. 'Especially over a pool of red-hot lava.'

No-one found this funny, so they continued the next few miles in silence. The higher they climbed, the sparser the vegetation. A recent lava flow had stripped the slopes of trees and left in their place a landscape strewn with dull black, blocky boulders. The vog was now settling a few metres above the ground, making it difficult to drive. The temperature had dropped further and they had wound up the windows. Nathalie had shifted into a lower gear, making progress slow. She kept turning her wrist to check the time. They were half an hour late already. If the chopper had been booked out, or this cloud didn't clear, it would be a wasted journey. Perhaps Dan was right; she should have just bought some archive. Did she really need this shot, or was she doing it just for the thrills? They hadn't filmed a frame on the B-roll. The afternoon may have been better spent poking around at the OTEC plant, asking awkward questions of some of the Marine Corps engineers. The problem was she didn't even know what she was looking for. Geoff had been so vague. 'A great opportunity to make an investigative documentary', he had persuaded her. She was all for that but it was so frustrating. Scientific documentaries were difficult enough but at least there was an outline script, a kind of plan. With the other sort of thing you had to shoot from the hip, make up a story as you went along. All she had to go on so far was a couple of disasters at sea, which could have been coincidental, and an oddball senator who liked his arse being whipped. There were a few common threads such as Marine Corps and the discomfort of scientists when the UNCLOS Treaty was mentioned. Other than that, not a lot. That is, unless Bernard Lake had something up his sleeve. It certainly felt like he was about to spill the beans. Nathalie hoped he wouldn't get cold feet in the morning. She was so engrossed in these thoughts that she hadn't heard Charlie tell her that they had arrived.

'You've missed it, the turning's back there, a large pair of wire gates with a massive sign on it, "Big Island Helios". That's what he said, wasn't it?'

'Oh yes, sorry. I was miles away. Hold on, I'll turn around.'

She swept the Jeep into a tight three-point turn and drove up to the gates. Luke jumped out and held them open while she manoeuvred through. Before them was a high-fenced compound topped with barbed wire. In the centre was a hard-core surface the size of two tennis courts and to one side, a large, corrugated iron-roofed hangar. There was not a helicopter in sight. Luke suggested that they park up while he tried to find someone in charge. Nathalie cut the engine and waited. A few minutes later Luke appeared from a small concrete side building with a sallow-skinned man in overalls. A pilot, thought Nathalie, no helicopter. She wound down the window as the pilot approached the Jeep. He introduced himself as Malakina and declared that he thought they weren't coming.

'Sorry, we were held up,' said Nathalie, glancing at Charlie. 'Any chance of a ride?'

'Most of the choppers are out. We do have one left in the hangar. I understand you want to fly with the doors off. If you wait here, we'll fix that and bring it out for you. Cash in advance, okay?'

Nathalie nodded and suggested to Charlie that he should get his gear off the roof. The plan was for Dan and Luke to sit with the Jeep while she and Charlie took a trip to the volcanic vent. Charlie had done this sort of thing before and had brought with him some bungee ropes to attach the camera to the top of the chopper door frame. He also wore a thick leather belt with a chunky swivel clip that could be fixed to the cabin floor. Although he had never had to use it in anger, it always made him feel safer when he was leaning over the side. He handed Nathalie a magazine case.

'You should put a sweater on and have a scarf for your face. The last time I did this in Japan, the molten rock was so close that I could feel the heat and smell the sulphur. It was amazing, a glowing red tube pushing through the jagged black slope of the volcano. Let's hope this cloud lifts and we get something as good.'

It wasn't the cloud that stopped them getting the shot. They heard the whir of the blades and watched as the maroon-coloured helicopter shuffled out of the hangar. It parked close to the Jeep and Charlie approached to attach his bungee ropes. As he turned to ask Luke to bring the camera he suddenly caught something out of the corner of his eye. 'Hold on a minute, Luke, I just want to check something.'

Walking over to the tail of the helicopter, he ran his finger along the paintwork. He pointed to a large crack in the narrowest part of the fuselage, saying, 'I don't like the look of this.' He turned to the pilot, 'Have you seen this before?'

The pilot walked over, gave a sideways glance and mumbled that it was nothing, probably just a crack in the paintwork.

'Doesn't look like just the paintwork to me. Have you got someone who could check it over?'

'We have the best safety flight record on Hawaii, but if you insist …' protested the pilot. 'We also have one of the best aeronautical engineers. If you wait a minute I'll ask him to take a look.'

Charlie looked apologetically at Nathalie. 'All these guys say they have the best safety record. Better safe than sorry, yeah?'

Nathalie nodded in agreement. She was desperate to get off the ground but if Charlie had any doubts, so did she. Then a very strange thing happened. Luke started to laugh hysterically, so much so that he fell on the ground, holding his sides. Dan looked up and joined in. She asked them what they were doing. They were too far gone to be able to answer. All they could do was to point in the general direction of the hangar. Coming out of the door was the engineer with the best safety record on Hawaii. His right leg was plastered from his toe to the top of his thigh and he was swinging slowly on two crutches towards the helicopter.

Charlie shook his head in disbelief as the man walked up to the tail blade and, after a brief inspection, began to strap it with gaffer tape. Nathalie got out of the Jeep and took charge of the situation. She knew Charlie would go up if she asked him to. From the expression on his face it was obvious that he was not keen. To save his pride she walked up to the pilot and explained it was her decision and that they didn't have insurance for such things. They weren't backing out of the deal and, if they had another helicopter, they would like to film the volcano; if not, they might be able to come back another day. The pilot shrugged and told her that it was the last helicopter in the hangar. By the time the others had got back the visibility would be too poor for flying. Take it or leave it was what he seemed to say.

Nathalie had visions of tomorrow's newspaper headlines, *British Film Crew in Helicopter Crash,* followed by an explanation of a reckless trip over an erupting volcano in a door-less helicopter with a faulty tail blade. The weather was poor, the volcano might not co-operate, and she could probably get better archive, anyway.

'We'll leave it,' she told him and, with difficulty, helped the apoplectic Luke and Dan into the back of the Jeep.

It was getting late in the afternoon and it would take a few hours to get back to the hotel, so they decided to call it a day. Luke and Dan were still laughing like a couple of schoolkids. Nathalie told them if she heard the words 'safety record' or 'archive' once more she would not be responsible for her actions. Charlie kept quiet; it was obvious that he hadn't liked pulling out of the shot.

'It was my decision, right?' said Nathalie forcefully. 'The visibility was rubbish anyway. I'm glad you spotted the damage, it gave us a good excuse to pull out.' Despite Charlie's weak smile, she knew he wasn't at all happy.

The vog lifted as they descended. A different sort of Hawaii revealed itself; a palm tree-fringed coast edging onto an iridescent sea. The interior of the Jeep began to heat up again. A poolside break would give them time to cool down and an opportunity to regroup for the next day, which was going to be a long one. They agreed to meet by the pool bar after checking over their kit and having a shower. Nathalie helped unload the Jeep before retiring to her room. She slung her bag on the bed and opened her laptop to log on to the hotel's WiFi. There was a long e-mail from Geoff.

Haven't phoned because of the ten-hour time difference. Also, easier to get this across in writing. Any questions and you can ring me 7.00am UK time, that's 19.00 this evening for you.

Nick Coburn has been in touch with your French mate Philippe at the UN and dug up more info on Cronkar. Looks like there are some political shenanigans going on. We are trying to get you an interview with Cronkar's replacement.

We've also checked out Marine Corps. They are an international marine engineering company dealing mainly in oil rigs but they've got a lot of fingers in other pies. They supplied sediment charts to the drilling ship that went down. I discovered that they're working on a wave power machine near the island of Majuro. At the moment they're having a row with a Japanese mining ship in the area. I'd like you to take a detour and get some footage of both. Stefanie is fixing flights and hotels for you. Charlie Linde is signed up for two weeks. You'll have to extend the contract for sound and sparks. I've told Ocean Tech that the wave machine is en route anyway and would be a good addition to the energy movie. Naturally, I've not mentioned our other plans so ask Charlie to keep mum on that. See attachment for programme proposal. Geoff.

Okay, so I've got to act as a diplomat as well as a production manager and film director, thought Nathalie. He's got me to do his dirty work and Ocean Tech to pay for the travel costs. Par for the course then.

She clicked on the attachment – a one-page proposal typed onto Bagatelle's notepaper. *Proposal for a one-hour investigative television documentary. Working title – Oceans on Fire.*

He'd even pinched the CNN report title. She read on. The background gave information on climate change, the United Nations Convention on the Law of the Sea and investment in ocean energy. This was followed by a claim that there were people trying to disrupt these schemes; corruption of officials and the sabotaging of natural energy projects. It concluded that the programme would investigate the facts and point fingers at the culprits.

It all looked very daunting and Geoff must have realised this because she noticed that a second e-mail, timed ten minutes later, was now in her in-box.

Nathalie, don't worry about not shooting to a script. The story will develop as we find out more. Get the pieces of the jigsaw and we will make them fit a picture.

Best, Geoff.

She clicked on the 'reply' button. It was all very well for Geoff; he'd been making these seat-of-your-pants' movies for years. How should she answer? One pathetic photo of a Marine Corps engineer was all she had gathered so far. There was always tomorrow. If Bernard Lake came up with something she might be able to report a coup. She filed the e-mail and closed her laptop. Her reply could wait.

Professor Lake was preparing for his dummy run. He didn't want to look a fool for the camera the next day and besides, he quite liked driving this new sub-aqua machine. The controls were intuitive, a bit like a car. Pressing the right pedal with the ball of your foot made it go forward, with the heel backwards. The left pedal made it go up and down. In front of him was a touch-screen display. This powered up the sub, controlled the lights and monitored the depth. The life-support system included two externally mounted oxygen cylinders with electronic monitoring within the cockpit. He had checked the pressures and all looked fine. Pulling down the acrylic entry hatch he marvelled at the view; a complete 260° angle of vision. He fired up the engine and began the descent. The water flooded over him and the lights pierced into the gloom. Tomorrow he would have to navigate around the newly deployed underwater buoy. For now, he would take a simple trip around the harbour. Besides the front and back thrusters there were two angled side-thrusters which enabled him to move at between three and four knots in any direction. During his first lesson, guided by the voice of an instructor, he couldn't believe how easy it was. Now he had become quite an expert. He liked this quiet underwater world, with no-one to hassle him. That's why he had decided to rehearse in the late afternoon when most of the operators had gone home; no-one to bother him on the communications' intercom.

He pressed down the pedal to descend even further. He checked the monitor – well within the limits; this thing would go down to six hundred metres, if necessary. Not much to see except for a few shoals of jellyfish. The offshore engineering and the pipe laying had killed off most fish in the harbour. Shame about that. Still, the eco-nature of the plant would more than compensate. A shape suddenly loomed up in front of him. In an instinctive reaction he squeezed on the side-thrusters. Only a seaweed-encrusted anchor chain from one of the supply boats. His heart rate had raced and his respiration increased. A near miss, it could have been dangerous; he would have to stay more alert. He sniffed at the air inside the capsule. Something a bit odd. A pungent sort of smell, a bit like smelling salts. He touched the keypad to bring up the life-support monitors. The first oxygen cylinder was low so the second had kicked in. The smell was getting worse and he began to recognise it – ammonia. Some idiot must have mixed up one of the cylinders with the heat exchanger fluids. Still, he had enough oxygen in the first cylinder to get back to the pier. He would just shut the second one down. The smell was unpleasant and he felt a bit nauseous but he could cope with it.

He turned the sub around and headed back towards the docking station. If he made a straight line it would only be a few hundred metres. As he pressed on the foot controls, his breathing became more difficult and his throat began to swell. Strange, he had encountered ammonia many times in the heat exchanger room and it had never affected him like this before. Perhaps it was the confined space. Then the symptoms hit him. His throat started to burn and he slowly began to lose vision. He felt around in the cockpit and winced as his hands touched the controls. His skin felt on fire. Pain like a knife stabbed his abdomen as he struggled for the VHF communication system. He tried to cry for help. All that came out was a paroxysmal cough and a mouthful of blood. The submarine lost power and slowly sank to the bottom of the harbour.

Eleven

A cordon of striped plastic police tape spanned the entrance. Luke jumped out of the Jeep to show the officer their pass. He was held in animated conversation for some time before the tape was lifted to let them through. Dan opened the door for him as the Jeep stopped on the other side of the barrier.

'Some sort of incident; he wasn't keen to let us through. But it's a small community here. I know his boss well, chaperones us on the *Hawaii Five-0* shoots. I said we'd check in with him at the main gate.'

'Incident? What sort of incident?' asked Nathalie, anxiously. 'I hope they haven't launched the buoy yet, they promised not to do it until later in the morning.'

'Didn't say,' said Luke. 'We'll soon know, though; that's the captain in the police car up ahead.'

The police car straddled the road; no siren, only flashing lights. Luke jumped out and ran up to the uniformed officer sitting in the car's open doorway. They greeted each other like long-lost friends and then fell into deep debate. Luke was waving his arms around and the officer was pointing towards the harbour. After some minutes the policeman returned to his car and backed it away from the road. Luke ran back to the Jeep.

'Sounds serious, they got a call early this morning. Someone had reported the theft of a submersible. Now it seems some divers have found the thing at the bottom of the harbour. It could have broken loose or something. They're bringing it up now.'

'Will they let us in?' Nathalie was anxious to get a shot of this.

'Brett says we can follow him. He doesn't mind us filming as long as we don't interfere with the salvage operation.'

Charlie looked concerned. 'Are you sure this is a good idea, Nathalie?'

If there was a table Nathalie would have kicked him under it; instead she made do with one of her best glares. 'Of course it is, Charlie, it's B-roll stuff.' Her next words were mouthed silently. 'Just what we need.'

Two machines cut loose within a few days of each other. She might be jumping the gun but it would look good on TV. They'd missed the first shot of the Lone Ranger disappearing into the sea; they could fill that with shots of the deployment and the empty wake afterwards. Now, thanks to Luke's familiarity with local law enforcement, there was the chance to get some real action. She followed the police car slowly through the plant's perimeter gate. The harbour wall was out of sight beyond the row of Portakabins that acted as offices. The police car pulled up alongside a stack of enormous yellow pipes which stretched for many metres towards the sea. Why were these marine installations always yellow, wondered Nathalie as she watched a crane lunging dangerously in the blue sky above them. Brett's gestures from the driver's window indicated that they should park behind him. As they unloaded the gear an open-topped Jeep full of hard-hatted engineers rushed past them. Luke slung the tripod over his shoulder and marched towards the harbour. Charlie took the camera out of its case and Nathalie carried the lens box. Dan followed behind with his sound gear. They didn't run but there was a professional expectation in their step as they strode towards the salvage site.

Engineers in overalls were milling around the pier. A small group of office workers looked out of place as they watched from a distance. The underwater buoy was still in situ, while the crane that was supposed to deploy it was now being guided into a new position on the outer harbour wall. The operator could just be made out in the cabin through the scratched glass window, pulling on levers like a controller in a signal box. A policeman, who was talking into his radio, spotted the film crew and gestured to them to stop where they were. A pile of aluminium chemical drums were nearby and Nathalie asked Charlie and Luke to use them to get a higher vantage point. Charlie seemed a little reluctant but Luke stabilised the tripod spreader on three of the drums by weighing it down with a few heavy rocks. Charlie handed Nathalie the camera while he clambered onto the drums. Once in position, she held it up to him and he placed it in the tripod bowl. Using a long lens he focused the camera on the end of the crane. Now he could make out two frogmen in the water. One was gesturing to a crane driver to lower the vast hook in a position beside them. The chain moved closer and the diver caught hold of it and made a downwards movement with his other hand. Moments later he disappeared into the green gloom.

Nathalie stood on tiptoes in order to get a better view but at five-foot four, she had little chance. 'What's going on?'

Charlie was concentrating on the shot; he panned the camera to the crane operator, counted to ten in his head, and then slowly panned back to the water, turning over all the time.

'Not a lot yet; two frogmen in the harbour guiding the crane driver. One guy's gone down with the hook under the water. I'll cut the camera now and keep a shot locked off on the chain. As soon as it starts moving I'll turn over again. Dan, I don't know if you can pick up any sync sound from here, but if you want to record, I'll give you the thumbs up for a back slate.'

Nathalie was used to this. When filming on the hoof it was difficult to put a clapperboard in front of the camera so the editor could synchronise the sound with the picture later. Instead, it was common to clap the slate upside down at the end of the shot. This time, they had unloaded the Jeep so quickly they had forgotten the slate. She decided to improvise.

'We can hear the crane from here. Dan, as soon as you see Charlie's hand turn the camera over, start recording.' She shouted up to Charlie, 'Charlie, when you've finished the shot, whip-pan down to me and I'll clap my hands.'

Charlie nodded, and then hunched back over the camera. It was now nearly nine o'clock in the morning and the sun was rising quickly. Charlie asked Luke to shade the lens to stop the flair coming off the water.

'It's going to start moving,' interrupted Dan, pressing the headset to his ears. 'He's started to shift the gears.'

'Okay, Luke, leave it,' said Charlie, putting up his own hand to shield the sun. 'Turning over, Dan.'

Nathalie couldn't see a thing so she let them get on with it. Either the sub would be fished out of the water or it wouldn't. She had seen Charlie's camerawork on the sonar vessel. He was cool in excitable circumstances and kept his lens focused and still; no dashing from one shot to another with the danger of missing both. Even without the amplification of the headphones she could hear the crane shudder into action. From where she stood she could see the pulley at the top of the iron latticework. The chain had started to rise. She badly wanted to shout some sort of instruction or encouragement but she kept her mouth shut. The chain and the time moved slowly. Each magazine only contained ten minutes of film. Nathalie looked at her watch; only sixty seconds had passed. She looked back at the camera, concentrating on Charlie's finger resting on the zoom bar; it hadn't moved. Then, gingerly, Charlie adjusted the angle of the camera which rested on the bowl. His finger gradually started to twist the zoom bar. She could imagine the shot slowly creeping in.

'Holy shit!' cried Charlie, almost falling off the chemical drums. His face suddenly turned away from the camera and with a violent retch he vomited his breakfast onto the ground.

Luke grabbed the tripod to stop it from falling. Instinctively he steadied the camera and put his eyes to the viewfinder. Dan helped Charlie off the drums and supported him as he sat on an equipment box. Nathalie didn't know whether to go to Charlie or to the camera. Dan was holding Charlie's head between his knees and so she decided on the camera. She scrambled up onto the chemical drums alongside Luke, who was still filming.

'What's going on?'

'Take a look for yourself,' said Luke. 'But I hope you've got a better stomach than Charlie, it's not a pretty sight.'

Luke held the camera mount still as she put her right eye to the eyepiece. On changing places they had put the camera out of focus; all she could see was a blur. She slowly moved the zoom bar. Piece by piece the picture came into view – first, the shiny surface of the acrylic entry hatch, which was attached to the cylindrical hull; then, on changing the depth of field, a shape within the dome. As she pulled the focus further she understood why Charlie had vomited. The cockpit was smeared with blood; the occupant's face was contorted, tinged with blue and wore a mask of agony; yet, despite this mask, there was no doubt who it was.

It was Bernard Lake.

'The man's dead?'

'That's what I said, Geoff.' Nathalie put her left finger in her ear so that she could hear him more clearly. 'Apparently he'd been down there all night, no-one knows why; could have been that he got his foot stuck on the descent pedal and couldn't get it off. The police were already here. Someone thought the sub had been stolen. Not so though, it seems that he was taking it for a trial run. We filmed the salvage, it was terrible, and his body was in a hell of a state.'

'How are the police treating it?' Geoff's voice sounded like it was coming from next to her now, rather than halfway around the world.

'Treating it?'

'Suspicious, or possible homicide, I think they call it there.'

'I don't know, we can't get near them yet; they've taped off the whole area. I do know that they have called for a coroner, though. My plan was to try to get some interviews when the commotion has calmed down a bit. We've got something going for us, in that the sparks is a friend of the senior police officer here. I just thought I should let you know what's happening.'

'Absolutely, although you sound like you know what you're doing.'

'I'm doing what I can. You said you wanted stuff on ocean sabotage. I'm no detective but in my view I think you're getting it.'

'Nathalie,' Geoff's tone of voice had softened.

'Yes, Geoff?'

'If you think this stuff is getting too … you know, too dangerous, you can always come home. I've no problem with that.'

'I know, Geoff, but now we've started, I'd like to finish. Two incidents at sea could have been coincidence; three, I don't think so.'

'If you're sure …'

'I am in the right place.'

'Okay, get what you can in the rest of your day and return to Oahu first thing tomorrow. Stefanie has contacted a travel agent there who has your air tickets and hotel booking for Majuro. She's sent you details by e-mail. And, Nathalie …'

'Yes, Geoff?'

'If at any time you feel that you could be in trouble, telephone me, day or night; is that clear?'

'Very clear, Geoff,' she said, shutting off the handset.

The pier side was now a hive of activity. An ambulance had arrived and men could be seen running between the installations. The submersible looked undamaged as it lay at a slight angle on the dockside. The cockpit dome had been left open and the body removed. A small group of engineers were being held back while a police photographer went about his business. Charlie had recovered, having drunk a glass of water, and was now being over apologetic. It wasn't like him; he had filmed many gruesome things. The shock, early breakfast, and the heat had made him lose it for a while. He was fine now and eager to get some interviews in the can. Nathalie was right about Luke's policeman friend. He was being more than co-operative and had agreed to do an interview himself after the coroner had done his stuff.

The crew set up their equipment as close as they were permitted to the submersible; a good backdrop for the interviews. Nathalie asked Luke if he could persuade any of the Marine Corps engineers to say something. To her surprise he turned up with their supervisor.

Nathalie shook his hand. 'Terrible tragedy. Did you know Bernard Lake well?'

'We've only been here a few days, last-minute contract, so can't say I did. Your colleague said that you'd like to interview me but I'm not sure how much I can tell you.'

'Oh, just a bit about your involvement here and what you think might have happened. If you stand over there and look at me I'll ask you a couple of questions. Don't worry if you fluff your remarks, we can always cut and do it again. Are you okay with that?'

He nodded and so Nathalie stood to one side of the camera while Luke held a reflector disc to help illuminate the Marine Corps supervisor's face. Dan lowered his microphone until Charlie gave him the edge of frame and, when they were all settled, she gently began her questions. She asked him his name and position and, once more, how long he had been working at the OTEC plant. As he started to relax she probed a little further. What did he know about the submersible and how was his relationship with Lake? He didn't seem at all fazed by these questions. Their priority was to launch the underwater buoy; Lake had kept them away from his precious submarine. As for the relationship, there wasn't much of one. Lake was a strange man who blew hot and cold; seemed a little reluctant to have them on the site. He just put it down to eccentricity; the guy had a reputation for being a scientific genius. After a few further questions Nathalie realised that she wasn't getting much more so she asked Charlie to cut the camera. She had expected the engineer to be more nervous and evasive. Instead, he was cool and straightforward with his answers. It was evident that he either had nothing to do with the incident, or he was a very good actor indeed. Maybe there was someone else on his team who was involved. She asked if any of his crew were willing to talk.

'They won't be able to tell you any more than me, and with all this going on, we're going to be pretty busy. The reason I gave you this interview is so that you don't need to disturb anyone else and we can get on with things. So, if you don't mind ...'

Nathalie thanked him and let him go. No point in pressing the point; she would get more out of the afternoon by not antagonising him.

Later in the day, a calmer atmosphere had spread around the site. The deployment of the underwater buoy had been cancelled or postponed, yet there was still the routine maintenance of the plant to be done. The office workers had returned to the Portakabins and the engineers had dissolved into the background. Business as usual, except for the eerie sight of the loan submersible resting on the concrete pier. The ambulance and coroner had long gone and apart from the captain's car, so had the police. Luke had told Nathalie that Brett had needed little persuading to be filmed. On the *Hawaii Five-0* shoots he was always on the periphery of the action, holding traffic back or advising on police procedure. Today was his turn to be the focus of attention and it looked like he was going to make the most of it.

'He says we can film him right next to the submersible,' said Luke. 'He can tell us what they know so far. He's really into this movie stuff, so don't be surprised if he tries to direct the shots. If you play along I think he'll give you what you want.'

Nathalie nodded knowingly. 'Good work, Luke. I'll let him be Cecil B. DeMille, if he produces the goods.'

'I don't think he's heard of Cecil B. DeMille,' laughed Luke. 'Steven Spielberg, perhaps. Just keep him sweet.'

They made their way to the pier, past the cylinders and tubes of the heat exchanger plant and across the scrub towards the crane derricks. The killi sedge grass protruded through the dark, blocky soil, causing them to pick their steps carefully. Brett was waiting for them beside the submersible.

'Want a hand?'

'No, we're fine, thanks,' Nathalie accentuated her British accent. 'It's very good of you to give us this interview.'

'No problem. I thought you would like to start by filming me here, then the camera could follow me to the cockpit, where I could point out the things we've been investigating.'

Luke wasn't joking about the Spielberg bit, but she played along. 'That sounds good. Charlie, we'll do this hand-held. Dan, do you think you can follow him or would you prefer a radio mic for this one?'

Charlie gave her a 'what the hell is going on here?' look. Dan, who had been talking to Luke, said that as it was a tight frame he wouldn't have a problem with the boom. Brett did that sort of thing with his neck that rugby players do before a game, and stood with his legs apart in front of Charlie and the camera. Charlie looked at Nathalie and, getting no response, put the camera on his shoulder and pointed the lens at their interviewee. Nathalie asked Brett to tell his story in his own way, in his own time.

'Turnover sound, picture, mark it, and …,' Nathalie paused for Luke to move the clapperboard out of the way. 'Action!'

Brett behaved like a first-time daytime television presenter. He started by dramatically telling the camera how they had been called out to the OTEC plant early in the morning about a stolen submarine.

'Sounded more like a job for the Marines,' he grinned. 'When we arrived we were told it had been found at the bottom of the harbour.'

His face became more serious as he described the salvage and the discovery of the body of Professor Lake inside the capsule. He didn't spare the gory detail of what they had found when they opened the hatch – a twisted body with agony frozen on its face; and dried blood everywhere, which had been coughed up by the deceased. The professor's left foot had been found fixed on the descent pedal. It was this that had sent the sub to the bottom of the harbour. Rigor mortis had set in and the controls were well and truly jammed. Brett beckoned the camera over to the cockpit and pointed to the foot controls. He suggested to Charlie that they take a close-up of him moving the pedal backwards and forwards with his hand to show how it worked. Nathalie nodded her approval and they took the shot.

Brett now moved triumphantly around to the rear of the machine.

'Now I'd like to show you something …' He unclipped the two life-support cylinders that were attached to the back of the vehicle and held them next to each other. 'If you look at these markings …,' he waved Charlie backwards, 'take a long shot of this.'

Dan was about to interrupt, to say that he was getting directions mixed up with the interview, but Nathalie simply glared at him and wound her finger around in a circle to indicate that they should keep recording. Brett was on a roll.

'You see, the one on the left is faded and there doesn't seem much difference. Now, zoom in closer. Got that?'

'We're getting it,' said Nathalie, watching Charlie's zoom bar. 'What's your point?'

'The point is that the one on the right is a regular oxygen cylinder, whereas …' Brett paused for dramatic effect, '… the one on the left is full of ammonia gas.'

Twelve

Nathalie stared at the canister in the police officer's hand and, for a moment, forgot her role as a film director.

'Is that what killed him?'

Brett was about to reply when she gathered herself and instructed Charlie to re-position on a tight shot of the officer's face.

'Sorry, Brett, if I can call you that. Just explain in your own words what this means.'

The policeman composed himself and looked straight into the camera's lens. 'Ammonia is pretty nasty stuff and most people would jump to the conclusion that it was this gas that killed him. In fact, as soon as we found it, that's what we thought.' Brett did another of his dramatic pauses. He was enjoying this. 'But we're police officers and trained to go beyond the obvious. We got the engineers to check out the systems on the sub; it's got a computer recording of every move the pilot makes.'

Ham actor or not, this speech was going to make good television. Nathalie indicated to Charlie to keep the camera fixed on Brett's face; they could take cutaways of the sub's systems later.

Brett was now in his stride. 'The computer records show that, yes, Lake did open the ammonia cylinder but he must have smelt it as he immediately closed it again. The coroner is pretty sure that there wasn't enough ammonia released to kill him.' He held up the cylinder once more, not realising that it was out of the camera's frame. 'We checked the cylinder, and it agrees with the computer. Which begs the question ...'

Now was a good time to pause, thought Nathalie. She told Charlie to cut the camera and praised Brett for his presentation, explaining that she wanted to reposition the camera on a mid-shot and pick up again on the investigation. Her mind was racing. A change of shot would be a good idea to help with the editing, but really, she was buying herself time. How much could she squeeze out of this guy and what shots would she need to make good cutaways? Would the engineers reconstruct their computer analysis, for instance? The officer had insisted on looking down the lens like a television presenter, rather than to the side like a normal interviewee, although they had started so she would have to continue in that way. She stood directly behind the camera so he wouldn't keep glancing at her and asked him to once more pick up on the story.

'Turnover, Charlie. Okay, Brett, if the ammonia didn't kill him, can you tell us what your current theory is?'

Brett stretched himself up to his full height and struck a strange pose, holding his arms out in front. He had obviously seen this in some CNN broadcast. 'The police are keeping an open mind on this case. The body has been sent for autopsy and the investigation is continuing.'

Nathalie wondered whether she had blown it by pausing the interview. 'You must have some ideas, do you think there was any foul play?'

'My personal theory is that it was an accident. Lake normally didn't let anyone touch the submarine. The ammonia cylinder had faded markings and could easily be mistaken for an oxygen one. As soon as he realised he'd made a mistake he switched it off and, according to the computer, headed straight for the docking station. But the ammonia may have made him feel nauseous and for some reason he got his foot stuck on the descent pedal, although the coroner did seem concerned about a couple of things.'

Brett had paused again but this time not for effect; Nathalie could see that he was wondering if he had said too much already. She pressed him further.

'A couple of things?'

Brett turned away from the camera lens and spoke directly to Nathalie. 'Off the record, there were some things he couldn't explain.

First, the skin on his hands was seriously burnt and then, why so much blood?'

Brett had said 'off the record' yet Nathalie knew that although she hadn't got the picture, it was very much on the record on Dan's digital sound recorder.

They used the rest of the afternoon taking close-ups to cover their two interviews. The engineers were surprisingly co-operative in showing them the submersible's on-board computer. As Nathalie directed the shots on the quayside she couldn't help but feel some sort of unease at the back of her mind. Here she was filming an accident, or was it a crime scene, when she should have been recording the late Professor Lake. Now she would never know what he was going to tell her. Possibly just a scientist moaning about a cut in funding and a group of freelance engineers he hadn't asked for, but maybe not. When they had finished the last shot of the day she decided to share her concerns with Charlie.

'Odd, don't you think? Lake was about to give us some lowdown on Marine Corps and the next day he's found dead.'

Charlie stopped packing the camera into its case and pointed to the schedule. 'Odd is hardly the word for it, now we've been asked to go to Majuro to film a wave power station that's being worked on by Marine Corps engineers. Aren't you worried about that?'

'A bit, but even if these things aren't just accidents, they're not targeting us; they are scuppering the installations. And isn't this what we're here for?'

'Not originally. I thought we were doing a film on climate change and ocean energy. It's bloody obvious that we are poking our nose in now. Does your boss know what he's getting us into?'

'You know he does. I thought you agreed.'

'Yes, but now a guy's dead. And it's not just me; I'm concerned about the safety of both of us.'

'Well, you needn't worry about me. I'm picking up the tickets from a travel agent tomorrow morning. If you don't want to come I'll have to get another cameraman. Are you with me or not?'

Charlie didn't have time to reply as the assistant director of the plant came into the room.

'I see that you have finished here. Is there anything else we can do?'

It was obvious that the man was still in shock and coming to terms with his responsibilities for the facility.

Nathalie was at a loss for something appropriate to say but managed to mutter, 'No, but thank you for all of your help in such difficult circumstances.'

He nodded awkwardly and shuffled off to have a word with one of the engineers.

Nathalie and Charlie rejoined the crew and, in silence, they drove out of the compound.

In the evening, showered and made up, Nathalie took the short walk down the staircase to the hotel lobby. She found Charlie sheepishly sitting on a bench, waiting for her. Dan and Luke had taken the Jeep to meet some friends along the coast, so they had decided to stay in and eat in the hotel restaurant.

Charlie nodded towards the bar. 'Fancy a drink first?'

'Why not? Neither of us is going to be driving this evening.'

The bar was empty apart from a lone pianist in the corner. They sat on two of the faux fur-topped chrome bar stools. Charlie beckoned the barman over and half turned to Nathalie.

'What are you having? This one's on me; I think I owe you an apology.'

'Ice-cold beer, please; and apology accepted, if you're still coming on the shoot.'

Charlie ordered two beers and swivelled on the bar stool so that he was looking her straight in the eye.

'I was just worried about your safety, and mine, I must admit. If I was on my own it would be different, but with a ...'

'A girl,' interrupted Nathalie. 'Is that what you think of me – a girl prancing around the Pacific, playing at being a film director? If that's what you call an apology then you can …' She felt the blood rise in her face, her anger getting to the point of no return. She caught the astonished glances of the barman and pianist in her direction. Her voice must have been rising. She inhaled deeply through her nostrils and closed her eyes briefly, before placing her two palms down upon the bar.

'I think we should have this drink and then I'm going to get a meal sent up to my room. What you do is your concern.'

'Nathalie, I'm really sorry, I didn't mean … I know you're not playing, it's obvious you've shot this sort of stuff before. You're right, it was a sexist thing to say. After all, it was me who let you down today, vomiting all over the place. It won't happen again.'

He put his hand on hers but she withdrew it immediately. 'I wasn't worried about that. You were the first to see it and it must have been a shock. It's the patronising bit that gets me. Are you really saying that if I was a bloke you'd be hesitating about going to Majuro?'

'What can I say? You're right. Wrong call. No place for old-fashioned prejudice. Forgive me.'

'No, I won't. But if you stop grovelling and come on the shoot tomorrow, I'll have dinner with you. How's that?'

The pianist had stopped playing and was obviously straining to hear their conversation. The barman was just standing there, warming their two ice-cold beers in his hands.

'What are you two looking at?' snapped Nathalie, taking a beer from the surprised barman. 'Can you give my friend here his beer before it reaches room temperature and tell the restaurant that we will be a few minutes' late.'

The long queue of customers at the car rentals' return jangled their car keys impatiently as they waited for their deposits. The stocky glass-eyed man behind the desk was in no hurry. The closer to take-off time, the less they could complain. It was a system that worked.

Nathalie had already abandoned her prepared speech on faulty air conditioning and broken door locks in order to get a discount. She would be lucky to get her deposit back at this rate. The plane to Honolulu was already on the runway; maybe she should just throw the keys at him and run. The queue shuffled forward another step. Her watch said ten past eight, only forty minutes to go. At least she had had the sense to send the crew on ahead. They would have checked the equipment in by now. Dan and Luke had cheerfully accepted a trip to a coral atoll and another five days' pay. They had a shoot on Oahu lined up in a week's time; fortunately, it was possible to get them a return ticket that fitted their schedule. Charlie had behaved well over dinner and had committed to both films but, that morning, there was no doubt there was some distance between them. She hoped that would change; there was nothing worse than a cameraman who wasn't on your side.

'Next!' At last she had come to the front of the queue. She pushed her papers and credit card forward and waited for the refund. Just in time as the Kona Airport announcer was giving the boarding call.

Honolulu Airport was bustling with Japanese tourists. Nathalie left Charlie to watch the luggage carousel while she peered over the exit barrier for the travel agent. A piece of white card appeared, floating above the heads of the milling crowd. On it, in crude capital letters, was marked her misspelt name, *MS TOMSON*. She hailed the small boy who was holding it above his head. As he handed over the papers he held out his hand in expectation. She put five dollars into it and without a word he turned and disappeared into the throng.

'Thank you,' said Nathalie out loud to herself.

Charlie had that sort of look you have when you push a door that needs to be pulled. The three of them were standing alongside the now familiar pile of aluminium boxes, watching the empty carousel.

Luke was the first to speak. 'It's always the legs.'

'It doesn't matter when you check them in, they're always last,' moaned Dan.

Nathalie pointed to the strips of rubber spewing out of the black cylinder containing the tripod. 'It seems I've brought you luck, here they are. Better hurry or we'll be late for our connecting flight.'

The Continental aircraft looked as if it had seen better days. Nathalie squeezed into one of the worn red seats next to Charlie. He smiled at her for the first time that day and offered her his iPod. She belted up, slipped on the headphones and closed her eyes to the soporific sounds of Enya.

Some time later she was woken with a jolt. She looked at her watch. They weren't due in for another three hours. She turned to Charlie, who was peering out of the window.

'What's going on?'

'Unscheduled stop. Take a look.'

She undid her seat belt and stretched over him to peer outside. They were sitting on a grey piece of tarmac in the middle of the ocean. A few rusty outhouses were scattered to one side and what looked like an electrical generating station on the other. In the distance was a large, threatening, dull black military aircraft. The pilot's voice came through the speakers.

'Please remain seated and do not leave the aircraft. We have stopped for routine maintenance and should be airborne again within the hour. Thank you for your patience.'

'Routine maintenance, my arse,' said Charlie. 'This place was shut down as a commercial runway years ago. We've got a problem, Houston, more like it.'

Nathalie was now almost sitting on Charlie's lap in her attempt to see more. 'Where are we?'

'Johnson Island, I think. Don't see where else it could be, only two hours out of Hawaii. There's nothing else out here. It was once used for nuclear testing and storing chemical weapons.'

'You're joking.'

'That's what I've read. It's all shut down now, though.'

'What's that black thing doing on the runway then?'

Charlie put his head beside hers. 'See your point, another emergency stop, perhaps?'

Their cheeks were almost touching and Nathalie could smell the muskiness of his skin, a comforting smell considering the situation; a forced landing on a tiny, polluted atoll in the middle of the Pacific. It was almost with reluctance that she sat back in her seat when the steward came around with the complimentary drinks.

Charlie sipped his whisky. 'Any more news on our Majuro shoot?'

'No more than I told you over dinner last night. Geoff's told me to expect an e-mail when we arrive. That's if this thing ever gets off the ground again.'

'Doesn't look promising,' laughed Charlie, squinting out of the window. 'They've got a guy looking into the engine with a torch and a spanner in his hand.'

'You're not serious?'

'No, really, take a look.'

Nathalie squeezed across his lap once more and shook her head in disbelief as she watched a man in a short-sleeved shirt halfway up a ladder that was leaning against the plane's wing. 'At least it's not a hammer,' she joked. 'Call the steward, I think we deserve another whisky.'

The one-hour announced delay was optimistic, for they had been on the runway nearly three hours before the pilot told them that they would be on their way. There were only so many times that you could read the in-flight magazine, so Nathalie and Charlie had spent the time drinking whisky and making up. As far as she was concerned, it was business as usual and perhaps a little better than that as she now felt she had stamped her authority on the situation. The whisky had made them sleepy and so they spent the next four hours to Majuro leaning against each other, fast asleep.

Neither of them saw the landing on the amazing strip of runway built like an aircraft carrier on the edge of the atoll. Majuro is a croissant-shaped island, thirty miles long, and at the narrow ends, only one hundred yards wide. In places you could stand in the middle and throw a stone in the water on both sides. The heat hit them like a treacle Jacuzzi as they stepped off the plane. The hotel Robert Reimers' shuttle bus was waiting outside the tiny terminal. A few tourists squeezed in beside them as the driver clumsily stored their equipment on the roof.

'Hey, hold on there,' shouted Charlie, 'that stuff's fragile. Pass me that camera box, I'll keep it on my lap.'

The driver was reluctant to do this – luggage went on the roof, passengers in the bus. Charlie squared up for a fight. 'There's no way you're putting that on the roof, tied up with that tiny bit of string.'

Charlie was six-foot two and had the biceps of someone who was used to carrying heavy camera kit around. The diminutive driver backed down. So began the uncomfortable twenty-minute journey along the solitary road around the atoll.

'I wonder if they sell many Sat Navs here,' said Luke, smiling at the lady opposite who was grimacing every time the camera box nudged her elbow.

Nathalie looked through the palm trees to her right at the open ocean and then to her left across the wide lagoon. In the distance she could just make out the other tip of the island, fringed with more palm trees in the haze. A crescent speck in the middle of miles and miles of water. What on earth did people do here for a living?

The Hotel Robert Reimers had an unimpressive façade – a narrow car park fronting a low-rise building – which on first sight looked like a Midwest Motel but, as they entered the hand-carved wooden-walled lobby, it had a charm of its own. Hand-crafted ornaments adorned the walls and to the far side of the reception desk was a window and a terrace overlooking the lagoon. Nathalie put her papers on the counter.

'We have a reservation for four rooms for one night and we would like a table in the restaurant this evening, please.'

There was a long pause while the young receptionist leafed through the travel documents. She tapped on her antiquated computer and stared at the screen for a while. Nathalie could never understand why it took so long to complete such a simple task.

'Is there a problem?' she said, more by way of asking the girl to hurry up rather than if there really was one.

'I'm afraid there is, ma'am. You see these documents show your reservation for last night. I'm afraid that tonight all the hotels on the island are completely full.'

Nathalie grabbed back the travel documents. 'Impossible, I just picked these up this morning. Look, it says four rooms for Wednesday night.'

'Yes, ma'am, but today is Thursday. Your travel agent should have known. When you flew here from Hawaii you crossed the dateline.'

Thirteen

The lobby fell silent for a while. Dan and Luke sat quietly on two of the aluminium boxes that were blocking the doorway. Charlie braced himself for the torrent of abuse that his director was about to deliver to the receptionist. Instead, Nathalie was ice-cool. Here they were on a coral atoll in the middle of the Pacific with thousands of pounds' worth of equipment in heavy boxes and there was no room at the inn. She knew that nothing would be done by shouting and so she spoke calmly.

'And you say that there are no other rooms free on the whole of the island?'

The receptionist shook her head. 'No, ma'am, there are only a few places to stay here.' She waved at the grimy computer terminal on her desk. 'I've rechecked them all, nothing until tomorrow night.'

'Well, I'm afraid that we're out of here tomorrow night.' Nathalie gestured to her crew and their equipment. 'As you can see, it's tonight that we have a little problem.'

The receptionist shrugged and gave Nathalie a look that said it wasn't *her* problem. At that moment a young man in a shabby white coat with brass buttons passed through the lobby and opened a side door with a key that he took out of his pocket. Nathalie just caught a glimpse of an untidy room with a single bed in the corner.

'You have staffrooms here?'

'Yes, ma'am.'

'I suppose we could sleep on the beach.' Nathalie pulled a bunch of ten-dollar bills from her bag and began counting them out onto the desk. 'As you can see we have rather a lot of expensive equipment that needs to be locked up.' She looked into the receptionist's eyes and could see from the woman's expression that the penny, or rather the wad of ten-dollar bills, was dropping.

It was going to be cramped. They were offered two small, single-bedded rooms. The waiter and the houseboy seemed quite pleased with their remuneration and thanked them repeatedly as they removed their meagre belongings. Dan and Luke moved half of the equipment into one of the rooms while Nathalie and Charlie took up the other.

'Cosy,' said Charlie, squeezing in the last lens box.

But Nathalie wasn't listening; she was hunched up on the single bed, trying to get a connection to her laptop. 'No signal; I thought the travel agent said they had WiFi.'

'You mean the travel agent who said they had booked us four rooms for tonight.'

'They've got an e-mail address so they must have some sort of connection. We've not got a lot of time. I'd like to shoot this afternoon. Strip down the gear to the bare minimum, and tell Dan and Luke to do the same. I'll ask reception if they can get into my Hotmail address to see if we've got an update from Bagatelle.'

Before Charlie could make any comment Nathalie leapt over the boxes and into the corridor. The hotel's internet access was slow and expensive but eventually she downloaded her e-mails. For another fee she was allowed to print her attachments. She took them into the sunshine to look them over. Bagatelle's researchers had found some more background on the dispute between the wave power station and a Japanese exploration ship. The offshore wave machines were being set up by an American company as some sort of trade-off for military presence. Eventually the power generated would be used by the islanders but any patent rights during the development phase would remain the property of the company. Everything was going swimmingly until a Japanese research vessel had come on the scene, claiming their right to explore for underwater minerals. The Second World War action between America and Japan in the area didn't help. The Japanese ship wanted access to the waters around the atoll. The American wave power station was claiming that this would interfere with their development work. Now there was a stand-off. The Majuro authorities, not wanting to upset either, were referring the case to the Marshall Islands' central government. Nobody was happy which, as far as Geoff was concerned, would make good footage for the documentary. Unfortunately for Nathalie he didn't suggest how to get this footage. She was hoping for contact names and some sort of filming schedule. Instead all she was given was a 'to whom it may concern' letter asking for permission to film sequences for a rather vague and benign documentary on ocean research.

'He's done it again,' she ranted, waving the printouts at Charlie.

Her cameraman still had his head in the camera box, screwing an all-purpose lens onto the mount. 'Done *what* again?'

'Oh, never mind!' snapped Nathalie. 'Haven't you finished that yet? I want to get to the harbour ASAP, there won't be much light left to shoot anything soon.'

'Harbour? I thought …'

'Change of plan; ship today, wave power station tomorrow.'

'I thought the whole reason for coming here was the wave power station. Why the harbour?'

'Because it would take us hours to get to the wave power station and I want to see if we can get some footage of this mining vessel.'

'And how do you propose to get on this ship?'

'Charlie, I'm tired. All you seem to be doing is making obstacles. I've got us a room, and I'll get us on the ship. Meet me outside in five minutes with the others. I'll see if I can get the shuttle bus to take us to the harbour.'

The quayside was deserted and the mining vessel was the only large ship in port. A lone gangplank with a slack rope handrail was placed alongside. Nathalie asked the shuttle bus driver to collect them at dusk and told the crew to wait on the quay. She went aboard and looked around. It was like the *Mary Celeste* – no-one to be seen.

'Hello?' She walked towards a varnished cabin door. 'Anybody there?'

Not a sound. She pushed at the door and it swung open. Inside were a wash basin and a double bunk dimly lit by a small porthole.

She jumped as a head wrapped in a knotted white handkerchief peered over the top bunk.

'Jesus, you frightened me,' she said, staring into the glowering eyes of the Oriental face.

'Who are you and what are you doing on my ship?' The voice was soft, yet authoritative and spoken with a heavy Japanese accent.

'I'm terribly sorry, I'm Nathalie Thomson, a film director from England, and I was hoping to ask permission to film on this wonderful ship.'

The captain's quarters were tiny with a low ceiling. He sat opposite her and placed two small blue china bowls on the table. In one corner a steaming pot of tea rested on a hotplate. Spread out on a side table were marine charts scattered with a number of DVDs. The captain noticed the direction of Nathalie's glances.

'Yes, Miss Thompson, we take video too. Perhaps you would like to see?'

He got up slowly and she thought he was going to pass her a disc. Instead he walked over to the teapot and poured some of its clear green liquid into the two bowls. She sat in silence while he regained his place and raised one of the bowls towards her. Mimicking his action, she sipped some of the thirst-quenching tea.

They must have been poised on opposite sides of the table drinking tea for at least a minute before Nathalie broke the stalemate.

'The video, you said that you would show me your video.'

The captain, who continued looking at her with his calm watery eyes, gently placed his tea bowl on the table and picked up a silver coloured remote lying nearby.

'Of course. This may save you a lot of trouble. We film all of our operations at sea. Perhaps your English television would like to use this.'

Nathalie turned her gaze to the television set. The monitor flickered into life. Burnt into one corner were the words '*copyright ASCO International*'. The picture quality was quite good but the camera work was terrible. A bunch of sailors in orange overalls were on the deck in the middle of the ocean. They were using a crane to lower a contraption which resembled one of those fairground grabbing machines; the ones that always drop the cuddly toy before you can get it into the slot. The sailors were more successful. A wobbly close-up of them opening the grabbing bucket revealed some strange shiny nodules sitting on a base of sand. These were picked out carefully and placed onto a plastic specimen tray. The video camera lurched upwards to find a man walking towards the objects with a measuring gauge.

'Manganese nodules.' The captain said this in reply to Nathalie's un-asked question. 'They form on the seabed over millions of years. The metal ore is valuable. The problem is that it lies three miles under the ocean. One day it may be possible to mine these nodules but not today. Until then, we do surveys for the scientists.'

All very interesting, thought Nathalie. Although none of this was very helpful in getting footage for either of her movies. The video was of non-broadcast standard and the subject matter hardly relevant. Geoff had said that there was some sort of row going on between this vessel and the nearby wave power station. Shooting material on this subject was going to be quite sensitive. She decided to take the diplomatic tack.

'Great video,' she exclaimed, 'though I'm afraid we can't use DVDs for editing. We have to shoot it on 16mm film. Would it be possible for us to do that?'

The captain took another slow sip of tea from his bowl. Nathalie waited patiently; she realised that in Japanese culture it is very difficult to say an absolute no to anyone. Eventually, he placed his bowl on the table and laid his hands face down on either side. Apart from the normal Japanese-accented 'L' instead of an 'R', his English diction was clear and deliberate.

'We have two small problems, Miss Thompson. At present we are in port because there is a misunderstanding between my government and the government of the United States. This concerns the permission to explore the seabed in the nearby region. Secondly, even if we could put to sea, this would not be possible today.' The captain looked at her resignedly and shrugged his shoulders. 'All crew on shore leave.'

Hardly small problems, thought Nathalie. But Geoff was right, there was a dispute. All she had to do now was to get a controversial interview about this without frightening him off. She would have to tread very carefully; perhaps tackle him on an issue he was more comfortable with first. From the little conversation that he had made so far this was manganese nodules.

'It must be really skilful to get those nodule samples from such depths,' she began. 'It would be a great shame if we couldn't show that on TV.'

He put his head to one side but didn't say a word in reply.

'If we could get a couple of crew volunteers to help I'm sure we could re-enact some of the action in the harbour. I could point our camera towards the ocean. With a few shots of a ship's wake and a clever bit of editing I'm sure we could make it look like we were at sea.'

The captain's fingers began to drum on the table. It was evident that he was coming to a decision.

'All right, Miss Thompson, the cook is still on board. I'll ask him to go into the town to see if any of the crew would like to be film stars.' For the first time his mouth broke into a discernible smile. 'I must warn you, though, he may have a little difficulty as the crew have been at sea for three months and there is a famous house in the town that provides the company of Micronesian ladies. They have a reputation for great beauty.'

In the hope that the lust for fame would triumph over sex Nathalie asked the film crew to prepare by setting their gear on the deck. She sensed by his body language that Charlie was in a strange mood.

'What's up, Charlie, you have a problem with something?'

Charlie continued screwing the bowl of the Romford head onto the tripod. 'I don't get it; I thought we were trying to get ocean energy stuff. I don't see what this has got to do with either of the films.

Dragging up a couple of bits of stone from the ocean doesn't seem very cutting-edge investigative journalism to me.'

'Okay, keep your voice down, the guy speaks perfect English.' Nathalie dropped her voice to a whisper. 'I'm just doing this to keep him warm; when we get round to the interviews I can drop in a couple of questions on what he thinks about the territorial dispute. I think this is the sort of stuff that Lake was going to talk about. The United States put up an offshore wave power station, call it an island, and then start claiming the territorial waters around it.'

Charlie continued setting up his camera. 'Okay,' he said resignedly. 'You're the boss, although I still think we'd get better material from the wave power station. See if it really works, and if they've got the right to put it there.'

'I don't know what's wrong with you, Charlie, I told you we'll try for that stuff tomorrow. Believe me, if we can film this guy's pet subject and make him look good he is more likely to let slip something in an interview.'

Charlie shrugged his shoulders and clipped the magazine onto the camera. 'Okay, as I said you're the boss, I'm ready to roll.'

Nathalie needed a pouty cameraman like a hole in the head but she soon cheered up when she saw the cook return with three budding film actors from the brothel. Either the Micronesian girls weren't all they were cracked up to be, or they had run out of Viagra. The captain greeted them with a ceremonial bow and explained what they were expected to do. When Nathalie was told of the first exercise she realised that it was fortuitous that they were not doing it for real at sea. It would have been almost impossible to film. The sailors brought out a man-sized orange buoy with a pennant sticking out of the top of it. At its base was a small grab similar to the one she'd seen in the video. They placed a brick in the grab and began to haul the buoy over the side.

'Wait,' Nathalie shouted. 'Do that again, I need to get a shot of it.'

The sailors repeated the action under the gaze of Charlie's camera. This time the buoy sank to the bottom of the harbour. The captain explained to Nathalie that when it hit the bottom a spring would release the grab and the brick would fall out. Then the grab would snap shut again and pick up some of the bottom sediment. As the sediment would be lighter than the brick the buoy would eventually float to the surface. In the deep ocean this could take hours as it had miles to travel. At sea they would launch dozens of these buoys and circle the ship to detect them from their flashing beacons to pick them up later. The harbour was only twenty metres deep so Charlie had little difficulty in catching a shot of the buoy emerging on the surface; a shot that would not have been possible in the open sea.

'Great,' cried Nathalie. 'Now reposition so we can get a shot of them taking a sample out of the grab on board.' She turned to one of the sailors. 'Can we put one of those manganese nodule things into the grab to pretend it's been found on the seabed?'

It was evident that the sailor didn't speak much English for he just looked at her quizzically. She turned to Charlie for help but he was busying himself checking the gate of the camera. Nathalie pulled a handkerchief from her pocket and rolled it into a ball. She pointed at it and said slowly and loudly the words, 'manganese nodule.' She put the handkerchief into the grab and then stood back with an exaggerated gesture of surprise. The sailor got the idea. With a broad grin he rushed below deck. Minutes later he reappeared, triumphantly holding one of the iridescent metal objects that Nathalie had seen on the video.

'Manganese nodule,' he proudly declared.

They dramatised the sequence several times to get close-ups as well as the wide shot of the action. Each time the crew were becoming more enthusiastic and creative. When it was cut together Nathalie was sure that this scene would look just like it had been shot at sea. Only, having controlled the action, it looked far better than it would have done had it been filmed on the hoof. The rest of the afternoon went smoothly. More and more crew joined in the reconstructed scenes as news of the event leaked back to the centre of Majuro. It was obvious that the action here was hotter than in town. Even the ship's master had become relaxed enough to join in. The sun had started to set and a blood red orange backdrop rose from the horizon. Time for the interview, thought Nathalie.

The captain leant against the rail of the ship. Luke had positioned a small light to illuminate his face. The background of distant palms silhouetted against the burning sky contrasted with the pale character lines of their interviewee. The shot looked awesome. Even Charlie seemed to have perked up.

'Magic hour,' he muttered quietly.

They went through their ritual. Dan held out the boom and said that sound was rolling; Luke clapped the board and shouted the slate number; and the nod from Charlie indicated that he was framed.

Nathalie addressed her first question. 'Captain, we have filmed some exercises on your ship today. Could you explain in your own words what this vessel does and why it is doing it?'

The captain was as clear and succinct as he was the first time she had met him. No errs, ums or irrelevancies, the perfect interviewee. He explained about the amazing mineral resources of the sea and the different systems on his ship that could detect them. Currently, they were surveying manganese nodules. Nathalie asked him to explain what they were.

'A manganese nodule is a one to twenty-five centimetre ball of valuable metals; mainly manganese but also copper, nickel, cobalt and titanium. Currently, we think there are twenty-three million tonnes of these metals contained in these nodules in the deep ocean. That's more than the total known ore reserves on land. At present there is no economic means of bringing these nodules to the surface in huge quantities. Yet as Japan imports most of its minerals we feel it important to survey this possible future resource.'

Her interviewee appeared at ease so Nathalie thought it time to strike. 'So, if it's just to survey, what right has a new wave power station under development by the United States got to stop you working around the atoll?'

If she had touched a raw nerve the man didn't show it. He answered as calmly as he had for her other questions. He told her that the wave power station claimed that his vessel's presence in the area would interfere with their instruments. He denied this and said that he believed there was a more covert reason, that of the station attempting to set a legal precedent of ownership of the seabed under the UNCLOS Charter. In fact, they were suggesting that the artificial island could claim its own exclusive economic zone and the fishing and mineral rights within it. If his ship withdrew from the area it was possible that the United States would claim that Japan had conceded the territory.

'Out of stock,' interrupted Charlie, tapping the magazine. 'You said come light, I'm afraid that's the last roll of film we have on us. The rest of the stock is in the hotel.'

Nathalie turned to glare at him. She relaxed her shoulders just in time. He was right, she did say bring the bare minimum. 'Okay, the light has gone anyway and we've got some good material today. Let's make it a wrap.' She turned to her interviewee. 'Captain, thank you and your crew so much for all your help and hospitality. I do hope you settle your differences with the power station.'

To their surprise the shuttle bus turned up on time and the driver helped them store their gear inside. A few cold beers on the terrace bar of the Hotel Robert Reimers helped them forget their lack of sleep and the stresses of the day. Even Charlie had shaken off his sullen mood. Luke passed around some suspicious cigarettes that he had been given by one of the ship's crew and they all began to laugh, even at his poor jokes. The evening was warm and in different circumstances they would have stayed up all night.

Nathalie reluctantly stood up. 'Sorry, guys, another heavy day tomorrow. I think we should call it a night.'

They nodded and Dan and Luke staggered towards their quarters. Charlie helped Nathalie along the corridor. They stepped into their tiny room. The overhead fan slowly rotated, casting shadows over the walls. The floor was packed with camera boxes, leaving little place to stand. Hard against one wall was the single bed. Nathalie pushed her hands against the springs.

'There's no room on the floor so I suppose we'll have to share.'

Charlie gave her a wicked grin. 'Fair enough, but I must warn you, in this heat I don't sleep with any clothes on.'

Nathalie looked him straight in the eye. 'That's okay, neither do I.'

Fourteen

There was freezing fog on the M4. The traffic was backed up for miles and Geoff could hardly see the pinpricks of red light from the car in front of him. The Heathrow tunnel was crowded at the best of times so he had left the office an hour early but this was bad. Nick would really be pissed off with him if he was late.

'I'm burnt and bruised all over, haven't slept for two days, and you want me to go to the bloody Foreign Office for a meeting as soon as I've landed.' he had complained on the telephone. So Geoff had agreed to pick him up at the airport. He turned on the radio for the traffic reports. One announcement was devoted to air travel. There were delays on the JFK to Heathrow flights but no cancellations due to the specialist air traffic control facilities. With a bit of luck, if the plane was late, he would get there as Nick arrived.

It had taken all his influence to get an appointment with the Foreign Office. They normally hated unsolicited contact with the media. After several failed attempts he had approached a member of the House of Lords who had advised on one of his earlier Open University programmes. The guy had always been interested in television and Geoff had promised that if anything came of the meeting he was sure that another advisory post could be found. A few strings were pulled and hey presto, a senior official from the Foreign Office had agreed to give them an off-the-record meeting concerning the Law of the Sea Convention. He had thought he had scheduled it with plenty of time; he hadn't reckoned on this freezing fog.

Nick was waiting for him on the pavement just outside the arrivals hall. He threw his small hand luggage into the back of Geoff's Audi and jumped into the passenger seat.

'I thought my balls had enough torment – now you're trying to freeze them off.'

Geoff looked puzzled for a moment and then he twigged. 'You're the only person I know who would complain about having legitimate expenses for going to a sex club,' he laughed. 'While you've been having fun with the ladies I've had to put up with brown-nosing around the dusty corridors of power.'

'Yeah, but I don't suppose that you had to get your privates whipped to get the information; or perhaps you did, knowing that House of Lords lot.'

Geoff pulled the car out into the mainstream traffic. Fortunately, the fog was clearing and the motorway flashing signs had been switched off. The journey was still slow. However, things were moving and it was bearable. There was time for a debrief from Nick and a chance to get him up to speed with the agenda for the meeting. As they reached the Hammersmith flyover Nick repeated the story about Viveca Olsson and Senator Cronkar.

'Viveca, interesting name,' interrupted Geoff. 'If she's the age you say, she was probably named after Viveca Lindfors, the Swedish actress. Do you know anything about her background?'

'Who, Lindfors?'

'No, Olsson. Where did she come from, who are her contacts, what's her role in the UN?'

'Charday tells me she's the Senior Operations Manager for the Environmental Protection Agency. Used to work for Cronkar, now works with Cain. Swedish origin, but used to work for some energy company in the Far East. Think that's how she got her current job, some sort of green issues' convert. Not a lot more on her, unless you consider her legs – up to her armpits. No wonder she's named after a film star, she's a stunner.'

Geoff was used to Nick's banter; it sounded flip but if you read between the lines there was always some good information in there somewhere.

'So, what did you get out of the hostess at the nightclub, besides the bruised testicles? No "double entendres", just the facts, please.'

'Shame, I was just about to tell you that I was too tied up to ...' Nick broke off as Geoff turned his head sharply, nearly spinning the car off the road. 'Okay, I'll lose the jokes. As I told you on the phone, Olsson lubricated the guy with alcohol and put him in a car to Spankers with an escort. My friend Sadie said that when he arrived he was a bit disorientated. Viveca was nowhere to be seen and he probably thought that he had been taken to the wrong place by mistake. Sadie thought he was given a spiked drink because he started to become more compliant. By the time they took him into the private room I think he was well gone. Apparently the stuff that was going on in the area I was in was child's play compared to the private dungeon. I tell you, once you are strapped into those contraptions, you're completely at their mercy. Would have been easy to video it. Problem for Cronkar, he couldn't blame Viveca – she was nowhere near the place. Easy for her to say that the cab went to the wrong address. I wasn't in a position to grill Geena, the dominatrix, either, and it wouldn't have been any good if I had. She was pretty much in control of everything that went on in there and it would be easy for her to say that he paid for it. I don't think you'd get many of the customers prepared to be witnesses to say otherwise.'

'What about the escort?'

'No-one seems to have seen her since. Victor and Billy know most of the classy escorts in Manhattan but even they hadn't seen her before.'

'Victor and Billy?'

'Victor runs a fashionable New York nightclub called Pumas. I've known him for years. Billy's his sidekick. Between them they know all that you need to know about the ladies of the night. They said if someone really wanted to stitch Cronkar up it wouldn't have been difficult to get someone from out of town. I thought it best not to tackle Olsson until we knew more about what was going on.'

Geoff turned into Earls Court Road and headed for the Embankment.

'Right decision. If she's now working with Cain, either the agency think she's got nothing to do with it or they're complicit in the whole affair. What we've got to do is to find who has the most to gain from Cronkar's resignation. That's what this meeting is about.'

The Audi swept along Millbank and Geoff turned into Great College Street and down the ramp to the underground car park. The Foreign Office was only a ten-minute walk away and they had twenty minutes to spare, so they decided to stroll instead of taking a cab. Geoff dug into his jacket pocket and pulled out a necktie. He offered it to Nick.

'What's that for?'

'It's a tie.'

'Yes, I know what it is; why are you giving it to me? It's not my birthday. I don't wear ties anyway.'

'I know that, that's why I brought one along. The Foreign Office are a strange lot, old-fashioned etiquette and all that. I don't want to get off on the wrong foot.'

Nick held the pink and blue striped tie up to his open-necked khaki shirt. 'I'm not sure it goes with my complexion,' he said.

'It will if I give you a punch,' replied Geoff. 'Just put it on.'

By the time they had reached the corner of King Charles Street the two men had made their plan. No point in flannelling, the Foreign Office might be a stuffy lot but they weren't stupid. Bagatelle was a well-known production company that made investigative films. Geoff would come straight to the point. They didn't reveal sources but they wanted to know if there had been a change in policy from the United States since Cronkar had been kicked out. Nick, who had first-hand contact with Charday, would ask about Cain and his background. Geoff was to handle the more technical stuff about the treaty.

They walked through the central arch and introduced themselves to the security men. They were expected and after a quick ID check they were chaperoned up the State Stair. A golden arched ceiling towered above them, leading to a star-studded central dome painted with figures representing the world's states.

'O let the nations rejoice,' read Nick from the gold inscription. 'Bloody lot of rejoicing when I was in action, I don't think.'

When they had reached the landing their chaperone, who had either not heard or ignored Nick, led them down a door-lined corridor. He paused at one of the large panelled doors and using his knuckles made a soft tap.

'Come.' An Etonian voice came from the interior.

They were ushered into the room and asked to sit. Compared to the marble-pillared entrance hall the room was rather shabby. Buff-coloured metal filing cabinets lined one wall and a hodgepotge of different style tables were scattered around the room. A figure in a pinstriped three-piece suit could just be made out, sitting behind a desk against the large window. When their eyes had become accustomed to the light they could see a pale balding man with a grey moustache. Everything fitted their expectation of a jobsworth civil servant. They were to be pleasantly surprised.

'Farthing,' the man said. 'Matthew Farthing. Would you like some coffee?' Without waiting for an answer, he pressed the intercom button on his desk and asked his assistant to bring them coffee and biscuits. 'So, it's the Law of the Sea you've come about. Complicated business; nearly fifty years of negotiations and we are still no further in coming to an agreement. But knowing you TV guys, you've not come for a lecture, you've come for a good story. Fire away.'

Farthing was laying his cards on the table so Geoff decided to play his.

'Senator Cronkar. I believe you had some dealings with him during some of the most recent negotiations. What sort of man was he?'

'Ah, the sex scandal chap, I thought it might be him. I was surprised, frankly. Didn't seem like the sort of man to get caught. Brilliant negotiator. A good man too; finger on the pulse. We were getting on quite swimmingly.'

Not the sort of man to get caught, thought Geoff. Nothing about his moral compass.

A quiet knock on the door was followed by the entrance of a young man in a grey suit with a drinks' tray. He placed the tray on the desk and without a word left the office. Farthing began to pour the coffees.

'Milk?'

Geoff and Nick declined and leant forward to take the bone china cups. Nick accepted a biscuit gratefully, he hadn't eaten for hours. '*Were* getting on?' he questioned.

'Very pro-climate change, sympathetic to developing countries and the landlocked states. Twelve months of careful wording of the treaty appendices. All now past tense.'

Nick tried to swallow the last of his biscuit.

'I was at the UN a couple of days ago. Understand he has a successor.'

'Not actually met him. Suffered the fallout, though. Cain has put the brakes on everything that Cronkar started. We did some checks on him. Middle-of-the-road Republican with no great track record. Seems that the appointment has gone to his head. Extreme insular policies, climate change sceptic and anti-treaty. No sign of this in his recent past. Perhaps the top brass were getting cold feet. Could be a puppet changing his tune to rise through the ranks.'

'Which would make it very convenient that there was a vacant post,' said Geoff.

'We thought about that. Difficult to prove.'

Geoff looked at Nick sitting uncomfortably on the hard upright chair. Not if you're prepared to stick your bum out, he thought.

'What happens next?'

'Back to square one, I'm afraid. Not very good for those alternative energy types, not to mention the aggravation about the EEZs. Sorry, jargon for the area of ocean-bordering countries that they can exploit for resources. The bloody Falklands' row will start up again.' He said the last sentence with exasperation. Funny how civil servants see things. To Farthing, the Cronkar scandal meant a pile more paperwork.

'When are you meeting this guy?' Nick was eager to get a practical outcome from the meeting.

Farthing flicked through his diary, more out of a habit than necessity. 'Soon, as a matter of fact. There is a conference in Guam in a few days.'

Nick placed his empty cup back on the tray. 'Could you get us some tickets?'

'Would you have your cameras there? We could do with some good biased publicity at the moment.'

Nick looked for a response from Geoff, who was reaching for his mobile phone.

'Well, Mr Farthing, if you could get us some access then I think we could say it's a deal.'

The two men stepped briskly into the frosty air. Whitehall was teeming with office workers wrapped up from the cold. The sodium streetlights had come on, bathing the whole scene in an orange glow. Farthing hadn't known much more than they had, but it had been a successful meeting as far as getting an introduction to Cain was concerned. Geoff had already texted a message to Stefanie in the office. The coincidence of the location of the conference hadn't escaped Nick and he said as much to Geoff.

'Jammy bastard. Cain turns up in Guam and you've got a pet film crew in the area.'

'I wouldn't call two thousand miles away "in the area",' said Geoff, 'especially as it's in the wrong direction. I've asked Stefanie to cancel Nathalie's return ticket to Hawaii and change it for one in a westerly direction. Air travel from those islands is notoriously unpredictable. We'll be lucky if we can get in place in time.'

'Have you told Nathalie?'

'Not yet. I want her to keep her eye on Marine Corps for the moment. When Stefanie's fixed up some air tickets and local sound and lights in Guam, if there are any, I'll tell her the good news.'

They were passing a corner public house. The glow through the thick spun-glass panes was inviting. Geoff suggested that they stop for a drink. It was one of those old-fashioned city centre pubs that hadn't changed in decades; scrubbed wooden floors and panelled walls scattered with dusty fringed lamps. The evening trade had only just begun and there were plenty of seats. They found a quiet table in the corner at the rear. Geoff ordered two pints of bitter and carefully placed them on the beer mats. Nick downed half of his glass in one draft.

'You can't get that in the States. Eat your heart out, McSorley.'

Geoff had no idea what he was talking about. 'McSorley who?'

'Never mind. Tell me more about Marine Corps. You sent me some stuff but they didn't have any offices in New York so I didn't take it any further.'

Geoff related what he had found out so far. On the face of it, a reputable ocean engineering company employing groups of engineers spread all around the world. Internet research, Companies House and outfits that had used them all showed a clean track record. They had even found citations of glowing praise. However, the troubling facts were that Marine Corps' engineers had been on site for two ocean project disasters and had supplied survey maps to a third. Bagatelle had discovered a leaked pre-publication report on the demise of the *IOD Revolution*, the fated drilling ship. It was rumoured that the ship had gone down as a result of puncturing a sub-seafloor gas bubble. Receipts found in the drilling projects offices revealed that the engineers who had supplied the earlier sediment surveys to the ship were from Marine Corps. Geoff rose to order another round but Nick got to the bar before him. He waved a ten-pound note at the barman.

'My round, I think.' He turned to Geoff. 'And knowing all this, you've let Nathalie put her head in a noose on another Marine Corps' project?'

Geoff shrugged. 'We've no proof of anything, could all be coincidental. The wave power project isn't Marine Corps' – they just have a few engineers on-site, like they do on other stuff in the ocean.'

Nick concentrated on getting the two brimful glasses of beer back to the table without spilling them. He took a sip from one and with the back of his hand, wiped the froth from his mouth. 'So, what's the connection between these so-called accidents and the Cronkar-Cain affair?'

'We've no idea, it's just that it's a bit strange that a climate change sceptic is pushed into power at the same time that renewable ocean energy companies are getting some bad press. Possibly a motor industry or an oil connection, too early to say. That's what I hope we'll find out in Guam.'

'You want me to go over there to check this guy out? Could get heavy if people like the CIA are involved. I know Nathalie's capable but …'

'Capable, and she won't arouse suspicion; a nice young woman with a friendly documentary film crew, or a war-torn guy with strapping biceps – who would you trust?' Geoff reached for Nick's empty glass. It was obvious it was going to be a long evening. 'Besides, she's into her stride now; should have got a good relationship with her cameraman. When you do those shoots, you get a sixth sense; things start happening for you.'

Fifteen

Things had certainly started happening for Nathalie, although she wasn't exactly sure that they were the right things. She woke up with a blinding headache. Charlie was already dressed and preparing his camera for the day's shoot. She wrapped a sheet around herself and tiptoed between the boxes towards the small basin in the corner of the room. Charlie looked up.

'You okay?'

Nathalie splashed some lukewarm water over her face. 'Not sure yet. You?'

'I'm fine. Do you want to talk about it?'

She was about to say 'talk about what?' but thought better of it. 'Perhaps later.'

Charlie continued rummaging around in the equipment boxes. 'How many rolls of stock do you think we'll use today?'

'How many have we got left?'

'Five.'

'Better bring them all. Today's our last day here and if Geoff wants us to pick up some more shots in Hawaii on our way back, we could always get some stock there.'

'Okay, five it is. I'll load up two in the magazines. Twenty minutes should be fine for the morning session unless you have a long interview planned.'

'I don't have anything planned yet. Depends on what we find when we get there.' Nathalie looked at her watch, the only thing she was wearing. 'The wave power guys have arranged for a boat to pick us up within the hour.'

Seeing that she was looking uncomfortable Charlie made his way to the door. 'I'll let you get dressed. I'll grab a couple of coffees and meet you on the veranda in ten minutes.'

Nathalie nodded and picked her way carefully back to the small bed, where her clothes were lying in a dishevelled heap. After pulling on her jeans and T-shirt, she looked around for her rucksack. She found it squashed under one of the boxes and pulled out the notes she'd made on the wave station. Pushing them into her back pocket, she headed for the veranda. The sun was searing hot and the three guys were sitting in the shade with their eyes closed. They were missing a spectacular view. The veranda was perched on the shoreline overlooking the lagoon. In the distance you could pick out the fringes of the atoll, white sand and lush palms. The ocean was becalmed in this natural harbour and reflected the cloudless sky. The narrow sandy beach in front of them sloped away to form a turquoise border. An ideal holiday location for any couple. But it wasn't the two of them, there were four, and they weren't on holiday. She would have to concentrate on the task in front of her. Luke, hearing her footsteps on the boardwalk, opened his eyes and pulled up a chair. He looked as fresh as a daisy. Sparks were like that – they could fill themselves with alcohol and soft narcotics and still get up the next morning with no ill-effects.

'Charlie ordered you a coffee. I hope it hasn't gone cold.'

Nathalie took the beaker from him and took a life-giving sip. 'No, it's fine, just what I needed.'

The other two were now sitting upright, waiting for the day's briefing. Nathalie once more had to decide how much to tell them.

'I expect Charlie's told you we're being picked up by a boat in the next half-hour. The wave power station is located several hundred metres outside the atoll. I've been told it's quite a substantial structure so we should have no problem in setting up our gear. Before we begin shooting they're going to give us a guided tour to show how the thing works. Charlie, I'd like you to check out the best camera positions. I'll see if I can get some of their operators to do a bit of business to make some sort of narrative. Luke, I've no idea if there are any filmable interiors on this thing. It's worth you bringing a small lamp along in case we need some basic lighting; a redhead should do.' Nathalie suddenly remembered that she had broken her golden rule. Always speak to the soundman first; stop them feeling like a bridesmaid.

'Sorry, Dan, I wasn't ignoring you. Just that it's atmos in the morning. I'd like you to be prepared for exterior interviews in the afternoon.'

Dan removed the bored expression from his face. 'If you are going to shoot any from a distance, I could bring a radio mic.'

'Perfect, we might do a shot of the station from the boat. And guys, I don't just want the operation to look like clockwork. If it looks like they're messing things up, keep rolling. I want the reality of these things, not just a sanitised version.'

Charlie looked at her knowingly. 'You mean if Marine Corps try to fuck things up, get it in the can,' he whispered from behind his hand.

Their boat was punctual. The small aluminium motorcraft pulled up at the hotel's jetty. One of the two occupants jumped out to tie it up. He looked like an American marine – crew-cut, bronzed and muscles that strained at his white T-shirt. His partner was slighter and had the appearance of a Pacific islander. His origin was confirmed by the lilt in his voice.

'You going to bring all that stuff?' He was pointing at the camera boxes on the jetty.

''fraid so,' said Charlie, passing him the magazine case.

It was a tight fit yet they made it. The water was nearly up to the gunwales but the marine didn't seem too worried as he opened up the outboard and headed for the neck of the island. The moving air and spray did a lot for Nathalie's headache; it was much cooler here in the centre of the lagoon.

Luke pointed to the gap in the atoll. 'I hope this thing's got a pump, it's going to be a lot choppier out there.'

He was right. As soon as they had passed the tips of the atoll the waves hit them. Luckily the boat was built for it. It tossed and rolled and apart from the odd shower of spray, it stayed dry. The power station could be seen in the distance. Two vast platforms loomed over the ocean surface. Between them stretched a series of bright orange objects linked by some sort of flexible tubing. Today the sea was calm but even in these conditions Nathalie could see the objects bobbing up and down in the water, no doubt making electricity from their movement. Their craft was aiming towards one of the platforms. On closer inspection, it was a sort of operational base. Small coloured Lego-like outbuildings were perched on top of it. The area to one side of them was just about big enough to land a helicopter. Somebody had really put a lot of money into this enterprise. Was American military presence on Majuro that important, or was there really something in this business about territorial ownership around artificial islands? She would soon find out.

An aluminium ladder dipped into the water. The platform was surprisingly stable considering that, unlike an oil derrick, it was floating; not founded on pillars stretching to the bottom. Their boatmen grabbed onto the rail.

'You climb up, we'll get a crane to lift your equipment,' shouted the islander.

Charlie looked at the precarious boxes heaving up and down in the small boat. 'I'll stay with the equipment. Luke, make sure those crane guys know what they're doing. I'll secure the stuff on at this end; you and Dan unload it at the other.'

Luke gave him the thumbs up and made his way up the ladder. Once Nathalie and Dan were alongside he checked out the cage that they were going to lower into the boat. It was a wooden palette encased in a large rope mesh. A guy in a hard hat, with the name 'Marine Corps' plastered all over his overalls, slipped the crane hook through one of the loops. The palette lurched its way downwards. The first attempt nearly landed in the sea. The second was more accurate. The guy with the crew-cut grabbed onto the cage and steadied it as best he could. Charlie and the islander strapped the gear onto the wooden base with bungee ropes. When the last box was on, the islander gestured to the crane driver to haul away.

'Wait,' shouted Charlie, 'I'll ride with it; prevent anything from sliding off.'

Before they could stop him he was inside the cage, holding onto the boxes with all his might. Nathalie watched, open-mouthed, as Charlie and the camera gear spun towards her. The palette was nearly level with the platform edge when the crane's chain slipped. The jolt nearly threw Charlie and one of the cases into the ocean. At the last moment he grabbed onto the case and a rope to steady himself. With his body half hanging over the side he was pulled to safety.

'Bloody fool, hitching a ride with the equipment,' said Dan.

'We would have all looked bloody fools if I hadn't,' spat back Charlie. 'The camera was in that case.'

They were interrupted by a man with a large bushy beard. 'So you made it, just, I see.' Noticing Nathalie, he held out his hand. 'Welcome aboard Station Salt One. Bring your equipment into one of our offices and I'll let you know the procedures.'

Nathalie couldn't get the name of Captain Haddock out of her head as she followed the chief of the station into his office. He gave them a place to store their gear and handed out hard hats.

'As you have noticed this is a floating structure and it can be quite precarious, moving around. Surfaces can be slippery, so watch where you are treading. Before I give you a guided tour, have you any questions?'

Nathalie dug the notes out of her back pocket. 'You called the station Salt One,' she said. 'Why is that?'

Nathalie's 'Captain Haddock' stroked his woolly beard. 'A couple of reasons. We are on salt water and it's the first in the area but also, it's an acknowledgement to the man who started this wave power stuff, back in the late seventies. A guy called Salter, an amazing engineer. Worked out that you could get power out of waves by transferring the energy to an object that moved up and down with the water. Problem was, to get the most energy out, he needed an object with a front but no back so he came up with a shape looking something like a duck. It's what we've based this plant on; Salter Ducks.'

Nathalie leant forward. 'So why has it taken all this time for them to be put to use?'

More stroking of the beard. 'Long story, but the long and short of it is that he was stuffed by a committee who were assessing his invention. Rumour goes that they were nuclear scientists. Some number cruncher underestimated his energy efficiency by ten times. Threw the idea out. Very convenient for the nuclear power lobby, put ocean energy back by thirty years. Now we've got another fly in the ointment.'

Nathalie was about to ask him what that was but he was already walking towards the door.

'Now, if you don't mind, I have a lot of things to do, so if I can hand you over to my senior engineer he will give you a quick tour to show you how things work.' Noticing Nathalie's wide-eyed expression he added, 'I know you'd like to film an interview, and I'm quite happy to do so. Not until mid-afternoon, though, I'm afraid.'

'Mid-afternoon is good,' said Nathalie, following him onto the platform.

The senior engineer was an affable man with a ruddy complexion. He looked as if he had been at sea for most of his life. He escorted them around the floating platform and showed them where the huge chains were anchoring it to the bottom.

'There is a lot of technology on this station,' he laughed. 'You wouldn't believe it but the most difficult part of this installation is to keep these things still. Four bloody great chains and some ballast is all we could come up with. Still, we haven't broken loose yet.'

He explained that the platforms had a number of functions: the main one, to hold a string of bobbing orange ducks between them; the other, to act as a collection centre to relay the electricity to the island. They trod carefully towards the guard rail overlooking the string of ducks.

'Now it's these things that we want to keep moving,' said the engineer. 'As you can see they're strung out between the platforms and joined together by those metre-wide floating tubes. It was a hell of a job bolting them altogether; as soon as you got one in place another started to float away. As I said, it's not the high-tech stuff that's difficult; at sea it's basic engineering.'

Nathalie was already running the story through in her head. It would look spectacular on film. The bright orange objects floating on the sea with the vivid backdrop of the sky behind them.

'So, what's the high-tech stuff?' she asked.

The engineer's eyes lit up. 'If you click this safety line to your belt I'll take you out and show you.'

Nathalie attached the line to the harness she had been given to wear and the engineer opened a gate in the guard rail. He gingerly stepped onto the narrow floating platform and gestured for her to follow. It was weird, just like walking on an air-bed. Thank goodness for the thick orange rope that acted as a handrail. After about ten metres the floating walkway widened out onto a small ledge. Nathalie suddenly felt a rush as she confronted the object in front of her. The Salter Duck was massive, the size of a large car. She would have described it as teardrop-shaped rather than a duck. The nose of the teardrop was facing the incoming waves and bobbing as they passed. As this happened her head was filled with a loud noise.

'What's that?' she shouted to the engineer.

'It's the pendulum inside the casing. Every time a wave passes, this pendulum swings to capture the wave's energy; as much as ninety per cent of it, which makes it one of the most efficient alternative energy machines on the planet. The pendulum moves pistons, which in turn pressurise hydraulic oil. We push this hydraulic oil back to the platform through a motor which generates the electricity.'

'Did you say ninety per cent?' asked Nathalie. She had read a lot about alternative energy since taking this project and fifty to sixty per cent efficiency was thought to be good.

'That's exactly what I said; this thing's the holy grail of ocean energy.'

Nathalie turned to face the engineer and suddenly noticed the logo on his overalls. She had become so absorbed in those enormous machines that she had almost forgotten her remit for the investigative documentary. Perhaps it was time to get back to the safety of the floating platform to ask this guy a few questions of the more political kind.

They picked their way back along the narrow linking gangway. The sun was high in the sky and the light perfect to show the contrast of the bright orange wave machine against the tropical sea. Charlie and Luke were waiting for her. No sign of Dan. Charlie noticed Nathalie looking around.

'Dan's gone walkabout. Said he would grab some atmos around the platform.'

'He should have waited,' replied Nathalie irritably. 'There's a sound out there that I want synched with the pictures.'

She briefly explained how the system worked and the shots she wanted: the waves moving in; the ducks moving up and down; and the way that they were connected to the walkways and platforms.

'Charlie, why don't you set up the camera by the first duck. Luke, go and find Dan. I'll see if I can rustle up any engineers to pretend they are bolting the ducks to the walkways, a sort of reconstruction of the thing being put together. If we can get all this in the can before lunchtime we'll be free to do the interviews inside this afternoon. Then we won't have to worry about the weather.'

Charlie looked up at the sky, not a single wisp of cloud. But she was right. Shoot now while you have good, even light. Many's the time he had been under directors who wasted time in taking pretty shots they didn't need because the light looked good. It only took a few minutes for cloud to be drawn across the sky, ruining the more important pictures that had been left to the end of the day. This woman was good. He thought back to the night before. What did she think of him?

'Okay, you guys, let's get on with it,' said Nathalie, striding towards the platform's crew base.

The engineers seemed pretty keen to help. Now they had constructed the installation, the work had become more routine;

testing the output, making sure that the ducks weren't cast adrift and maintaining the generators and transformers. Play-acting for a film and pretending they were putting the plant together sounded a good idea. They described how they had bolted each section of the floating walkway to the ducks. The walkway wasn't just a simple linking device, it also carried all the hydraulic and electrical cables to the platform. It would be dangerous to start to uncouple the whole thing now; instead they could pretend that they were tightening the last four huge bolts that locked the things together. The thespian volunteers were reaching into the tool chest for the enormous wrenches when the senior engineer rushed into the building.

'What the hell is your guy doing out there, all on his own? I thought I told you people to keep with a member of staff at all times.'

Nathalie went with him to the platform's guard rail. 'My fault,' she said. 'I asked him to set up his camera. I should've asked.'

Charlie had somehow managed to get onto the walkway between the ducks. They could see him trying to position his camera.

The senior engineer cupped his hands and shouted for Charlie to keep still while he sent a workboat to fetch him. It was the wrong thing to do. Charlie looked up in surprise and in doing so slipped. He desperately tried to secure the camera.

'For Christ's sake, get that boat!' screamed Nathalie as she watched his body plunge into the water under the relentless nodding machine.

Sixteen

The workboat was still attached to the aluminium ladder. To Nathalie it seemed as if the platform crew were moving in slow motion. Nothing could have been further from the truth. These men were well trained, no shouting or flurry of panic, just a smooth and efficient passage towards the rocking machinery. Luke had appeared at the platform's edge and was attempting to climb over the guard rail to get onto the floating pathway. He was pulled back by one of the engineers.

'We don't want two of you in there! Let them get on with it.'

Luke realised that the guy was making sense. The boat was nearly there, he would only complicate the mission. Nathalie and Dan had joined him at the rail, straining their eyes to try and make out what was going on. They all felt helpless. One of the boatmen was now in the water. The other had tied the boat up to the nearest platform adjoining the duck. Charlie's body was nowhere to be seen. Nathalie felt sick; why on earth hadn't she made sure that Charlie was supervised? She suddenly realised that her feelings were not to do with the fact that she was responsible for the crew, it was all about Charlie. The diver in the water broke through the surface for air and then submerged again. She could just about make out the man in the boat playing out a line. It was a dangerous rescue attempt. If the diver got too close to that machine … she didn't dare to think what might have happened to Charlie.

A man on the platform came over to them. 'I think they've got him.' He began talking on a communication's device to the man in the boat. 'What state's he in?'

Nathalie stared anxiously at his face, waiting for the reply. The guy put the handset to his ear and shook his head.

She almost grabbed the handset. 'Is he …?' She didn't finish her sentence because the man had turned away from her and was running towards the docking bay. Nathalie followed, almost slipping on the deck as she did so.

As the workboat pulled up by the platform she felt someone restrain her from going towards the edge.

'You will only get in the way,' said Luke. 'They know what they're doing; they have a resus team on standby.'

They watched at a distance as the station crew hauled Charlie's body onto a stretcher. Within minutes they had wheeled him into the first aid centre. Nathalie ran up to one of the boatmen. He spoke before she could blurt out her questions.

'He's alive. Completely out cold, but he's alive. I think he hit his head as he fell in. Maybe a good thing. Because he didn't struggle he didn't get caught up in the machine. We found him floating just below the surface. I don't think he's got too much water in his lungs.'

Nathalie closed her eyes and took a deep breath. 'Thank you,' was all that she could manage to say.

'No problem. Not a great place to hang around on though. It's normally the rule to go out in pairs; I'd have thought our boss would've told you that.'

'It's all my fault, I asked him to take the shots. I should've known better.'

The boatman shrugged. 'Maybe.' He paused and then turned to glance at the wave machine. 'Oh yes, and I think he may be in luck with that one. I've a feeling that his camera is still out there on the walkway.'

When Nathalie was at last allowed into the first aid room she found a pale-looking Charlie on a couch, propped up by a pillow.

He gave her a weak smile. 'Sorry about all of the fuss. Did they find the camera?'

Nathalie shook her head at him. 'Typical, you've nearly died and all you can think about is the camera! As a matter of fact you threw it on the walkway as you fell in. They're out there retrieving it now, we think it's okay.'

'*Think* it's okay?'

'Yes, think it's okay. But you are more important than the camera, why didn't you just drop it and save yourself?' She smiled. 'I'm in enough shit already, letting you go out there all on your own. If you had drowned, it would have been my fault.'

'But I didn't go out there on my own. A maintenance guy from Marine Corps helped me along the walkway. Said I would be fine if I kept both my feet on the ground and left me to it.'

'Well you should've asked him to stay with you. What on earth did you think you were doing?'

Charlie tried to get up but was gently restrained by a medical orderly. 'My job,' he said, resignedly lying back on the couch.

'Well, you're lucky that these guys are experts, otherwise you wouldn't be able to do your job,' chided Nathalie. 'You'd be under one of those thrashing machines.'

She pulled one of the orderlies aside and whispered a question in his ear. The orderly didn't attempt to hide the answer.

'He swallowed a bit of seawater and has a bit of concussion. A few hours' rest and he'll be fine.'

'I'm fine now' said Charlie. 'We've got a shoot to do this afternoon, and I'm the only one who can operate the camera.'

'You're not moving,' ordered Nathalie. 'And we haven't got the camera yet. It's still out there, next to one of those damn ducks.'

Charlie didn't put up much of a fight. It was obvious that in his state he could hardly walk properly, let alone handle a camera on a moving wave machine. Nathalie pacified him and took control. She asked one of the engineers if he would be good enough to rescue the camera from the floating walkway and told Dan to prepare for an audio interview with the chief engineer after lunch.

'We have enough pictures to cover most of the sound. If Charlie and the camera are okay, at the end of the day we could get an establishing shot to stick on the front,' she said practically. There was no way she wanted to miss out on this interview. Perhaps not having the camera for a while was a good thing. She might get some more candid stuff about the mining ship dispute without the glare of the lights.

Lunch consisted of a few dried sandwiches, which they snacked upon while sitting on the equipment boxes in one of the featureless offices. None of them were hungry. After further reassurance from the medical orderly Nathalie had left Charlie in the medical room. In two hours they would do some tests; he should be fine. An engineer and boat man had made their way out to the floating platform. Charlie had kept on about the fragility of the camera and they assured him that they would pick it up with care.

Luke was wondering what to do with the remains of a second sandwich when a commotion was heard on the platform deck. The three of them rushed out of the office, praying the camera was still in one piece. The camera was the last of the engineer's concerns. There was an instability on one of the structures. If it wasn't fixed soon the whole installation could break apart. A man with a huge battery-powered wrench was rushing towards the docking station. The sea conditions were getting worse and the boat was rising and falling against the aluminium ladder. Nathalie saw someone in the boat throw an object to an engineer on the platform. So much for treating the camera with care. The man caught it deftly and put it down beside him before reaching down to steady the pitching craft. The wrench man jumped in and the boat powered away. Luke made his way to the camera, picked it up and brought it back to Nathalie. He sounded relieved.

'Looks okay. Charlie should check it over, though.'

Nathalie was as desperate as Luke to know that it worked. Getting another camera in the middle of the Pacific wasn't an option. Two hours wasn't going to make much difference so she suggested that they store it in a dry place and wait for Charlie to recover properly. They were brought up suddenly by a loud crash. A cup had fallen onto the floor. Their concern about the camera had almost made them forget about the stability of the wave station. They ran outside to find a hive of activity. The platform workers had launched a second boat and were loading it with equipment. This was proving difficult as the platform lurched alarmingly.

'Shit, hope this thing isn't falling apart,' cried Luke.

A passing engineer heard this and stopped to reassure him. 'This is normal. It's just that the sea conditions have become worse. Don't worry, if that duck shears off, you really will know it.'

'Great,' said Luke.

The clear sky had become obscured with haze and a chill filled the air. The prevailing wind was now bringing white crested waves, which crashed against the oscillating machinery. The blistering idyllic tropical morning seemed a lifetime ago. They could still make out the fringe of the atoll in the distance but it had become a smudge on the horizon. Only a few hours ago they had been sipping coffee on the hotel's veranda. Now they were on a bucking platform with an injured cameraman in danger of being cast adrift. Dan beckoned them over to the handrail and pointed to the workboats. They were returning at a leisurely pace to the platform.

'Panic over, I think.'

'I wouldn't have called it a panic …' The senior engineer's voice came from behind them. 'Over, I would agree with.'

Nathalie asked him for the details.

'Unusual, a main connection bolt came loose. If it had become much worse, the whole installation could have sheared away from the platforms; millions of pounds worth of damage. He was a bloody fool, but your cameraman did us a favour. If he hadn't slipped and left his camera on the walkway we may not have noticed it until the next scheduled maintenance. Could have been too late by then. Still, it's fixed now, business as usual. Now you wanted that interview …'

They set the audio recording equipment up in his office. Nathalie asked him to relax in a chair while she sat opposite. Dan fixed a directional mic on a stand and placed it just above the senior engineer's head.

‘What did you have for breakfast?’ he asked. The senior engineer looked puzzled. ‘It’s just for a sound level. Anything will do.’

Nathalie intervened. ‘Perhaps you could begin by telling us your name and position here. As we have no picture at the moment, it’ll be a good ident for me, as well as helping Dan with his levels.’

The engineer began nervously. ‘My name is Max Friedlander. I’m the Station Head and senior engineer of Salt One, the wave power installation that you are now on.’

Dan nodded to indicate that the levels were fine. Nathalie was keen to relax this guy so she sat back casually and started to ask questions about how the station worked. After a few minutes, when she saw his shoulders begin to drop, she made her move.

‘Max, you said earlier that there was another fly in the ointment. What did you mean by that?’

Max Friedlander began the familiar habit of stroking his beard. ‘I was telling you about the scuppering of Salter’s plans, back in the 1980s. The nuclear lobby weren’t very keen for his work to succeed. I don’t think I’d be spilling any beans to tell you there’s probably another lobby trying to scupper this lot.’

Nathalie leaned gently forward in her chair. ‘Another lobby?’

‘The various agencies of the US Government seem to have taken a recent U-turn. A few months ago everything was hunky-dory – money thrown at us, golden boys of ocean energy research. Now it’s proving difficult to buy something as simple as a screwdriver.’ Friedlander moved uneasily in his chair. ‘No, that’s an exaggeration. A few days ago we tried to order a new consignment of materials. Routine stuff. Strange messages came back that we may not be able to purchase them under this year’s budget arrangement.’ He rustled through some papers on his desk, as if looking through some accounts. ‘The last time I checked the budget was fine, plenty of cash. I made a few phone calls.’

Nathalie waited for the outcome but nothing was forthcoming. Max continued fidgeting in his chair, looking around the room nervously. Nathalie decided to wait a little longer. Eventually he began to speak.

'I think someone in the Environmental Agency is stirring up trouble with the military. There was an internet leak that this island offshore power station is a trade-off. *The New York Times* picked it up. It wasn't front-page news but it has done some damage. As I said, I'm not giving any secrets away because it's all over the newspapers. The message is that the United States are doing this thing just so that they can have a military base on Majuro. Nothing about the fact that we are pioneering the most efficient alternative energy scheme on the planet.' Max leaned back in his chair and shook his head sadly.

Again Nathalie waited patiently.

This time Max didn't continue. He rose from his chair and walked towards Dan, who was crouching on the floor beside his recorder.

'Would you mind switching that off for a minute?' he asked quietly.

Nathalie nodded towards Dan, who cut the recording.

Max turned to Nathalie. 'I'm not sure how much you're going to use of this material or how it fits in with your story.' He paced his office, obviously making a decision about what to say next. 'As you will appreciate, it's not going to do our project here much good if you put it out that we had a small mishap with the installation connections this afternoon.'

Nathalie opened her eyes a little wider, expectantly but still silent.

'Let's put it this way, I have a trade-off. If you can ignore that small matter then I'll give you my real opinion on our so-called "fly in the ointment".' He pointed at Dan's sound recorder. 'I'm afraid it will have to be off the record – I can't be seen to be associated with these views. However, I'm sure your television journalists have other sources you could follow up.'

Nathalie tried not to appear too eager. She pulled out her notepad. 'No mention of a loose bolt, off the record and unattributable,' she said casually. 'Do you mind if I take notes?'

Friedlander made his way back to his chair but instead of using it, decided to perch on his desk. He pulled out a well-thumbed scientific magazine from a drawer and waved it at Nathalie. 'I think our fly in the ointment is in here. And this time it's not nuclear, it's oil shale.'

Nathalie had heard the term before but wasn't too sure about its relevance to the wave power station. 'Oil shale?' was all she could offer.

Friedlander opened the magazine, found the page he was looking for and folded it back. He handed it to her. She looked at the article. It was from the American Chemical Society, and you probably had to be a chemist to understand it. She was grappling with the sentence about high molecular weight solid polymers when Max Friedlander unwittingly got her out of the predicament.

'Not a difficult equation,' he said. 'Scientist selling new technology for squeezing oil and gas from oil shale, and a recent heavy investment by some of the largest corporations in America. And do you know who has the largest stocks of shale oil in the world?' He didn't wait for the answer. 'The United States of America. Two trillion barrels worth of it.'

Max placed his arms behind him and rested back on the desk. It was a pose suggesting that he had just given her the answer to all the questions she needed to ask.

Nathalie made a note of the article on her pad and handed the journal back. 'So, you're suggesting that money has been deflected away from your project to this new energy source,' she proffered.

Friedlander took the magazine and stood up in exasperation. "Deflected" isn't quite the word I would use. Don't you get it? This is corporate corruption and political bribery on a grand scale.'

'Corruption?' questioned Nathalie.

He began to pace up and down his tiny office. 'Okay, let me spell it out for you. But before I do, it's off the record. I've no actual proof, it's all circumstantial.'

Nathalie held her relaxed pose. 'So why don't we start with the word "allegedly"', she said with a smile.

'All right, allegedly in recent weeks two huge corporations have purchased vast amounts of oil-shale-bearing land in Utah. At the same time this article from the American Chemical Society is claiming that squeezing oil and gas from these rocks could be economically viable;

more viable than current ocean energy projects, for example. Now, coming from the press yourself, I don't expect it has escaped your notice that there has been quite a bit of bad publicity about ocean energy projects recently; it's not safe, it's unreliable and anything else they can think about printing. All this has coincided with a change of staff in the bureaucratic hierarchy. I'm an engineer, I'm not one for coincidences. Politicians need money to campaign for more votes. Large corporations have a lot of money. I find it strange that the senator who is pro-law of the sea and pro-alternative energy should suddenly be replaced by a climate change sceptic who refuses to sign the treaty.' It was a rant, but a good rant. Nathalie used the pregnant pause to catch up with her notes.

'So, the oil-shale lobby is fixing the comparative price of extracting gas from shale and extracting power from the sea and persuading politicians to steer away from ocean energy,' she surmised.

'In a nutshell, but it's not me who told you so.'

'So what's all this got to do with your dispute with the Japanese mining vessel?'

'Probably nothing. It's just that this bloody ship has turned up at the wrong time. More armoury for the anti-UNCLOS treaty lot. All we're worried about is that they might interfere with the station. We are still at the research phase and need good figures for energy conversion. If they start ploughing up and down, messing with the wave formations, then someone is bound to question the statistics. Problem is, they have turned it into a territorial dispute; muddied the waters, so to speak, saying we are claiming that we are an artificial island with territorial rights. Lot of bloody nonsense! Now it's even gone to government level and is being debated in the Marshall Islands' Senate. It's the last thing we need.'

Nathalie understood his frustration. He was being attacked on all sides: economic pressures, a political scandal and fighting a poor safety record of ocean projects. No wonder the guy didn't want her to mention the loose bolt.

'I'll do what I can to check your story. If there's any truth in it you can be assured we will get it out there. Just one more thing, though. I noticed that a lot of your staff come from Marine Corps. How do you find them?'

'Yes, at least fifty per cent of our engineers are freelance. They're really good at their job. Nothing but praise for them. Look at the way they rescued your cameraman. He probably owes them his life.'

Seventeen

The small workboat chugged its way back to the lagoon. Charlie, who had been given a clean bill of health, sat in the prow, clinging onto his camera box. Nathalie was pleased with her day's work. The camera and Charlie were both in good working order. She had got her final establishing shot and enough material to work on for both of her documentaries. Now she was looking forward to a good meal, back on dry land. It had been Dan and Luke's last day and they were both in 'wrap party' mode.

'You'd better let me help you with that onto the pier,' said Luke, pointing at the camera box. 'You seemed determined to jump into the water with it today and I don't want that to be third time lucky!'

'That's not even worth a reply, Luke,' said Charlie, sadly shaking his head.

Dan was staring back at the wave power station. 'Glad to see the back of that one,' he said. 'Crap food and a platform that won't keep still. Can't wait for a plate of grilled fish and a beer. Thank God we're going back to Hawaii tomorrow. One more night in that cupboard with Luke and I think I'd go stir crazy.' So much had happened that day that Nathalie had almost forgotten their accommodation arrangements.

'I'm sure Bagatelle can find their way to paying your bar bill tonight as compensation, Dan. When Geoff hears about the dateline fracas, I wouldn't like to be the travel agent on the end of the telephone. I'm sure he will get more than his money back.'

'I'll have Charlie's share,' chipped in Luke. 'I've heard somewhere that you're not supposed to drink alcohol after concussion.'

The boat was entering the mouth of the atoll. The sea became calmer and the clouds were clearing, revealing the setting sun. Charlie was on the point of telling Luke that if he didn't shut up there would be another case of concussion but thought better of it. The light was sensational. The atoll fringe was becoming like a silhouette cardboard cut-out against a sky of fire. Ignoring Luke, he opened the camera box, clipped the magazine onto the SR body and put the camera to his shoulder. There was about a minute left on the roll. He slowly panned the horizon and waited to hear the click-clicking of the final frames passing through the gate before taking his eye from the eyepiece.

'End credits and cut,' he said, smiling at Nathalie. 'You'll like that one.'

Minutes later the boat pulled up at the hotel pier. They said their goodbyes to the boatmen and stacked the equipment into their small rooms. The barman lined up four golden glasses of beer. Charlie ran a finger down one of the glasses, making a smooth line in the condensation.

'Ice-cold in Alex,' he said.

Dan looked puzzled, 'Alex?'

Nathalie took her beer and downed it in one. 'John Mills, British actor, 1958.' She offered her empty glass to the barman and waited for a refill. 'Great film, set in the Second World War; these guys cross a desert, dreaming of cold beers in Alexandria.'

'Sounds weird,' said Dan. 'Better plot lines in *Hawaii Five-0*.'

'Doubt it,' said Charlie. 'They really knew how to make movies then.'

Luke joined in. 'Never heard of it; sounds like one of those crap Brit films. Now, *Saving Private Ryan*, Tom Hanks, that's a war movie.'

Their banter was interrupted by Nathalie's mobile phone, a text message from Geoff, asking her to urgently download her e-mails.

'God calling,' she said, slipping down from the barstool. 'I'd better check this out.' She smiled at Charlie. 'Let me know who wins.'

The young woman they had met on their first day was still on reception. Nathalie asked her once more if she could use the hotel's computer to download her e-mails. The girl shrugged and pushed the scruffy tariff card towards her.

‘Yeah, I know the price, just add it to the bill,’ said Nathalie, pushing it back. She walked around the counter and pecked at the soiled keyboard. People were always complaining about internet speeds in London; they should try Majuro, she thought. It took fifteen minutes to make a connection and another five to download the e-mails from her Hotmail site. By now she was starving so she paid another eye-watering fee to have them printed off. She would read them over dinner.

The crew had already started without her when she returned to the veranda restaurant. The sweet smell of barbecued fish filled the air. Luke beckoned her over, enthusiastically.

‘This is fantastic!’ he muffled through a mouthful. ‘I’ve asked them to put one on for you. I hope you don’t mind.’

‘Mind?’ exclaimed Nathalie. ‘I’d have killed you if you hadn’t.’

The timing couldn’t have been more perfect. The moment she sat down she was presented with a large plate. A silver scaled fish with the charred bars of a barbecue grill striped across its back spilled over the sides. She leant over to take in the aroma. The waiter returned with half a coconut shell filled with steaming spiced rice and wished her bon appétit. She nodded her appreciation and put her e-mails to one side. What could be more urgent than this? She pushed her fork into the white flesh, closed her eyes and took in the first succulent mouthful. It was only then that she looked up to see the other three looking at her.

‘What?’

‘Charlie said your face would be a picture,’ laughed Luke. ‘We thought of shooting it and calling the movie, *Barbecue-hot on Majuro*.’

By the end of the meal the table had filled with empty Corona beer bottles. The sun was gone and the waiter had lit the paper lanterns that wafted around the veranda. There was no other ambient light but their eyes had become used to the orange glow that reflected on each other’s faces. The mood was mellow and conversation had been replaced by a satisfied silence. They leaned back in their chairs, sipped cold beer and listened to the lapping shoreline. Nathalie was almost dozing off when she suddenly remembered her e-mails.

'Oh, shit,' she exclaimed, 'Geoff bloody Sykes! I've got to read these e-mails. Sorry, guys. Keep the bar tab going. The light's a bit dim here. I'll just take these back to the room to see what he wants.'

She grabbed the papers that were beside her and made her way back to the room. It was even more of a mess than last night; boxes and film cans everywhere. She picked her way over the obstacles and lay on the unmade bed. The first e-mail was a long one from Geoff. The opening sentence made her sit upright. *Change of plan.*

It was the first time Nick had taken the Oresund Bridge. When Stefanie had given him his tickets to Copenhagen Airport he politely pointed out that he was going to Malmö, Sweden, not Malmö, Denmark, if there was such a place. She just replied with one of those Stefanie inscrutable smiles and told him he would be taking the bridge. The word 'bridge' turned out to be a bit of a misnomer. The bridge runs nearly eight kilometres from the Swedish coast to the artificial island of Peberholm; the rest of the link is by a four-kilometre tunnel into Denmark. The taxi driver at Copenhagen Airport had said that it would take less than an hour to get to his destination on the Western Harbour in Malmö. Nick observed that it was an extraordinary feat of engineering.

The Danish cabdriver's English was impeccable. 'True; extraordinary engineering and extraordinary costs. We are still paying for it.'

Nick sat in the back of the cab and put his papers to one side as they emerged from the tunnel. 'Yeah, it must have cost a fortune. Why a tunnel and a bridge?'

'They had to avoid interfering with air traffic from Copenhagen Airport, give a clear channel for ships, and prevent ice floes from blocking the strait. Apparently this was the best solution.'

Nick stared across the Oresund waters through the strobing struts of the bridge. 'Looks a bloody good solution from here; the view is amazing.'

They slowed to stop at the tollbooth on entering Sweden. There was some sort of customs post but no-one bothered to ask for Nick's passport.

'Welcome to Sweden,' said the driver, putting his foot down on the pedal.

They kept on the ring road for a few kilometres before turning into the centre of town. Rows of new apartments lined the highway.

'A lot of new development around here,' commented Nick.

'Yes, a few years ago this area was an old polluted shipyard. Now it's a showpiece for the environmental set. Houses powered by renewable energy; local buses from residents' waste. Waterfront cafe life and a place for innovative economic development is how the brochures tell it. I think they would have been better off reviving the shipping industry. They sacked nearly six thousand people you know.'

The taxi driver sounded bitter. Possibly an old sailor, Nick thought. The car rumbled as they travelled over newly cobbled streets bordered by the Western Harbour on one side and a row of brightly painted low-rise buildings on the other. Number 47 was a small terracotta four-storey block. No sign advertising Marine Corps. Nick got out, paid the driver and made his way to the front door. It was slightly set back with a row of labelled buttons on the right-hand wall of the alcove. The one he was looking for indicated the third floor so he pressed it and put his ear to the entry speaker. No reply. Nick turned to see the cab driving off. Stefanie had said it had all been arranged. He hoped he hadn't come on a wild goose chase. He pressed the button again, this time harder and longer. A crackle came through the speakerphone. It was indecipherable and probably in Swedish so Nick spoke his name very slowly and told the aluminium grill that he had an appointment with Marine Corps. Another indecipherable message from the speakerphone but, this time, a loud buzz told him that someone had unlocked the front door. He let himself in and made his way up the concrete stairway. At the top of each set of identical steps was an identical landing with two sets of frosted panelled doors. Each door was painted in primary colours and contained a small, removable nameplate. These were no bespoke offices; floor space to rent at reasonable prices for limited periods, thought Nick. Not a promising permanent location for a major marine engineering company.

He was expected, for on the third floor he found the bright blue painted door held ajar. Lukas was the stereotypical Swede; six-foot two, flaxen hair, blue eyes. He greeted Nick with a warm handshake and invited him in with impeccable English. The office was as uninspiring as the staircase. Pictureless cream walls and economy IKEA furniture. A laptop and telephone were placed on two of the three desks. Lukas seemed to be the only person in the office. Nick accepted the offer of a cup of coffee and sat at one of the desks while his host went behind a small screened-off area, presumably the kitchenette.

'Been here long?' asked Nick.

'About six months, we were in Gothenburg before.'

'Taxi driver said it's very eco-friendly.'

'They say so but that's not the reason we moved. Sugar?'

'No, thanks. So what do you think of the area?'

Lukas appeared from behind a screen holding two china mugs of coffee. 'It's okay, a bit soulless, but some good restaurants and coffee shops. No, the reason we moved here was the rent – incentive schemes for young businesses.'

Nick took the coffee from him. 'Thanks, I thought that Marine Corps were well-established.'

'Yes, they are, *years* of engineering experience.' Lukas said the last line as if he were making a radio commercial. 'It's a franchise; offices all over the world. A very thorough vetting procedure though. We had to jump through a lot of hoops to get the brand. Got some good engineers in our team too. Your secretary said you were looking for some good engineers.'

'Early days, I hope she told you that.'

Lukas smiled. 'Oh yes, we weren't expecting a contract today. She said you were making tentative enquiries about going into some sort of alternative energy project. Wave powered turbines wasn't it?'

Nick threw him some drawings that Bagatelle's researchers had mocked up. He had told Geoff that he knew fuck all about mechanical engineering but he had persuaded him that all he had to do was let the other guy do the talking.

'These guys are keen as mustard to tell you everything they know when they're selling something,' he had said. 'Soften them up and then ask a few questions.'

As usual, bloody 'know-it-all' Geoff was right. Lukas eulogised about energy-producing wave turbines and was all for taking him on a trip to Norway to see one of the latest prototypes they had been working on.

'Might take you up on that, in time,' said Nick, retrieving his papers. 'As I said, it's early days.' He put the drawings into his briefcase then looked up suddenly, as if he had just remembered something. 'You sound a competent outfit but there is one thing that worries me.'

Lukas sat upright, 'If it's the offices, I can assure you that …'

Nick interrupted him. 'No, it's not that; it's these accidents.'

Lukas' complexion reddened. 'Accidents?'

'Well, incidents at sea concerning Marine Corps; there seem to have been rather a lot recently.'

Lukas was visibly shaken. 'Incidents, what incidents?'

Nick calmly counted the events on his outstretched hand. 'One, a drilling ship goes down; two, a sonar is lost; three, a submarine sinks with man on board and four …'

'I know, I know. Well, I don't know about the drilling ship but the rest … terrible publicity for us. Head office is all too aware. Don't hear from them normally; they leave us alone to do our own thing. Now it's a conference call once a week. It's nothing to do with us, I can promise you. All our projects have been fine, just a string of bad luck with some of the other franchises. They are not even connected.'

Nick put his hand up to indicate that Lukas was overselling his case. 'Not connected?'

'Different franchise on each project. The Californian group had the worst. Someone actually died on a Hawaiian job they were working on. Really bad luck. Marine engineering can be heavy-duty stuff but the safety checks are notoriously thorough. Usually a lot fewer accidents than land-based projects; mining, for instance. Problem is, the whole of the Ocean Renewable Energy movement gets a bad name.'

Lukas suddenly stopped his rant. He looked at Nick and put his head in his hands. 'Shit, I'm sorry! I've really blown it, haven't I? I'm just a hands-on engineer. The marketing guy is out today, gave me the job of seeing you. I really hope I haven't put you off. We are good at what we do. The Malmö group has not had one marine accident, and there is a bright future for ocean development, I can assure you.'

Nick decided to use the vulnerability of the moment to dig a little more. 'Another company I was thinking of looking up are called Ocean Tech. Know anything about their track record?'

Lukas was evidently puzzled by the change of tack. 'Ocean Tech?'

'Yes, have you heard of them?'

'Sure, but they're not exactly in our league. In fact, they opened up offices quite near to here. Nils dropped in on them.'

'Nils?'

A worried look came over Lukas' face. 'Our marketing guy, who I told you about. He's going to kill me for messing this up.'

Nick leaned back in his chair in an attempt to make him more at ease. 'You haven't messed anything up, Lukas. In fact you've done your company a favour. There's nothing more our outfit hates than people trying to cover things up. Your honesty does you proud. A straight-talking engineer who knows about marine turbines, that's what we're looking for.' He glanced at his watch. 'Nearly twelve. You said you had some good restaurants; let me take you out for lunch.'

It was a more relaxed Lukas who showed him the harbour front. Despite the bitter weather people were sitting out under canvas umbrellas warmed by heaters; all eco-friendly, Nick was assured. The cobbled areas turned to bleached boardwalks. Office workers streamed out of their buildings and milled around, taking in the ocean air. The two of them did not look out of place as they turned into the restaurant bar. An everyday business meeting over a seafood lunch and a glass of white wine. Nick was a master at getting information. By two o'clock he had the name and address of every Marine Corps executive and office around the world, where the expertise was and who you could trust.

A shrewd judge of character, he would have bet his house that Lukas wasn't involved in any espionage. If someone at Marine Corps was up to no good Lukas didn't know them. The headquarters were in Tokyo. Maybe he would have to check them out. That would be up to Geoff, it was his money. And, on the topic of money, Geoff would be more than interested in Lukas' lowdown on Ocean Tech. This was a surprise. Nick had thrown in the questions about Ocean Tech to change things around and to imply that he knew more than he did about ocean research. The answers he got were more than he bargained for. Ocean Tech used to have offices in the area. They had only been there a few months when they had moved out. Lukas described them as an amateur lot, who were looking into diversifying into alternative ocean energy. When they had first arrived Nils thought they might be a potential client for Marine Corps, but no such luck. Later, a trade magazine revealed that they were a failing oil exploration company that had been taken over by a large organisation based in Japan. They had tried to find out who these people were but they seemed to have nothing to do with the marine business. Now they had shut up shop they were no longer of concern. Not to Marine Corps, thought Nick, but Geoff Sykes would have more than a passing interest in the guys putting the money up for his latest film.

Eighteen

Nathalie stared at the e-mail. It told her to send 'sound' and 'lights' back to Hawaii and to catch a plane on to Guam with her cameraman. It sounded simple, the way it was written, but there she was, stuck on a desert island in the middle of the Pacific with no idea of its erratic airline schedules or how Charlie would take to the idea. She glanced at her watch. Geoff would be in his office. Normally, she was reluctant to phone him while on a shoot. She knew he liked his directors just to sort things out, that's what they were paid for. This was different, and she did have that stuff on oil shale to tell him about. The internet connection here was in the Stone Age so a phone call it would have to be.

'Hi, Nathalie, how's things? Get my e-mail?'

'Yes, Geoff. Just about. We are on the fringes of the World Wide Web here. I've got some information, could you phone me back? Stefanie's got the number of the hotel. My mobile doesn't work and this is costing me a fortune.'

Five minutes later the hotel receptionist put Geoff's call through to a telephone in the lobby.

'I'm sitting comfortably, got the file in front of me. Off you go.'

She told him about Max Friedlander's theory concerning the oil shale business and its conflict with the marine energy projects. It could be just another conspiracy theory but it did sound all rather coincidental; the more she heard about Governor Cain and his actions the more it looked as if there was something in it. It definitely looked as if Cain was mixed up in this thing somewhere.

'Well, I can stop you there,' Geoff's voice was distant but still audible. 'You're going to have the chance to ask him. That's why we're sending you to Guam. The Foreign Office says he's attending a conference there. It's a great opportunity and we've got you access. Stefanie's drafting you some details as we speak. Hang on, she's waving at me now,' Geoff's voice went off mic. '*What's that? Oh, okay.*'

Nathalie was wondering when she could get around to the topic of shoot and travel arrangements but Geoff beat her to it.

'Stefanie says she can arrange all the Guam stuff at this end, but flights are proving a little difficult. The airlines say it's a bit hit and miss on the Pacific island hoppers. Say you have a better chance of doing it at your end. Hope that's okay. Look, got to go now. Sounds like you're doing a great job. All the stuff you need will be in Stefanie's e-mail. Good luck.'

The crackle coming down the line told her he'd hung up.

'That's great, Geoff, thanks a lot! We've plenty of time to check out flights and things, don't you worry,' said Nathalie sarcastically. 'Have a good day.'

It was late, she was tired and the airport was closed. She made her way back to the room. Charlie was on the single bed, fully clothed and fast asleep. The night was warm. She grabbed her rucksack and went back onto the veranda. The lagoon was magical – navigation lights dancing on the water against a palm fringed horizon. Using some of her clothing as a pillow she lay down and watched the stars. The night soon took her into a deep sleep.

'Wake up, sleepyhead, 6 am. Time to catch our flight back to Hawaii.' Charlie sounded bright and cheerful.

Nathalie unscrewed her eyes. The sun was already up, reflecting against the water and giving quite a glare.

'Hawaii?' The fragments of her mind shuffled together to reconstruct the picture. 'Oh yes, Hawaii'. She lifted her stiff body from the hard planks of the veranda. 'Ask Luke and Dan to join us for an early breakfast, I've got a few things we need to talk about.'

The hotel cook didn't seem to mind rustling up a few sweet

pancakes and a steaming pot of coffee that early in the morning. Nathalie paid the hotel bill and added a tip to persuade the receptionist to print off Geoff's latest e-mail while they ate. Dan and Luke were glad that Bagatelle hadn't asked them to go to Guam; they had another job waiting for them in the US. Charlie just shrugged his shoulders; they had come this far.

'Okay, get the kit on the hotel shuttle bus and we'll head for the airport. Let's hope that there's a flight for us, Charlie.'

Even at this early hour the sun had risen enough to heat the tarmac. The shuttle bus wheels made sticky noises as they made their way down the single central highway to Amata Kabua Airport on the south side of the atoll. On arrival they'd been too tired to take in the scenery. Now they had time to look out of the windows and be amazed at this crescent of sand and lush vegetation in the middle of the Pacific. As they closed in on the airport the land either side of the single track road became narrower and narrower. Vast stretches of ocean lay on both sides. How on earth did humans find this place and what made them make it their home? The sand bar was now barely twenty metres across. The metalled road occupied four metres of this, nowhere near wide enough to land a plane. Nathalie was asleep when they landed. How had they done it? The answer was evident at the airport gate. The inhabitants of Majuro had built what could only be called an aircraft carrier on the end of their island. The concrete slab stretched to the far tip of the atoll.

'Bloody hell,' she muttered under her breath. 'Did we land on that?'

The shuttle bus driver pulled into the departures bay and helped them move their kit into a small, pink coloured, flat-roofed concrete building. It was early but a few passengers were already sitting on the metal and canvas chairs that lined the waiting room. A fan idled slowly above their heads. It didn't seem to be doing anything; the room was stifling. Nathalie walked up to the lone attendant sitting behind an open hatchway.

'We have return tickets to Hawaii but we would like to exchange two of them for an onward trip to Guam. Is there a flight today?'

The attendant didn't even bother to look at his monitor. 'We take off in one hour. Would you like aisle or window seat? No refunds, I'm afraid, you will have to pay full price.'

One hour's time? Nathalie couldn't believe her luck. Hang the price. She had prepared herself for the guy to say there wouldn't be another flight for a week. Handing him her Visa card, she asked for two seats close together. She looked over her shoulder and shouted to Charlie. 'Good job we got up early. That plane on the runway is ours. Get the camera gear checked in.' In her excitement she had forgotten all about Luke and Dan.

'If that's your flight, when's ours?' shouted Dan from the doorway.

'I'll just check,' replied Nathalie. 'Store your bags in the corner over there.'

She waited patiently while the airline clerk printed out tickets, and then asked him about the return flight to Hawaii. He looked puzzled. 'Return flight?'

'Yes, the one the four of us were going to take.'

Once more the man didn't even look at his monitor. 'There is no return flight today, Ma'am. There's no flight to Hawaii for another six days.'

Nathalie rummaged through her bag for her old tickets. She was about to thrust them under the nose of this jobsworth when it dawned on her. The dateline.

'Dan?'

Dan finished tipping the driver and turned to Nathalie.

She took a deep breath. 'Would you mind asking the driver to hang on for a bit?'

There was little time to be diplomatic. The passengers for the Guam flight were already boarding. Nathalie had gleaned that in this part of the world possession was nine-tenths of the law. If she and Charlie didn't grab their seats someone else might. Luke and Dan accepted her promise to refund their hotel and flight bills. There was nothing she could do about them missing their next job though. She hoped they would try to treat the next week as a sort of holiday although she stopped short at mentioning the words 'Pacific island in the sun'. All things considered, they took it quite well. Having said that, it was probably all they could do; their return flight had departed yesterday. That time of year flights to Hawaii were once a week. No matter how much they discussed it the situation wouldn't change. They shook hands.

'Okay, you two, get on that plane,' said Luke, shaking his head. 'If we can't get back in that hotel room I'm going to text you every day to rack up the guilt. Let us know how the rushes come out, Charlie.'

The two of them made for the exit and started to pack their gear back on the bus.

The island hopper was a Continental thirty-seater. It was surprisingly full. Nathalie had taken a window seat and peered out as it taxied down the thin concrete strip. It looked as though it was going the wrong way until she realised that the aircraft needed the whole runway in order to take off. The nose of the plane hung over the sea at the end of the runway before the pilot turned on a sixpence to point it in the other direction. The familiar seatbelt sign and a rumble of rubber wheels. The old plane shook as it slowly gathered speed. At one point it didn't look as if they would make it but at the last minute the nose lifted and the craft almost skimmed the palms as it lumbered into the air. Even the locals looked relieved as the captain switched on the cockpit intercom.

'Good morning, everyone. I hope you enjoy our island-hopping trip with Continental. We shall be stopping off at Pohnpei and Truk on our way to Guam. Those historians among you may be interested in the shipwrecks around Truk. Just before we land I'll tilt the wings so that you can get a good view. Have a nice day.'

And have a nice day to you too, thought Nathalie. As long as you can lift this thing into the air off these tiny strips of sand. The aircraft had now levelled out and she felt secure enough to get her bag out of the overhead locker. She looked over at Charlie in the window seat of the other aisle. He was already fast asleep. Still exhausted from his trauma at the wave power station most likely. The more rest he got, the better. Still standing, she unzipped her holdall and pulled out the sheaf of papers that had been printed out at the hotel. She sat down, belted up – you could never be too careful on these old planes – and unfolded the tray on the seat in front of her.

Geoff's last e-mail was a long one. It outlined his meeting with the Foreign Office. There was a profile on Governor Cain and some background on the Guam conference. 'Ocean Development' was the vague umbrella title. Under this there were several lectures and workshop sessions. 'Oceans and Climate Change', 'Sharing Ocean Resources', and 'Alternative Energy from the Sea', were the three that were highlighted. She was informed that they would be met by a junior British Foreign Office official, who would give them access to film these sessions. On the second day they would also be given the opportunity to interview Governor Cain. Cain had been told that a British television crew wished to give a balanced view of the conference – those for the Law of the Sea Treaty and those against. As far as Geoff was concerned the canvas was blank and Nathalie should dig as deep as she could to get to the truth of the matter. Since speaking to her last, Geoff had Bagatelle's researchers look into the oil shale business. It sounded like a good lead. If she could make any connection with Cain and the shale fracking business it could form a good exposé – there were a few background notes on this but the rest of the document dealt with what Geoff labelled as logistics: hotel, local sound recordist, sparks, equipment and travel plans. She hoped these plans were better than the last lot.

She slept through Pohnpei but was woken when the pilot dipped the wings of the plane to show passengers the sunken ships around the Truk Lagoon. The captain's voice broke over the intercom.

'Well, here we are, folks. Those on the starboard can see what is known as the ghost fleet of Truk lagoon.' The continual commentary was similar to those on tourist bus trips rather than a scheduled flight across the Pacific. 'More than fifty major ships from World War II litter the seabed, making this the best wreck-diving destination on the globe. In 1944, the Americans launched Operation Hailstone or, as some know it, the Japanese Pearl Harbor.' Nathalie peered out of the window to see what he was talking about, but she was on the wrong side; all she could see was blue sky. She listened to the captain's well-rehearsed commentary about how three days of bombardment left wrecks with cargo holds full of fighter aircraft, tanks and human remains. As he was explaining the fact that divers held the site to be haunted she felt the aircraft shudder. Her irrational fear was quelled by his next sentence.

'Now, before we land I'll circle and tilt to the port side so that you other guys can have a look.'

The plane banked and Nathalie found herself pressed against the window as it tilted violently to the left. She was in no mood for grisly war tourism but she had little option than to look at the sinister shapes under the clear turquoise waters.

By the time the plane had touched down, with a fairly bumpy landing, both she and Charlie were wide-awake. The pilot had told them that they would be stopping to refuel and any passengers who wanted to stretch their legs were welcome to take a walk outside. Nathalie beckoned to Charlie and he nodded in agreement. The air hit them like a warm soup; a contrast from the cool, metallic taste of their air-conditioned cabin. They made their way across the tarmac to a series of low-rise white-painted buildings. The captain strolled alongside them; white short-sleeve shirt, cap tilted jauntily to one side. They reached a wicker fence. No-one seemed at all bothered about security or passports so they walked through the gate. A narrow, palm-fringed road spread out in front of them. On one side in a clearing was a faded, pale green building. The sign indicated that it was some sort of shop. They climbed the two board steps and walked into a small room lined with wooden shelves. There was hardly anything on them apart from two packets of soap powder and a few tins. Some sort of washing line hung diagonally across the ceiling. A pair of pants, either new merchandise or a recently washed pair belonging to the proprietor – who could say? – was pinned to it by a clothes' peg. Nathalie looked at Charlie and tried not to laugh. Pan-faced he gazed back at her and then turned to the wide-hipped woman who appeared from a backroom.

'Have you any cold cola?' he asked.

The woman explained that she didn't sell drinks but they could get some at the airport. After thanking her, they hurriedly left the shop before breaking into merciless giggles.

'We could always ask her if she wants a floor walker,' said Charlie. 'What a weird place!'

There were no other items of interest on the street so they decided to return to the airport to make sure they didn't miss their flight. The captain was outside, leaning against a fence with a pale amber drink in his hand.

'Well, she was right about getting a drink here,' said Charlie. 'I only hope that there's no alcohol in that one.'

They bought two lukewarm colas and sat on a veranda on the edge of the tarmac. An old aluminium DC7, stripped of its paintwork, sat on the runway, looking as though it was posing for a black-and-white film.

Charlie looked at it dreamily. 'Pity my camera's in the hold.'

Nathalie put an arm on his shoulder. 'No, it isn't. You haven't got any stock left. And on that score, I should fill you in about Guam. Bagatelle has arranged sound and sparks and eight rolls of film for the conference.'

'What sort of film stock?'

'Four fast, four slow, plenty.'

'Who's the sparks?'

'No idea, don't think we have much choice on Guam. I'm sure you'll cope.'

'So we're going to film this Cain guy. What's the angle?'

Nathalie went through Geoff's e-mail and the possible idea that Cain was involved in oil shale. Anything that aided ocean energy development could damage the oil shale business. She was going to use the interview opportunity as a means of getting him to admit this on camera.

When he had heard that they were going to Guam to film the conference, Charlie had seemed disinterested but on learning about the oil shale story he seemed to perk up. 'Oil shale fracking? I've heard all about it, did a corporate on it some time ago. They stick this pressurised fluid down a fracture in the rocks to force out oil and gas. Apparently there's thousands of tons of the stuff in the States, the answer to all their energy dreams. Couple of problems, though. The eco-warriors are worried about groundwater pollution, and the real estate business about earthquakes. Quite a bit of opposition. If Cain's involved in it then he's got his hands full. It would also make sense that he wouldn't be on the ocean energy bandwagon. Sounds a good plan to see if it all ties in.'

Nathalie felt a wave of relaxation pass through her body. She had her cameraman back.

Nineteen

Despite the early start, the time taken at their stopovers meant that the plane was delayed and they weren't taxiing down the Guam runway until late in the afternoon. Bagatelle had booked them into the Ramada Hotel, only a few hundred yards from the airport. To avoid lugging the gear all over the island the idea was to check it into security lockers and pick it up in the morning on the way to the conference. Charlie wasn't happy with that but they came to a compromise. He would put the exposed rolls of film with a fresh T-shirt into his holdall while they would store the camera, lens box and legs at the airport with the rest of their luggage. The American airport staff were efficient but by the time they had their carné stamped and had filled in all the documentation for their gear it was getting dark. Both starving, they jumped into a taxi and asked the driver to recommend a restaurant nearby. They could always check into the hotel later.

'First time in Guam?' The taxi driver tried to take Charlie's holdall.

'I'll keep that,' Charlie clutched the heavy bag to his chest. 'Sure. We would just like somewhere nice to eat, by the sea if that's possible.'

'Got just the place – the Beach Bar and Grill on Tumon Bay. Best chicken skewers on the island.'

'How far?'

'Ten minutes at most.'

Nathalie put her overnight bag next to Charlie on the back seat. 'Sounds good to me, let's go.'

The taxi swung out of the airport and into a neon-lit road. Nathalie did a double take when she noticed the road sign – *Marine Corps Drive*. She was haunted by that name. This had to be a coincidence. She didn't point it out to Charlie. He hadn't mentioned anything about his accident, if that's what it was, since they had returned from the wave power station. The taxi turned off the main avenue and onto a small side road that led to the sea. The moon was full and lit up the shoreline, a familiar scene. They were getting used to these tropical paradise backdrops. A row of beach bars fringed the sand. The car drew up at one of them.

'Tell them Jerry sent you,' said their driver. 'You'll get a free cocktail.'

'Thanks,' said Nathalie, counting out the number of dollars that she had noted on the meter. 'Can we have your number? We have to check into the Ramada after dinner.'

The driver handed her a small card. 'My last fare is at eleven, need to finish after that.'

'Make it eleven then. We'll meet you here.'

The suitably named Beach Bar and Grill was a large stilted wooden building on the edge of the sand. Lanterns were strung across the roof, giving it that welcoming tropical island feeling. The waiter led them to two chairs by a thick wooden table under the thatched veranda.

'Jerry who?' was the response at the mention of their driver.

'No matter,' laughed Nathalie. 'Just bring us your menu please. We're starving!'

They ordered Tinian Beach burgers and two cold beers. The waiter warned them that the Tinian sauce would be hot, and he wasn't kidding. They lined up more beers to put the fires out. Charlie began to ask Nathalie how she was going to get information from Governor Cain.

'Not tonight, Charlie. Let's just sit back and relax and take in the ocean. You had quite a day yesterday. We'll put our heads together tomorrow to work out the shoot.'

Charlie nodded thoughtfully. 'Okay, I just wanted you to know that I'm still with you.' He took a bottle from the table and stepped off the veranda onto the sand. She watched him as he kicked off his shoes and trailed his bare feet in the edge of the sea.

Eleven o'clock came and Jerry was late. They rang his number but there was no reply. Half an hour later a taxi drew up in the now nearly empty car park.

'You going to the Ramada?'

They picked up their bags and made their way to the taxi. 'Yes, did Jerry send you?'

'He got a fare to the other side of the island. You're lucky, I'm on my way home.'

The guy was in a hurry. They were thrown about in the back of the taxi as he headed inland. The hotel was no palace. Convenient for the airport, Geoff's logistics sheet had put it. Convenient for the budget, thought Nathalie. The lobby looked deserted except for one small, dark-haired man behind a tiled reception bar. They put their bags on the floor and Nathalie placed their passports on the counter.

'Two people, three nights, Thompson and Linde,' she said in a tired voice.

The man looked as tired as she felt. He tapped lazily at the keyboard and stared at the monitor. Several minutes passed and he was still tapping.

Nathalie turned to Charlie. 'Why do they always do this? All I want is the numbers of our rooms, not for him to write a bloody novel!'

'Sorry, no Thompson.'

Nathalie felt her blood rise. Charlie must have noticed for he put his hand gently on her shoulder. 'Thompson and Linde,' he said slowly and gently.

'No, sorry; no Thompson or Linde.'

Nathalie started to rummage in her bag for Geoff's e-mail. The man continued tapping. 'Oh yes, I see what's happened.'

Nathalie sighed, 'Great, just give us our keys and tell us the numbers of our rooms. We'll find our own way.'

'Sorry, I can't do that. The booking was for yesterday.' He was about to continue but Nathalie was exhausted. She slammed her fist on the counter and shouted at the man.

'Okay, it may have been for yesterday but we have three nights so can we have the second of them now.'

The man stood his ground. 'Sorry, because it was a no-show, we have rebooked the rooms. It's a busy time, we are full up.'

Charlie could see that Nathalie was about to garrotte the man behind the desk. His voice was calm. 'Well, I for one don't plan on sleeping in another broom cupboard. This isn't Majuro, there must be hundreds of hotels. We've only hand luggage, let's go and look.'

Nathalie narrowed her eyes at the receptionist, picked up the passports and followed Charlie silently out of the lobby, thinking about all those things she would do to Bagatelle's travel agent who had obviously used their dateline data from the first booking. They looked around the poorly lit hotel car park. The taxi driver had gone. No-one was to be seen except a lone uniformed police officer leaning against his car near the entrance.

'Maybe this guy can help. Must be a Marriott or Holiday Inn around here somewhere,' said Charlie, striding towards the police car. Nathalie folded her arms and waited. She would have gone back to the reception and tiraded that supercilious little man until he had given them a room. She watched the conversation in the distance. Much waving of arms and animated debate. After a few minutes Charlie beckoned her over.

'This officer agrees with the guy at reception. It's a busy period, the island is pretty well full up. But he does have a suggestion.'

'Which is?'

'His brother's a security guard on a self-catering apartment block in the hills. If we want he'll give us a lift.'

It sounded suspicious. A stranger offering you a lift at midnight to an unspecified apartment block on a small tropical island. Well, it was a police car and she was shattered.

'Nothing ventured,' said Nathalie, nodding to the policeman as he opened the rear door for her.

The officer asked if they were on holiday as the car made its way up a series of steep winding roads. He seemed more than interested when they said that they were part of a film crew in Guam to film the ocean resources' conference. There was either something very creepy about all of this or the guy was just a bored police officer on nightshift. They had come to a part of the island without streetlights. It was difficult to see their surroundings but the headlights of the vehicle picked out scrub on either side of the road. Nathalie was imagining the worst when the car pulled up at a gated area of apartment blocks, half of which were only partly built. A young man jumped out of the guardhouse.

'Harry,' he shouted. The two brothers embraced and after a short conversation Charlie and Nathalie were led into what they could only describe as a luxury show home. Fifty dollars a night, hot and cold running water, but no services or food. They could stay as long as they liked. Nathalie handed over one hundred and fifty dollars and thanked Harry for his help.

'No problem. If you like I'll pick you up in the morning and take you to the conference. Sounds a real interesting job you've got.'

The apartment was stunning. Marble floors, gold taps in the bathroom, a king-size bed. They were right about the hot and cold water, and all the power worked, but the fridge was empty. They looked at each other in disbelief. Nathalie was the first one to speak.

'I'm not sure if this is legal but I feel wiped out and that bed looks very inviting. You happy to share it?'

Their policeman, come-taxi-driver was as good as his word. At eight o'clock sharp they heard the wheels of his car scrunch outside their apartment.

'Sleep well?'

'Perfectly, thank you.' Nathalie locked the door behind her. 'You've been very kind. Are you sure this is all okay?'

'No problem. You've come all this way to film our small island, it's the least we can do.'

The police car even waited at the airport while they recovered their camera gear. The officer shook their hands as he left them at the conference hall.

'You make sure my brother looks after you. Have a good time in Guam.'

'Not a lot of crime in Guam then,' said Nathalie quietly as the car pulled back onto the highway.

The two young men in the anteroom of the conference hall looked like rookies; American marine-type haircuts, pressed blue jeans and gleaming white trainers. They rushed up to Nathalie to help with the matte box she was carrying. She indicated that it was fine and introduced herself and Charlie. They were both called Paul, which was going to be a bit confusing. So Paul the sound and Paul the sparks it became. Fortunately, Bagatelle hadn't messed this one up and there were passes waiting for them at the main door. They were ushered into a side room and asked to wait for the assistant to the British delegate, who would chaperone them on the shoot. Nathalie didn't like the word 'chaperone' but she was really there for Cain on the second day so she put on her best behaviour. Simmons, she never got his first name, showed them where they could set up in the conference hall. The three seminars Bagatelle had asked for were fortunately in the same room. The two young Pauls set up their lights and microphones under the patient eye of Charlie and they waited for the delegates.

The conference was as boring as it could be. Poorly lit PowerPoint slides and monotone speakers outlined the pros and cons of ocean development. Cain appeared briefly in order to comment on what he called the 'novelty' of ocean energy schemes; how they were experimental, unproven and in their infancy. His speech was bland and hardly what one might call aggressive or provocative. At the end of the day Simmons came up to them and politely asked if they would like to go to the 'evening bash' as he coined it. As he promised a chauffeur-driven car to their accommodation at the end of the event they gratefully accepted. They now had their full luggage with them so Nathalie took her case to the ladies' washroom and pulled out a cotton dress. It was creased to hell but in this heat it would soon straighten out. She met Charlie in the foyer and took the elevator to the third floor, where the party was being held.

'Nice dress, looks good on you.'

'Your T-shirt doesn't look so bad. Good job it's not black-tie, though.'

They got out of the third floor and mingled with the delegates. In the far corner was a face that Nathalie thought she recognised.

'There's someone I know over there, would you mind?'

'No problem. I'm heading for the buffet anyway.' Charlie disappeared through the crowd.

She had only seen him on Skype but Philippe Charday was unmistakable. A slight, sallow, bearded young man with that inquisitive stare.

'Philippe.'

'Nathalie Thompson, quelle surprise!'

She was a little taken aback when he kissed her on both cheeks. Although their cyber relationship had broken the ice long ago this was the first time she had met him in person. They took a glass of champagne from the waiter and found two upright chairs in a quiet corner. After small talk about her experiences of Guam and the bizarre policeman the conversation turned to Senator Cronkar and Governor Cain.

'I told your friend, I was so sorry to let you down.'

'Friend?'

'Nick Coburn. We had a long chat about the Law of the Sea in New York.'

'Nick? A long chat on maritime law? Must be a first.'

'No, he was very interested, especially when I told him that Cain turned the department's policy on its head.'

'That's why we're here.'

'Still making the UNCLOS programme then?'

'Not exactly, that was scrapped after the Cronkar affair. This is another job, a lot more interesting. Could be on broadcast TV.'

'Oh, so you're the crew with the British delegation. You've got an interview with Cain tomorrow?'

'That's right. How did you know?'

'I was asked to help set it up. Cain wasn't too keen at first but when he heard British television wanted to give both sides of the story he decided to play with the ball. British rules of cricket, I think he called it.'

Nathalie smiled. 'It's "play ball", but I think I'd prefer it your way. How's Cain being received?'

Philippe looked nervously around the room. 'It's a nightmare. Everything we set up in Publicity has been torn up. Now it's brakes on the Law of the Sea Treaty, renewable energy research on the backburner, and "à l'attaque" on United States oil shale reserves. Last week we were asked to find statistics that showed that oil shale fracking wouldn't affect climate change.'

Now it was Nathalie's turn to look around the room. 'There are rumours that he has investments in oil shale. Any truth in that?'

Philippe looked genuinely surprised. 'Where did you hear that? I'm sure that someone on Capitol Hill would have raised it. Conflict of interest. I don't think even Viveca would allow him to get away with that.'

'Viveca?'

'Viveca Olsson. She's practically running the show at the moment. Cain's the government representative but she's the "senior ops manager"; does all the day-to-day stuff. I mentioned her to your friend Nick. He seemed quite interested. Recently she's become even more hands-on. Cain doesn't make a move without her. Now she has us running around, trying to cut budgets on everything. Ocean resources used to be the flavour of the month, now we've been told to put projects on standby.' Philippe looked bitter. 'I know I must sound like a whingeing employee but this isn't what I came into this business for. Even this ocean conference is window dressing.'

'And what about all these so-called accidents in the maritime business? Has Cain or this Viveca woman ever mentioned the name Marine Corps to you?'

'Marine Corps? I don't think so.'

They were interrupted by a delegate seeking Philippe's attention; something about a display board for tomorrow's seminars. Philippe excused himself and hurried off to the other side of the room. Nathalie's eyes followed him. The party was now getting into full swing. People started to gather on the dance floor and move to the music. Most of them looked a little clumsy, arms and legs flailing awkwardly in the air. She took another glass of wine from the waiter's tray and leant back against the wall to people-watch. The lights dimmed and the music turned to a slower number. Couples shuffled around the floor. She scanned the faces to see if she could see Cain. Instead she saw a tall blonde woman in close contact with Charlie – *too* close in contact. The woman was practically climbing inside him; more of a romantic clinch than a casual dance. She felt the pressure rise inside her chest. Who was this woman? What was Charlie doing with her? Last night in the apartment they had had … well, she didn't know what they had had. Lovemaking or just casual sex? And not for the first time. Bloody cheek! Okay, maybe the first time had been for a bit of comfort but now she felt they were becoming quite close.

'What a shit!' The woman next to her looked astonished; Nathalie hadn't realised that she had spoken out loud. But now she was so angry that she didn't care. 'Fuck you, Charlie Linde!' she said more loudly and stormed out of the reception room.

Twenty

The lobby was dark. A car light beam raked the ceiling as it passed through the glass door entrance of the conference centre. Nathalie sat on the last step of the staircase with their luggage and camera gear on a trolley beside her. She felt a fool. They had been promised an official car to take them back to their accommodation. It was booked for one o'clock in the morning. She had been sitting on this step for nearly an hour and it was still only five to. She kicked out at the wheels of the trolley. It lurched forward a little, the dimpled aluminium lens box on the top nearly toppling off. She had tried to calm down but she was still seething. Now she had to face the guy and even share an apartment with him. She heard the noise of the elevator and a green light made a dinging noise as it reached ground level. The doors parted to reveal the beaming face of Charlie.

'Great, I wondered where you were. And you've loaded all the gear up. Fantastic.' Charlie seemed totally oblivious to her glowering stare.

There was no way she was going to have a shouting match in the lobby and so she stepped out of the shadow of the staircase and pushed the trolley towards the exit.

'See if our car's arrived,' she said abruptly.

The glass plate automatic doors parted as Charlie jumped in front of her. A large, black Ford saloon with tinted windows was just pulling up at the crescent of tarmac that fronted the building. Charlie tapped at the window and a large, suited gentleman got out of the car and helped them put their luggage in the trunk. The camera tripod wouldn't fit but Charlie said he would rest his legs on his legs. Neither the driver nor Nathalie smiled at the joke. The driver didn't get it and Nathalie was not in a humorous mood. Thinking she was just tired, Charlie opened the rear door for her and without another word got in the other side and gave the driver a piece of paper with their apartment address.

The limousine drove slowly and silently past the governor's house and the cathedral before it turned into the gravel winding road that led into the hills. The inside of the car was now pitch black except for the glowing dials on the instrument panel. Nathalie had spent the last hour planning what she was going to say. Now here in the back seat of a car with the tripod case banging against her legs she was back at square one. Did she have any right to lay into him? Perhaps he wasn't as fond of her as she was becoming of him. She shouldn't have had sex with him anyway. He was her cameraman. The lone king-size bed was a problem but they were adults; they could just sleep in it.

Harry's brother greeted them at the gatehouse and cheerfully manhandled their equipment into the apartment. Nathalie was unsure about tipping him or the driver but the discovery that she only had large denomination bills solved the problem. She thanked them both and locked the door behind her.

Charlie was the first to speak. 'Do you want to shower first? I want to make sure the cans are labelled properly. The Pauls seem a bit green.'

'Sure.'

'You okay?'

Nathalie was making her way to the marble-tiled wet room and pretended not to hear. She showered and pulled on an old T-shirt and a pair of briefs. Charlie was still in the lounge so she went straight to the bedroom and climbed into bed. Despite the air-conditioning it was still hot so she made do with a single top sheet. By the time he had finished messing about with the film can and had showered she was poised on the edge of the bed, pretending to be asleep.

Charlie dropped his towel on the floor, got in beside her and shuffled over so that he was touching her back. She flinched.

'Hey, are you okay?' His voice was gentle.

When she didn't respond he asked again. 'I know you're not asleep. Are you okay?'

Nathalie remained facing the wall in the foetal position. 'No, I'm not okay.'

'What's the problem?

'You are.'

'Me?'

Nathalie was becoming tired of this game so she sat upright in the bed and turned to look Charlie in the eye.

'Yes, you. I'm wondering what I'm doing in bed with a naked man who, a few hours earlier, was crawling all over a six-foot leggy blonde.'

Charlie reddened a little. 'Oh, that?'

'Yes,' said Nathalie calmly, 'that.'

'I can explain.'

'That's what they all say.'

'Just let me have some airtime.'

Nathalie leant against the headboard and folded her arms. She didn't say anything so Charlie told his story.

'The leggy blonde, as you call her, is a big wig in the Environmental Protection Agency. She works with the guy we're filming tomorrow, Governor Cain. She's Swedish, we speak the same language. I thought I might get some information out of her.'

'And to do that you had to put your tongue down her throat.'

Charlie sat up and leant against the headboard alongside her. 'No.' He drew out the word in protest. 'She was a bit clinchy in the dancing, I suppose, but I thought if I played along she might talk more freely.'

Nathalie sat staring into the room. 'And did she?'

'As a matter of fact she did.'

They both sat there, upright, in the spacious marble-floored bedroom with no sound except for the low humming of the inefficient air conditioner. Nathalie was the first to break the silence. 'And did you?'

'Of course not. It was just a dance. Who do you think I am? I don't go sleeping around with every girl I meet. And ...,' he stopped mid-sentence.

'And?'

'… and you are the first film director that I've had a relationship with. Not very professional, I know, but …'

'*Mea culpa*,' interrupted Nathalie. 'I shouldn't have encouraged you.'

'Well, what do we do now?'

Nathalie turned towards him. 'Act like professionals. We've got a film to make. You said that this woman talked. What about?'

The drizzle hung in the air over Soho Square. Nick Coburn folded down his collar and skipped up the steps leading to the entrance of Bagatelle's production office. He waved cheerily at the girl behind the reception desk and made his way straight to the elevators. She was about to ask him to sign the visitors' book when the doors opened and he disappeared inside. Geoff had seemed unconcerned about his report on Ocean Tech. 'Got the development money in the bank and we've got bigger fish to fry,' was his comment. The meeting had been set up for three-thirty; it was now quarter to four but Geoff knew that Nick wasn't the punctual sort.

'There you are, you late bastard,' was Geoff's opening greeting.

Nick sat down in the old leather armchair facing Geoff's desk. 'Nice to see you too.'

Geoff threw a set of files at him and without ceremony launched into a monologue, more for his own benefit than Nick's.

'Checked your concerns over Ocean Tech and you could be right. Only an answerphone in the last twenty-four hours. But that's not a problem. If they've jumped ship, they've paid up-to-date, and if they've just relocated, we can pick up their little project later on. In a way, it would be good if they were out of the picture. This new movie could be quite a coup. Even got the BBC and Channel 4 fighting over the rights.'

Nick was used to Geoff's enthusiasm over the most recent thing on his desk. 'So what's the next move?'

'That's what I wanted to talk about. We've put a researcher onto your list of Marine Corps addresses. Current feedback is that they seem a fairly autonomous lot. Don't have much to do with each other, just the franchise name. And before you ask, yes, we will be looking a bit more into the background of Ocean Tech. It's not about the money but it's a bit odd that they didn't mention their Malmö office or their big-time backers in Japan.'

Nick began to wonder what his role was in all of this. 'Who's your main contact at Ocean Tech? Want me to flush him out?'

'Their media guy? A chap called Oyama. Hisoka Oyama. No, that's not a priority. A lot of these companies hot desk. I don't want to start pressing the panic button and find that he's just gone on holiday for a week.' Geoff Sykes eased himself out of his swivel armchair and made his way to a large whiteboard at the end of his office.

'No, what I want you to do is to concentrate on these ocean project disasters.' Geoff picked up a felt tip from its holder at the bottom of the board and started to write.

'So what have we got? Ocean drilling ship sinks and catches fire. Still no adequate explanation from the investigation team.' A large question mark is scrawled on the board. 'Next. A sonar device disappears into the ocean. A guy is nearly killed and it looks like someone has cut the rope.' Geoff writes the word '*sabotage?*' next to his sonar column. 'Finally, we have a tragic submersible accident in Hawaii. This time a guy does get killed. The Hawaiian police are a bit cagey on this one. Open verdict at the moment but Nathalie has a hunch that there was foul play.'

Nick sat back in the chair and watched with interest as the whiteboard turned into something like a scene out of a police criminal investigation. Geoff picked up a red marker pen and made a dramatic circle around his list. With an even more exaggerated flourish he extended the circle into an arrow pointing to the other side of the board.

'Okay, now let's look at the main players. All three incidents have connections with Marine Corps. Engineers on-site at the time.' Geoff scrawled the word '*PLAYERS*' onto the board and began to write names underneath.

'So far all we have is Lukas, and what was the other guy's name?'

Nick shook his head in amusement but seeing Geoff's intense expression decided to play along. 'Nils. Nils something, the marketing guy at Malmö, but I didn't meet him.'

'Okay, Nils. At least that's a start.'

'Yeah, but I'm not sure about the involvement of these guys. Lukas was real naive, I'm sure he knew nothing about this stuff.'

'We don't know that yet, and we'll add to the list when our researcher gets more information on Marine Corps.'

Nick shrugged his shoulders. 'This all seems a bit random. We've not got any evidence that any of these things are connected.'

'We're not lawyers; we don't need forensic evidence, just a story for a television audience. If we can make a connection, great; if not, we'll show the pictures and let them make up their own minds. There's definitely a programme in this – terror at sea, sex scandals, conspiracy theories, that sort of thing.' Geoff exchanged his red pen for a black marker. 'And talking about sex scandals …' He scrawled the name '*CRONKAR*' onto the board. 'Guy photographed being spanked in a sex club moments before the ratification of the Law of the Sea Treaty.' Geoff dramatically swept a marker pen arrow to a third column and wrote out the letters '*UNCLOS*'.

'You can add our leggy Viveca to that column,' chipped in Nick. 'That lady's name seems to crop up in all sorts of places. "Crop" being the operative word,' he added with a smile.

'And now she's working for Cain, the guy who's turning US ocean energy policy on its head.' Geoff continued filling in his whiteboard. 'Shale fracking, that could be the answer to all of this stuff. If Cain is knee-deep in oil, we could have a great conspiracy storyline.'

Nick tilted his head sideways to read the remainder of Geoff's graffiti. 'Okay, Boss, Nathalie should have that one covered. What's our next move?'

Geoff threw the worn-out marker pen into the bin and made his way to his computer. 'I've been thinking about that. My hunch is to check out other ocean energy projects with poor track records. See how many threads we can feed back to Marine Corps or the Viveca-Cain partnership. I've asked Stefanie to put a few things into my inbox, let's see what she's come up with.'

It was getting dark outside. Either it was dusk or heavy cloud had set in. They had both lost track of the time. Nick leant over Geoff's shoulders and rested his arms on the desk. The computer screen glowed brightly, the keys below dimly lit by the art deco angle-poise. Stefanie had done her homework but few fitted the bill until they came across an experimental tidal plant in the Philippines. The project was fraught with problems. And, more to the point, it was just under a four-hour flight from Guam.

The two Pauls rushed out eagerly to greet the taxi. 'No police escort this time, I see.'

Nathalie was in no mood for banter. 'Help Charlie with the camera gear. I'll go in and check on Cain. We're running a bit late.'

She swept into the conference hall and showed her badge to the desk. 'Could you contact Philippe Charday for me? I believe he's booked out the room for us to film the governor.'

The young man at the desk responded with a smile and punched in an extension line on his phone keypad. Charday must have been waiting, for after a few polite grunts he put down the phone and told Nathalie that Governor Cain's aide, Viveca Olsson, would be down shortly to show them to the room. Nathalie bristled slightly at the name but nodded and turned to help the crew move the equipment into the lobby.

Minutes later the long, slender legs of Olsson could be seen coming down the staircase. As her head came into view she smiled and held out her hand to Nathalie. Nathalie responded slightly begrudgingly.

'Good morning, Miss Olsson. I understand that you have a room for us. Could the lighting guy recce it before we move all the equipment in to see if it's okay?'

Olsson ignored the rather prickly request and gestured to the desk clerk. 'Ben, please show the film crew to room 106. Our media people have checked it out for suitability for filming an interview. While you do so, I will stay here with Miss Thompson. I would just like a few words with her.'

Nathalie felt the control being swept away from her. But this woman was on her own territory and there was nothing she could do about it.

'Fine, if that's what you want. Charlie, take the kit with you and set it up for a one-to-one, sound only on interviewer situation. If there's any technical problem with the room let me know.' She turned back to Viveca Olsson, 'Now, Miss Olsson, what exactly are these few words you would like to have?'

The combat looked a little one-sided – six-foot Viveca Olsson in her cream tailored pencil skirt suit, and five-foot four Nathalie Thompson in crumpled T-shirt and faded jeans.

'Before the interview, Miss Thomson, I would like to present the senator with a list of your questions. Do you have them written down or shall I ask one of our secretaries to type them out for you?'

Nathalie produced a professional smile. 'I'm sorry, Miss Olsson. In response to your first question, I do not. And I'm afraid I wouldn't want to waste your secretary's time because we are professional broadcast documentary makers and we tend to ask questions on an ad hoc basis in response to the answers. There is no script, unlike some of your environmental corporate videos.'

Olsson stood her ground. 'The senator likes to prepare himself for these interviews so that you have very clear answers for your television programme. Our American documentary makers have always been pleased to present their questions beforehand.'

'I'm afraid that's not the way we work, Miss Olsson. Even if I did give you some questions now I'm sure that they would only change through the course of the interview. I wouldn't want to waste your or Governor Cain's time. Also, I understand that Mr Cain is an extremely astute politician and will be able to field any questions that I may pose.'

Olsson took a deep intake of breath, but before she could answer this upstart of a girl, Ben came running down the staircase, saying that Governor Cain wished to see Miss Olsson immediately. Olsson turned on her heel and made her way towards the staircase; as she did so, she turned briefly to Nathalie.

'You have exactly one half-hour with Governor Cain, Miss Thompson, not a minute more. I would be pleased if you, and your crew, leave the premises as you found them and vacate the building by midday.'

'Absolutely, Miss Olsson,' replied Nathalie. 'Thank you so much for making arrangements for us and being so welcoming.'

Ben tried to stifle his amusement as he and Nathalie watched the woman in the tight skirt try to navigate her way gracefully up the stairs. As she didn't turn back the two of them could only guess at the expression on her face.

The interview started off on a bad note. The senator had obviously been told about Nathalie's refusal to hand over pre-prepared questions. He patronised her from the outset.

'Now, young lady, many of the issues we deal with here are highly technical, so if you don't understand some of the answers please stop me and I'll try to simplify them for your audience.'

'Oh, I think my audience will be quite capable of understanding the issues, Governor. Paul, please mark it and turnover, Charlie.'

Paul, the sparks, placed the clapperboard in front of their interviewee and gently clicked it shut. 'Oceans, slate one hundred and forty-six. Take one. Interview with Governor Cain.'

'Camera rolling,' said Charlie, and Nathalie took control.

Twenty-one

The governor sat back in his chair. He had done this a thousand times. Listen to the question intently, ignore it completely, and then say what he wanted to say by prefacing the answer with 'What I think is ...'

Nathalie was prepared for this tactic. She began the interview by asking a few innocuous questions; the timing of the conference, the role of the United States in the sharing of the resources of the sea. Cain rolled out his usual palliative replies. As soon as Nathalie saw he was getting comfortable she went on the attack.

'I met a Doctor Phelps the other day; we were on a sonar vessel at the time I recall. He said that your government was hiring him to map the whole of the underwater areas surrounding the coastline of the United States. Sounds a big project. Why haven't you advertised it in the conference?'

Cain was taken off guard. Of course they hadn't advertised it. It was meant to be kept under wraps. The agency didn't want the world to know that it might be exploiting these unclaimed territories in the future. He paused before making a reply. The silence was broken by the sound of a door opening in the corner of the room. Nathalie turned to see Viveca Olsson walking in. She put a finger to her lips and turned back again to address her interviewee. Olsson's entrance seemed to have unnerved him further.

'I believe there is some mapping; not a major project, just normal ongoing research and exploration. Not my remit I'm afraid. My predecessor, Senator Cronkar, initiated those things. I haven't inherited the responsibility.'

'But you did inherit the responsibility of ratifying the Law of the Sea Treaty,' Nathalie quickly interjected. 'I believe Senator Cronkar was all for the idea. Why didn't you sign?'

Cain shuffled in his chair and looked up at Olsson. He had been preparing a political answer about underwater mapping. Now he was caught flat-footed on another topic entirely. What had his media training taught him? Yes, that's right, deflect the question. 'Senator Cronkar was a disgrace. I don't think it's my place here to discuss his impropriety; the media has explored that avenue thoroughly enough already.'

'I wasn't asking you to discuss his personal life,' said Nathalie calmly. 'I was merely enquiring why you reversed the decision to sign the treaty.' She put her head slightly to one side and widened her eyes, waiting for an answer. Cain, once more, glanced up at Olsson.

Nathalie turned the dagger. 'Wouldn't be anything to do with oil shale fracking, I suppose?'

Charlie's lens was tracking in slowly onto the discomforted face of Cain when the shot was obscured by the body of Olsson moving into the set.

'Sorry, people, your half-hour is up and I am afraid that Governor Cain has a very important steering committee to attend.'

Nathalie didn't need to look at her watch, she knew that they had ten minutes left, but Cain's rattled expression and an interrupted interview on camera was all she needed.

'I'm sorry too,' she said loudly for the microphone. 'I would have loved to have heard about Governor Cain's involvement in shale fracking and its conflict of interest with the development of ocean resources.'

'This is ridiculous …,' began Cain, but the rest of his sentence was lost as Viveca Olsson steered him swiftly out of the room.

'And cut,' said Nathalie quietly with a smile on her face.

An hour later, the Pauls handed over the sound sheets and wished them well. They were still unsure of what had happened in that room but it was none of their business and they were thankful for the early finish.

'Coffee?' Nathalie was feeling good. She was sure that Geoff would get something out of that footage, and Olsson hadn't even acknowledged Charlie.

'Why not?' said Charlie. 'I'm sure we could leave this trolley load of gear with Ben at reception.'

Ben was all too pleased to look after their camera equipment. 'No problem. There's a small staff cafe on the first floor, but before you go, I've got something for you.' He rifled around in his desk drawer. 'Here it is; an e-mail from your office. Came in fifteen minutes ago.'

Nathalie took it from him and made her way to the staircase. 'Another of Geoff's world tour missives I expect. Where do you think he's sending us this time?'

They both pored over the printout while sipping their institutional coffee out of Styrofoam cups. It slowly dawned on them that Nathalie's quip was turning out to be true. The first page was crammed with technical jargon. It described vertical axes turbines, tidal fences and caissons, whatever they were, and the megawatts that could be produced by harnessing the tides. The next contained clippings from various journals.

Problems for the San Bernardino Straight project.

Political instability halts tidal power scheme.

Accident or sabotage? Ocean power thwarted again.

Nathalie groaned when she looked at the maps. 'It's in the Philippines.'

Charlie turned the papers towards him to get a closer view. 'What's in the Philippines?'

'The power station.'

'So what of it?'

'More problems with ocean technology; possible Marine Corps' involvement. He wants us to investigate.'

'Well, if it is the Philippines, it's only four hours away and at least it's in the right direction. We could fly back to London from there.' Charlie noticed the glum look on her face. 'Cheer up, I'm in. One last shoot, okay?'

'It just had to be the Philippines. I worked on a film there some time ago; had a very bad experience.'

Charlie put his arm around her. 'Well, I'm here this time.' He grinned. 'What could possibly go wrong?'

They took a taxi back to the apartment, planning their evening meal on the way. The row over Olsson seemed an age ago. Charlie pointed to the tourist brochure he was holding. 'This place looks good, not too far from our digs and a good local menu. They've even got morcizas.'

'Morcizas?'

'Chicken neck stuffed with meat, peppers and garlic.'

'Chicken neck?'

'Well, they do great burgers too.'

'No. When in Guam ...'

'Okay, chicken neck it is.'

The taxi drew up at the gatehouse and the guard let them in. Nathalie left Charlie to unload the gear and check the magazines while she sorted out her papers and prepared notes for the phone call she was about to make to Geoff. He had signed off by asking her to call him to discuss the arrangements. It was now six-thirty in the evening, 8.30 am London time. Geoff would be in the office waiting for her call.

'Nathalie, great to hear from you. How did the shoot go?'

She told him about Cain and his awkwardness in fending the questions on the Law of the Sea; also about Olsson's interference and the abortion of the interview.

'Guilty, your honour,' chipped in Geoff. 'Nothing better than a suspect terminating an interview on camera. Always makes the headlines. We are still checking on his possible holdings in oil shale, but as I said to Nick, we're not in a court of law. All we have to do is show a part of the jigsaw; the audience can fill in the full picture. I would say the stuff we've got on Olsson, combined with these ocean accidents, is a good start.'

'Olsson?'

'Yeah, Nick's found a link with her and the Cronkar scandal; but enough of that. Before the line goes down, let me fill you in on the ocean power plant.'

Nick took the next five minutes to outline their plot; ocean sabotage around the world and conspiracy theories involving the oil shale business. He briefed her about their ongoing investigations into Marine Corps and the idea of looking into other ocean power disasters.

'A bit of fortune there. A tidal power station on your doorstep with a catalogue of problems. You've been to the country before so travelling around should be a piece of cake. And talking of travelling, I'll hand you over to Stefanie; she's been sorting out the tickets.'

Nathalie sighed in exasperation. 'As you know, Geoff, the Philippines isn't my favourite place, and I've yet to tell you about Majuro.'

But she would have to wait to tell him about the incident on Majuro because he had taken another call and handed the phone to Stefanie.

'Sorry, Nathalie, it's me here. I'll pass you back when he's finished his other call. Meanwhile, I've got you a flight to Manila tomorrow morning. Tickets will be at the airport. I'm arranging for sound and lights to meet you off the plane. The next bit of the journey is pretty tricky because the power station base is on a small island near Northern Samar; I'll e-mail you a map. I think there are daily flights there, so I'll book you in for one night in Manila and try to book your internal flights for the next day. Geoff says there's a university lecturer near the location who could get you an introduction to the tidal plant.' The phone muffled as Nathalie heard Stefanie put her hand over the mouthpiece. '*What's that, Geoff? Yes, I'm explaining that now. Okay, I'll tell her.*' The line became clearer. 'Geoff says I'm flooding you. I'll put it all down in an e-mail when I have more information. He suggests you log into WiFi at the airport tomorrow morning. Can you be there by 8 am Guam time?'

Nathalie said that she could and Stefanie said her goodbyes. It was only when the phone had been put down that Nathalie realised she hadn't finished the things she wanted to talk about with Geoff. But it was obvious that he was insensitive to her history in the Philippines and the wave power station incident could always wait. In fact, she would put it in an e-mail now and send it when she was at the airport tomorrow morning.

'Chicken necks?' A shout came from the shower.

'Well, if you didn't take so long in that thing I'd be washed, changed and ready by now.'

'You could always join me.'

She had to stop herself from grinning. Things were nearly back to normal but she wasn't quite ready for *that* yet.

'Pass. Just let me know when you're finished.' She walked through to the lounge and opened her laptop. The more she typed about the events on Majuro, the more she began to wonder what had really happened.

Nick Coburn rarely stayed in one place for long. That month he had rented a one-bedroom flat in Pimlico. It was close to Westminster, the seat of power, and a short bus ride to Soho, home of the media. Since leaving the army he had been a jack-of-all-trades, but in recent years, he had found a niche working for magazines and television. He had contacts and field experience and the ability to go where normal researchers feared to tread. Geoff Sykes from Bagatelle Productions had used him a number of times. He liked working with Geoff; the work was varied and interesting, and despite Sykes' miserly reputation, well-paid. The problem was that Geoff was like a kid. He would get all excited about the latest project, throw a lot of questions and opinions up in the air, and then move onto something else while leaving you to do the groundwork. So, in front of him, he had a stack of files which had been carefully put into his rucksack by Stefanie.

He lit the small gas fire in the grate and kneeled on the large Afghan carpet that covered the floor. A freebie and a good acquisition; at least there were some perks of the trade. He sorted the paperwork into three piles – Marine Corps, Ocean Tech, and the US Environmental Protection Agency. The Marine Corps files were a mess – some notes from his trip to Sweden, lists and lists of Marine Corps offices, and speculative notes on engineers who worked at the various ocean project sites where Nathalie had filmed. He had no idea how Geoff was going to make a film out of this lot. Okay, if these guys had sabotaged some of the plants, what was in it for them? The guy Lukas in Malmö certainly didn't fit the bill of a saboteur and surely, by closing down ocean projects, they were doing themselves out of a job. Under the pile of addresses he found the leaked report on the sinking of the *IOD Revolution*. The official report had still yet to come out. More conspiracy or just red tape and bureaucracy? The Marine Corps survey people were based in their head office in Japan. Now he knew their exact address; on the coast, only sixty kilometres from the capital. He liked Tokyo. Maybe Geoff would fork out some petty cash for him to take another look.

It's strange what the psyche will do. Half an hour later, Nick was sitting cross-legged on the floor, eating out of an aluminium take-away Bento box. He was now sorting through the Ocean Tech files and cross-checking them with an internet search on his laptop. The more he dug, the less he found. The history on the internet showed that Ocean Tech was an insignificant marine drilling outfit barely breaking even. A year ago it seemed to have been taken over by a large conglomerate; a pyramid of companies with a difficult line to trace. Their new website showed an interest in climate change and energy from the sea. A large company using a small franchise to put a toe in the water. Nothing suspicious about that, but the fact that their Malmö office had shut up shop and that Geoff's sponsor had gone AWOL was another story. Geoff hadn't asked him to check up on Hisoka Oyama, their media officer; he wanted to give him a little more time to call in but Nick thought that was a mistake. Why would a guy throw a few thousand dollars at a project and then disappear for a few weeks?

Ocean Tech's head office was also in Japan. Nick checked the address on Google maps. Better still, in Tokyo itself. Now Geoff might be interested in that, two for the price of one. Maybe he would even send Nathalie and Charlie there to get some interviews on film. And Charlie, wasn't he introduced to Bagatelle by Ocean Tech in the first place? Nick wondered whether Charlie had any idea about his evasive promoter.

Nick put the wooden chopsticks into the now empty Bento box and took the last pile of paperwork into his small kitchen. He crushed the box and threw it into the bin, slapped the files onto the worktop and switched on the small espresso machine. It was getting late and he had promised Bagatelle that he would have his recommendations on their desk first thing in the morning. He was better at a night stakeout than rifling through paperwork, and strong black coffee was the only answer.

The Environmental Protection Agency file was the thinnest and he had left it until last. Cronkar, Cain, Charday and Olsson; most of the notes were his own. Why had Olsson stitched up Cronkar? Had she a deal with Cain? Was he pulling the strings? And Charday's comments on the Law the Sea …? Was this big-time politics with the United States trying to grab more resources under the unclaimed ocean floor, or just a guy wanting a better job? Geoff had said that Nathalie's interview seemed to suggest neither. 'It's all about greed,' he had mooted. 'A guy with a shale fracking business doesn't want the climate change lobby and the ocean power lot to fuck up his business,' were his actual words.

Nick wasn't so sure. No matter how much research he and Bagatelle's team had done on the web, none of them could come up with a link with Cain and any fracking company.

'These guys are clever,' Geoff had said. 'They have a thousand ways of distancing themselves from company boards, but when the oil flows in, so does the money.'

It wasn't Nick's job to argue. It was Geoff's film. He could show what he wanted. Also, he liked the sex scandal angle; a senator literally whipped out of his job so that another guy could take his place and change US ocean policy. At least Nick had personal proof that Viveca Olsson had some part in this. Maybe he should recommend taking another trip to the States, put Olsson on the spot and this time without having his balls spanked. The espresso machine was demanding his attention, so he put more coffee in the container and turned the lever. He was sure his caffeine receptors were blocked with years of abuse. He could hardly keep his eyes open. One last double and he would have to make a decision. Olsson, or Oyama, New York or Tokyo? He selected Geoff's Bagatelle address and took the coffee cup from the base of the machine. Nick downed the creamy liquid in one and sat down to compose his e-mail. At the last minute, he made up his mind.

Suggest you fly me to Tokyo. It's time we got to the bottom of this Marine Corps outfit. Can check out Ocean Tech at the same time. They are within close radius. You may want some of this stuff on film. Tokyo only a four-hour flight from Manila. When Nathalie and Charlie are through with their tidal power station I'm sure they would like me to buy them a beer. Nick.

He clicked on 'send', snapped the laptop shut and made his way to his inviting but unmade bed.

Twenty-two

Guam International Airport was unnaturally quiet. For a pleasant change, the security checks were swift, efficient and genial. Nathalie left Charlie in the departures lounge, hugging his rolls of exposed film – he refused to let them go in the hold – while she searched for a spot to download her e-mails. The Philippine Airlines' clerk couldn't have been more helpful. She even offered to print out some of the map attachments.

'You going to Samar?'

Nathalie took the maps from her and began to study them. 'Apparently. You know the island?'

'Very well, my family come from there. It's a holiday?'

'Not quite, we're working. Making a film on alternative power.'

'Northern Samar is very famous for that. They're building a huge tidal power station.'

'So I hear. Are there any nice hotels around there?'

'The main power station office is on Dalupiri. It's a very small island. Here, you can see it on your map; it's just off Samar. There are no hotels there but you can hire bungalows. If you have the time, I could look it up on the computer.'

Nathalie thought of the way in which Bagatelle booked accommodation. Price first, cleanliness and proximity from location a good second. 'You're an angel. That would be fantastic, just in case my company haven't found anything suitable yet.'

The airline clerk shuffled around on the keyboard and after a few minutes printed out a brochure. *Octopussy Bungalow Beach Resort*, read the headline. The pictures looked amazing; white sands, emerald seas and cute little palm-thatched bungalows. There was even a step-by-step description of how to get there.

'Great,' said Nathalie, putting all the papers into her bag, 'I'll send you a postcard if we get there.'

The woman smiled. 'You do that. Have a great trip.'

The flight was uneventful, four hours later and they were passing through the Ninoy Aquino Airport arrivals lounge. A young taxi driver was waiting there for them, holding up a hand-crafted placard. He drove them and their equipment the few hundred yards to the Manila Airport Hotel. You would hardly call it a luxury hotel but it was in the airport complex and it looked clean enough. The driver helped them into the reception with their gear and lingered after Nathalie had paid his fare, waiting for a tip. She only had hundred dollar bills so she asked Charlie if he had any spare change. He dug out a ten-dollar bill and the driver thought it was Christmas.

Nathalie made her way to the desk. 'Well, no dateline this time so let's see if there are any other gremlins in the accommodation arrangements.'

But the check-in went as smoothly as the flight; two adjacent standard rooms on the ground floor, with easy access for the equipment. The receptionist handed her some tickets.

'These were sent to us by your travel agent. The flight to Catarman tomorrow leaves early at six o'clock so I've arranged for some bread rolls and fresh fruit to be in your room for this evening. You will be able to get some hot coffee out of the machine at the airport. Would you like a wake-up call?'

Nathalie stepped back in amazement. Was this woman vying for a job as a production assistant? Wake-up call, prearranged breakfast; would she be offering a massage next?

'Yeah, that would be great. Could you order us a cab for the terminal too?'

'No problem. I see you have a lot of equipment. I'll get you a large Jeepney.'

Nathalie was familiar with Jeepneys, decorated aluminium Jeeps based on the old American military design. They looked like something out of a funfair but were a practical way of getting around.

'Thanks, that's more than helpful. One final thing, is there anywhere we can get a bite to eat around here?'

'Sure, there's our coffee shop around the corner. They've got pancit, fried chicken, and sandwiches. But if you want something more…,' she moved her head from side to side, searching for the word.

Nathalie gathered that she was wondering whether these travelled Westerners would prefer something more gourmet. 'No, the coffee shop sounds fine; I love pancit, and thank you again.'

'What's pancit?' asked Charlie as they made their way to the restaurant.

'Stir-fried rice noodles. You can get them with all sorts of stuff – fried pork, prawns, vegetables – they are really tasty.' She shook her head and grinned. 'A lot better than chicken necks.'

'I said you could have a burger, it was you who wanted to go native.'

'Yeah, but weren't they terrible?'

'Too right, but can I trust you on this pancit?'

'Try it and see, and if I remember correctly it was you who recommended the chicken necks.'

They both laughed and grabbed a tray for the self-service. The pancit smelt wonderful. Good food, a receptionist from heaven and rooms right next to the airport. She just had to text Stefanie the details on the Island Beach Resort and they could take things easy for the rest of the evening. Things were on the up.

The four-thirty wake-up call came all too soon. Bleary-eyed, the two of them dragged the metal boxes into the Jeepney. They munched their bread rolls and fruit on the short ride to the terminal. It was an internal flight so the check-in was relatively easy and Nathalie had plenty of time to log into her e-mails. Stefanie was relieved and thankful to take on board her recommendation of the Octopussy Bungalows and had booked half-board for three nights. She had also finalised their contact details. The university lecturer, a Doctor Flores, would meet them at Catarman Airport and assist them in getting access to the tidal power station. The final call came over the tannoy and she hurriedly began to pack her laptop into its case.

'Hi, I'm Spike, your film crew.' Nathalie looked up sharply to locate the source of the Antipodean drawl.

'Film crew?'

'Well, audio guy with digi-recorder and a couple of redheads. How does that sound?'

'Not like a full film crew. Stefanie said there would be two of you.'

'A bit short notice, I'm afraid; I'm all she could get. She did say that most of your stuff would be exterior but I brought a couple of lamps just in case.'

'The two redheads, yes, very good of you. What did you say your name was?'

'They call me Spike.'

Nathalie glanced at his gelled-up hair. 'I wonder why, but I suppose if you're all we've got,' she said with a grin.

'Best sound in the Philippines. As you've probably guessed an Aussie but I also speak the local lingo; might be a bit of help out in the sticks.'

Nathalie held out her hand, 'Okay, Spike, welcome on-board. Let's go into the departure lounge and I'll introduce you to Charlie.'

The flight was on time. A short hop over the Sibuyan Sea and they were in Catarman. The airport was typically provincial; a low-rise, green-roofed building next to a series of corrugated iron warehouses masquerading as aircraft hangars. The single runway was surrounded by scrub and palm trees and a few Filipinos offering their wares on makeshift market stalls. They descended the steps of the propeller plane onto the tarmac and waited for their gear to be unloaded onto a trolley. It was blisteringly hot and the overhead fans in the terminal did little to make things any better. Nathalie looked around for Doctor Flores. There weren't many people so it shouldn't have been difficult to pick him out.

'Welcome to Catarman. I'm Tala,' said a diminutive young woman. Then seeing the surprise on Nathalie's face, 'Doctor Flores, from the University of Eastern Philippines.'

Nathalie recovered quickly and shook her hand. She was ashamed of assuming that the doctor would be a man and hoped that Tala had not noticed her blushes. 'Nathalie,' she responded, turning to the two men, 'and this is Charlie, the cameraman, and Spike, our sound recordist.'

'They said that you would have a lot of equipment so I've brought the university minibus. I hope that's okay?'

'Perfect. Can we go somewhere to have a chat about planning our days? Stefanie has told me that you can get access to the tidal power station.'

'Of course. Your company has told me what you require and I have mapped out a schedule for you. If you follow me we can talk about it in a cooler environment at the university.'

The university campus sat among forested mountains and rice fields, facing the Pacific Ocean. Tala drove the minibus through a decorated archway, past some playing fields, and drew up in front of the building bearing a large sign labelling it as the Nonconventional Energy Centre. Two young men eagerly helped them move their equipment into an air-conditioned room, and Tala invited them to sit around a large teak conference table. It was obvious that the university had set out to please; nothing was too much trouble. Cold drinks were brought in and they were given a brief PowerPoint presentation. The first image was one of the central Philippines. Tala pointed out the three small islands that lay in the straits between Samar Island and Luzon. She explained that the tidal surges between these islands held enormous natural power and the university, in conjunction with an international engineering company, were attempting to turn this into electricity for the whole of the Philippines.

The doctor turned from the screen to the intently watching faces. 'I'm sorry if I sound so excited,' she said, 'but it really is exciting. It could revolutionise the lives of millions of Filipinos.'

'Don't worry,' said Nathalie. 'We understand. Go on, we'd like to know how it works.'

'All right. The next part of the presentation was made for our students. Please stop me if it becomes too technical.' She changed the slide to a photograph of a strange-looking bridge.

'This is the first stage of the project. It's a tidal fence composed of a number of individual vertical axis turbines, which are mounted within the fence structure known as a "caisson". Think of it as a large turnstile, where the water can be forced through huge turbines. The turbines have a variable speed direct-drive magnet generator. They can change the force of the water into either AC or DC electricity depending on voltages and distances to the nearest connection point of the grid.' She looked up again. 'I'm going too fast for you?'

'Not at all,' said Nathalie. 'Is it possible to film this thing or is it all underwater?'

'There's a road bridge that goes over the top but we could get you a boat to film some of the structure from the water. You won't be able to get a very good picture of the turbines but I might be able to gain access to a dry chamber where they're doing some testing. It's usually off-limits; they're worried about safety issues, but if you're going to give them some good publicity we might persuade them to let you in.'

'And interviews? Would you be prepared to go on camera; and perhaps an engineer from the project?'

'Certainly, we need all the publicity we can get. There are a lot of doubters about this scheme, especially because of some recent incidents.'

'Incidents?'

Doctor Flores reddened a little; it was obvious that she was wondering whether she had said too much. She tried to backtrack.

'When I say incidents, there's always teething problems with innovative technology projects. But the engineers seem to be overcoming these.'

'Any of these from Marine Corps?'

'Marine Corps?'

'Yes, a marine engineering company; they are often hired to troubleshoot ocean projects.'

'I'm not sure. We deal more with the academic side – power output, efficiency ratios, and so on. You'll have to ask the plant manager about that one.'

Nathalie didn't push the subject. She wanted to keep her powder dry for when the camera was running. She steered the conversation towards more practical things and mentioned that they had a reservation at the Octopussy Beach Resort.

'Oh, you'll like it there. It's a holiday place really but it's very convenient for the Tidal Fence. I was planning to take you out tomorrow morning. I'm afraid I have lectures this afternoon. Have you directions to get there?'

Nathalie pulled out a sheet from her bag, 'Journey to Octopussy Bungalow Resort. Full details of how to get there from a wonderful lady at Manila Airport. Don't worry about us, we're quite resourceful. What we would really like is for you to meet with us tomorrow morning and introduce us to the plant manager so we can do a recce.'

'No problem, let me know the bungalow you're staying in and I'll pick you up around eight-thirty. Here's a number to call a Jeepney. I'm sorry, I've got to rush, my students will be waiting.'

Spike had looked bored during the presentation but now he seemed to have cheered up. 'Holiday resort, eh? Let's go! If we get there early we could do a bit of snorkelling.'

Normally Nathalie would have taken affront at this attitude but there was nothing she wanted to waste precious film stock on today so she went with the flow.

'Why not? Charlie and I have had a whirlwind round-the-world tour and it's time we had a break.' She looked at her directions. It's about fifty kilometres to Victoria, where we can get a bangka. I'll give the Jeepney company a call.'

The Jeepney guy said he would be there in ten minutes. Ten Filipino minutes meant that he pulled up forty minutes later. He was surprised by the eight metal boxes but was extremely helpful in loading them when he heard that he was being paid a bonus. The coast road was bumpy, but not impassable. The ocean on their right-hand side looked inviting and they couldn't wait to get out of this stifling tin can for a cooling-off dip. Victoria consisted of a few grass huts and some pulled-up bangkas on the clean white sand. The bangkas, or outrigger canoes, had colourfully painted struts that were tied onto their bamboo stabilisers. Not a soul was to be seen. The Jeepney driver leant on his horn. Within seconds two young Filipino men came bounding out of the trees. They were naked from the waist up and wearing cut-off faded jeans and flip-flops. Charlie and Spike had to fend them off from throwing the camera kit into one of the bangkas. The bangka boys got the message and stood back while the gear was carefully stowed aboard. Spike was as good as his word with Tagalog, for he chatted to them, explaining that the equipment would be damaged if it got wet. The short journey took twenty minutes. The young lads pulled up at the pier and took their dollars gratefully. Nathalie apologised that she didn't have any pesos.

'I wouldn't worry about that,' said Spike. 'US dollars are better than a tip, less devaluation than the peso. I wouldn't bother changing your money if I was you; the dollar goes a long way in the Philippines, even out here.'

They could see the resort from the pier and the boys offered to help them carry the film equipment to the reception. The married couple who ran the place greeted them like long-lost family and showed them to a small thatched bungalow perched on the sand. It looked a bit like a house out of a fairy-tale. A small open-board staircase lead to a white and blue painted veranda. Inside were two small rooms with three single beds and a sort of living-kitchen space.

Spike looked Nathalie and Charlie up and down. 'What's the sleeping arrangement here, guys?'

Was it that obvious? thought Nathalie, before telling him, 'Men in the room on the right, and I'll take the one on the left. And as it is your gear, you can put it in your room. I'm fed up with sleeping with metal boxes.'

The owners had promised them a barbecue at dusk, so after storing and checking the gear, they changed into their costumes and ran over the ten metres of hot sand into the inviting waters. The sea was as good as it looked and they splashed around like ten-year-olds for the next hour. The sun sets fast in that part of the world and it wasn't long before long shadows swept the beach. They ran back to the bungalow to find a table laid with bowls of rice and a milk-fish sizzling on the barbecue.

'Hey, you guys, can I come on more shoots with you?' Spike grabbed some plates and started serving up. 'I'm more used to being shacked up in a Manila Marriott, preparing for an interview with the CEO of an insurance company.'

Nathalie took a plate of fish from him. 'We've done our share, she told him.' She handed a second plate to Charlie. 'At least I have.' She thought back to her corporate film days. 'You should work for Sheila.'

'Sheila, a good Aussie name.'

'She wouldn't have liked it pronounced like that.' But at that moment Nathalie didn't care what Sheila liked. That part of her business seemed a thousand years away: sitting in the lobby of a Boston hotel, waiting for Cronkar; Sheila asking her to wipe the tapes that were never recorded. That was making a lot more sense now. She pushed the whole thing to the back of her mind and stared out at the horizon.

Spike sat cross-legged on the sand next to her and started to fork some of the aromatic flakes of fish into his mouth. 'I bet you don't get to see many sunsets like this.'

'Oh, I don't know,' said Nathalie wistfully, thinking of her and Charlie's trip around the Pacific. 'Maybe six or seven.'

'More like nine or ten, I think,' chipped in Charlie, joining in the game.

Nathalie took her turn. 'Perhaps it was eleven, could have been twelve.'

'Up to twenty, perhaps?' said Charlie, laughing, fending off the fish bones being hurled at him.

Twenty-three

Geoff was in a bad mood. Instead of sitting in The Ivy Club cradling a cup of their Lavazza espresso he was in a cab heading towards Horseferry Road. The head commissioner of docs had changed again. It was easy with Derek, an informal chat in the club and a decision on what programme would fit what slot. Now he would have to start all over again. Probably some young man or woman who had failed to succeed in getting a film director's job and who thought they could make a programme by sitting at a Channel 4 desk. Geoff's past experience with a new young gun had been a disaster. Instead of keeping to their brief of being a commissioner, one who commissions programmes and attempts to make a balanced viewing schedule, the woman had wanted to be producer, director and even at one point composer for one of his documentaries: 'I took the rough-cut home and my mother didn't like the music. Could you replace it with something more modern.'

It wasn't a question, it was a statement. Geoff had paid one of the top guys a fortune to write the score, and this woman wanted her mother to choose it. He only hoped the new guy would be better. He could hardly be worse than that … he stopped himself from getting more annoyed. No point in going in there with all guns blazing. He had to think of a more delicate strategy. The problem was that his latest bunch of proposals hadn't been commissioned yet. Derek had given a firm promise on the oceans' project but nothing was signed. He had spent all of Ocean Tech's money to date and the current shoot was being funded out of his own pocket. Derek had wanted to fund the completion of the film and take a share of the royalties. The other option was that Bagatelle would finish it on their own and sell the non-exclusive rights around the world. The attraction of the documentary would depend on how far they could prove any sabotage and how many big names they could point fingers at. The subject had United States and Far East appeal so the market could be huge. But it would be good to get this new guy into his confidence, so a Bagatelle Channel 4 co-production might be the way to go. Also, it would be less risky using their upfront production money.

He tipped the cab driver and strolled up the steps to the glass and steel-fronted reception. The woman at the desk recognised him and put a call through immediately. Minutes later, the lift opened and he was greeted warmly by a red-haired young man.

'Geoff Sykes, I presume. I'm Julian Barnes, the new commissioner of documentaries, not the writer. Derek has told me a lot about you. Would you like a cup of coffee before we go up?'

Geoff never refused a coffee, even an institutional one out of a machine. They rode in the elevator to the fourth floor, holding their scalding cardboard cups. Julian said that he would have liked to have accepted Geoff's invitation to The Ivy but as he had just taken up the position he had a full schedule. He hoped that Geoff hadn't minded having the meeting in his office.

'Perfectly understandable,' said Geoff, moving his cardboard cup from hand to hand. 'I just thought you might like to get out for a bit and have a proper cup of coffee.'

'Another time. I don't want to be seen as swanning around picking up favours, even if it is only a cup of coffee, the minute I've taken up my position. It wouldn't look too good. Ah, here we are, first door on the right.'

For a man who looked as if he could be his son, Julian went about the business fairly maturely. He had read Geoff's proposals and had spoken to Derek about the discussions so far. They talked through a number of the embryonic ideas and agreed that they would review them again when full costings had been worked out. There was one large file remaining and Julian opened it with a flourish.

'Now this oceans' project looks interesting. I know Derek has discussed funding it ...' he sat back in his chair and tapped the table nervously with a pencil, '… and I know that it must be frustrating, having a young interloper take over and upsetting the apple cart. But it would be irresponsible of me to just rubberstamp this. I'm not saying that we are not going to fund it, it's just that it looks a little flaky on the conspiracy theory thing.'

'Flaky?'

'There doesn't seem too much of a narrative. Also, I'd like to know the reveal.'

'Reveal? This isn't a game show; it's a documentary and that's what we're doing, documenting things. Until we finish the filming we won't know what the outcome is.'

'That's my point, there might not be any; outcome, that is.'

'There's always an outcome. We've got footage of major ocean incidents around the world; ships being sunk, sonar devices being sabotaged, even a guy being killed in a submarine. Too many events to be a coincidence. Something's going on here. A US senator is fired so that someone with a different policy view can take his place. We even know the woman who set it up. What more do you want? Look, you know that the BBC is interested in buying the rights. If you don't want to fund it then they'll buy it as soon as we've finished. We couldn't offer it to you at that stage because they would want unique UK distribution.'

'Well, perhaps you could present us with more of a definitive storyline.'

'Waste of time, the storyline is shifting every day. The more we probe into this thing, the more intriguing it gets. This very minute we're shooting a tidal plant in the Philippines. It's incredible. Thousands of pollution-free kilowatt-hours delivered to a nation like the Philippines. It's a godsend, but what's happening? Delay after delay, major accidents, political unrest and who knows what? I've got one of our best directors on the job. If there is a conspiracy out there she'll find it. This programme is big, really big, prime-time viewing. Do you realise that two-thirds of our planet isn't owned by anybody. The resources of the oceans are vast; wars have been waged over less.

If someone wants to scupper these assets they must have a very good reason. Now I'm offering you the opportunity to be part of this story when it breaks, reveal or no reveal. I can't give you more time because the money is being spent on filming as we speak. Are you in or not?'

Julian repositioned himself in his chair. He hoped that not all of his producers would be like this. To date most of them had been grovelling and sycophantic and couldn't bend over far enough to please but, if Bagatelle's track record was anything to go by, this guy would deliver.

'Okay, you seem passionate enough and from the last couple of programmes I've seen of yours, you can tell a good story. The Channel's in; contract dependent, obviously. Can you send in your production manager on Wednesday?'

'Sure thing,' said Geoff, rising from his chair 'You won't regret it.'

And I bloody well hope *I* won't, he thought as he walked out of the Channel 4 office.

Doctor Flores was as good as her word. At eight-thirty sharp she pulled up on the Octopussy Bungalow Resort sands in the university workboat. The kit was stowed aboard and they made their way a few kilometres around the coast to the power station. It was huge. A vast, yet incomplete roadway stretched towards the mainland. It was supported by a concrete lattice-work that could be seen plunging into the clear waters. At the pier head stood a white cubic building with simple aluminium-framed windows and a darkened glass-panelled door. It seemed very out of place on this island of thatched roofs and stilted huts.

They were expected. The director of the plant invited them warmly into his office. Coffee and hot rolls were served and they were given another presentation, this time in the form of a video. A wobbly helicopter shot was accompanied by a narration explaining that the project was planned in four phases. Four enormous fences that would link the three small stepping-stone-like islands between Luzon and

Samar. Phase one would connect Dalupiri to the mainland. This was partially complete and would act as a commercial demonstration for the rest of the project. The images cut to grainy pictures of a massive turbine. It was being installed in the gloom of a concrete chamber as the stilted voice of the commentary explained how the rotor shaft was made of alloyed steel covered with a corrosion resistant coating. The end credits were almost as long as the film; obviously the corporate video company wanted to make their mark. The director ejected the VHS tape from the antiquated machine.

'You might want to use some of these pictures in your film; I think the helicopter shots show the tidal channels very well.'

Nathalie accepted the tape. It was easier than telling the guy that: one, the pictures were non-broadcast quality and unusable; and two, even if he had commissioned the video he probably didn't own the copyright of the images.

'Thanks, it was very interesting. Now, would it be possible for someone to show us around for a quick recce, then we can work out what we could shoot this afternoon?'

'Sure. I've asked our chief engineer to give you a guided tour. Doctor Flores and I have a few items to discuss. We could meet up again here about twelve for lunch, how does that sound?'

'Perfect. Lead the way.'

They were all given hard hats and introduced to the chief engineer, a rather stern Canadian, who began by giving them a lecture on health and safety. Despite the ominous start, the tour was thorough. They scrambled into a powerful rib that was moored alongside the university workboat. Within minutes they were skimming along the water alongside the tidal fence.

'This is the best view of the underwater turbines,' shouted the engineer above the roar of the outboard motors. 'Some of the caisson structure is above the waterline but the turbines are stacked up to fifty metres down. The water is very clear here and you will be able to make out the ones near the surface. I'll cut the motor so that you can have a look.'

They leant over the rubber casing of the rib and peered into the deep emerald sea. The tops of the shimmering turbines could be made out just below the surface.

Nathalie cupped her hands and shaded her eyes. 'Great atmospheric shot,' she commented. 'But it won't exactly show how the thing works.' She turned to the engineer. 'Doctor Flores mentioned that you might be able to give us access to one of the turbines in a dry chamber. That would be really helpful if you could.'

The engineer looked into her beguiling eyes. 'I'm not sure,' he said. 'We're testing a turbine in there. There's an automatic timer that turns it on from time to time. There's very little room, it's dark and it could be dangerous.'

'Lighting is all about balance. If it's very dark, we need very little lighting to film, just a single 1K lamp. Perhaps we could pick a time when the turbine's switched off. It really would help show the scale of these things.'

The engineer looked around the boat. 'I'd need to be there with you, and it's not possible to get the four of us in the chamber.'

'That's okay. As long as you can get Charlie, a lamp and his camera in there with you I'll leave it up to him to get the shots.'

The discussion continued over lunch until the engineer reluctantly agreed and they scheduled in a slot towards the end of the day. The weather and tides were perfect for the exteriors. They would shoot the tidal fence from the water, then move onto the walkway, and film the turbine chamber last in case the light was fading. This all fitted in well with Doctor Flores and the director, who agreed to do their interviews in the power plant office the next day.

Spike was more helpful than he looked. He acted as clapper loader and sound recordist with consummate ease. The exteriors were soon in the can and, as agreed, the chief engineer led them towards the dry chamber. They stopped at a large metal manhole on the tidal fence walkway. *DANGER. AUTHORISED PERSONNEL ONLY* was inscribed on its surface. The engineer pulled out two metal levers and eased the heavy lid onto its side. Nathalie peered into the void. A long metal ladder descended into the darkness.

'I'll go down first and you can hand me the film boxes,' directed the Canadian brusquely. 'The cameraman can follow me. The rest of you stay here. We don't have much time because the generator is timed to come on soon.'

Charlie followed him down the ladder. The others waited, listening to the clanking metal and muffled voices. It seemed like an age before they reappeared. Nathalie took the camera while they cleared the last few steps.

'Any joy?'

'I think you'll like the shots; the turbine is bloody huge! I gelled the redhead and gave it a bit of orange glow. It looks amazing in that place. It's like a mediaeval dungeon down there.'

'Great, I can't wait to see the rushes. Okay, you guys, that's a wrap. It's getting dark and Tala has said they will give us supper here. I'm sure you're both starving.'

They ate with some of the tidal plant crew in the canteen. Platefuls of steaming goat stew in a rich tomato sauce. They were tired and hardly a word was spoken as they spooned in the piping hot mouthfuls. The chief engineer had to leave and said his goodbye, but suggested they stay for coffee. Tara Flores had promised to take them back to their bungalow within the next half-hour so they agreed to wait in the canteen for her. Nathalie looked out of the window; a row of neon lamps blinked along the tidal fence walkway. The silver streak dancing across the waters became suddenly obscured by a cloud passing across the moon. At least she had got her exteriors today. If the weather turned tomorrow she could always do the interviews inside. She turned to Charlie to ask where he thought it was best to set up the camera. But he was not there.

'Where's Charlie, in the men's room?'

Spike drained the remains of his coffee. 'No, I don't think so. He mentioned something about losing a "teddy". Must be some kind of mascot.'

'No, it's short for teddy's arsehole. It's that chamois bit that fits over his eyepiece. Which way did he go?'

Spike pointed to the door leading to the outside gangway.

'Oh shit, I hope he hasn't gone back to that chamber in the dark. Stay here and wait for Tala. I'll go and fetch him.'

Nathalie pushed at the exit bar and walked into the warm evening air. She strained her eyes to peer along the gangway. No sign of Charlie. Fearing the worst she made her way the hundred metres to the chamber hatch. She groaned as she found it wide open.

Bloody Charlie Linde! All over a scrap of chamois leather. Why couldn't he have waited until the morning? She made a cone out of two hands and shouted down the shaft. No reply. Her mobile phone was the only light she had. She switched it on and put her foot on the first rung.

'Charlie, are you down there?' Still no reply.

The shaft was deeper than she had imagined. There was a chill in the air, a contrast with the soup of the warm tropical atmosphere above. Even with the phone light she had to feel for each rung with her feet. After what seemed an age she descended into a concrete-lined cavern, about six feet by six feet. She pointed the phone to the far corner but the light was too weak to make out any definition. There seemed to be a dark void in the floor. She gingerly shuffled towards the edge and peered downwards. Her light caught the edge of a gigantic steel curved blade; evidently the top of the turbine. She listened for a moment and thought that she could hear a scuffling sound from below.

'Charlie, is that you, what the hell are you doing?'

The noise stopped abruptly.

'Charlie, if it's you, get out of there. It's not worth it for a stupid eyepiece cover.' Her voice echoed eerily around the chamber.

Going down on her hands and knees she tried to take a closer look. The bowed fin-like metal structure curled into the distance. At last she saw him, holding onto one of the blades.

'Are you okay? How in God's name did you get down there? Can you climb up on your own or do you want me to get some help?'

Charlie opened his mouth to reply but Nathalie didn't hear the answer. There was a terrible rumbling sound and a huge metal grate descended from the ceiling. She tried to pull back but it was too late. She was thrown to one side with a sharp blow to her head. The steel grill pinned one of her hands to the floor but she didn't feel it, she was out cold.

Charlie, in shock, tried to scramble up the turbine shaft. The vanes were only centimetres from the walls. Then another noise, more dreadful, filled the chamber. With a deafening, grinding sound the blades slowly began to turn.

Twenty-four

There was a working lunch in the boardroom of Bagatelle's Soho offices when the call came through. Stefanie was alone in Geoff's office. She held the telephone to her ear and the blood drained from her face. After listening, she tried to gather her normal efficient composure, and after some minutes asked a few succinct questions. She put down the receiver, checked a number on Geoff's computer and punched it in on the telephone keypad.

'This is the third time that the BBC has let us down,' said Geoff, munching on his sandwich. 'There's nothing wrong with the film director we've chosen.'

A lean bespectacled production manager shrugged her shoulders. 'It's that new commissioning editor of *Horizon*. Thinks just because it's a programme about astronomy he needs someone with a Ph.D.'

'Ph.D.?' The scriptwriter nearly spat out his mouthful of crisps. 'I'm writing the damn thing, I haven't even got one!'

'I'm obviously exaggerating, but ...'

Everyone's eyes turned away from the production manager to stare at Stefanie who, unlike her unflappable self, had crashed into the office.

'There's been a terrible accident,' she said, visibly shaking. 'It's Nathalie and Charlie in the Philippines.'

Geoff ordered everyone out of the boardroom. He helped Stefanie into a chair and calmly asked her what had happened. She began by describing the dry chamber turbine.

'Nathalie?' Geoff interrupted, 'Nathalie, is she all right?'

'I'm not sure. She's in a local hospital, concussion and a crushed hand.'

Geoff sat back in his chair. 'Doesn't sound too bad. By the way you came in, I thought ...'

'It's Charlie, he was actually in the turbine shaft. Sounds appalling.'

'Is he in the hospital with Nathalie?'

'No, they wouldn't describe his condition on the telephone but apparently he's in a terrible state. The power station helicopter has taken him to Manila.'

'We're insured; get an air ambulance to fly him back to London.'

'Already arranged, Geoff. It's the first thing I did.'

'See if you can get me that local hospital on the telephone, and then ring Nick. Ask him to cancel his flight to Japan.'

'No point, he's already in the air. Stay here, I'll get the hospital on the phone for you.'

Geoff waited in the boardroom for what seemed like an age before the telephone blinked. He grabbed the receiver and Stefanie told him that she had a Philippine doctor on a crackly line. The doctor was reassuring. He was keeping Nathalie in hospital overnight as a precaution. She had mild concussion after being knocked out by a metal grille. Unfortunately her left hand had become trapped and she had broken the proximal pharynx in the third and fourth fingers. He had put them in splints and had given her analgesics. She was resting at present but was attended by one of her film crew, someone called Spike. Geoff enquired about Charlie but the doctor had no knowledge of his condition as the patient hadn't been brought to the hospital but transported directly to Manila. Before Geoff could ask if he could be put through to Spike the telephone line went dead.

Spike sat on a rattan chair and stared at Nathalie's pale face on a rather grubby hospital pillow. The cream paintwork was chipped on the iron bedstead, which was one of twelve in the airless ward. Mosquito nets threw eerie shadows over the pale plaster walls. It was getting light outside and the noise of the crickets mingled with the coughs and groans that surrounded him. He hadn't slept for a single minute during the night, his mind turned over and over again, re-visualising the horrors he had experienced the evening before. He was still finishing his coffee in the power plant canteen when all hell had broken loose. Red lights and sirens everywhere. He had run with the engineers towards the turbine chamber. The rest was a bit of a haze. A rescue guy had climbed down the hatch and retrieved the unconscious Nathalie but it took a while before they could get at Charlie. Because of the obstruction the emergency cut-out had caused the machinery to stop but not before taking off Charlie's arm and half of his face. After the emergency crew had brought what was left of him to the surface it hadn't take long for the helicopter to airlift him off the walkway. Spike was still in shock and glad that Nathalie had not seen it. She had recovered half an hour later but was in such a dazed state that no one had yet told her what had happened. Now here he was, six o'clock in the morning, keeping vigil. The phone vibrated in his pocket. He took it out to look at the illuminated screen; an unknown number. He pressed the green key and held the phone to his ear.

'Yeah, Spike here.'

The voice on the end of the telephone was as clear as if the man had been in the next room.

'Is that the sound recordist on Nathalie Thompson's shoot?'

'You could say that, who's asking?'

'Geoff Sykes, executive producer on the film. How is she?'

'She's been in an accident.'

'I know that. Can't get through to the hospital. It's taken hell and high water to get hold of your number. How is she?'

'Asleep. I'm with her now.'

'Where are you?'

'In the ward. They're keeping her in overnight. The doctor says she should be okay, though.'

'Thank God for that! Are *you* okay? What exactly happened?' Spike told Geoff that he was fine and as much as he could about the accident. Charlie had returned to the turbine room to look for some missing equipment. Nathalie had followed him and a timer had started the machinery. A security grille had knocked her out and the turbine was about to make mincemeat of Charlie when a safety mechanism had kicked in. He tried not to be too graphic about the injuries but Geoff had already had a report from Manila. An air ambulance was flying Charlie back to the UK as they were speaking. He was in the best possible hands.

'Spike, you sound a caring sort of guy. Can you do me a favour?'

'Sure.'

'Tomorrow, talk to the doctors for me; find out if Nathalie is really okay. I mean really okay, still capable of working.'

'I can do that.'

'I want you to ring me. If she is not fine we'll fly her back. Don't let her make the decision; she'll want to carry on anyway.'

Nathalie stirred in the bed next to Spike. He put the phone closer to his mouth and whispered into it. 'And if the doctors say she's okay?'

'Get her to ring me, say I want her to go to Japan. A colleague of hers, Nick Coburn, will be there waiting for her. And Spike …?'

'Yeah?'

'If she is okay, are you available to fly there with her? We will need a soundman.'

The main tower of the Shinagawa Prince Hotel looked like a vast domino on its end. In the gloom of mid-morning Tokyo it could have been a double hundred rather than a double six as the windows blinked their lights. Anonymous, multi-storeyed and clean, just as Nick Coburn preferred. He had checked in earlier and was returning after a brief stroll around the area to get his bearings. The girl in the lobby passed him his card key as he asked for a coffee to be sent to his room. He tucked the newly purchased cheap laptop under his arm and made for the elevator. Thirty storeys later and he was logging into the hotel's WiFi in his bland standard double room overlooking the heart of the city. He had heard the news about the accident on his arrival at the airport and was tempted to try and contact Nathalie. But Geoff had told him that everything was under control and that he should concentrate on locating contacts and setting up a shoot in Japan. As soon as there was any more news he would be the first to know. He rechecked his mobile just to be sure and seeing no message started to concentrate on the job in hand. The small encrypted memory stick that he carried with him contained most of the links that he required. He logged into the Imagica site, one of the most established post-production houses in Japan. Geoff had asked him to find a 16mm cameraman with camera and stock, not so easy in today's world of digital video. A dying art, Geoff had said. He also needed the developing laboratory to process the exposed film stock that Nathalie was carrying with her. If she was fit to carry on then she would be asked to take the stock to Japan. Geoff was worried that the rolls of negative had been travelling through X-rays and heat for too long and that it was time to get them safely back to London. Nick found the number and prayed that they would speak English. He needn't have worried. The man at reception was not only bilingual but invited him for a tour of their offices. Developing film, no problem. Finding a documentary film cameraman with good English also no problem. Nick made an appointment for mid-afternoon and ticked that one off his list. Now for Ocean Tech and Marine Corps … His phone rang.

'Geoff, must be important, what time is it there?'

'Half past two, in the morning that is. Just sorting out this bloody mess.'

'Nathalie?'

'She's fine, just spoken to her. Her hand's a bit of a mess but the doctor's given her the all-clear. I've told her to stay where she is today and get a flight to Tokyo via Manila tomorrow morning your time.'

'You sure she's okay?'

'I told you, she's fine. Got a sound guy called Spike with her, helping out with the arrangements.'

'Arrangements?'

'Yeah, getting the flights, handling the film stock, and packing up Charlie's gear so it can be couriered to London. And talking about Charlie, Nathalie knows he's being flown back but hasn't been told the extent of his injuries. Let's keep it like that.'

Nick shook his head into the phone.

'Nick?'

'Yeah.'

'Did you get that?'

'Shouldn't we tell her?'

'No point in worrying her, there's nothing more anyone else can do. Anyway, how are your arrangements going?'

'Good, so far. Got someone who will develop the stock and, with a bit of luck, a cameraman who shoots film.'

'At bloody last, a country with a real sense of art. If he shoots film there's a strong chance he'll be good. None of this video "wham, bam, thank you ma'am" stuff. And Ocean Tech and Marine Corps?'

'Give me a chance Geoff. Just been in the country a few hours. About to get hold of them when I'm interrupted by this English guy eulogising about out-of-date production techniques.'

'Fuck off, Coburn! Let me do my business and you get on with yours; frightening these engineer bastards and getting them to tell us what the hell is going on in our oceans.'

'Think you need to get your head down, Geoff. A bit of rest might make you in a better mood.'

'I'm going, and Nick ...'

Nick turned his gaze to the ceiling, 'Yes, Geoff?'

'Nathalie, look after her.'

Two hours later and Nick had discovered the mystery about the missing Mr Oyama. One of the staff at Ocean Tech's headquarters had told him in broken English that Oyama was on sick leave and the office had shut down temporarily for a short holiday break. Nick thought this a strange coincidence and highly unlikely but pursued the difficult conversation and managed to persuade the company to entertain a short visit from Bagatelle's film crew. An essential part of your corporate ocean film, Nick had insisted. An arrangement was made for the afternoon of the next day. He had less luck with Marine Corps. An answerphone kept telling him that they would call back but they never did. His earlier research had indicated that Marine Corps' head offices were in the coastal town of Port Sajiama. He rechecked the address on Google maps and made some enquiries on how to get there. It was a little far for a taxi and the best bet seemed to be by rail. He tried to book tickets on the internet but the website was impenetrable, even using the British flag symbol to obtain a translation. By now he was getting hungry so he decided to make some enquiries at the hotel reception on his way out to a nearby restaurant that he had seen earlier. He was in luck; the receptionist had a relative on the coast and had made the journey many times. Within minutes she had printed out four open return tickets for him. The number of tickets reminded him that Nathalie and Spike would need accommodation. He booked two single rooms, on the same floor as his, for the next three nights. Geoff had said Nathalie would arrive the next morning but he hadn't stated a time. At least he would have rooms for them and their kit, whatever hour they arrived.

The restaurant was as good as it looked from the exterior. Colourful photographs of food were displayed in the window. He ordered miso soup, followed by sukiyaki. A wide-eyed girl in tight jeans and T-shirt cooked and served him the beef, vegetables and tofu at the table. He looked around; none of the waitresses were wearing traditional costumes and the clientele were all obviously from local businesses. He was pleased with himself for not landing in a tourist site but almost regretted it when it came to the dessert. None of the staff spoke English. They had managed to interpret his pronunciation of sukiyaki but when he tried to order something sweet there was nothing but confusion. He ended up with a savoury sushi dish, paid the bill with a credit card and left with the cute smiling waitress bowing him to the door.

Imagica Studios were impressive. Only fifteen minutes by taxi from the hotel, Nick arrived a little early. The receptionist brought him a cup of jasmine tea and said that a senior staff member would be down in a few minutes. He was as good as his word, and Nick was given a guided tour around the digital suites and film post-production facilities. Operators gazed intently at huge television monitors displaying everything from 3-D animation to live-action car chases. Nick mentioned again about the processing of 16mm film. No problem. Much less throughput than there used to be but they still had the facilities to develop and print. If required, they could ship the developed negative and a one light print to London by secure courier. Nick had no idea what a 'one light print' was so he gave them Geoff's personal e-mail and asked them to put all the details in writing.

'Mr Coburn?' An accented voice came from behind them.

Nick turned around to see a handsome young Japanese man. He was well-dressed and tall for his race.

The Imagica staff member introduced him. 'This is Hiro, Hiro Nakamura, one of our top freelance documentary cameramen. He has credits for NHK, Discovery Channel and the BBC. If you want, we can put up his showreel.'

'Hi Hiro, have you got a 16mm camera?'

Hiro shook Nick's hand. 'Yes, an Arri sixteen. She's quite old but she hasn't let me down yet.'

'You speak impeccable English, you shoot film and, if you're free in the next three days, you're hired. Never look a gift horse, that's what I say.'

Hiro looked confused. 'I certainly am free but what is a gift horse?'

'It's something you don't look in the mouth,' said Nick, laughing. 'Forget it, stupid English idiom. Means I'm lucky to have found you, if you're happy to work for us, that is.'

'Sure,' said Hiro, still looking a little confused. 'When would you like me to start?'

They spent the next half-hour discussing equipment, film stock, rates and locations. Nick explained that he knew little about the filming process and that the director and soundman were flying in the next day. What he did know was that they would be filming some sensitive interviews in a couple of offices. Hiro said that he was used to having a sparks but if the sets were not too complicated he would bring along a couple of lamps. When Nick told him about the Ocean Tech location in Tokyo he seemed a little surprised.

'It's a bit of a rough area; rundown warehouses, that sort of thing. Doesn't sound the sort of location for a big maritime outfit.'

'The more I hear about Ocean Tech, the more it fits,' said Nick. 'This thing could get a little heavy; are you up for it?'

'Sounds interesting. I was worried it could be a corporate self-admiring job. Don't worry, I've filmed some documentaries about the Gokudo. Some of my best work.'

'I hope it won't get that bad, just some evasive guys in a two-bit ocean engineering company. All the same, I smell a bit of a rat. I just want you to be prepared.'

'My camera is good at smelling rats,' said Hiro with a grin. 'If there is one I am sure we can sniff it out.'

Twenty-five

It was mid-morning when the taxi pulled up at the Shinagawa Prince Hotel. Nathalie climbed out of the cab to be met by a warm bear hug from Nick Coburn. She winced slightly as he touched her wounded left hand.

'Sorry, a bit clumsy. How are you?'

'Only a flesh wound,' she smiled wistfully. 'Here, meet Spike, our soundman, medical orderly and everything else.' Nick shook hands with Spike and helped him take their luggage out of the taxi.

'Thanks,' said Spike, pushing the hotel trolley into the lobby, 'The Imagica courier collected the exposed stock at the airport. Said that they would ship the agreed order to Bagatelle by the end of the week. Here's the receipt.' Nick took the piece of paper and put it in his wallet.

'Great, I'll text Geoff to confirm that everything is okay. Now I expect you two would like to take a shower and have a bite to eat.'

The hotel had about a dozen restaurants in its multiple tower blocks, but today was about planning rather than eating so they met for a light lunch in the Cafe 24 restaurant, near the base of the East Tower. There were few people about and plenty of space so they pushed a couple of tables together and laid out their paperwork.

'Before we start,' began Nathalie, 'how's Charlie?'

'No more news, I'm afraid, Nathalie,' replied Nick, avoiding her eyes. 'The air ambulance got him back to London. He's in the best place.'

'That's what everybody says when it's pretty serious. It *is* serious, isn't it?'

Nick shrugged his shoulders, 'So I hear but I guess all we can do is wait and hope for the best.'

During the short interchange Spike avoided getting involved by asking the waiter for some drinks. Nathalie sensed the awkward atmosphere and realising she wasn't going to get any more information, turned to stare at the map in front of her.

'Just either of you tell me the first bit of news you get, you promise me that?'

'Of course, Nathalie, but in the meantime there's nothing else we can do. You sure you're up for this? Geoff says he will fly you back any time you want.'

Nathalie shook her head. 'No, I'm fine. What do they say about falling off a horse? If you don't get back on immediately … I just want to be kept in the loop. Any news and I want to know it first, that's all.'

She shook off Nick's arm and asked him what plans had been put in place. Nick told her about Ocean Tech and the new cameraman, Hiro. He sounded the real deal and would be picking them up in his four-by-four within the next hour. Time was short so Nick thought it best for Nathalie to brief him on the drive to the location. What they had to do now was to eat and work out what they needed from the Ocean Tech interview.

'I don't go along with all this Oyama sick leave and the company holiday,' said Nick, munching on the burger the waiter had just put in front of him. 'I've talked to Geoff and he's not worried about upsetting his sponsor. He really wants to get to the bottom of all this. The guys in their office seem a bit timid and I've told them we just want to interview them for the corporate film, so don't frighten them off by going in too hard at the …' Nick stopped as he saw Nathalie's eyes boring into him. 'Okay, okay, sorry. You know your job; just trying to give you the background.'

Nathalie had gathered herself since talking about Charlie and now took over the meeting, scribbling down some notes while asking Nick a few probing questions. She then turned to Spike and discussed how to mic up these guys. The more unobtrusive they were, the more likely they were to catch slip-ups on camera.

'The innocent corporate female film director asking lots of nice, cosy questions, just before she turns into Mr Hyde, gets them every time,' said Nathalie, closing her notebook.

Hiro was as good as his word and turned up on time in his Toyota four-by-four. From the way he introduced himself and the gear he had with him Nathalie could tell that he was a seasoned pro. She went through the objectives of the shoot. A simple interview with Ocean Tech staff but, if he saw anything interesting or out of place, he should give her a nod and shoot a few surreptitious feet of film. Looking out of the window she noticed that the smart skyscrapers and office blocks were giving way to lower-rise shanty buildings. Huge storage buildings with rusty corrugated iron roofs began to line the litter-strewn highway. They were nearing one of the container docks.

'We are a few blocks away now,' said Hiro. 'The last time I was in this district someone spiked my tyres.' He glanced at Nathalie. 'If you can be spared, Nick, would you mind staying with the Toyota?'

'Yes, once he's done the introductions I'm sure we can release him to be a minder. That's your forté, isn't it, Nick? Better than this namby-pamby filming stuff.' Nick smiled, pleased to see that Nathalie, if not quite her old self, was playing the part. He gave her a mock salute. 'You're the boss.'

They pulled up at a grimy grey building with featureless metal-framed windows. Nick jumped out and took a closer look at the company nameplates which were screwed next to a pair of aluminium doors. Most of them were in Japanese but a few had English names under the script. Kiko Foodstuffs, Hisan Metallurgy and there, at the bottom, Ocean Tech. He pressed the buzzer and the door immediately clicked open. The shabby entrance space contained an old elevator. It didn't look safe but fortunately to one side was a battered door with a small wire glassed window. On it were the newly painted words 'Ocean Tech'. There was no need to knock as it was opened promptly to reveal a suited Japanese gentleman who placed his hands together and bowed in greeting.

'Mr Nicholas Coburn, welcome to our humble offices. I am afraid Mr Oyama is still unwell but we will do what we can to assist you. Please come in.'

Nick nodded in return and entered the offices – open-plan, with a number of screens obscuring workstations. There were about five female secretaries typing away furiously at computers. None of them looked up as Nick and the film crew followed their host through the aisles towards a prefabricated room that protruded into the soulless office space. Once more there was no need to knock as the door opened before they reached it. It was almost as if this was choreographed, Nathalie thought. The man who opened the door introduced himself as Mr Kobe and invited them to sit at the prearranged chairs that were placed in an arc in front of his desk. His companion slipped out of the office and closed the door quietly behind him. Mr Kobe apologised again for the absent Mr Oyama and said that the company had put him forward as a spokesperson for the film. He added that he was honoured and pleased to take part but Nathalie gleaned from his expression that this couldn't be further from the truth. After the preliminaries and the compulsory cups of tea Nick suggested that he leave them to it while he went back to the vehicle. He didn't attempt to explain the reason why.

'I'll come with you,' said Hiro. 'Just need a few more bits of kit. Nathalie, if it's okay with you, I'll leave you and Spike to arrange the interview set up. I think we need to ND those windows; the light will be coming in hard in the next hour or two. I've got some gel in the Toyota.'

Nathalie nodded her approval and asked Spike to set up the stands for the sound and lights. It was evident that Mr Kobe had never encountered a film crew before and he spent the time nervously shuffling around the room, getting in the way. Hiro seemed to take his time getting the gel from the four-by-four so the room was practically rigged when he returned. It didn't take him long to gel the windows though and within minutes the camera was on the tripod and ready to roll. Mr Kobe sat nervously behind his desk as Nathalie explained to him that he should try not to look into the camera and just chat to her as if they were alone in the room. She had done a lot of interviews but never with someone so jumpy as Mr Kobe. He shifted in his chair, shuffled papers on his desk and, no matter how many times she gently chided him, kept glancing into the camera lens. She began by asking some simple noncontroversial questions about why Ocean Tech was making a film on alternative energy. Was it to do with climate change, reducing oil resources or just an interest in pushing out the boundaries in the oceans? The problem was that Mr Kobe didn't seem to have any answers to these questions; he just kept repeating the same parroted lines. Ocean Tech was proud to sponsor such a film, a small company with high ambition, the joy of ocean exploration. When pushed on what this high ambition was, all he could muster was how proud they were to have it. This wasn't going as Nathalie had planned. The idea was to get him relaxed on comfortable territory and then stick the knife regarding conspiracy and sabotage. But Mr Kobe didn't seem to have any comfortable territory; perhaps it was just cultural and linguistic difficulties. She was just about to give up when she noticed one of the documents that he was nervously fingering in one hand. She nodded furtively to Hiro, who lightly tipped down the lens and rotated the zoom bar.

Nathalie distracted her interviewee by asking a question. 'Mr Kobe, I see that your company also has an interest in ocean mining. Isn't that a research document that you have there?'

Mr Kobe dropped the papers he was handling as if they were hot coals.

Nathalie continued. 'When we were in the Pacific, filming a wave power station, we had the opportunity to get some footage on a deep-sea mining vessel. They were Japanese. I'm sure we could incorporate these shots into the film somehow if Ocean Tech has an interest in this area.'

Hiro had now repositioned the camera to take a close-up of Mr Kobe's reddening face. He looked around the room as if searching for some assistance but of course there was no-one there except the film crew. He started to play for time.

'Sorry, my English is not very good. I do not understand your question.'

Oh yes, you do, thought Nathalie. Strange that you have spoken to us in perfect English so far. Perhaps she had struck a nerve. She rephrased her question.

'Ocean mining, is it of interest to Ocean Tech? We have some film that you could use in your programme.'

'Ocean mining, yes. No, we are interested in ocean energy.'

'But you also seem to have some interest in ocean mining. I think that is a very recent paper, yes?'

Mr Kobe looked down at his desk and seemed surprised to find the papers on it. 'This is not my office or my paper. You will have to ask Mr Oyama.'

'But I thought Mr Oyama had made you spokesperson for this interview?' Nathalie paused and sat back to make the silence even more uncomfortable.

Mr Kobe tried to gather himself. 'Ocean Tech are honoured to make a film on ocean energy. We hope that our ambitions can be achieved by hard work and investigation.'

'Yes, but do you have any ambitions regarding ocean mining?' persisted Nathalie, putting her head to one side and smiling invitingly.

Mr Kobe seemed to lose it. He looked at his watch and stood up, almost hitting his head on the sound boom. 'I'm afraid that our time is up. We are an ocean company, Miss Thompson. We have many papers on ocean affairs in the office. This does not mean to say that we have any ambitions regarding them. I wish you well in the completion of our small film. If you have any further questions I am sure Mr Oyama will answer them when he returns.'

The interview was over. Nathalie accepted the situation and told Hiro to cut. She shook Mr Kobe by the hand and told him that she hoped he would be happy with the final film. The awkwardness in the air remained while they struck the equipment and carried it back to the Toyota.

'Any joy?' asked Nick cheerfully.

'Maybe,' replied Nathalie.

'Sounds enigmatic.'

'It is,' she said.

The train was fast. Hiro had offered to take the Toyota, but as the parking was known to be bad and Nick had already bought the tickets, they were all happy to go by rail. Marine Corps still hadn't answered their calls so they had decided to wing it. They had made an early start, hoping to arrive mid-morning and catch them unawares. Port Sajima is a small fishing port, with restaurants attached to the markets, which will prepare the fresh fish or cook it in front of you. Hiro told them that if Marine Corps weren't at home at least they would have one of the best fish lunches they had ever tasted. They took two taxis for the short hop from the station to the seafront address that Nick had obtained from his research. The cab drivers looked a little taken aback by the metal boxes of kit and tried to charge extra for luggage but Hiro was having none of it. He thrust a wad of yen into their hands and told them that if they stopped arguing they would be used for the return journey. The drivers reluctantly agreed and handed over their cards with telephone numbers.

After their experience the day before they looked out for a derelict building but to their surprise the Marine Corps offices were as far from the Ocean Tech offices as could be imagined. The glass revolving door was set in a smart stainless steel office front. Either side were manicured shrubs in refined oriental pots. Nick went up to a small television screen set into one side and pressed the intercom button. After a few seconds a western face appeared on the screen and an American voice came out of the speaker.

'Hi, Marine Corps, how can I help you?'

Nick noticed that above the screen was the small lens of a camera. He looked into it and smiled. 'Hi, Nick Coburn here. I work for the UK film company Bagatelle Productions. We're making a film on ocean resources and hear you guys are experts in the field. Is there someone there who could chat to us for a minute? I did ring to make an appointment but I'm afraid I couldn't get through.'

'Sorry about that, we've been having problems with our telephone lines. Looks like you've come a long way. I'll try to see if there is someone free to talk to you.'

The screen went blank and Nick explained the situation to Nathalie. 'So far, so good. I've not told them that I have a television crew with me. They might balk at that so perhaps you should hold back while I suss out the situation.'

But he needn't have worried. The guy on the screen came to the door to meet them and didn't seem at all fazed to see a full film crew and their equipment standing on the seafront. They were ushered into the spacious lobby to sign the visitors' book and then made their way in the elevator to the fourth floor.

'You're in luck,' said their young escort. 'The CEO is free at the moment and said that he would meet with you.'

Once he discovered that Bagatelle were making a programme on ocean resources that would be televised the CEO could not have been more welcoming. Within the hour they were fully rigged in the boardroom, with Mr Marine Corps himself sitting in the interview chair. Nathalie began in the time-old way with a sound check.

'Before we start, could you just tell us your name and what you had for breakfast.'

The CEO had obviously been filmed before because he answered without hesitation and in perfect English. 'My name is Mr Asai and this morning I had miso soup, boiled rice and some lightly broiled fish.'

Nathalie noticed the word 'broiled' rather than 'grilled', also the slight accent, suggesting an American university education.

The interview started well. Mr Asai was obviously keen to advertise Marine Corps' expertise in ocean engineering. He explained that their franchise was a world leader in the exciting new world of ocean resource development, from power stations to deep sea exploration. He was articulate, comfortable and amenable. Nathalie decided it was time to become Mr Hyde.

'You're obviously proud of your expertise and successes but what do you feel about the increasing number of . . ., she paused, 'I can only call them disasters at sea, where your company is involved?'

Mr Asai remained calm. 'Would you like to elucidate?'

'As you may know we have been filming ocean energy projects around the world and there seems, what shall I say? more than a coincidence of catastrophes.'

'Such as?'

There was no need for Nathalie to look down at her notes. 'One, the sinking of the *IOD Revolution* drilling ship; two, the loss of the sonar, Lone Ranger, in the seas surrounding Hawaii; three, the death of Professor Lake in a submersible involved in an ocean thermal energy project; four, the near-loss of a critical component of a Majuro wave power station; and last, but not least,' a tear came to Nathalie's eyes as she recalled Charlie's predicament, 'a terrible incident in the Philippines involving a tidal power turbine.'

Mr Asai waited patiently for Nathalie to collect herself before composing his reply.

'We have heard of some of these incidents and I must agree that many of the projects employed some of our franchise members of staff. We have investigated them thoroughly and are as upset and mystified as you appear to be, Miss Thompson. To date, at no point can we find any evidence of negligence by any Marine Corps employee. However, we continue to reappraise our health and safety procedures. Until this year we had an unblemished record and we trust that this series of accidents were down to pure bad fortune. Ocean engineering is a dangerous occupation.'

'Damned right it is!' snapped Nathalie angrily. 'My cameraman is fighting for his life right now because of your Philippine ocean engineering.'

Mr Asai lent forward, almost reaching out his hand in sympathy. 'I'm extremely sorry to hear that, Miss Thompson, but I have to tell you that the Philippine tidal plant has never employed any person from Marine Corps.'

Twenty-six

The scheduled Virgin flight left Tokyo at a very respectable time. They said their goodbyes to Spike over breakfast and waited for Hiro, who had insisted on taking them to the airport. Nathalie had called the London Hospital at least half a dozen times since they wrapped at Marine Corps, but still there was no more news on Charlie. 'In intensive care, stable, but no improvement', was all she could get out of them. It felt strange, almost naked, getting into the Toyota land cruiser without any film gear. Nathalie sat in the front while Nick stretched his legs in the back.

'Strange set up, that Ocean Tech outfit,' said Hiro, not taking his eyes off the road.

'You could say that,' replied Nathalie. 'Sorry we couldn't get more out of him, he was obviously just a stooge.'

'Not the only one.'

'Meaning?'

'The secretaries. When I was getting the ND gel, I asked one of them how long she had worked there.'

'And?'

'Just that morning. All of them, hired from a temp agency. Told to copy-type from a book.'

Nathalie stared at the dull, unlit neon signs on the buildings alongside. 'It's beginning to make sense.'

'More to you than to me. I've enjoyed working with you; sorry we couldn't shoot more slates.'

'Likewise. Two inconclusive interviews. I expect you are used to more exciting stuff.'

'From what you've told me you could have a good programme. Anything else on the horizon in Japan, let me know. There aren't many people left shooting film.'

'Yeah, I expect Geoff will die using celluloid. I like it too but you have to admit that digital has come a long way.'

'True, but it's lost a lot of camaraderie. Camera assistants, clapper loaders, sound separate from the picture. Cutting rooms used to be a social event. Now it's darkened rooms full of people staring at computer screens.'

It had been a regular discussion between film crews, film versus video. Probably one of the last, thought Nathalie. In years to come film-makers would not have heard of jargon such as 'one light print' or 'an optical'. She ought to enjoy it while it lasted.

'Here we are, departures on the right,' said Hiro suddenly. And moments later they were left, baggage on trolley, the land cruiser disappearing into the traffic.

'Nice guy,' observed Nick.

'Yeah,' said Nathalie wistfully. 'Only known him a few days and it feels like saying goodbye to an old friend.'

Heathrow was grey, dull and cold. Quite a contrast to Nathalie's recent landings. It was four in the afternoon by the time they collected their bags from the carousel. The flight had been over twelve hours so both of them were tired and uncommunicative. Nick switched his mobile on and found a text from Bagatelle. It told him that there would be cabs waiting for them at the arrivals' rank. One would take him to Bagatelle for a debrief and the other would take Nathalie to a private hospital for a check-up.

'Check-up?'

'That's what it says.'

'I'm knackered. What do I want a check-up for?'

'I suppose Geoff's worried about you, you know. Your hand. Being knocked out.'

'Geoff worried? Insurance demand more like it.'

Nick snorted. 'You're probably right. Best do as he says, though. He won't want you falling over in the cutting room without the right cover.'

Nathalie looked at her splinted left hand. Two fingers strapped together. It was sore, yes, but it hadn't given her much trouble in the last couple of days. 'Typical Sykes. I've just done a non-stop round-the-world trip for him and instead of letting me have a shower and chill out in my own place he wants me to go to a bloody hospital.'

'You think you've got it bad. I've got the short straw – a meeting with him, whiteboard and all. I expect he'll want enough information to fill a final script. I don't think we've got that, do you? More questions than answers.'

'Maybe,' said Nathalie, throwing her bag into the taxi. 'Got a nagging feeling about this one. I think we could be nearly there.'

The hospital was a small smart private one on the edge of Wimbledon Common. She was greeted like a guest at an hotel and offered coffee and biscuits before her appointments. The first was with a female orthopaedic surgeon not much older than Nathalie, who sent her for an X-ray and re-dressed her left hand.

'They did a good job, should heal up quite nicely. I'll write a report and send it to your GP. Would you like any more painkillers?'

Nathalie declined and was sent to her next appointment, an older doctor who checked out her balance and verbal reasoning. She seemed to pass with flying colours for he wrote out a letter for her and told her to carry on as normal but to go to her GP if she had any headaches or dizziness. Nathalie thanked him and ordered a cab to her Fulham flat. Who knows what state it would be in; she hadn't been there for weeks. But she needn't have worried. The flat was cold and damp but otherwise in much the same condition as she had left it. She put the immersion heater on, made herself a cup of black instant coffee and telephoned the hospital where Charlie was. They were still reticent about giving her much information but, when she lied and said that she was his sister, they said that it might be possible for her to visit the intensive care ward the next morning. After a hot bath and a takeaway pizza she crawled between the cold sheets of her hastily made bed and fell into a dreamless sleep.

Geoff Sykes was in a bad mood. The developed rushes were late coming from the airport and Nick Coburn had told him that all they had got from the shoot in Japan was a couple of crappy interviews. Not a lot for his money so far. He snapped at Stefanie to chase the courier and to tell the editor not to bother going into the cutting room before lunchtime.

Stefanie handed him his morning cup of espresso. 'I've already told Bob that he won't get the film before two o'clock. He says that's fine, he has to get a few bits and pieces for the edit anyway. As for the courier, it's not their fault the film is being held up in customs.'

'Bloody well get on to customs then. I've hired that cutting room for the week; every minute it's being unused it's costing us money.'

Stefanie and Geoff knew very well that Her Majesty's Customs could not, and would not, be hurried but she kept him happy by saying that she would see how things were progressing.

Geoff grunted. 'And Nathalie, where is she at the moment?'

'I think she's gone to the hospital, trying to see Charlie.'

'Oh, shit! I was worried about that. I didn't think they'd let her see him, not being a relative and all that.'

'Is he really that bad?'

'And the rest. I don't want her getting traumatised when she's just about to start an edit.'

'You don't mean that.'

'About messing up the edit, no. But it won't be any good for her, seeing the state he's in.'

Geoff was right, Nathalie felt sick when she saw Charlie through the window of the ICU unit. He was surrounded by tubes and ventilator machinery. Nothing unexpected there but she could hardly see his face. The unbandaged section was mutilated beyond description and it was evident that he had lost his right arm. The nurse who was with her put her hand on Nathalie's shoulder.

'Are you sure you want to go in there, dear? He's still drifting in and out of consciousness. You shouldn't be upset if he can't talk to you.'

Nathalie nodded.

'Okay then, I'll come in with you. Two minutes only, all right?' She nodded again and the nurse led her into the unit. Charlie's left arm was resting on top of the sheets and Nathalie gently took his hand.

'Charlie, it's me, Nathalie.'

Charlie didn't move. His only visible swollen eye-lid remained closed. Nathalie stroked his hand and gently whispered in his ear. 'You silly man; all over a stupid missing eyepiece cover.' Tears fell down her cheeks. 'I would have bought you a dozen when we got back.' The rhythmic pump of the ventilator filled the room.

'You'll be pleased to hear we've got the rushes back from the Far East. Can't wait to see them. I'll come in tomorrow to let you know what they're like.'

The nurse touched her arm to indicate that it was time to go. Nathalie leaned over to kiss Charlie on his exposed cheek. She pulled back with a start when his lips opened and he made a sound. She bent forward again to see if she could hear what he was saying. There were some gurgling noises but between them she thought she could work out a few words.

'What was that, Charlie, can you hear me?' There was no response. She squeezed his hand tenderly but he had stopped moving. The nurse gently guided her out of the ICU unit.

'That's enough for today, dear, come in tomorrow afternoon. I'll make sure I'm here.'

'Did you hear him? What he said?'

'No, dear. They do that sometimes, just a few noises now and again.'

'I'm sure I heard something, something like, "Lake, I didn't dream it." What could that mean?'

'I don't know, dear. You're obviously upset about seeing your brother. Why don't you go down to the cafe and have a cup of tea?' The word 'brother' reminded Nathalie that she had come under false pretences. She thanked the nurse and thought it best if she feigned making for the coffee shop. She followed the signs part of the way and then turned towards the exit and phoned for a cab.

The cutting room was in Wardour Street. Three flights up, a dingy concrete staircase led to a corridor of edit suites for dry-hire; dry-hire meaning that you paid to rent the room and the equipment but brought your own editor in. Most of the rooms contained 'Avids', or similar branded computerised editing machines, but two of them housed some of the remaining celluloid editing equipment in London. Nathalie knocked on the door and opened it to find Bob, one of Bagatelle's freelance film editors, sitting at the 16mm Steenbeck.

'Hi, good to see you again. Isn't it great to get back to cutting film?' said Bob, patting the blue editing table.

'Yeah, good to see you too; must have been at least eighteen months. Have the rushes come in?'

'About half an hour ago. I've been through the sheets and started syncing them up.' He handed Nathalie a couple of Manila folders. 'Geoff's left you some storyline stuff. Asked you to put the Ocean Tech film on one side for now and concentrate on the investigative documentary. Told me that you would know what he meant.'

'Anything else?'

'Yeah, admitted that the storyline was a bit vague at the moment. Said that the two of us would have to come up with a strong narrative pretty quickly.'

'Pretty quickly?'

'I gather that he has a meeting with Channel 4 to show some rough-cuts in a fortnight's time. Sounds like we've got our work cut out.'

Nathalie put the Ocean Tech project files to one side and flicked through the notes Geoff had made on the documentary. It was titled rather grandly 'Oceans on Fire'. Sounded like a lot to live up to.

'What's the print like?'

'Not seen a lot yet but what I have looks pretty good. Nice framing, good exposure, great locations.' Nathalie breathed a sigh of relief. If the pictures were good then they stood a chance. She already had an idea of how to start. While Bob continued syncing she flipped open her laptop and began typing.

VISION:	*NARRATION:*
Newsreel of the burning wreck of a drilling ship. Shots of the deep sea sonar slipping into the ocean, and a submersible containing a dead man being winched out of a harbour.	*Tragic accidents or sabotage? Why is it that there have been so many disasters at sea? And who are the winners and the losers if the oceans continue to be set on fire?*

Because of their late start Bob and Nathalie worked long into the evening. Yards and yards of film and audiotape hung in the film bins and Bob had managed to sync nearly a dozen rolls of film with the sound tapes. Nathalie had made good progress with her draft script and was itching to see some of the material. At ten o'clock she snapped shut her computer and looked over Bob's shoulders at the small Steenbeck screen.

'Have you done the Hawaiian OTEC shoot yet?'

'OTEC?'

'Ocean Thermal Energy Conversion plant. It's where we filmed those gruesome scenes of a dead guy being hauled out of the water. I was thinking of using it in the opening scene.'

'That submarine thing? Yes, great shots. A bit horrific, though.'

'That's the whole point, good TV. I just need to pop out to the loo. Can you put the roll up for me? Then we'll call it a day.'

Bob checked his charts and reached for a can on the shelf. He took out the roll of film, placed it on one of the Steenbeck plates and threaded one end through the viewing prism. The picture had just begun to flicker on the small screen when Nathalie re-entered the room.

'Terrible smell in there; I think the cleaner's overdone it with the Domestos. Okay, spin through, let's take a look.'

She was a bit disappointed with the first few feet of film. It was the Bernard Lake interview. There he was, sitting stiffly in his office chair, answering Nathalie's off-mic questions in dull monotones. He looked rather weird in those odd yellow overalls. Nathalie was about to ask Bob to spin through to the accident when a thought suddenly struck her.

'Bob, is there anywhere we can see these shots full screen?'

'What now?'

'Yes, there's something that is bothering me.'

'Well, there's a viewing theatre downstairs. It's nearly half past ten. It's bound to be free at the moment. Neither of us has eaten; why don't you grab a takeaway and I'll lace up the roll in the projector?'

'Good man,' said Nathalie. 'Indian or Chinese?'

Twenty minutes later the two of them were tucking into their Szechuan prawns, sitting in the back row of the small viewing theatre. The pictures looked brighter and more vivid on the big screen. They reached the part where Bernard Lake stood up between takes to have a drink.

'Bob, rewind and stop it there.' Bob looked confused. It was a poorly framed shot only exposed because the cameraman hadn't cut soon enough after the take.

'I know it's not usable, I just want to look at something in a bit more detail.'

Bob shrugged, put his carton and chopsticks on the adjacent seat and walked round to the small projection room.

'There, a couple of frames forward and freeze it there.' shouted Nathalie, walking down the aisle towards the large screen.

'That's why he died. They said there wasn't enough ammonia to kill him. Why didn't I think about it at the time?'

Bob came back into the room. From his expression it was obvious that he was completely mystified.

'Can't you see? It's on his overalls. I suggested that he change but he wouldn't. It was that smell in the loo just now, bleach. It must have triggered my memory. The day before he died Lake got angry with one of his workmen; he was trying to clean off some rust with bleach. Gave me a chemistry lesson; something about reduction potential.'

Bob was looking at her as if she'd gone mad.

'No, it's important, the chemistry lesson. The chlorine in bleach makes the rust set harder. Lake was so furious that he kicked over a pot of bleach and got it all over his overalls. Look at this shot.' Bob moved to look at the image where Nathalie was pointing. A large dark stain had covered Lake's overalls from his waist to his ankles.

'I still don't get it.'

'Chemistry experiment, I did it for A-level. I'm so stupid not to have thought about it at the time. I could have told the police.'

'What's the police got to do with chemistry experiments?'

'Everything, it could explain everything.'

Bob was shaking his head. 'Okay, Nathalie, sit down and in words of one or two syllables tell me what in the hell you're talking about.'

Nathalie stayed standing. 'Right, you can see from these rushes that Lake had a whole canister of bleach on his overalls. I bet you when we look at the shots of him in the submersible he's wearing the same overalls.'

'And?'

'The police noticed that one of the oxygen cylinders in the submarine had been replaced by a cylinder of ammonia but they didn't think that would actually kill him and they couldn't explain the burns on his skin.'

'So?'

'Here's where the chemistry experiment comes in. Lake was in a confined space. He must've opened the ammonia cylinder instead of what he thought was oxygen. If you mix ammonia and chlorine the bleach decomposes to form hydrochloric acid. This reacts with ammonia to form toxic chloramine and even amazingly dangerous hydrazine. That's why he looked like he did. He was blistered and blue, with blood all over his face. He must have died in agony. Apparently his foot was stuck under the pedal. Even if the gas didn't kill him he could have been incapacitated and eventually died from lack of air.'

'Gruesome,' winced Bob. 'So the guy who switched the canisters may not have actually tried to kill him?'

'My thoughts exactly,' reflected Nathalie. 'Someone may have just tried to frighten him off.'

Twenty-seven

When Geoff arrived at Bagatelle's offices at half past eight in the morning he was surprised to find Nathalie, pale faced, sitting on the steps waiting for him.

'Jesus, Nathalie, what are you doing here at this hour? Are you okay? The hospital said you were. Or have you taken a turn for the worst? I could always get someone to fill in for you for a few days if you need a break.'

Nathalie had rarely seen Geoff in this flappable state; must be the time of morning.

'I'm fine, Geoff, tired but fine. Let's go in and I'll tell you all about it.'

They were the first in. Geoff took a while looking for his keys but he was saved the trouble by Stefanie, who tipped up behind them carrying two Styrofoam cups of steaming coffee. She let them in and gave them the coffee.

'I bought them for Geoff and myself; our machine takes a while to warm up. Don't worry, though, I'll wait for it. You two look like you've got something to talk about.'

Nathalie sat in the familiar chair opposite Geoff's desk and sipped her coffee. Geoff was still looking agitated. He opened the palms of his hands and raised his eyebrows.

'Fire away.'

Nathalie told him about Lake and her ideas about the bleach and ammonia. Geoff listened patiently and then asked her what she thought they should do.

'For a start I think someone should telephone the Hawaiian coroner, or perhaps the police.'

'Won't that open up a can of worms? They might want you to go back there to give some sort of evidence.'

'I could always send a written statement. I'm sure you must have a lawyer who could give us some advice. I think it's important. Remember the photograph of that shifty-looking Marine Corps employee I sent you? Could be someone trying to put a spanner in the OTEC plant.'

'I thought Nick said that they seemed pretty clean.'

'You're right. I'm tired, I'm not thinking straight, and it still may point to it being an accident. But we shouldn't sit on this information. I think the Hawaiian police should be told.'

'Yeah, you're probably right. Why don't you type out a report, sign it, and I'll ask one of our lawyers to look it over and fax it to Hawaii? Have you got time this morning or are you needed in the cutting room?'

'Bob's still syncing. He doesn't need me until three. I promised to go in after I had popped in to see Charlie.'

'I heard you went in yesterday. How is he?'

'Terrible,' Nathalie sat back in her chair abruptly as her visit flooded back. 'He did manage a few words though, something about Lake, funnily enough. I thought he said, "Lake, I didn't dream it". What a weird coincidence.'

Geoff was just about to ask her more when they were interrupted by Stefanie, who popped her head around the door. She apologised but said that she thought they would want to see the gentlemen in reception immediately. He claimed to be the sole survivor of the sunken drilling ship, the *IOD Revolution*.

The one-legged man told his story. He had survived; just. He had blanked out the incident of losing his leg and the first thing he could remember was lying in the bottom of a rescue helicopter with a tourniquet around his upper thigh. The ocean below was strewn with flotsam, jetsam and flames. No-one else appeared to have made it. He had spent weeks in an Australian hospital in a state of shock. On discharge he had left determined to find out why the ship had sunk. He had been interviewed by the loss adjusters, who had accused him of drilling in unsafe waters. He had told them the account of how he had used specially commissioned charts and had even taken gas samples from drill cores as an extra precaution. He started to explain how if a drill string hit a gas pocket in the sediment it could burst and send a huge bubble to the surface that could envelop the ship.

Geoff and Nathalie took all this in with open eyes. The man was becoming increasingly passionate and began to rant.

Geoff held up his hand, 'Okay, calm down, Mr Armstrong. Why did you know we would be interested in this story, and how did you find us?'

Armstrong took a deep breath and pulled out a document from his inside pocket. 'Sorry, I was coming to that. Here.' He handed Geoff the papers. 'They were really trying to pin this thing on me but after some difficulty I found this.'

Geoff unfolded the manuscript. It contained the same receipts for the gas field survey that his researchers had dug out some weeks ago. The receipts were from Marine Corps.

His guest continued, 'I also got copies of the surveys; the originals went down with the ship. They were fine. No signs of any gas fields.'

Geoff handed the papers to Nathalie to see. 'And Marine Corps?'

'Exactly. I had to track them down to see why their charts were so inaccurate.'

'And did you find them?'

'After a lot of trouble, yes. They seemed to have offices everywhere, but in the end, I traced them to their headquarters in Japan. It's on the harbour-side near …'

'I know,' interrupted Nathalie. 'What did they say?'

'Here's the problem. They said they had subcontracted the charts to a company called Ocean Tech.'

Armstrong paused, seeing the reaction that this name had provoked.

'You know them?'

Geoff looked at Nathalie, and Nathalie looked at Geoff. Neither spoke for a while. Then Geoff broke the silence.

'We might do. Go on, what happened next?'

'That's the point, not a lot. They gave me Ocean Tech's contact details, and told me about your visit. They said you were making a television programme about disasters at sea. I telephoned Ocean Tech six or seven times but couldn't get an answer. I also visited the address on their card but the building was empty. My last resort was you. I thought if you knew Marine Corps, and were making an investigative documentary, you might shed some light on the situation.'

It was a long speech and Sam Armstrong took a deep breath before settling back in his chair to wait for an answer. For a while there was nothing but the sound of hard rain hitting the windows of Geoff's office. It was still morning but the cloud cover made it look like a winter's evening. Geoff leant forward and switched on his angle-poise. He then steepled his hands and placed them under his chin. He thought for a while before bursting into action.

'Right, we do know Ocean Tech; they're meant to be sponsoring one of our films. What you are saying confirms what we have been thinking for some time. They are not a very straightforward outfit.' He retrieved a small card from his top drawer and handed it to Armstrong. 'Is this the number that you were given?'

Armstrong took it and held it under the angle-poise lamp.

'Yes, that's the one.'

Geoff picked up his phone and began pressing the keys.

'Well, why don't we call them now?'

The speaker-phone emitted the international dialling tone and then they heard a burst of Japanese. This was followed by the monotonous hang-up tone. Geoff pressed another button on the telephone.

'Stefanie, please could you ask one of the researchers to go to Inamo, dial Ocean Tech's number and ask one of the waiters what the hell this bloody woman is saying on the other end. And while we are waiting would you kindly bring Mr Armstrong another cup of coffee.'

Geoff explained to Armstrong that they had been suspicious about

Ocean Tech's motives for some time. Initially they claimed that the film was to promote their interest in ocean development. It seemed that they were a minor ocean-drilling business that had been taken over by someone with money to use as a toe in the water for ocean power. At first Bagatelle hadn't been too worried because they had paid the development costs upfront but recently they had become quite evasive. Bagatelle's freelancer, Nick Coburn, had travelled to Malmö and discovered a closed-up satellite office, then their media officer had gone walkabout. Finally, Nathalie had experienced a strange atmosphere when filming in their Japanese HQ. On hearing this, Sam Armstrong interjected. He turned to Nathalie.

'So, you filmed at those offices?'

'That's right.'

'When I got there, they looked empty, not a soul in sight.'

'I'm not surprised.'

Geoff looked startled. 'And why is that?'

'I was going to tell you. Our cameraman discovered that all of the secretaries were temps, only drafted in for that morning. The whole thing was a set-up. Why I don't know. What I do know is that Mr Asai was very uncomfortable when …'

She was interrupted by a young researcher, who barged into the office, mobile phone in hand.

'Stefanie told me that you needed this urgently.'

'Would be manners to knock,' said Geoff laconically. 'All right, what was the woman saying?'

'It's a standard telecommunications message. The line is out of use.'

'Great,' said Geoff. 'Close the door on your way out.'

Sam Armstrong knocked back the final dregs of his coffee. 'So, what do we do now?'

'Well, Mr Armstrong, I don't know what you are going to do but it's evident that our esteemed sponsor has disappeared. What we are going to do is, rather than make a film *for* them,' he looked at Nathalie, 'I am going to suggest to my director that she makes a film *about* them.'

Nathalie left Nick negotiating a film interview with Sam

Armstrong. She made her way through the rain to a nearby cafe bar. Not that she wanted another cup of coffee, just a private space to make her phone call. It took a while to get through to the hospital but eventually, when she did, her heart sank. No, unfortunately she couldn't visit Charlie that afternoon, he was scheduled for another operation. After some persuasion the ICU nurse told her that it was to relieve the pressure from a haematoma on his brain. Nathalie put down the phone. After five minutes staring out of the rain-streaked window she decided the best way of dealing with it was to get back to work. The cutting room was only in the next street and although Bob would still be busy syncing, she could use the room to draft out some of her plans. The company would be comforting.

Bob wasn't too pleased to see her though, 'I thought I told you I wouldn't be ready until three,' he said as she entered the cutting room.

'I know, I promise I'll keep quiet and sit in a corner. Just want to use the space to draft out a storyline. I won't get in your way.'

'That's what all the directors say. This job is faster when you're on your own.'

'I'll fetch you drinks and lunch, how about that? That will save you a bit of time.'

'Okay, deal, but don't get me involved in any conversation. You know how we'll end up telling old stories about the industry.'

'Not another word,' said Nathalie, pulling up a stool to a workbench and taking out her laptop from its case. She spent the morning looking at her notes on Ocean Tech. She read through the part concerning the change in portfolio, the new backers and their disappearing acts in Malmö and Tokyo before adding a paragraph about their involvement in the sediment gas surveys. The pictures were not great to cover this section of her film: an interview with Mr Asai; newsreel of a sunken ship; and a rostrum shot of the survey. Geoff would no doubt persuade Sam Armstrong to tell his story on camera but that was still just another talking head. Also, all they had was conjecture and mystery. Why would Ocean Tech deliver such an inaccurate survey? And why disappear when you've just stuck a few thousand dollars into a corporate film? Perhaps it was just incompetence, they'd screwed up the charts and their backers had shut up shop to avoid being sued.

'How's your cameraman?' asked Bob.

Nathalie turned to see him with his back towards her, still spooling through the film.

'Bad news, he's having another operation. Sounds really serious.'

'Sorry for snapping at you earlier, insensitive of me.'

'You weren't to know.'

Bob carried on in silence and Nathalie returned to her laptop. A thought struck her. Charlie, of course. He had worked with Ocean Tech before. In fact it was Ocean Tech who had recommended him. He would know more about their background. She tried to remember his conversations about them. Something to do with Mr Oyama and why Charlie could speak Japanese. That seemed a lifetime ago. Sipping Piña Coladas and walking along moonlit beaches. Now he was being wheeled into an operating theatre for emergency surgery. Who knows how long it would take him to recover, let alone to be well enough to talk about Ocean Tech?

The day dragged slowly. She strolled around the streets of Soho at lunchtime to look for a sandwich for Bob. Pret A Manger did a good chicken wrap, so she bought two and took them back to the cutting room. Bob worked through, munching on his wrap while he threaded up the machine with the other hand. Three o'clock came and went, and it wasn't until half past four that he finally turned to Nathalie with both thumbs up.

'Let's go into the viewing room to celebrate,' he said. 'The pictures will look really good in there. What rolls would you like to see first?'

Nathalie walked over to the shelves and picked out one of the cans. 'Geoff's asked me to start on the Ocean Tech story first, so why don't you put up this one.'

Mr Asai's office appeared on the screen. It looked a lot better than it did in reality. Hiro had lit it well. They listened to the first part of the interview.

'Nervous sort of guy,' commented Bob.

'You wait, he throws a wobbly right at the end. I want to use that part, especially the bit where he cries off the interview.'

The camera slowly crept into the document on the desk. It was so close up that they could read the title of the paper – *Dawn for Resources in Deep Seabed. Manganese Nodules Mining System.* After a few seconds the picture crept out again to see a wide-shot of the uncomfortable-looking interviewee struggling to answer the questions.

'Hold it there,' cried Nathalie abruptly. 'Freeze the picture on that shot.'

'We shouldn't do this too many times,' said Bob, getting up to go into the projection room. 'You'll burn the frame in the film if you pause it too long.'

He wound the film back to the image that Nathalie wanted and went back into the viewing room to see what she was interested in looking at.

'There,' said Nathalie, pointing with her pencil, 'on the wall behind him.'

'A lot of photos and diagrams pinned to the noticeboard. What of it?'

'Yes, but look at those photos. Pictures of huge underwater mining machinery, and they've got a logo plastered all over them.'

Bob took the reading glasses from his forehead and peered intently at the screen.

'Yes, I can just make them out, some capital letters in a diamond shape.' He spelled them out. 'A. S. C. O.'

Nathalie squinted at where Bob was looking. 'You're right, and these photos aren't pictures of models or mock-ups, they're the real thing. And I've seen that logo before. Can you fetch the rushes that were shot in Majuro? I'd like to double-check.'

The shots of the Japanese mining vessel were impressive. Charlie was a very good cameraman. The film looked like it had been shot in the middle of the ocean, whereas Nathalie knew they had been in the harbour all the time. In their orange overalls the crew contrasted vividly with the piercing blue sky. They scurried around, deploying the various bits of equipment. Nathalie remembered when she had first seen that logo. It was on the DVD that the captain had shown her. She hadn't thought much about it at the time but now she could clearly see that on the pocket of every overall was emblazoned the ASCO symbol. The captain had told her that it was a research vessel, surveying manganese nodules as a possible future resource. From the photographs in Ocean Tech's office there was no such 'future' about it; ASCO were mining ocean floor manganese now. No wonder the ship was in dispute with the wave power station. If the power station claimed the seabed around it as a right of ownership, then who would own the nodules?

'Seen enough?' asked Bob.

'Thanks,' said Nathalie, scribbling down a few notes. 'Let's now move on to the reel with the interview of the Japanese captain.'

While Bob shuffled back into the projection room, Nathalie stared at the observations in her notebook. How did those photographs turn up on that noticeboard, and why on earth would Ocean Tech have detailed and confidential plans of another company's activity?

Twenty-eight

The Fulham flat still felt cold and damp. Nathalie rummaged around in the broom cupboard and pulled out an old fan-heater. It had been raining all day and she closed the curtains and switched on all the sidelights to make the room cosier. Her head was spinning with the new revelations concerning Ocean Tech and this mining company called ASCO. Watching the footage of the manganese survey vessel with Bob had brought back memories of the shoot. Charlie seemed reluctant to film the vessel, and the captain had been very insistent in stressing that the ship was surveying, not mining. Both of these thoughts troubled her. There was something about Charlie's attitude that she couldn't quite put a finger on, but she could see now why the captain had been so fervent in telling her that ocean mining was not yet possible.

The photographs in Ocean Tech's offices showed the exact opposite. ASCO had fully operational deep-sea mining equipment. This was obviously a corporate secret that the captain did not want to reveal; so why all the clandestine behaviour about a few lumps of metal ore on the ocean floor? She plugged her laptop into the mains' socket; it might be a long evening. A grimace flashed across her face as, forgetting her splints, she had switched the power on with her left hand.

She opened the lid of the laptop and began typing with her right hand. The more she discovered about manganese nodules, the more she understood why ASCO would want to keep their operations close to their chest. There are about 500 billion tons of these nodules on the deep ocean floor. Although labelled 'manganese nodules', they also contain nickel, copper and cobalt. These minerals could produce high-strength alloys resistant to corrosion. They were used in products from batteries and magnets to jet turbines and generators. One internet site claimed that there were vastly more of these deposits in the ocean than on all of the continents put together. Anyone with the ability to mine these minerals would be floating on a fortune.

'So who exactly are you?' muttered Nathalie, typing the letters 'ASCO' into her computer.

It was no surprise to find that ASCO was a huge global mining corporation. Its CEO was a guy called Adachi. There was plenty of stuff on land-based mining systems in Africa and Australia but that was where their website ended. No more staff names, no details about any oceanographic operations. Nathalie rummaged around in her paper files, looking for any notes that would help fill in the picture. She found some old notes typed up by Nick; his meeting with Philippe Charday. There was a paragraph on the Law of the Sea Treaty. She remembered Nick telling her something about Philippe using Styrofoam coffee cups to explain the principal. Nick wasn't the greatest of writers so she read the paragraph twice. If it meant what she thought it meant then the signing of the Law of the Sea Treaty would halve ASCO's ocean mining profits. The idea made her think about Cronkar and her aborted corporate film for Sheila's Chiswick outfit. Didn't she have some old files somewhere? Before she could open the cabinet she was interrupted by the doorbell.

The director of Bagatelle Productions felt pleased with himself; Armstrong had agreed to be interviewed and didn't even want a fee. Getting publicity for his cause was payment enough. Geoff was quite happy with the turn of events concerning Ocean Tech. It meant that now he could dump their corporate film and use all the footage on his broadcast documentary. At the end of the day he had sat staring at the production notes on his whiteboard. Still a few loose ends. He was sure that Nathalie and Bob could come up with some narrative that had an investigative bite but he'd like to get the sex scandal in there somewhere. He had rung Nick and arranged to meet at the Coach and Horses in Greek Street.

'We'll go upstairs, a bit quieter up there,' shouted Geoff, as Nick strolled in the door, late as usual.

The two men found a table and sat over their glasses of beer.

Geoff got straight to the point. 'Viveca Olsson.'

Nick downed half of his pint. 'What about her?'

'I think you should pay her a visit.'

'I was wondering when you'd ask me to do that.'

'Well, I'm asking now. What do you think?'

'It's a good idea. Nathalie told me a bit more about her on the plane. Think she's pulling the governor's strings.'

'Bums spanked, strings pulled, what more does this woman do?'

'She's involved in this story somewhere, that's for sure. Right up her long legs to her armpits.'

'You can't say that these days, Nick.'

'I just have.'

'I didn't mean …' Geoff looked passively at Nick's pathetic grin. 'Never mind, I just want to make sure she's in *our* story. Take a flight to New York and use some sort of ruse to meet up. Challenge her on your information about the Cronkar set-up and find out what she's got on Cain. I don't want to know how you do it but if you can get something on your camera-phone Bagatelle will pay for the footage.'

'Sounds good to me,' said Nick, offering his empty glass for Geoff to fill. 'New York's my kind of place.'

Two men stood at the door, holding a large crate between them. Nathalie looked around and saw a delivery van parked by the pavement. The crate was obviously heavy as one of the guys was having a problem holding it.

'Nathalie Thompson?' he panted.

He looked a bit overweight to be a courier but the van looked kosher so Nathalie said it was she.

'Package from Heathrow, need a signature.' The fat man tried to balance the crate on his knee while fishing for a document in his top pocket.

'You'd better put that down,' said Nathalie. 'In the hall will do.'

She tried to make out the strange labels on the container as the delivery men clumsily manipulated it onto the hall carpet. Who on earth was sending this thing at this time of night?

The silent man made his way back to the van as the fat man stuck the paperwork under her nose.

'Sign, here and here, and the time here,' he grunted.

Cheerful soul, thought Nathalie. She signed the paperwork and forced a smile. 'You're working late, must be difficult in all this rain.'

'Too bloody right! Traffic's murder, and we're overrunning; two more deliveries before we can knock off.'

'Well, thanks for your trouble. Any information on the sender?'

'On the back of the document, from foreign parts. Says it's fragile too. We've been careful so if there's any damage it's not our fault.'

'I'll check it over; if there's a problem I'll give your company a ring.'

But Nathalie's last words were wasted as the man had started to wobble back to his van.

She closed the door, sat on the crate and looked over the papers. 'Foreign parts.' Of course, it had the Philippine export marks stamped all over it. It had to be Charlie's possessions and camera kit. She had forgotten all about it. After the trauma of the accident she must have given her address for the return of his stuff. The crate looked a bit heavy to move so she went into her flat to search for something to open it. She found a large screwdriver in the back of one of the drawers and set to open the lid. It was full of smaller packages. She recognised the camera and lens boxes; the parcels in brown paper must be his clothes. One by one she carefully lifted the items out of the crate and placed them on the table in her living room.

She was waylaid by a file containing Charlie's old call-sheets and sat cross-legged on the floor by the fan-heater to leaf through them. They brought back a lot of memories. At the bottom of the pile was a call-sheet with John McCord's name on it. She remembered the first time she met Charlie Linde. It was at Heathrow Airport. She was waiting for John McCord, when Charlie turned up. John had had an accident and Charlie just happened to be in the right place at the right time. Charlie's papers were now spread out all around her. She caught her breath as she noticed one of them containing the name of Ocean Tech. It was Ocean Tech who had recommended Charlie. Quite a coincidence, one of their freelance cameramen being at the airport at the time of John's accident. A terrible thought flashed across her mind. What if it wasn't an accident? What if the elusive Ocean Tech wanted one of their own contacts to get information from the shoot?

She sat staring at the papers; weeks of travel were within their pages. Weeks where she and Charlie had become close, perhaps too close for a professional relationship. She tried to remember what he had said about Ocean Tech. He had worked for a Hisoka Oyama on corporate shoots and he spoke Japanese. Would Oyama have fixed it so that Charlie did the shoot to find out technical stuff about the ocean projects? Industrial espionage even? Nathalie heard a church clock strike twelve in the distance. She was tired and couldn't think straight, maybe things would be clearer in the morning.

She was about to go to bed when she thought it would be wise to just check over the camera gear. Those guys hadn't looked too capable with their transportation methods. She started to open the boxes. The lenses were neatly cushioned in their padded slots. Taking them out, one at a time, Nathalie peered through the glass. They seemed perfect, not a scratch on them. She felt slightly emotional as she reached for the camera case. Charlie's precious 16mm Arriflex. She unclipped the chrome catches and lifted the lid. The camera was there in one piece, nestling in its foam block. She started to lift the camera out of the case when a cold chill ran through her spine. She touched it with her fingertip to make sure she wasn't dreaming. The soft leather chamois cover was still on the eyepiece.

The bar in The Ivy Club was unusually quiet. Perhaps it was too early for the wheeler dealers, thought Geoff. He ordered a croissant and an espresso and sat back with a copy of the *Guardian*, waiting for Nathalie. She had rung him in the small hours, gabbling incoherently about some piece of missing equipment, or was it some sort of equipment that should be missing? Geoff had told her that he would talk about it in the morning; he wanted to get back to sleep and she should too. He had hung up on her and she hadn't rung back so it couldn't have been that urgent. He had sent her a text telling her to meet him at The Ivy Club at ten. It was now five to. If she had got the text then she would be coming up in the glass lift at any moment.

She was bang on time. 'Good morning, Geoff, I'm so sorry I woke you up last night. It was quite a shock, I didn't know what else to do.'

'No problem, sit down and I'll order you some breakfast. Croissant and coffee okay?'

'Oh yes please, a cappuccino if they have one.'

Geoff placed the order and watched as Nathalie laid out sheets and sheets of paper on the low table in front of them.

'What's this, the script?'

'No, not yet. Couldn't sleep a wink last night, so I spent the time sorting out my ideas. They sounded crazy at first but the more I wrote down, the more it all made sense.'

Geoff noticed that her eyes were moist. He rested his hand on her arm and told her to take her time.

'Okay, start at the beginning, what's this about some piece of missing equipment?'

'Well, that's not the beginning but it's what started me thinking. Late last evening I received a crate sent from the Philippines. It contained all Charlie's possessions that he left behind when you airlifted him out. I unpacked it to check that there wasn't any damage when I noticed that his eyepiece still had the teddy on it. You know, a teddy is …'

'Yes, I know what a teddy is. Go on.'

'Spike, our sound guy, told me that Charlie had gone back to the turbine to look for his missing teddy. But he can't have. It was on his camera all the time. He was so fastidious about his camera he would have known that.'

'So why *did* he go back?'

'That's what I asked myself. Then I thought of all the accidents and disasters we had encountered during the trip. Here, look, I wrote them down.'

She pointed to the fan of papers she had neatly displayed in order. Geoff picked up the top sheet and looked at the list. Nathalie took a deep breath.

'When we were in Hawaii there was a terrible accident. Professor Lake was killed in his submersible – I think someone switched the oxygen for ammonia. The trouble is that they didn't realise that he had chlorine on his overalls. When we were filming the recovery of the vessel Charlie had to stop filming. He was physically sick. It was bad but he was a hardened cameraman; it didn't seem natural. When I went to the hospital the other day Charlie said a few words. *"Lake, I didn't dream it,"* I thought he said. But it wasn't that at all. It was *"Lake, I didn't mean it."* I think it was Charlie who attempted to sabotage the submarine. He even had the occasion to switch the canisters; he was outside when I was talking to Lake in the lunch break.'

Geoff remained silent while taking all of this in. He now pointed to the paper in his hand. 'And this list?'

Nathalie closed her eyes in despair. 'It shows that Charlie had the opportunity to sabotage all of the projects. He was on the deck of the ship when the sonar cable was severed; he was rescued from the wave power station where a bolt had come loose; and he was in the tidal power turbine shaft, seemingly looking for an eyepiece cover which was on his camera all the time.'

Her eyes had become wet with tears. Geoff handed her his handkerchief just as the waitress brought them the cappuccino and croissant.

'Thank you. I think I'll have another espresso, double, please.'

'Certainly, Sir,' said the waitress, looking slightly embarrassed.

Geoff sat back on the couch and waited for Nathalie to compose herself. The waitress returned with his coffee and he downed it in one. It was his turn to take a deep breath.

'If Mr Linde is our saboteur, what do you think his motive is?'

'I don't know, at least I'm not sure; he does have a connection with Ocean Tech.'

Nathalie told him about Charlie's relationship with Mr Oyama and her suspicions about John McCord's so-called accident. She explained the strange relationship between Ocean Tech and ASCO and wondered whether Ocean Tech had anything to do with the mining business.

'We filmed the manganese survey vessel because I thought it might fit in somewhere with our ocean resources' film. It seemed a good opportunity but Charlie was really reluctant to do it. Now I think about it, if Ocean Tech and ASCO were partners, and Charlie was working with Ocean Tech, he wouldn't want to publicise the mining activity. It's obvious they want it to be secret. God, this is a mess.'

'Not a mess, Nathalie. Sounds like a great story to me. Our little sponsor seems to be the villain behind this piece. All we have to do now is find out if they really hired Charlie Linde to fuck up these ocean activities and, if they did, what the hell are they doing it for?'

Nathalie took a sip of the cappuccino and pushed the croissant around her plate. She had lost her appetite. 'What should we do now?'

'The first thing is to talk to Charlie Linde. I could go to the hospital this afternoon, if you like.'

Nathalie shook her head. 'No, I should do it. We had such a good relationship. Why, oh why, did he get involved in all of this? I still can't believe a guy like Charlie would do all those things.'

Geoff pointed to her fan of papers. 'Looks like he did, though;

you've got the evidence right here.' He signed the waitress's chit and got to his feet. 'I've got to get back to the office. Find out when you can speak to Charlie, then get back to the cutting room and put your head into making this film. Let me know how you get on. No rush, finish your breakfast first.'

Nathalie watched as he smiled at the waitress and made his way to the exit. She had started to put her papers in her bag when the sound of Geoff's voice made her look up.

'Oh, I nearly forgot! I've sent Nick to New York on a fishing trip. Big catch, I hear; it's called Viveca Olsson.'

Twenty-nine

'Bitch, bitch, bitch!' muttered Nathalie aloud, stomping along Wardour Street towards the edit suite. With recent events she had almost forgotten about the name Olsson. Well, if Geoff wanted her in the film, she would do so with relish. She had her own axe to grind but she recalled Geoff saying that Nick had found a link between that woman and the Cronkar scandal. Nick's notes were so muddled that she hadn't had time to go through all of them yet. She would make it her first priority after she had rung the hospital.

'Cup of coffee?' offered Bob as she entered the cutting room.

'Just had one, thanks.'

'Putting this manganese survey scene together; it all seems to make sense. Shots look great. I've cut in some ship's wake from another roll and it looks just as if you are miles out at sea.'

Nathalie would normally have been excited by those words, after all they had filmed it on a static vessel in twenty-foot of water. Today she had other things on her mind.

'Great, Bob,' she said, trying to sound enthusiastic. 'I'll keep out of your way and let you get on. I have a few things that I must do.'

Bob shrugged and turned back to the edit table. Nathalie put down her bag and went back into the corridor. The hospital number was plugged in under favourites. How inappropriate, she thought. After the usual voice messages and rerouting of operators she at last got through to the ICU nurse. No, sorry, it was not possible to visit Charlie Linde that afternoon. He was still unconscious and recovering from the operation. As soon as there was any news she would be the first to be told.

Nathalie decided it was useless to press any further and so she thanked the nurse and returned to the cutting room. Best to throw herself into her work. She picked up Nick's notes that she had left in a pile on the floor. Half were typed and half written in his scrawly handwriting. She took out an A4 pad and eased the top off a ballpoint with her teeth. Nick had first come across Olsson when meeting Philippe in New York. She précised his opening paragraph.

Viveca Olsson, Senior Operations Manager, Environmental Protection Agency, used to work for Cronkar now assigned to Cain. Swedish national, ex-employee of undisclosed energy company in Far East.

She left out the part about the long legs and being a tough cookie. The next lot of notes were in almost indecipherable handwriting. She made out that he had met someone who had seen Olsson putting Senator Cronkar in a taxi bound for Spankers Nightclub. She wondered whether it was the real name of a club or just Nick's stupid joke. It appeared that at the club Cronkar said he was waiting for Viveca but Olsson didn't turn up. Meanwhile he was laced with booze and being filmed while his arse was whipped. Nick always did have a nice turn of phrase. Nathalie filled the next few pages with her own memories: her conversation with Charday at the conference in Guam; how Olsson seemed to be controlling Cain and influencing the ocean resources projects; the fact that Philippe hadn't heard her mention anything about Marine Corps. But that was all spurious now. The question she should have asked was had she anything to do with a company called Ocean Tech? She omitted her confrontation with Charlie concerning his encounter with Viveca and recorded a few notes on Olsson's influence on the Cain interview. She then drew a line under her notes and wrote a brief summary.

Manipulative woman controlling the actions of the US Environmental Agency. Influencing the signing of the Law of the Sea Treaty and steering the department's policy away from ocean energy development.

She held up the sheet of paper; her conclusion looked impressive. This was a massive political scandal but she couldn't help returning to her personal relationship with Charlie. If it was Charlie who was sabotaging the ocean projects then he too would be steering people's interest away from ocean energy development. It was the part she had left out that was hurting her most. Charlie's intimacy with Olsson at the conference party. He had told her that he was only trying to get information for the film. She wasn't convinced then, and she was less convinced now. They were both Swedes, and their encounter was too familiar; far too familiar for a first-time meeting and an informal chat about ocean politics. What was their real connection?

'You going to stare at that piece of paper all day or are you going to help me cut the next scene?' Bob softened his chastisement with a grin.

'Sorry, Bob, I'm still having trouble with the structure of this narrative.'

'Okay, why don't we both take a break, sit down and have a brainstorm over a cup of tea?'

Nathalie put down her papers. It sounded like a good idea. She was becoming too wrapped up in her emotions to deal objectively with the story.

'Not a bad suggestion, Bob. It would be good to get a third eye on the project, someone who hasn't been too close. Let me tell you a bit more about Ocean Tech, ASCO and a woman called Viveca Olsson. See what theory you can come up with.'

Nick strolled along East Houston Street. He preferred this end of New York. There was sunlight in lower Manhattan, less of the oppressive skyscraper shadows. The Gem advertised itself as 'A boutique hotel in SoHo surrounded by iconic cast-iron buildings balancing Bohemia and sophistication'. In reality it was a no-fuss collection of rooms in a neat, characterless building. Just what Nick wanted. He checked in at the tiny reception area, threw his bag in his room and immediately left to take a walk around East Village.

After purchasing his normal items, a cheap laptop and a pay-as-you-go phone, he made for a deli with free WiFi and checked out the stores in the area. He was in luck – there was an Army Surplus a few blocks from a surf shop. He would be able to get all of the items he needed. After checking his watch, he dialled Geoff's mobile. He got his answerphone.

'Hi Geoff, I've landed and all is okay. I've blocked the number on my new phone but I'll e-mail it to you. Can you find out if Charlie's mobile was sent back with his stuff? If so, I'm going to send you a telephone number. Use Charlie's phone to text it the following message.' He looked around at the other customers before speaking slowly into the mouthpiece. 'Geena getting greedy, need to cover some tracks, meet me in Spankers Nightclub at midnight.'

Now all he had to do was call Philippe Charday. He dialled him at the UN Environmental Agency office.

'Philippe, it's Nick Coburn, how's things? I wonder if you could do me a favour. Can you let me have Viveca Olsson's mobile number?'

Bob fished out a thermos from his rucksack. Despite the fact that there was a good working kitchen down the corridor it was a habit of his to bring his own pre-brewed tea. He unscrewed the outer lid, and then the inner one that was sitting underneath like a Russian doll. He filled both with the steaming, milky tea and handed the smaller cup to Nathalie.

'Thanks,' she said, taking a first sip. It was sweet and sticky, really awful. 'Great,' she lied.

'I've read your plot notes and looked at all of the rushes but why don't you tell me what you know in your own words?' suggested Bob.

Nathalie found it difficult to know where to begin. She opened by describing some background on Marine Corps.

'At first we were suspicious about Marine Corps. They seemed to get everywhere, everywhere there were accidents or disasters.' She stopped, once more thinking about Charlie.

Bob took a gulp of tea, 'Go on.'

'Well, it seems that this was a red herring. It's not surprising that they showed up at ocean projects. They're a franchised marine engineering company with set-ups all around the world.' Nathalie threw Bob a file. 'It's this lot we should have been looking at.'

She told him about Ocean Tech, how they had commissioned a film, suggested Charlie as a cameraman, and had provided false ocean floor gas charts. She paused while Bob read through the notes. After a while he looked up and pointed to the film cans on the shelf.

'So this is the same outfit that had information on the ASCO mining company that you showed me in the viewing room?'

Nathalie nodded.

Bob handed back the file. 'Looks obvious to me. ASCO didn't want anyone sniffing around the ocean floor where they were hoping to mine minerals so they bought a ghost company, Ocean Tech, and used them to sabotage projects.'

Nathalie blinked. 'You really think it's that simple?'

'Yes. If I wanted to get at some valuable stuff on the seabed, I wouldn't want anyone else owning the area, or even poking their noses around the place. What better thing to do than make ocean development risky or unpopular?'

'You think that this Law of the Sea Treaty thing is also to do with it?'

'Why not? If what you've told me about it is true, and everybody signs up, ASCO would have to make two mining sites and give the profits of one of them to the international community. It's a no-brainer – stop people signing it.'

Nathalie stared at him. He was right. That was just what Viveca Olsson had engineered. The more she thought about it, the bigger this thing got; and what's more, Charlie must have been part of it.

Nick felt a bit stupid in the long khaki raincoat. He had wanted a waxed Barbour but that might be stretching Geoff's expenses too far.

He had opted for the nearest thing in the Army Surplus Store when purchasing his other item, now tucked away out of sight in his shoulder bag. Geoff had listened to his voice-mail and e-mailed a reply. The night should be an interesting one. It was half past eleven, early for Spankers, but he needed the time to set things up. To his surprise there was already a queue at the door – the usual suspects in raincoats or bizarre gear. He took his place at the back and waited in turn. After a few minutes the burly bouncer grunted at him.

'Dress code.'

Nick opened his Mackintosh. The doorman looked askance at the rubber wetsuit. Nick could see that he was weighing up whether this was a fetish or real scam. Nick fumbled around in his bag and pulled out a World War II gas mask. The guy nudged his head towards the door and let him in.

The last time he had visited the club he had done so with a VIP card. This time he had no such access so he pretended to be a regular and headed towards the locker room in the basement. As he had no locker key, he took off his Mackintosh and shoved it under a bench in the corner. He put on the gas mask and tried to walk without inhibition into the bar. He sounded a bit like Darth Vader as he ordered a drink from the waitress in her leather mini-kilt and studded bra.

'Sorry, I didn't get that,' she mouthed.

Nick pointed to the Johnnie Walker bottle behind the counter. How he was going to drink it through this thing, God only knew.

She got his drift and poured out two fingers into a tumbler. 'Ice?'

He shook his head and she took his credit card and stamped his hand with a number. 'Show that when you want another, or a special service, and we'll charge it to your account.'

Nick was about to ask her what 'special service' was when he remembered the attentions of Sadie on his last visit. He put his thumbs up and sat at the bar, wondering how to drink his whisky without showing too much of his face. The evening was hotting up. Couples and threesomes were starting to enjoy the equipment in the dungeon. One trouserless guy in a red jacket and top hat was being locked in a cage by a girl with a bullwhip, wearing nothing but a tiger's tail. Nick would have liked to have studied the outcome of this scenario but he had a job to do. He scanned the room for the dominatrix Geena, and sighted her engaged in an earnest conversation with one of her cigarette girls. It was time for him to make his move.

At first Geena thought the man in the gas mask wanted a hostess for the night, but when Nick tore it off and explained his business she took little time in showing him to her private office. She was none too pleased to find the Cronkar story plastered all over *The New York Times*. She had agreed to do the set-up because she thought the client was out for revenge on a wayward husband. If she had known that the guy was a senator in the United States Government she wouldn't have touched it with a riding whip. Nick smiled at Geena's choice of words.

'Well, this client would like to do a little payback for the senator. How much did she pay you?'

He suspected that Geena upped the fee a little but he agreed to match it. She looked at the stamp on his hand.

'Okay, done deal; I'll take the fee from your account. It shouldn't take me long to set up the room and brief the girls. I suggest you put that mask back on and watch the show. When she arrives, I'll tell her that … what did you say his name was?'

'Charlie.'

'Yeah, right … that Charlie is waiting for her in the members' dungeon. After that I'll leave it to you and the girls.'

Nick nodded, pulled his gas mask back on and walked into the bar. It wasn't long before he noticed her enter the room.

Viveca Olsson was wearing a corseted black leather cat-suit with zips in all the wrong places, or all the right ones, depending on how you looked at it. She stood at the entrance, holding her head high, surveying the room. The kilted waitress slipped out from behind the bar and whispered in her ear. It was fortunate that she was wearing six-inch heels or else there was no way she would have reached. Olsson stood for a moment, and for one worrying instant Nick thought that she had become aware of the ruse. But after a few seconds she smiled at the girl and followed her towards a small red studded door in the far corner. Nick waited for a full minute before following.

Behind the red door was a series of stone steps leading downwards to an arched portico. The air felt damp with a musty smell. If they were trying to create a mediaeval feel they had certainly achieved it. Beyond the portico was a dimly lit room, its rough walls illuminated by red spotlights. At the centre of the room he noticed the same mediaeval-style rack that he had seen in the Cronkar photographs. He looked around the room for Olsson. He didn't notice her at first but then saw her in the shadows of an alcove. Two of Geena's so-called hostesses stood on either side. Nick made his way over to speak to them. As he got closer he stopped in his tracks. Olsson was against the wall, upright, arms above her head locked into iron manacles. She looked furious; she might have been shouting obscenities but she couldn't as they had also placed a gag in her mouth. As she saw Nick, her eyes widened with fear. It dawned on him that he was still wearing the gas mask. Normally this outfit would have appeared somewhat ridiculous but in this environment he must have looked terrifying.

He peeled off the rubber contraption. 'Good evening, or should I say morning, Miss Olsson. Viveca, isn't it, like the famous film actress?'

Viveca struggled in her chains and made a gurgling sound through the gag.

'Oh, I'm sorry, you're a bit tied up at the moment. I'm Nick Coburn, a friend of Nathalie Thompson, who is a friend of Charlie Linde.' Nick paused while he let all this sink in.

'I asked these young ladies to keep you here, so we could have a chat.' He glanced at the two scantily-clad girls on either side. 'I didn't realise how creative they would be in their restraint but you have to give it to them, don't you?'

Olsson narrowed her eyes and made more threatening, grunting noises.

'I wonder if our escorts are the same as those who tied up Senator Cronkar for you.' Nick gestured towards the rack in the middle of the room. 'Only he had the "special", didn't he? Photographer and all.'

The two girls gestured as if to ask Nick if he wanted them to give Olsson the same treatment.

'Oh, I don't think there will be a need for that. I'm sure if we ask Miss Olsson not to scream the place down we can take off her gag and have a civilised conversation. Don't you agree, Miss Olsson?'

Viveca Olsson looked towards the girl with the whip and nodded vigorously. Nick asked the girls to take off her gag but told them to leave the manacles on for the moment. He wanted to show Olsson that he was serious, implying that any lies would be met by repercussions from the hostesses. They seemed a little too anxious for that eventuality he thought, and hoped Olsson would sense that too. Her eyes widened as he began to unzip his wet suit.

'Oh, don't worry, Miss Olsson, I'm not here for one of your sex games. I was just going to show you this.' He put his hand into the wetsuit and pulled out a mobile phone. 'Yes, it's Charlie's, and …'

'You bloody …' began Olsson.

'Bloody cheat in sending you a text from someone else's phone? Or bloody clever chap in working out your involvement with the Cronkar setup?'

Olsson shut her mouth and dropped her head. She knew that the game was up and in her position she had no way of wriggling out of it.

'That's better. Now why don't you tell me how you and Charlie first met?'

Olsson, still staring at the floor, started to whisper. 'It was in Japan, just a chance meeting.'

Nick glanced at one of the girls, who prodded Olsson with her whip.

'They can't quite hear you, Miss Olsson, and I know they're dying to play some more games, so why don't you speak up a little?'

Nick knew this was the moment when his reluctant interviewee was going to come clean. She raised her head and stared at him defiantly, straight in the eyes.

'Charlie and I used to work for a company called ASCO in Japan. We are both Swedish and we share the same culture. It wasn't long before we became an item.'

'Intimately and sexually involved?' interrupted Nick.

'Yes, intimately and sexually involved. But you make it sound dirty. It wasn't that, it was a whirlwind romance and we lived an amazing extravagant lifestyle in an exotic country.'

'Extravagant?'

'Yes, we were so carried away that we started living beyond our means. After a while, about a year ago, we stumbled across an opportunity to get some money out of the company.'

'Embezzle, you mean?'

'If you want to call it that; their pay was crap and we found a way of topping it up. Look, could you ask them to unlock these manacles, they're chaffing my wrists.'

'In good time, Miss Olsson. I take it they caught you?'

Viveca straightened her spine to release some of the pressure on the restraints. Nick couldn't help noticing how her breasts stretched against the tight soft leather of her cat-suit. Olsson noticed his reaction.

'If you let me go, I could be quite co-operative, you know.'

Nick snapped back into inquisition mode. 'I think you're going to be co-operative anyway,' he said. 'Now, you are telling me about how you were stealing ASCO's money ...'

Olsson pouted and continued. 'You're right, they caught us and threatened us with jail.'

The Swede seemed to have lost her arrogant demeanour and was becoming quite tearful. Nick decided it was time to unlock her chains and asked the girls to leave them alone. He sat beside Olsson on a crude bench by the wall. She rubbed her wrists as she told him about the blackmail.

'There was no choice. Do as we were told or go to jail. They set me up with a glowing CV from a fictitious energy company and I got a job as Cronkar's aide. At first all I had to do was to do everything I could to dissuade him from signing the Law of the Sea Treaty. Drop a few convincing arguments in here and there, get him to meet some high-powered treaty sceptics. But it didn't work – Cronkar wouldn't play ball. ASCO were on my back so I devised a plan to ruin his reputation.'

'The spanking scandal.'

'That's what the press called it; it worked better than even I had hoped for. He resigned the next day and ASCO gave me a pile of money to bribe his successor.'

Nick put a hand on her knee. 'And Charlie?'

'Charlie also made a deal, getting bad publicity for ocean technology projects. I didn't ask too many questions but I'm sure it involved sabotage.'

'And it got worse here too, didn't it? Did you know he killed a guy called Lake?'

'Charlie, kill someone. Never!'

'You don't think so?'

'Call him, call him now, he'll tell you it's not true.'

'So you haven't heard about the accident?'

'What accident? An accident involving Charlie? What have you done with him? Where is he?'

Nick got up and stared at her. A six-foot diva dressed in head-to-toe leather, yet curiously looking a vulnerable mess. He walked out without saying another word.

Thirty

'Dead?'

'I'm terribly sorry.'

Nathalie stared at the small telephone device in her hand that had just given her the terrible news.

'When?'

'During the night. I'm afraid he didn't come round after the operation. He was in no pain and wouldn't have known about it.'

She was too numb to cry.

In the following days everybody commiserated with her and sent their condolences. Geoff had said that he would find out if Charlie had any close relatives and organise everything with the hospital. Nick Coburn heard the news on his arrival back in the UK and had a long telephone conversation with her. She explained that she had seen the condition Charlie was in and half expected this but his death had still come as a severe shock. Almost on autopilot she had asked how he had got on with Viveca Olsson. Nick had spared her most of the details but outlined the facts of the ASCO blackmail and the manipulation of Cronkar and Cain. When pressed, he admitted that Charlie had worked for the same company and had been under similar threats. He omitted to mention the sexual relationship, not thinking it relevant at this stage.

As soon as Geoff received Nick's report he called a crisis meeting. Nathalie, Nick and Stefanie walked into the boardroom to find Geoff busy on the telephone. He waved at them to sit down as he carried on his earnest conversation with Channel 4's commissioning editor.

'This is dynamite, Julian. We've now got information to implicate huge corporate corruption. This thing goes right to the top of the US Government. Yes, I know we need independent sources. Don't worry, this is watertight. Topical? Of course it's topical! Alternative ocean power saboteurs, climate change lobbyists, shale fracking, it's got it all. How soon can we deliver?'

Geoff looked around at the small team in front of him.

'A week, maybe two.'

He waved them down as they started to open their mouths in protest.

'Great, I'll send someone round with the schedule. You just let me know the prime-time slot.'

He put down the phone and addressed the meeting.

'Yes, I know it's not very long. But it's possible.'

Nick put his hand up. 'You say we've got sources.' He turned to Nathalie. 'Sorry, but I've got to say this. Our key witness, Charlie Linde, is dead.'

Geoff leant back in his chair and raised his hands in the air. 'There's enough evidence that he did it, and we have footage to back it up. Cut rope on the sonar, wave power guys talking about loose bolts, even the shots of chlorine on a dead guy's overalls. And there's Olsson.' He sat bolt upright as the thought struck him. 'Olsson, we'll need her testimony on film. Nathalie will be too busy editing. Stefanie, can you arrange a film crew in New York?'

Nick intervened. 'Hold on, the woman gave me this stuff under, what shall I call it, duress. How do you know she'll talk on camera in the bright light of day?'

'Good point.' He glanced at his watch. 'Why don't you telephone her now, make some sort of negotiation? The rest of us will take a break and we'll meet back here tomorrow morning. Nathalie, did you get that?'

Nathalie was staring at her notepad in a complete daze. She had hardly taken in anything of the meeting.

'Nathalie, take the rest of the day off while we sort this out. I'll personally go around to Bob's cutting room this afternoon to give him some directions.'

Geoff closed the meeting and left for his office.

The three of them sat for a while in stunned silence. Then Stefanie got to her feet. 'Nick, you can use my office to make your phone call. Nathalie, sit here a while and I'll make us both a cup of tea.'

Nick made the call. Olsson's mobile was out of action so he called her at the Environmental Agency. Her extension there wasn't working either. His last resort was Philippe Charday.

'Viveca? I thought you might have heard. She's disappeared. Her desk was cleared yesterday; my boss told me that she had been posted overseas. Sounded strange so I checked all the UN registers. No sign of her on any list.'

'I'm not surprised,' said Nick. 'If you want to keep your job I suggest you let sleeping dogs lie.'

'Sleeping dogs?'

'Yes, English phrase for leaving things alone. It's up to you, Philippe, but that woman's bad news. If I discover where she went, I'll let you know.'

Nick suspected that he wouldn't find out anything. She had either been whisked away by ASCO or Cain had given her some hideaway in exchange for her silence. Geoff was going to be really pleased about that.

But Geoff had other things on his mind. He was halfway down Wardour Street when he was stopped from going any further by a barricade. Fire engines and police cars were everywhere. He spotted their editor Bob milling around with some of the crowd.

'Bob, what's up?'

'It's a bloody disaster! I worked through the night yesterday so I've just got in. They won't let us go any further. The building with the edit suite has gone up in flames. Cutting rooms and film have all been burnt to a cinder.'

Geoff looked at the black smoke billowing up in front of them. 'But we've got the negative?'

Bob looked despondent. 'That's the point, we haven't. It was delivered to the cutting room along with the print. It's all gone. The whole lot's bloody gone! I'm sorry, Geoff, but your film's finished.'

Thirty-one

It was one of those rare blazing British summers. Three months had come and gone since the cutting room fire. Nathalie sauntered across the green oasis of Soho Square. Girls in bikinis lay beside shirtless young men on the grass, soaking up the sun. Bob had been right about the film being finished. Nothing had remained from the fire. The insurance company still had to establish whether it was an accident or arson but they had paid out handsomely. Not enough evidently to compensate for the painful emotional hours but enough to pay the bills. Geoff had been quite resigned about the whole affair. He was already into other high-risk documentaries. He had offered Nathalie one of them, but when she said she wasn't ready, he gave her some titbits researching the science curriculum for a schools' programme. That's what she had been doing today, looking for stuff on photosynthesis on the internet. She was getting bored and she knew it. Maybe it was time to look for something more adventurous.

It was lunchtime by the time she got home. She unwrapped her Pret A Manger sandwich and sat down to watch the midday news. First came the normal silly summer season stuff; *It's a Scorcher* and *Brighton Beach Belles* made the headlines. She sat up as the topic switched to the international news. A familiar face appeared on the screen – Governor Cain was issuing forth on the reasons why the United States were continuing to block ratification of the Law of the Sea Treaty. So, he was still holding office. She was really sore that they couldn't hold him to account and she still wondered whether it was Olsson's bribe or his oil shale interests that made him lobby against the treaty and the climate change protagonists. Perhaps a bit of both. She switched the television off in disgust and picked up her copy of the *Guardian*.

'Proper news,' she told herself.

But when she reached the middle pages she found she couldn't get away from it. There, in a small column, was an article explaining that due to engineering difficulties and the frequency of accidents many ocean engineering projects were being put on hold. Ocean energy was now seen as risky and uneconomic. The Philippine tidal fence was cited as one example. The news made her furious and think of ASCO. She turned to the business pages to check their share price. No relief there. ASCO's profits had risen sharply as their development of ocean manganese fields continued to flourish. Nathalie folded up the newspaper and stormed out of her front door.

'We've been through all of this before, Nathalie,' said Geoff, handing her back the newspaper. 'You have to move on. There are thousands of crooks in the world getting away with it. We'll catch some of them in our films but you can't win them all. You had a great story and great footage that you got in the most difficult of circumstances. Think of it as a learning curve.'

'But the bastards have got away with it, and we've still got some evidence in the files.'

'Yes, but we're a film company, we make films. And at the moment we haven't got any footage to show. We are not a detective agency, Nathalie.'

Geoff made his way to his filing cabinet and pulled out a thick folder. He placed it in front of her and turned it round so she could read the cover. *Noxious Nightmare,* read the title. *A proposal for an investigative documentary on a pharmaceutical scandal*.

'Now, take that home, read it and tell me if you want to direct it.'

Nathalie played with the edge of the front cover. Seeing her long face Geoff laughed. 'Come on, Nathalie, worse things happen at sea.'

Nathalie wasn't amused. She picked up the file, put it roughly in her bag, and walked out.

She took the tube back to Fulham. Long shadows heralded the end of what should have been a perfect day. Geoff's last insensitive quip had brought back memories of Charlie. She still wasn't sure whether he had any real feelings for her or had duped her completely. If he had, he was extremely good at it. She put the key in the door, entered the flat, and placed her bag on the table. It was time to get this thing out of her mind once and for all. Her cupboard was full of old 'Oceans on Fire' folders. She started to sift through them to see what she could throw away. On the top was a copy of her final script.

'Maybe not a detective agency but I'm sure someone could make use of this,' she muttered to herself.

The newspaper was in her bag, she found the page, and the name of the journalist. She dug out a large manila envelope, addressed it to '*The Guardian*', and popped the script into it. She would post it tomorrow. Feeling more satisfied she sat down with a cup of coffee and idly started to flip through Geoff's documentary brief when she heard a noise from her letterbox.

On the doormat was a battered postcard. A faded photograph of a coral atoll was on the front. Looking at the postmark she noticed that it had taken months to reach her. She turned it over to find it was from Luke and Dan, signed with a smiley face.

On it they had scrawled the words

Wish you were here.
Instead of us!

Also by Martin Granger

When the *Southern Mariner*, a huge cargo ship, is hijacked in the Far East, young TV journalist Nathalie Thompson is sent to investigate the story behind the theft.

Joining forces with Philippine coastguard Peter Ramos, she embarks on an exciting quest that plunges them headfirst into the dark and dangerous world of piracy. But, when another thousand tonne freighter with its million-dollar cargo disappears and its American captain is killed, events start to spiral out of control.

Together, Nathalie and Peter must find the courage to confront a force on the high seas that stands above the law, and escape from a violent world of guns, corruption and cold-blooded murder.

MANILA HARBOUR

One

Crossing at night in the Yamaha-powered outriggers would be hazardous. At their narrowest point the Malacca Straits are only two kilometres wide and yet they are one of the busiest shipping lanes in the world. High-sided freighters move in and out of Singapore like bees to a hive. They might easily make flotsam out of the wood and bamboo bangkas without even noticing them. But then being noticed was the last thing Eduardo Cordilla wanted.

There were four men on each craft, not many for the night's work, but it was not unknown for fishing boats to use less. The bamboo poles skimmed along the water, suspended by their spider-like feet from the painted hulls. Anyone on the beach glimpsing the two boats through the intervals of moonlit cloud would not have been unduly concerned – it was usual practice for fishing to be done at night. No doubt large butane lit lanterns would be raised on masts to attract the fish when the bangkas had reached the fishing grounds. Seen from the shore it could look like a city of lights at night only to reveal a stretch of empty sea in the morning. This evening only Benny Serdiajio noticed anything out of the ordinary. Lying on the floor of his stilted shack he turned over and rested on his elbow to listen more closely to the outboards – Yamaha 200's, rich fishermen.

Not more than two nautical miles away the *Southern Mariner* was slipping her moorings and being guided into the channel by the pilot boat. When the thirty-thousand tonne freighter was underway she would join the main shipping lane that was lit up like a motorway. It would take a while for her to reach the Phillip Channel, where the winking lights of the other cargo vessels and oil tankers became fewer as the ships spread out from the narrow straits into the open sea. The bangka crews had prepared for that. Eduardo Cordilla checked his watch. If his calculations were correct they were right on time.

In the middle of the channel there was not another boat in sight. Nothing but the dark, cold lapping water and the occasional glow of a cigarette from one of the bangkas. Eduardo cut his engine and shouted to the others to do the same. The men moved silently around their crafts. Ropes were tidied and boxes strapped down. They had done this before, but despite the outward calm they were nervous. Busying themselves was a way of relaxing. The bangkas looked like a cross between Viking warships and something out of a *Star Wars*' movie. The raked-back cabins were placed towards the stern. A few paces behind, the deck of the crafts tilted like oriental pagodas over the water. The front of each vessel was open apart from a small stretch of canvas; cover for the chests that lay in the centre of the hull.

'Open her up,' Charlito Cordilla snapped at one of the crew.

A man began to unfasten the chest. Inside was a long coil of thick metal rope. Without a word he handed it to Charlito. On one end of the rope was welded a large clasped hook. By the small lantern on the masts of the vessel they slowly hauled the hook over the side and secured it onto the other bangka's gunwales. Although it was nearly midnight the air was warm; humid tropical air that made the shirt stick to your back. The rope was heavy, and greased to hold back the rust. It was difficult to handle. Droplets of sweat ran down Charlito's moustache.

'No hurry', he panted, 'plenty of time.'

Eduardo lit a second cigarette and pushed the flip-top pack into the back pocket of his Levi's. Real Levi's, not the imitation label from Hong Kong. A man conscious of his appearance even on a night like this. 'The boat hook,' he muttered quietly, the cigarette still between his lips.

A long bamboo pole with a metal-strapped end was placed in his outstretched hand.

'Cast off and let them drift. I'll signal when to start up.'

The crews of the two craft acted instantly as they always did when this pale Filipino with his soft American accent calmly gave instructions. The pole was eased against the side and the two bangkas floated apart. The metal rope between them slowly sank into the ocean.

The Cordilla brothers looked at the sky; the clouds were still gathering. Less and less of the moon's upside-down crescent appeared between them. The evening had started clear, but now the time was closing, the blacker the better.

The bangkas were still within hailing distance but Eduardo went to his cabin and removed an Eveready black rubber torch from a lacquered hardwood drawer. Back on deck he pointed it like a pistol at the other boat and pressed the switch through the spongy rubber cover. Three flashes, a moment of silence, and then the Yamaha outboard kicked into life. The throttle was closed, leaving a throaty, rhythmic echo of sound in the air. Slowly, Charlito's bangka moved away until all that could be seen were three pin pricks of light. Eduardo paused a while before kneeling to shine his torch into the sea beyond the metal rope that was hanging over the side. Within minutes the beam caught the snake of metal rising in its glare. Cordilla flicked the torch upwards – three more flashes and the outboard fell silent. The bangkas continued to drift apart and then a sudden jolt. The men held onto the masts to steady themselves. They peered into the sea between the two craft – just below the surface, a long and sinewy umbilical cord threatened like a serpent. They sat and waited.

The massive hull ploughing into the steel rope nearly took Charlito Cordilla off his feet. The bangka was caught like a marlin on a line. The two crews wrestled with their bamboo poles to stop the vessels' outriggers smashing to pieces as they were dragged in towards the freighter. From the air it would have looked like two strange oriental water skiers being pulled along by the massive ship. Within minutes the bangkas were held close against the metal cliff of the freighter. The tyres roped to the sides helped cushion the impact and the vessels were soon speeding along, three abreast.

The first grappling hook fell back into the water but the second throw was more successful. The prongs held fast onto the freighter's superstructure. The eight masked men clambered up the vertical painted rust face like expert mountaineers. In the shadows any crew member who had been on deck would have seen the outline of their backpacks – AK-47's, lethal equipment that could pump out six rounds a second but, as expected, not a crew member was in sight.

The first thing that Seaman Rivera could remember was seeing Chief Officer Castellano walk out of the chart room with both hands on his head. It looked comical and it took him a while to connect this bizarre behaviour to the man behind. A short man, something strapped over his shoulders, with dark-skinned hands, grasping a pistol pointing at Castellano's head.

'Captain, you captain?' snapped a voice. Tomas Rivera couldn't move, think or speak.

'Officer? *Officer*?' screamed the man. In his state of suspended animation it dawned on Tomas that he was being asked a question.

'No, no officer! Seaman! *Seaman*!' he heard himself screaming back.

'Down! *Down*!' shouted the man, waving the pistol wildly about in front of him. Rivera fell to the deck and heard a crash as a bullet smashed into the starboard side radar. A figure stepped over him. Tomas half opened an eye to see a large knife being pulled from a belt hanging at the waist. He began to shake. The knife slashed downwards, once, twice. The cables of the VHF radio and the bridge telephone to the engine room hung lifeless.

Rivera closed his eyes and lay as still as he could, which was difficult. He felt nauseous, and his body was involuntarily shifting from side to side. It had a life of its own and wanted to be anywhere but here on the cold metal bridge deck. His hands felt the ribbed coils of the hastily applied paintwork. It was green, applied too thickly and had dried as molten lava with a wrinkled crust. It was vivid green; he remembered having to remove the stains from his cheap white T-shirt with gasoline from the ship's stores.

'Captain, captain, where captain?' screamed the voice. It seemed to echo through the metal dark into his ears.

Castellano muttering, a shuffle of deck shoes or bare feet, a groan, a muffled clang. Then a terrible whining noise, cold fear flushed through Tomas' body as he began to hallucinate.

Castellano's voice in the distance, 'I have children, a wife,' but it was not now spoken in quiet, subservient tones; it was awful, pitiful, pleading. 'Please don't kill me, *please* don't kill me, *please* don't …' the sentence ended in a gargle of sobs.

The apprentice officer, Francis Tsang, was woken by the shot. He was in his cabin on the second deck. Fully awake, he rushed to his door, opened it, and instantly closed it again, throwing the lock. Two hooded men brandishing machine guns were running down the gangway, throwing open doors as they went. He heard another shot interspersed by a short scream.

The boatswain also on the second deck opened his door to see the captain tied up with a rope in the alleyway. Shaking, he ran to the toilet and locked the door.

Salvador Rocco banged on the bulkhead to alert the second engineer. There was no need to wake him. After a quick interchange they decided to leave their cabins through the portholes. Dropping down on the deck, they made their way to the stowage hold and lay on the floor in silence.

Charlito found Eduardo on the deck, staring out to sea. 'We've secured the captain and the chief officer and there's a guy on the floor shitting his pants in the wheelhouse.'

'The others?'

'Not giving any problem, the radio is out and they didn't have time to send a message. A pushover; shall I get the guys to round them up?'

'Yes, tell them to keep their masks on and get a lifeboat ready. The sea's calm enough, they should be able to reach the shore without too much trouble.'

Charlito turned to make his way to the metal ladder. Without looking back, he shouted some words into the air: 'You're too good to them. Chuck them in the drink, that's what I would do,'

Eduardo laughed, he doubted it. Charlito was his crazy elder brother, but not that crazy. Years ago he had worked tirelessly in a garage repairing jeepneys, those Filipino-decorated versions of Second World War jeeps. All to raise money to get Eduardo into naval college. Well, if they got this ship to their destination then he would be paid back handsomely. Eduardo had met his paymasters at Annapolis; they'd picked him out on graduation day. He was the only one not throwing his hat into the air. When a close friend asked him why he hadn't done it, he had thrust the cap into his friend's hands and told him he could keep it. The two suited Malaysians had spotted the air of discontent and had made their approach. But that was years ago and, step by step, he'd become enmeshed in this business. Charlito could be a fool sometimes but he was a good mechanic and game for anything. When he had been offered the opportunity to join Eduardo he had jumped at it.

'Are you going to leave us to do all the fucking work, or are you going to keep pretending to keep watch?' his brother's voice came from the deck above.

'You keep to your part of the deal and I'll keep to mine,' called back Eduardo. 'Have you got those guys into the lifeboat yet?'

'A couple are missing but don't worry, we'll flush them out.'

'The captain?'

'He's still tied up by the wheelhouse, started to make a fuss so Roscoe hit him over the head and he's bleeding a bit.'

'A bit?'

'Okay, quite a lot. I think we should bandage him up before we stick him in the boat.'

'Well, get on with it. Are you sure he's all right?'

'Yeah, a few aspirin and he'll be fine,' laughed Charlito. 'I'll get Roscoe to play nurse.'

'Give him time to recover, don't move him until he's fit to stand. We've got time; we need to stay on this course for a while to avoid attracting attention. You do one more sweep of the ship to make sure you've got everyone and then send two of the guys back with the bangkas.' Eduardo started to climb the metal rungs of the ladder. 'I've finished here, I'll come up there and start the paperwork.'

Eduardo reached the main deck, scowled at Roscoe and stepped around the captain, avoiding the pool of blood seeping across the alleyway. Peeling the ski mask from his head, he slipped into the cabin. His breathing was smooth and even. Like a hunter returning from a day's sport he gently placed his AK-47 on the table and manoeuvred himself into the captain's chair. The desk was basic, an unfinished letter on the surface and an untouched revolver in the top right-hand drawer. Taking a ship couldn't be easier. One revolver and a fire hose against half a dozen heavily armed thugs. Actually stealing it took a little more guile. He found the safe instructions carelessly left in a bottom drawer. Ships were home to Eduardo. Without looking around he made straight for the safe, knelt down and laid the instructions beside him. Everything was as he expected: the documents and the ship were as good as his.

About the author

Martin Granger has been making documentary films for thirty years. In that time he has won more than one hundred international film awards. His work has ranged from directing BBC's *Horizon* to producing a BAFTA nominated science series for Channel 4. His novels, although fiction, are based upon his experience in the film industry. He lives in Wimbledon with his wife Jacqueline.

www.martingrangerbooks.com